# TO THE
# WATERS
*and*
# THE WILD

# TO THE
# WATERS
*and*
# THE WILD

*a novel*

BY

# S.C. McGRATH

Seanachie Press

For permission requests, please address Seanachie Press at:
seanachiepress.books@gmail.com

Published 2019

ISBN: 978-0-9914493-2-3 pbk
ISBN: 978-0-9914493-3-0 ebk

*Editing by Jennifer Sawyer Fisher*
*Book design by Stacey Aaronson*

Printed in the United States of America

This is a work of fiction. With the exception of certain recognizable historical figures and events, all other characters and scenes in this novel are entirely the product of the author's imagination.

*For Roger, Katie, Duncan, Scarlett, and Fulton*
*with all my love*

*To the waters and the wild*
*With a faery, hand in hand,*
*For the world's more full of*
*weeping than you can understand.*

—WILLIAM BUTLER YEATS

# PROLOGUE

*S*HE SOARED OVER THE OCEAN, SEARCHING THE horizon. Far in the distance the outline of land was visible. She flew closer. Soon mountains and valleys took shape and muted colors became bright and clear. Never losing sight of her destination, she dipped her shoulders first one way and then the other, sweeping back and forth through the air, rejoicing in her flight. Abruptly she dove and followed the rugged coastline, low enough to see the current rippling along the surface of the water and feel the spray from waves that broke against an off-shore wind. High surf pounded sandy beaches, interrupted only when a rocky point signaled a protected cove. Then the current's force waned and weaker swells moved slowly to shore until met by a freshwater creek rushing into the ocean, diluting its salty weight momentarily. Upstream, the creek curled through an inlet of green and yellow grasses and craggy copses. She could imagine lush meadows beyond, beckoning her inland.

In an instant the coastline changed. Sandy shores gave way to towering cliffs with huge, granite fingers jutting into the ocean and barring her way. Thick clouds blocked the sun and the smell of acrid smoke and the tumult of a desperate battle assaulted her. The wind that had moments ago buoyed both her body and spirit now buffeted her mercilessly. She struggled forward, her mind roiled by dark, chaotic thoughts. If she faltered, all would be lost.

Her body was but a feather against the powers of nature, and so she cast aside all fear and allowed the wind to grab her, sending her twisting and tumbling through the air. She gained strength with each second of its embrace and soon was flying in accord with the wind as it carried her far out to sea and then back, skirting perilously close to the granite cliffs. Looking ahead she saw a massive promontory. Eagerly, she flew toward it. The clouds had now disappeared and the sun's rays felt warm against her skin. She rounded the promontory and a wondrous sight awaited her. There, perched in hollows along the cliffs were what appeared to be cottages. But not the stone, mud, and thatch cottages she knew. These were magnificent, with sharp angles, multiple levels, and sometimes reflective surfaces that gleamed against the bright sunshine. She flew closer and noticed a footpath winding precariously down to the ocean.

On that path was a man.

# CHAPTER ONE

KEELIN OPENED HER EYES.

"Only a dream," she sighed.

No, that was not true. It was *the* dream, visiting her with ever increasing frequency over the past year and leaving her with the same feelings of both exhilaration and frustration. Sometimes, like today, it also left her with a fleeting sense of apprehension tinged with melancholy. Beautiful and familiar, the dream drew her in, delighting her senses, only to abruptly end before she reached the cliff's edge.

To be so close and not to see his face, she thought angrily.

"But I was flying! I felt . . . *free!*" she exclaimed, her anger forgotten as quickly as it had risen. She stood up and absently brushed leaves and twigs from her damp, wrinkled clothing. She frowned slightly, scanning the heather-dotted meadow that spread across the upper reaches of her family's land. Bordering the meadow was a great oak forest. Keelin came here in search of healing herbs that grew in the shadows, protected by the oaks' sheltering branches. She also visited the meadow to escape. It was her secret refuge where her racing mind could relax.

"Do you ever dream of flying, my handsome Rua, with great wings of gold?" Keelin asked the powerful horse grazing quietly nearby.

Rua raised his head and responded with a low whinny. He calmly walked over to her, nudging her hand with his soft muzzle.

"Of course you do not," said Keelin, stroking the stallion's sleek neck. She was the one who wanted to fly away, not her magnificent Rua.

"I just don't understand why the gods would choose such a life for me. I am sure, however, that you, my big red beast, will always be my fearless protector," Keelin said, laughing off her doubts.

It was then that she felt the chill of evening. The warmth of the late summer sun had all but disappeared, and the damp of evening was setting in. She had slept longer than she had intended. Her mother must be worried, thought Keelin, her expression softening.

Keelin picked up the satchel she always carried to store the herbs, flowers, and roots she collected and walked over to Rua, who had resumed grazing while she gathered her belongings. He towered over her, the top of her head barely reaching the middle of his shoulders. At the touch of her hand on his left foreleg, he slowly bent one knee and lowered his heavy body, allowing Keelin to spring onto his back, her rough linen skirt hiking up around her knees.

"All right, Rua," whispered Keelin into her stallion's ear. "Let's go." With only the lightest of pressure from Keelin's slender legs, Rua charged forward, sensing her excitement and welcoming the signal for speed.

Taking a short cut across the gulley that divided her family's land from their neighbor's, Keelin would reach home in a fraction of the time, avoiding the longer but safer path down the mountain.

As the stallion's stride lengthened, Keelin felt the wind grab her loose blouse and hold it billowing behind her like an air-filled balloon. She never tired of this wonderful race home. Charging down the mountain—the hedges, trees, and sheep a mere blur—left her breathless and exultant. Speed was intoxicating, and riding Rua was the closest thing to flying she had ever experienced.

Keelin knew that many of the villagers looked askance at her riding astride a stallion, thinking it "shameful." What does it matter, let them talk, Keelin thought as Rua approached a large hedgerow, cantering in a ground-covering stride. As if performing a wonderfully choreographed dance, Rua met the hedge perfectly and sailed over it, landing lightly on the other side.

Keelin had just reached the stone wall that bordered the main road and slowed Rua to a walk when she heard the sound of someone singing. The notes were clear and the voice pure. The song told of love and loss and had a melancholy turn like so many of the songs of Keelin's people. The lilting melody rang through the air with such beauty that she was transfixed. In her sixteen years she had already seen the effects of brutal warfare, disease, and old age. It had been scarcely five years since the last battle between the neighboring clans, and she remembered vividly how few families had been spared the horrors it had wrought. How many new songs would she hear about those brave, doomed warriors?

The singing stopped abruptly, awakening Keelin from her reverie. She was greeted by a far less mellifluous voice.

"So it is the wee Keelin who has trespassed on our land again and frightened our sheep in the upper pastures," remarked a tall young man who stood alongside a small herd of dairy cows, his dog at his feet.

Keelin's eyes narrowed and her muscles tensed with anger. She hated the fact that she was small, almost tiny if she were to admit it. Her diminutive stature was made even worse because her parents were both tall, as were most of the people of her clan. When she was younger she would fly like a crazed terrier at anyone who dared to slight her. The girls of the village learned quickly to avoid any mention of her height. The boys, on the other hand, delighted in teasing her. Now it was only Brian, standing insolently in front of her, who still teased her. Strangely enough it was Brian who had put an end to the boys' harassment. He warned them off, and no one wanted to face his wrath.

"It wasn't I who scattered the sheep but you with your frightful crowing," said Keelin with an edge to her voice. Seeing that the barb had hit home, she added, "And what is a mighty warrior doing herding cows? I thought you considered such menial tasks beneath you."

Brian's dark eyes swept over Keelin, making her feel distinctly uncomfortable. "There is always that spare moment between slaying dragons and vanquishing foes," he said with a jaunty smile. "Besides, herding cows is one of the few tasks of the farm I do enjoy."

"And I can imagine why," said Keelin, unable to suppress a giggle. "The poor beasts are but captive listeners to your unceasing songs of glory. At least I see that you heeded my advice and have taken them down to the eastern brook. I told you they preferred the grasses there. Is not their milk sweeter now?"

"Yes," Brian said with a grin, "their milk is nearly sweet enough to quell the bitter taste I always get from seeing the likes of you. Don't you ever comb that tangled mass of hair, you little witch?"

At that he laughed and turned to drive the cows home. His dog, a fine collie, gave a happy yip and bounded around the cows, biting at their legs and keeping them on the narrow road. Startled by the dog's sudden movement, Rua snorted and pawed the ground, impatient to be off as well.

Keelin smarted from Brian's words. Yes, she knew her hair was wild and tangled, but as hard as she tried to keep it neat and plaited in a long braid, it never failed to come loose when she was riding Rua. She was somewhat self-conscious and, if truth be known, sensitive about her looks. Keelin knew she was no beauty.

Curse him, she thought angrily. Brian knew just how to irk her. Admittedly, Keelin had always enjoyed the challenge of their verbal duels even though, as often as not, he got the better of her. Of late, however, Brian seemed to avoid her, and when they did meet he was often aloof and his comments were dismissive. She heartily disliked him. Perhaps she would never marry and instead live the life of a priestess like her intimidating and formidable teacher, Nuala. But no, that was not the life for her, whatever the gods may think.

"Let's go home, Rua," she muttered distractedly, trying not to think too much about her troubling future.

As she and Rua made their way slowly down the road, she called and waved a greeting to Pádraig, one of the clan's finest warriors and, although considerably younger than her father, Conall's closest friend. The two men had been spending a great deal of time together of late, often walking out onto the fields where no one would chance to hear their conversation. Conall would always come back with his face grave and full of purpose.

Pádraig returned her greeting. "Good evening to you, Keelin. Hurry home, your mother is beginning to despair, sure that you and Rua have come to grief."

KEELIN REACHED HOME just as the last rays of sunlight glowed on the whitewashed walls of the family cottage. The split-rail fence surrounding the outer reaches of the yard cast long shadows on the bare ground. The yard was quiet and peaceful. Keelin could still see the roses and other flowers that grew in front of the cottage, lining the path to the door. On this late summer evening, their glory of color and scent had waned along with the heat of the season, but there were still those stalwart few, their petals reaching toward the sun, heedless of the inexorable approach of winter.

My mother's flowers, thought Keelin, they never fail to soothe my soul with their delicate beauty. Few people of their clan bothered planting flowers, finding little use for them, and preferred instead to focus on their vegetable gardens, which brought food to their tables. Conall also thought Saraid's flowers were a frivolous extravagance, but he quietly indulged her. Naturally gentle and reserved, Saraid had a calming influence on all, especially on Conall, tempering his mercurial swings of mood and consoling him when demons darkened his soul.

What few people guessed, and even fewer saw, was Saraid's steely determination and cold countenance once provoked. Recently, when Conall's brooding melancholia turned to angry combativeness that had him shouting orders and cursing violently at the slightest provocation, Saraid stood watching him, her white face grim, waiting for his ranting to cease. Then she told him in a clear, stern voice that if he continued to behave like a brutish animal, he could go sleep with the pigs, for she would not tolerate him in her home any longer. Without another word, Saraid turned from him and resumed preparations for dinner. Conall stormed out of the cottage only to feel regret later for provoking Saraid's censure, knowing he had deserved it. Conall also knew that Saraid would never mention the incident again or tally up her grievances against him.

THE TRANQUILITY OF the yard was abruptly shattered when a little brown and white terrier came charging from the direction of the vegetable garden, greeting Keelin with high-pitched barks, his short legs fully extended in his enthusiastic race to reach her. Successful, he bounced around Rua with his tail vibrating and body wiggling. Rua pinned his ears and angrily struck out at the manic little creature with a foreleg. The terrier jumped high into the air, easily dodging the stallion's lethal strike.

"Rua, behave yourself! Riley means no harm and is just happy to see us," Keelin reproached sternly. "Riley, go to the cottage this instant. My jealous Rua would like nothing better than to quiet your yapping for good." She watched as the little dog pranced happily toward the cottage, his right hind leg taking its peculiar little skip every few strides.

It was Saraid who had brought Riley home several years ago from one of her trips to the village. He had been the runt of the litter and Saraid had taken pity on him. When Conall came home he found the little pup curled up next to the fireplace, asleep on one of his old shirts. At first he was angry and exasperated with his wife. Conall loved his collies, but they had a purpose: they were working dogs who helped herd and look after the sheep and cattle.

"This wee terrier," reasoned Conall, "will be of no use whatsoever." He glanced down again at the little pup and shook his head.

Saraid looked resolutely at her husband. "I am sure he will make an excellent mouser." Saraid's words were prophetic. Riley took to his job with such enthusiasm that before long, not a mouse or a rat could be found anywhere near the cottage yard. He also delighted in guarding the vegetable garden, always ready to chase any rabbits who ventured near. Quite often now, Riley would come strutting into the cottage, a rabbit in his mouth, and proudly present it to Saraid.

AFTER GROOMING AND stabling Rua, Keelin ran to the cottage. She was famished, and as she opened the door she was met with the savory aroma of stew and freshly baked bread.

"Keelin, thank heaven you are home safely," greeted Saraid as she stood stirring the stew. "Have you washed up yet? Your father has gone to fetch your Uncle Liam, and as soon as they return we will eat."

"No, not yet," said Keelin, kissing her mother on the cheek. "I wanted to bring the herbs I gathered from the meadow inside before I washed. They are very rare and I feared they might become moldy from the evening damp. If that were to happen, Nuala would surely give me the evil eye."

"Speaking of Nuala," said Saraid frowning, "she visited here today."

Keelin stopped short, at once alert, and looked at her mother.

The Priestess was not one to make social calls. "What brought Nuala here?" she questioned, noting the fine lines of tension on her mother's brow.

Saraid hesitated for only an instant and then responded, "Your uncle Déaglán has returned from his voyage."

"I thought perhaps she had come to complain about my sorry lack of scholarship. I try her patience far too often," Keelin admitted, relieved. Almost as an afterthought, she asked, "Did Uncle Déaglán bring news of importance?"

Saraid smiled, the lines on her brow erased. "I spoke to Nuala only in passing and she made no mention of you. She wished to speak with your father and did not share with me the nature of Déaglán's news. Undoubtedly we will learn more this evening. Now go wash up before the men return. I don't know what is keeping them."

When Conall and Liam eventually entered the cottage, Keelin was helping her mother serve dinner. As Liam stepped across the threshold, he inhaled deeply and smiled. "Ah, rabbit stew. Thank you, clever Riley. I do appreciate your hunting skills."

Saraid, looking up from ladling the stew into a large bowl Keelin held, laughed. "Yes, and this rabbit greatly outweighed him, I assure you."

# CHAPTER TWO

*T*HE LARGE ROOM WAS WARM AND DIM, LIT ONLY by a single lantern and the glow from the fireplace. Conall's collies and Liam's wolfhounds lay in front of the stone hearth. Riley was curled up at Conall's feet. The family ate at a large, rough-hewn oak table and the chairs they sat on were of finely crafted yew wood, adorned with intricately carved designs.

Keelin had hardly touched her meal. The hunger she had felt earlier was gone, replaced by nervous anticipation. After learning that Nuala's visit had not been about her failure to master impossibly long history and poetry recitations, Keelin's curiosity regarding Uncle Déaglán's news was roused. She remembered her mother's tense expression and felt a vague, though seemingly irrational, uneasiness. Uncle Déaglán's rare visits to Eire were always occasions of celebration, and the news he brought of faraway places always captivated Keelin.

Déaglán was Saraid's older brother, although Keelin did not think they looked anything alike, except that they were both tall and slender. Whereas her mother was beautiful and graceful, Uncle Déaglán seemed almost nondescript and ordinary. His clothes usually hung loosely on his long, lanky body and his dark brown hair was invariably unkempt looking. Of course, Keelin knew her uncle was anything but ordinary, being a navigator of high repute. He had always loved the sea, and with the death of his young wife, Maeve, and their infant son in childbirth, it was the sea that gave him his only respite from grief. Many believed he was favored by the gods and that they protected him during his long voyages. Keelin thought it more likely that Déaglán's closest friend and confidant, Fearghus, the powerful High Priest of The Dagda, aided him. Among his many gifts, Fearghus could foresee the coming of storms and fair weather.

Keelin did not share her uncle's love of sailing vast oceans. She could not imagine spending lonely and endless days and weeks at sea. No, it was not her uncle's skill as a navigator that impressed Keelin but his adventures in Eoraip, the continent that lay to the east, far from her island home. She loved his fantastic tales of the mighty Romhanach Empire and its intrigues. She would hang on his every word, wishing she could visit all the wondrous places he described. She could not imagine a more exciting life than that of an adventurer in foreign lands. When Keelin had mentioned as much to Nuala recently, the priestess reminded her that only on Eire did women stand equal to men under the law.

"You would not be allowed to travel freely as Déaglán does in Roma," Nuala had cautioned. "A woman is no better than the property of her father, and then of her husband when she marries. Would you wish to rely on trickery and wiles to gain your ends in such a land? I think not, my bold Keelin. No, you belong here in Eire where your gifts are valued, as a Priestess of The Dagda."

Keelin did not want to think about her "gifts" tonight and how she often felt as much a prisoner of her fate as those poor women in Roma. Mentally shaking herself, she turned to her father and studied him. He had been unusually quiet tonight, gruffly answering questions and not inviting conversation. His dark moods were not uncommon, but this evening she sensed in him a rare solemnity. Even her Uncle Liam, who loved nothing better than a lively discussion during the evening meal, was oddly subdued. Once, Keelin had started to question her father about Uncle Déaglán's news, but her mother cautioned silence with a slight shake of her head. Keelin could do nothing except impatiently wait until her mother deemed it time.

It was not until Conall had finished his meal, pushed back his chair from the table, and absently welcomed Riley as the little dog sprang onto his lap that Saraid spoke.

She took in a deep breath. "Conall, it is time you shared the troubling news Déaglán has brought about the Romhanach and whatever else has been plaguing you since early summer."

Conall had been deep in thought and looked blankly at his wife for a moment. Then, after exchanging a brief glance with his brother, Liam, Conall straightened in his chair and squared his shoulders.

"Déaglán has indeed brought troubling news from Eoraip. Nuala spoke with him yesterday and has told me that there is little doubt the Romhanach are planning an invasion of Eire, possibly as early as next spring. However, I will be better able to assess the Romhanach threat by speaking with Déaglán myself. I will ride to Fhianait tomorrow to see him."

"The Romhanach threat?" Keelin looked at her father in disbelief. The Romhanach Empire had always fueled her dreams, had stirred in her a strange reverence. Nuala often referred to Romhanach medicinal treatments and surgeries, and many of the medical manuscripts Keelin studied were penned by Romhanach physicians. It seemed impossible that such an empire could pose any danger to Eire.

"Indeed, Keelin, the Romhanach threat," responded Conall. "The Dagda has long cautioned us that it was only a matter of time before the Romhanach turned their covetous eyes toward Eire. Yet, I and my fellow chieftains ignored The Dagda's admonitions. We have been too preoccupied with battling each other." In an effort to temper the news, Conall added, "Of course, any number of events may occur to forestall the invasion."

Saraid was not deceived. "Conall, I understand that you wish to spare Keelin and me undo worry, but we are not fainthearted and prefer to know what lies ahead."

"Aye, you must know the truth. Déaglán's news seems only to confirm what we have known since early summer. The Romhanach will invade Eire." Conall spoke softly, staring into the fireplace. The flames had died back, and now only the glow from burning embers remained. Riley whined faintly and licked Conall's hand, sensing his master's distress.

"Might Uncle Déaglán be mistaken?" questioned Keelin, wishing to break the stifling silence in the dark, warm room. "It may be only one of his fanciful tales, for why should he know of Romhanach intent?"

Liam spoke then, a wry grin on his face. "Déaglán may be a bit mad, but his tales are anything but fanciful. You see, Keelin, your Uncle Déaglán is a spy for Eire. The Dagda has long cautioned Eire's chieftains of the threat posed by the Romhanach, but it is Déaglán who has provided the details of their perfidy and evil."

Roused, Conall said, "Eire's only real hope of repulsing an invasion is for our warriors to unite. Nuala has assured me that the priests and priestesses of The Dagda have alerted all of Eire's chieftains of this imminent threat and have convinced them to meet at Tara in a fortnight. There we must agree to form a united warrior force. Déaglán and I will leave for Tara within the week. Pádraig will remain here, acting as chieftain in my absence."

"Surely our warriors are superior to any the Romhanach may have," proclaimed Keelin, her violet eyes flashing.

"Eire's warriors are second to none," exclaimed Conall, his anger rising. "But how can we defeat the Romhanach when we are divided and always at war with one another? Our warriors' prowess will mean nothing against the Romhanach legions, with their superior numbers, discipline, and weaponry. Absolutely nothing!" Conall banged his fist on the arm of his chair, startling Riley. "We must stop waging war against each other and unite. That is our only hope. Think of the powerful resistance we could muster if the finest warriors from every clan in Eire fought as one!" Stirred by the vision, Conall added, "Many of those warriors will be from our clan, one of the most notable being young Brian."

"Yes, Brian has a most vicious temper," declared Liam with relish, completely unfazed by Conall's violent outburst. "Did you hear, Conall, that Brian nearly bested Pádraig yesterday with sword and spear? I truly do love that boy's bloodlust."

Saraid frowned and looked at Liam disapprovingly. "Brian may be an admirable warrior, but he is not a brute. One has only to listen to him sing and see how his younger brothers and sister adore him to know of the kindheartedness he keeps so carefully hidden. He has had much to endure."

Liam scoffed, a wicked gleam in his eyes. "Yes, dear Saraid, Brian does indeed keep that sweet nature of his hidden, *very, very* deep. Though I do agree he has a most beautiful voice, and it will undoubtedly be of considerable use in rousing the warriors to battle when the time comes."

THE NEXT MORNING Saraid stood alone in the cottage yard, watching Conall ride away. She sighed and glanced down at Riley, who sat at her feet. "Come Riley, we had best get on with the day. Let us go see if any rabbits have invaded my vegetable garden while we slept." As soon as Saraid said the word "rabbits," Riley pricked his ears and was off, running toward the garden as fast as his short legs would carry him. Saraid had just started toward the garden when Keelin burst out the front door. She wore a plain linen skirt and blouse, both slightly wrinkled and worn, and her hair hung loosely about her shoulders.

"You look as though you are being pursued by demons," said Saraid.

Keelin abruptly stopped her mad dash the moment she noticed her father riding away on Rua, the two now far beyond the cottage yard. She had had a restless night, finally falling into a nightmare-filled sleep in the early morning hours and not waking until after sunrise. She had missed saying goodbye to her father and Rua, but at the moment she had more worrisome concerns.

"I *completely* forgot that I was to meet Nuala at dawn this morning," said Keelin breathlessly as she walked toward her mother. "I am already horribly late." Keelin braided her auburn hair as she spoke, her fingers quickly weaving the thick locks into a long plait. Frowning, she asked, "Do you believe the Romhanach will invade?"

"I believe they will."

"We will slay them all and spill every last drop of their cursed blood," declared Keelin, purposely not meeting her mother's eyes, knowing they would be filled with reproof. Rising up on her tiptoes, Keelin kissed her mother's cheek, and then turned and ran toward the barn. "I should be home by sun-down," she called over her shoulder. Though perhaps not, thought Keelin, knowing Nuala all too well. She will probably torture me with some odious task late into the evening to punish me for my lack of "punctuality and dedication."

As Keelin hurriedly completed her morning chores, she concocted an excellent excuse for her tardiness. She actually enjoyed inventing elaborate excuses to present to Nuala. It was a challenge of the mind, and Keelin's skill at protecting her thoughts from the priestess was increasing. Initially, Nuala's austere manner and unrelenting demands had overwhelmed Keelin, making her feel unworthy. She was awed by the priestess's vast knowledge, not only in the art of healing, but in every discipline imaginable. Nuala had only to look at Keelin with those piercing, perceptive eyes to make her feel oddly vulnerable and ill at ease, the priestess being the only person who had ever truly intimidated her. However, Keelin's irrepressible nature could not be stifled for long, even by the formidable Nuala. Keelin soon learned that Nuala's power to read her thoughts was not absolute. She could sometimes fool the Priestess and that was all the inspiration Keelin needed. Though never disrespectful, she took a certain wicked pleasure in testing her increasing power, secretly delighting in the effects of her mischief on Nuala.

Keelin was soon running across the fields, hoping she would catch up with Nuala before the priestess reached the village. At first heedless of the wet grasses, she quickly found it increasingly difficult to run, her damp skirt clinging to her thighs and grabbing her ankles with every stride.

"Curse it!" she muttered, lifting the hem of her skirt to her knees as she continued to run. Keelin thought long skirts and dresses very silly and quite impractical for almost everything and had said as much to Nuala, indignant that women could not wear trousers. To her surprise, Nuala had not been in the least shocked, smiling in amusement before raising an eyebrow in censure.

Having shed her shoes some distance back to cross a narrow creek, Keelin soon reached the main road, the only hurdle left being the stone wall. Shoving her shoes into her satchel, Keelin nimbly climbed the wall, threw one leg over the top, and then dropped down to the other side. In spite of the cool morning, Keelin was sweating from her run. She had just brushed back errant strands of hair that were plastered against her face and neck when she was startled by an unexpected greeting.

"Good morning to you, Keelin," said her cousin, Séamus, cheerfully. "I believe the fox went that way."

Keelin looked up to see Séamus and Brian, both on horseback, smiling down at her. Also looking at her with concern rather than amusement was Sinéad, a village girl Keelin's age and the miller's daughter. Sinéad was sitting aboard an open wagon filled with sacks of corn meal, a large gray draft horse harnessed to it.

"Very good, Séamus," responded Keelin sweetly. "I see that being dropped on your head as an infant affected your wit only modestly."

Séamus laughed good-naturedly. "Yes, luckily I have a very thick skull. But in all earnestness, Keelin, whatever possessed you to run across the fields this early in the morning? You are soaked from the dew."

"I am late. I was to meet Nuala earlier, but I suppose it is of no great consequence," said Keelin with as much nonchalance as she could summon. She was now painfully aware of her appearance, from her muddy feet and wet skirt to the strands of damp hair hanging about her face.

"You are in luck, then," responded Séamus, "for Brian and I saw Nuala not ten minutes ago on her way to visit Pádraig. She said that if we saw you, we were to tell you to begin your patient visits without her, that she will join you later this afternoon."

"Ah, that's grand," said Keelin, relieved.

"Nuala seemed irritated with you," commented Brian with a teasing, though not unkind, smile. "Tardy again?"

Keelin pointedly ignored Brian, her chin held high. She looked at Sinéad, who smiled back rather vaguely. Sinéad was a kind, sensible young woman and had all the makings of a good farmer's wife. Keelin found her painfully uninteresting. Still, Sinéad had calmly and skillfully assisted Keelin when she had set the badly fractured leg of Declan, Sinéad's younger brother. Their mother had fainted straight away at the sight of her son's mangled leg, but Sinéad had kept her wits about her. Sinéad's skill would be needed if the Romhanach do invade, thought Keelin, anger welling up in her, remembering the fearful wounds and death that all battles wrought, no matter the victor. She suddenly hated the Romhanach and their devouring ambitions, truly wishing to slay them all. How could she have ever admired them?

"Did you see . . ." Keelin hesitated, glancing first at Séamus and then at Brian, "my father this morning?" She was loathe to say more, not knowing whether news of the Romhanach had spread to the villagers yet.

"Séamus, I know you wish to escort Sinéad as far as the south road," said Brian. He and Séamus exchanged a brief look, Séamus's habitually cheerful expression sobering slightly. "I will meet you there shortly."

"I can think of nothing I would enjoy more," responded Séamus gallantly, smiling down at the deeply blushing though obviously pleased Sinéad.

Brian waited until the two were beyond earshot then turned to Keelin. "We did not see your father. Pádraig called for a warriors' assembly at dawn this morning and so we have just learned of Déaglán's news. Of course, Nuala has warned us of the Romhanach intentions for months, but not even your father paid her heed. Undoubtedly you have known for some time, being Nuala's favorite pupil and minion."

Keelin ignored Brian's jab and merely nodded, not wanting to admit that Nuala had shared nothing of the Romhanach threat with her.

"I hope they do not invade," Keelin blurted out, her anger and careless bravado of the morning replaced by apprehension.

"You cannot possibly fear the Romhanach! You would gladly cut the heart out of anyone who threatened Eire and suffer no qualms." Brian looked at Keelin with disappointment. "I expected you to be as eager as I for the battle and victory."

"Of course you are eager for battle!" said Keelin, frustrated by her own ambivalence. "You are a warrior. You will slay Eire's enemies, will drive the invader from our shores. I long to defend Eire as you will. You will battle the Romhanach and save Eire, whereas I . . ." Keelin could not continue. She stood glaring at Brian, mute.

"Must battle to save the wounded and dying," finished Brian, his tone softening. "I should not have forgotten your part in the last clan battle."

"Worse yet——" Keelin stopped before admitting she would be compelled to ease the suffering of wounded Romhanach soldiers on the battlefield. She would only be a hindrance to Eire's cause, such was her powerful instinct to heal.

"I shall magnanimously overlook your reluctance for battle, understanding its source," said Brian with a smile and broad sweep of his arm. "You may still accompany Séamus and me on our grand adventures after our victory over the Romhanach. In honesty, we would miss our dogged little shadow should you not be stalking us."

"Your adventures would be decidedly uninspired," responded Keelin, her lips twitching slightly, a crooked smile touching them. "For it was I who always imagined the most exciting and dangerous ones when we were children. Besides, I have no wish to accompany the two of you anywhere. I have dreams of my own after Eire's victory."

"Have you now?" Brian's dark eyes twinkled, and there was a patronizing look of mild interest on his face.

"Have you forgotten that I am a healer and will one day be a priestess of The Dagda?" shot back Keelin.

"No," said Brian, his tone at once becoming cool and unfriendly. "No," he repeated, "I have not forgotten, though why you would wish to become a priestess like Nuala is beyond me. Soon I will find you lurking in shadows, divining the will of the gods. Impressive to be sure, though not a life I would choose."

"It is not a choice but a destiny," responded Keelin too vehemently, stung by his retort.

Brian chuckled and looked down the road in the direction Seamus had gone. He picked up his horse's reins. "There is always a choice, Keelin. Do not let that old vulture, Nuala, tell you otherwise."

Keelin did not watch him ride off. Brian's words held more truth than she was willing to admit. She had no desire to be a priestess. Indecision plagued her as she walked toward the village. She was accustomed to bold, even precipitous action, and hated herself for what she perceived as weakness.

# CHAPTER THREE

ONALL AND DÉAGLÁN STOOD ON A BLUFF LOOKING
out at the ink blue waters of a large bay. It was dotted
with small, rocky islands that were uninhabited except by
screeching gulls and other sea birds. Fhianait, the small fishing
village where Déaglán lived when in Eire, lay some distance to
the west. When Conall had arrived, rain threatened but the men
had taken little notice, walking purposefully toward the bluff as
they skirted the shoreline, discussing the Romhanach menace.
By noon the clouds had lifted and fleeting patches of blue sky
appeared. Every now and then the sun's rays broke through,
reflecting off the ocean's dark surface for a few welcome moments. In spite of the brightening skies, the somber mood of the
men only deepened.

"Are there no warriors left in Sasanach bold enough to resist
the Romhanach?" asked Conall.

Déaglán knew the question was largely rhetorical and that
Conall knew the fate of Sasanach and her people almost as well
as himself. The Romhanach had begun their conquest of the
large island that lay east of Eire years before, at first facing
strong resistance. However, Sasanach tribes and fiefdoms, much
like Eire's clans, had been forever at odds with one another and

could not mount a united front to battle the mighty Romhanach legions. Tribe by tribe, fiefdom by fiefdom, the invaders attacked and overwhelmed the Sasanach. If the generals' demands for surrender were not met, entire villages, including women and children, were massacred, and captured Sasanach leaders were subjected to torture and humiliation before their executions. Romhanach brutality had struck terror into the hearts of the Sasanach people and there were few left who were brave enough to continue the fight.

"The men of the highlands are still fierce and ready to do battle," said Déaglán. "These rebels swoop down in quick, lethal strikes on Romhanach encampments and disappear just as swiftly. Few soldiers are foolhardy enough to give chase, knowing all too well that death by ambush awaits them in the highlands. But while the rebels make life more difficult for the Romhanach, they are no real threat." Déaglán felt a surge of emotion, re-membering one such raid, the rebels riding at full gallop, shout-ing as though possessed by demons, terrifying many of the younger and less experienced Romhanach soldiers. "I shall never forget the image of those brave men charging toward the enemy camp, intent upon wreaking as much havoc as possible, of spilling the blood of their accursed enemies!"

"There are no such men left in the lowlands?" asked Conall a second time.

"The Sasanach leaders and warriors of the lowlands have long since been killed in battle or executed, their women and children sold into slavery. The men who are left have little stom-ach for battle, many of whom have even embraced the harsh edicts of their new rulers. They are loathsome creatures, ex-changing freedom and honor for safety and order." His voice was filled with contempt, and Déaglán kicked a rock that lay at

his feet, sending it far beyond the bluff's edge and onto the
rocky shore below.

"I suppose there will always be men who are ready to give
their allegiance to whomever holds power, at whatever the price,"
responded Conall. "I do not understand such men, but I know
they indeed exist."

Both men were silent for some time, each contemplating
what lay ahead.

"It seems the circumstances are as dire as I had feared,"
said Conall at last.

Déaglán frowned. "Yes, alarmingly so. Yet, there may still
be hope, for all is not well with the new emperor, Domitian. The
Senate despises him and rightfully so, for he has made no pre-
tense of honoring their counsel, viewing them only as his servants. His insistence on being addressed as 'Master and God'
has only heightened the Senate's anger and humiliation. I did
not hear whisperings of any plot to assassinate him, but I would
not be surprised if there is one in the making."

"And the Romhanach military?" questioned Conall.

"Domitian has their support but not yet their allegiance. He
attempted to buy their loyalty by raising the pay of the legionnaires. While this has undoubtedly made him popular with the
rank and file soldiers and precluded threatened mutinies, it has
done little to elevate his stature among officers. Domitian desperately needs military victories to prove his worth as supreme
commander, thereby winning their respect." In spite of the seri-
ousness of Déaglán's words, he had become animated, caught
up in the drama that was unfolding. "Herein lies Eire's hope.
Domitian's legions have suffered serious defeats in Eoraip, both
in the conquest of new frontiers and in the quelling of rebellions.
Furthermore, there is a growing threat from the Dacian tribes to

the east. The generals of these legions have been clamoring for reinforcements, claiming victories cannot be achieved without additional men and weaponry. Likewise, Agricola, the commanding general of the legions in Sasanach, has requested reinforcements for the invasion of Eire. The victories achieved by Agricola in Sasanach have won him favor in the Romhanach capital and stand out in stark contrast to the debacles in Eoraip. And this is where the intrigue becomes very interesting." Déaglán smiled, clearly fascinated with the machinations of the emperor and his generals. "Domitian sent reinforcements to his generals in Eoraip, but has thus far ignored Agricola's request, though I heard rumors that an imperial dispatch was due any day. Agricola has grown impatient waiting for Domitian's response and has issued orders for the invasion of Eire in late spring or early summer, regardless of what the dispatch may contain. With the legions already stationed in Sasanach, Agricola can easily launch the invasion, though his forces are insufficient for a protracted war in Eire. Agricola is gambling that he will achieve an initial victory, or at the very least, establish a strong fortress on Eire. Either circumstance will almost surely result in Domitian granting the necessary reinforcements."

"What is the likelihood of the emperor granting such reinforcements before the invasion?" asked Conall.

Déaglán smiled with wry amusement. "I have had occasion to know the emperor quite well. He is neither decisive nor bold and not half the man that Agricola is. However, Domitian is cunning and cruel and a master at manipulation, as his enemies have learned all too well. He does not like Agricola, the general reminding him too much of his older brother whom he envied and despised. Therefore, he will taunt Agricola with his silence, hoping for precipitous action. He will withhold his approval of reinforcements, waiting to see the outcome of Agricola's initial invasion. If it is successful, Domitian will publicly declare victory over Eire and take credit for the invasion, readily approving reinforcements. But if Agricola meets with disaster, Domitian has only to reprimand him for his ill-advised and unauthorized invasion. Either way, Domitian will be satisfied."

Conall shrugged. "Without the unification of Eire's warriors, we will be unable to deliver a staggering blow to Agricola's legions, even if Domitian withholds reinforcements. Your optimistic suppositions will come to naught."

"Even with unification," Déaglán cautioned, "Eire's warriors face almost impossible odds. And we must protect Eire against spies and traitors to have any hope of defeating the Romhanach. If Agricola were to learn of Eire's unification, all advantage would be lost. Therefore, it is not enough to unite. We must be vigilant and wary, examining even the most seemingly untoward action with suspicion."

"Spies, yes, but traitors, never!" Conall spat the words out as if trying to rid himself of a bitter taste.

"You may loathe the idea of traitors to Eire, but you are not so foolish as to deny their existence. Furthermore, they are likely to be men of substance, with knowledge of our battle plans and strategy. Agricola's spies are very good, and they will carefully look for the discontented warrior or chieftain and entice him with offers of power and riches in a vanquished Eire. I have little doubt there will be at least one man, if not more, who will betray his people for ambition."

"You are a cynical man, Déaglán."

"Perhaps, but more importantly, I am a spy and know of what I speak."

AFTER AN HOUR spent discussing battlefield tactics and strategy, the men started their walk back to the fishing village. They had not gone far when Déaglán said, "There is something else I think you must know, for it portends in Eire's favor. However, I would ask that you keep what I am about to tell you in the strictest confidence."

"Of course," responded Conall, intrigued by Déaglán's suddenly cautious behavior.

"I was very curious about what this alleged dispatch from Domitian might contain, and if it even existed. A courier was expected within the week, and I decided to delay my departure from Sasanach until he arrived. I ignored my instincts as well as other telltale signs of danger and did not quietly disappear when I should have, such was my eagerness to discover what the courier may deliver. I was foolish because the odds of Domitian approving Agricola's request were negligible, but I wanted proof. As it turned out, I was imprudent and it nearly cost me my life. The day the courier arrived, without any dispatch for Agricola I might add, my identity was discovered."

Conall stopped in his tracks and looked sharply at Déaglán, who appeared almost chagrined, concerned more with his failure to elude detection than his capture by the Romhanach. "Continue," said Conall simply.

"I believe that under torture, one of the Sasanach captives may have betrayed me, but I had sensed danger for some time and do not blame the poor man. Romhanach torture is truly horrific and few can withstand it for long. I was imprisoned in a guarded cell located near the eastern wall of the fortress, awaiting Agricola's arrival the next morning. I knew I would be tortured and executed but could think of no way to escape. Miraculously, however, I did, and it was only with the help of The Dagda that I made it back to Eire alive." Déaglán looked pensively toward the ocean. "I admit I have many fancies and am given to talking to myself and with the gods on occasion. Much of my time is spent alone at sea or spying on others where I must always keep my own counsel. I have learned to live within my solitary world and am content there. Often at sea, when I can no longer keep my eyes open and fall into a restless slumber, I dream that my good friend Fearghus is there at my side, sailing my boat through rough waters or calling on fair winds where there had been for days only a deadly calm. Other times I dream of dear Maeve and she tells me that we will be together again in my next life, and that I will not be a sailor but a grand adventurer, scaling mountain peaks that reach the very heavens. I have always believed these to be dreams, however real they may have seemed. Now, after my escape from the fortress, I am not so certain. For you see, I had help that night from the Priestess Deirdre who seemed more a lovely phantom than a flesh and blood young woman. When I first heard her voice, I was lying awake on the cold ground of my cell, contemplating the horrors I would surely face in the morning." Noticing Conall's quizzical look upon hearing Deirdre's name, he added, "Of course, you do not know Deirdre. She is a priestess in a northern clan and was one of Fearghus's students. She is quick-witted and pretty, and it is said that she can gentle the most wild of beasts with just her voice or touch. She was once seen stroking the head of a great gray wolf as if it were a gentle collie."

Déaglán's voice had taken on a wistful quality and it seemed as if he was drifting into one of his peculiar reveries when he abruptly shook his head. "Conall, you must excuse me. I will get back to my strange tale. As I said, I was lying there, wondering if I would be able withstand the torture without screaming for mercy when I heard Deirdre calling to me. I looked frantically toward the guard but he didn't seem to hear her. I thought I must be going mad. I was not dreaming and yet I heard her voice as clearly as I can hear my own right now. Deirdre spoke again reassuring me that she was there to help me escape. She said there was a powerful storm approaching that should be overhead in less than an hour. It would bring deafening thunder and deadly lightning strikes that would set the fortress ablaze. The storm would wreak havoc on the Romhanach, killing many and creating confusion and panic, during which I could make my escape. She detailed a route that would give me my best chance for freedom." Déaglán paused, then added, "There was only one other strange occurrence. I had just escaped through a burning gap in the fortress wall and was running past the outlying cattle pens and soldiers' huts when I heard loud shouts over the din of the thunder. I was sure at any moment I would feel the burning pain of a spear or arrow as it pierced my back. Instead, I felt and saw Deirdre beside me, throwing her Dagda cloak over my shoulders and drawing me close to her body. The next moment I was in the shelter of the woods and Deirdre was gone."

"A strange tale to be sure," said Conall. "I have never doubted the powers of The Dagda, though it gives me pause that a young priestess would risk an open display of them. Why chance revealing such powers now? The priests and priestesses of The Dagda have always fiercely guarded their secrets, as if their very survival depended on it. There seems to be only one logical explanation for The Dagda saving you. They felt it critical that you live to bring us news of the impending Romhanach invasion."

"I am certain Deirdre aided me for just that reason. I am also certain that she and others of The Dagda will use their enchantments to aid us in our fight."

Conall shook his head. "The Dagda forbids its priests and priestesses to aid any man in war or bloodletting. No, The Dagda will not aid us."

"I do not agree," responded Déaglán. "The Dagda may not help us during the battle, but I am certain that my friend, the high priest Fearghus, will find some means to use the powers of The Dagda to help save Eire from destruction."

# CHAPTER FOUR

*K*EELIN WOKE UP IN A DARK MOOD. SHE HAD SLEPT only intermittently, with a nightmare plaguing her sleep and vivid images of the wounded and dying racing through her mind while awake. She did not know which had been more dreadful, her dream or her conscious thoughts. She was only surprised that her nightmare was not of battle scenes and death, but of Brian, at his most dismissive, and of her father, uncharacteristically passive and resigned. What did it mean? Keelin's dreams had always alternated between the wonderful and the savage. She was either flying joyously or fighting some fierce and deadly foe, whether man, beast, or disease. This nightmare had been horrible, but in a different way. Keelin had been powerless, unable to fight Brian, and left only with a fearful foreboding.

The nightmare replayed persistently in which she helplessly watched Brian, astride Rua, riding away on him—no, Keelin thought angrily, *stealing* him. Brian was dressed as a warrior going into battle. He wore a fine wool tunic of royal blue over a thick shirt of cotton. On top of the tunic was a three-meshed coat of mail, made of cold, refined iron. Around his waist was a wide belt of leather, carved with frightening images of wild boars and dragons. From that belt hung a sharp, single-edged sword. He held a long spear in his right hand, forged with twists and breaks along its entire surface so that any thrust would not only cut but also rip and tear as it was driven in and then recovered. His head was bare, his black hair reaching almost to his shoulders and the white skin of his face taut. Keelin had shouted at Brian, demanding that he come back.

Brian laughed in response. "Wee Keelin, you will not be needing Rua as a priestess of The Dagda. Rua is a warrior's horse and not a steed for a witch. Your father no longer needs him and I have a battle to fight."

Keelin, now frantic, called to Rua, commanding him to obey her and return. The stallion did not even turn his mighty head to look at her. Keelin then noticed her parents standing some distance away, watching Brian as he rode off. Her father was also dressed as a warrior, but his tunic was a blood-stained gray and he carried no weapon.

She ran to them and screamed, "Father, will you let Brian go and take Rua? You will need him for the approaching battle. Why do you just stand there?"

Her father merely shook his head. "Keelin, let Brian go. What he says is true. I no longer need Rua. My days as a warrior are over."

Keelin, tears streaming down her cheeks, looked beseechingly at her mother and saw only sadness and heartache written on the beloved face. Keelin turned and watched as Brian and Rua disappeared.

Sweating, and with tears in her eyes, Keelin would awake with a start.

All morning, while Keelin helped her mother and Uncle Liam with work on the farm, she agonized over the dream and what it might mean. It would be unbearable if her father were to die in battle. She could not bear it if the dream was a presage of his death. At daybreak he had left for Tara, accompanied by Nuala and Uncle Déaglán, and his departure had only heightened her anxiety.

I am being foolish, letting a dream affect me so, thought Keelin. She tried to reassure herself and turned her thoughts to the rest of her day, which would be spent visiting patients in the village and surrounding farms. However, she could not shrug off the troubling dream and felt renewed hostility toward Brian, who had played such a villain in it.

NELLIE NICKERED WHEN Keelin approached the pasture where the mare was grazing. She had decided to use the old mare on her patient visits today. Normally, Keelin and Nuala walked when making their rounds. The priestess insisted that it was good for the body and soul to be firmly connected with the earth and frowned upon any mention of riding or taking a horse-drawn cart. Although Keelin would never admit it, she loved to walk with the Priestess, intently listening to Nuala's lectures on medicine, often scrambling to keep up. But with Nuala away on one of her increasingly frequent and mysterious journeys, Keelin did not want to be alone and Nellie was always good company.

"So, my beautiful Nellie," Keelin said as the mare nudged her hand, "how are all your aches and pains today?"

Keelin had just turned five when her father had unceremoniously placed her astride Nellie, their reliable and stocky cart horse, with the instructions, "Now then, Keelin, ride her to the gate and back." Conall had soundly slapped the mare's rump and watched them trot away.

Nellie was now over twenty years old with arthritic knees
and pasterns, yet Keelin kept the mare sound and content. Each
day she mixed a special remedy in Nellie's bran mash that kept
the swelling and pain at bay.

"Yes, I see that you are quite well." She stroked the mare's
neck, knowing the remedy only slowed the progression of Nellie's
complaints. Keelin fervently wished that her healing powers were
stronger. There were so few diseases that could be cured. Keelin
now had sufficient knowledge to treat the sick and ease their pain
and suffering, and her otherworldly gift for healing was considerable, but she was not satisfied. Although she felt her power
growing daily, there was much she still had to learn from Nuala.
The priestess's unyielding manner and impossible expectations
often made studying under her intolerable. Yet Keelin could not
deny Nuala's brilliance. With no one but the priestess could she
master the art of healing. I *must* be patient, she thought with
grim determination as she led Nellie out of the pasture.

Nuala had accepted Keelin as a student of The Dagda
when she turned ten. Before then, the two saw each other only
infrequently. For her part, Keelin was in awe of Nuala but also
wary of her. Even from a very young age Keelin understood she
was different, had strange, otherworldly powers of the mind she
kept hidden as best she could. She instinctively knew Nuala possessed powers even stronger than her own. Therefore, she carefully avoided the priestess, not wishing to arouse her scrutiny.
Keelin eventually realized she had nothing to fear. Nuala rarely
even looked at her and, when she did, it was with cool disregard.
It was only after the incident with the wild boar when she was
nine that the priestess began to take notice of her.

Keelin had been excited that day. Her father and his brother,
Eirnín, along with Séamus and Brian, were going to hunt a large

stag that had been spotted in the northern woods. For the first time, Keelin's father had invited her to join them. Aunt Meghan, Eirnín's wife, had admonished both her husband and Conall when she saw Keelin about to ride off with the hunting party.

"A hunt is no place for a lass as young as Keelin. What possessed the two of you to even consider such a thing," Meghan proclaimed, her hands on her very sizable hips. Meghan was a big, sturdy woman with fiery red hair and a temper to match. She always spoke her mind and was never intimidated by Conall, much less her husband.

"Keelin can ride better than Séamus and will come to no harm," Eirnín answered, trying to placate his wife. "We will take great care of her, I assure you."

"Nonsense. Conall, I cannot imagine how Saraid must feel, you taking her dear lass and only child on a hunt. You don't know what you might encounter—wolves, wild boar—it's frightful." Becoming more incensed, Meghan was about to continue her harangue when Conall put up his hand and stopped her.

"Silence, Meghan. Saraid and I both agreed Keelin should join the stag hunt. I, for one, can think of a no more fearless and able companion."

Keelin swelled with pride as she rode off with the hunting party but dared not look at Aunt Meghan. Instead, she trotted Nellie up alongside her father who looked down and gave her a conspiratorial wink.

According to Uncle Eirnín, the big red buck was magnificent, with at least eighteen points on his antlers. Venison was highly prized in Eire and this buck would provide meat for her uncle's large family over the long winter. Séamus and Brian were both twelve and had accompanied the men on other hunts. Brian was already broad-shouldered and nearly as tall as the men.

Séamus, although naturally tall of frame, had not yet matured and was still considerably smaller than his best friend. Years before, Eirnín had taken Brian under his wing and had treated the boy as a son, knowing he received no paternal affection or guidance at home. Brian had responded with something akin to hero worship and loved Eirnín with steadfast devotion.

They had tracked the stag for nearly an hour when the hounds began to whine and behave strangely. They had been given the scent to track deer and became hesitant when they encountered the strong scent of another animal, especially the scent of a predator. Eirnín called the hounds to him and all but his youngest obeyed.

"Curse that young pup. Where did Béar go off to? I should not have brought him."

"It will be the death of him," said Conall, "for I fear the hounds have come upon the scent of wild boar and he will have no chance alone."

At that moment, they heard the rustle of bracken some twenty yards away and caught a fleeting glimpse of a massive boar as it disappeared into the woods. Conall turned to Séamus and Brian. "Stay here with Keelin and keep a keen eye for any more of the foul creatures. It is unlikely but you must take no chances." With that, the men galloped off in pursuit of the boar, the hounds bounding ahead of them.

Angry beyond words, Brian glared at Keelin. They had been sitting there for some time, the boys glowering at Keelin and she glowering right back at them, when they heard the agonized cry of a hound. It had come from the southwest, the opposite direction from the men's hunt. Keelin, without a moment's hesitation, kicked Nellie and was off in the direction of the cry, crashing through the woods, swerving around trees, and flattening herself against Nellie's neck as the mare galloped under low-hanging branches. Stunned for a second by Keelin's mad reaction, Séamus and Brian were quickly in pursuit. But while their horses were much faster, they were also bigger and the boys could not take the direct route that Keelin had. They were forced to check their horses repeatedly and steer around the tree branches that she had galloped under so recklessly.

By the time they reached the clearing where the attack had occurred, Keelin was already kneeling over the wounded hound. To the boys' horror, a wild boar was charging at full speed toward Keelin. They yelled a frantic warning to her but she ignored them, intent only on ministering to the pitiful hound. When the boar was but a stride or two away, Keelin looked up and with all her might commanded, "HALT!" Incredibly, the boar checked himself in mid-stride, but his momentum carried his massive body forward and one of his razor-sharp tusks pierced Keelin's chest. Recovering his balance, the boar seemed to look directly at Keelin. Then he spun around and ran from the clearing.

"Séamus, ride as fast as you can and bring back your father and Conall! I will help Keelin." Brian jumped from his horse and ran to Keelin's side. There was blood everywhere and he could not tell if it was Keelin's or the hound's. She had been knocked over by the boar but had righted herself and was again examining the hound by the time he reached her.

"Keelin!" said Brian as he knelt down next to her. "How deeply did the beast gore you?" Her woolen sweater was torn and covered with blood but Keelin seemed not to notice. When Brian attempted to inspect her wound, she brushed his hand away distractedly.

"I was dazed for a moment but I am not badly hurt. The boar just pricked me with his tusk. He must have decided to come back and finish off poor Béar. The big beast's first strike was a poor one." All the while Keelin spoke she was running her fingers gently over the hound's body. There was a large gash on his belly and his entrails were protruding from the open wound. He was panting but was otherwise still.

"Keelin, move away from Béar. I will put him out of his misery." Brian pulled a sharp knife from a sheath on his belt. Keelin caught his wrist in a vice-like grip.

"No!" she cried. "Béar is not fatally hurt. I know it looks dreadful but if we can get him to Nuala quickly, she can help him. I saw Nuala walking toward Uncle Eirnín's cottage when we left. With any luck she will still be there. Come now, help me with Béar so I can get on Nellie."

"I'll have no part in prolonging the poor hound's suffering. Curse you, Keelin, haven't you already done enough, almost getting yourself killed. Now move aside." Brian wrenched his arm from Keelin's grasp and tried to push her away, but she threw herself at him and wrapped her arms around his waist.

"Please, Brian! Béar appears to have no injuries to his vitals. I know I am right, please!" Keelin clung to Brian, her head pressed against his chest, her tears mingling with her blood on his shirt.

Brian glanced at the hound as he felt Keelin's body strain and tremble with the struggle to hold him tight. He sighed and returned his knife to its sheath, then stroked Keelin's hair.

"Don't cry, my fierce lass. We will find Nuala and she can try to work her magic on Béar." With that, he pried Keelin's arms from around his waist and gently wiped the tears from her eyes.

Brian walked over to where Nellie stood quietly and led the mare to Keelin. "Jump on Nellie and I will hand Béar up to you."

Keelin swayed as she stood up, lifting her hand to her forehead. Alarmed, Brian put his arm around her shoulders.

"I'll not let you ride alone. The three of us can ride on Rónán—and no arguments. You and Béar will be tumbling off Nellie, light-headed as you are." Brian whistled to his horse and Rónán came trotting over.

Instead of an angry retort, Keelin smiled amiably and allowed Brian to lift her onto Rónán's back and hand her Béar. Brian then jumped on Rónán and leading Nellie, they started back to Eirnín's cottage. They had gone only a short distance when the men, followed by Séamus, came galloping out of the woods. Keelin did not notice her father's expression change from fear to relief at the sight of her. Her thoughts were only of Béar. Leaning back against Brian's chest, she cradled the hound in her arms and murmured soothing words to him. Her father made no reproach and reined his horse alongside them.

When the hunting party reached Eirnín's farm, Keelin was relieved to find that Nuala was still there. The boys took care of the horses, while Eirnín held the hound and Conall walked with a protective arm around Keelin to the cottage. Conall had attempted to carry her but she refused his assistance and wiggled out of his arms.

"I am quite well," Keelin furtively whispered to her father, even though she still felt faint. She didn't want Nuala to treat her first, knowing that Béar was more seriously injured. She had noted that Brian's ill humor had slowly returned as they rode back to the cottage. He had undoubtedly begun stewing over the lost chance at hunting wild boar, thought Keelin. Forgetting his kindness in the clearing, she only remembered his anger at having to stay with her and his intention to finish off poor Béar.

The commotion of their arrival alerted Nuala and Aunt

Meghan. They emerged from the cottage door just as the men dismounted. At the sight of Keelin blood-stained and pale as death, Meghan gave a concerned cry and then leveled a sharp glance at Conall and her husband. She was ready to unleash a torrent of angry accusations, but Nuala took her arm and silenced her.

"The child is not seriously hurt and is only concerned for the poor hound Eirnín carries," she said firmly. "You may chastise the men for their folly later." With that, Nuala walked toward Eirnín and the hound.

"So tell me, Keelin, what happened to foolish young Béar, and why do you think I can save him?" Nuala took Béar from Eirnín and carried the hound to the cottage.

"Béar was attacked by a wild boar and has a large wound on his belly," said Keelin. "However, the injury is not fatal. The boar must have delivered only a glancing blow."

"Is that so?" said Nuala, not even glancing at the girl. "We shall see. Meghan, get a linen cloth and spread it on the table. Bring me plenty of boiling water and clean, dry rags."

When all was ready, Nuala placed the hound on the table and began examining him. Her long, bony fingers moved quickly and expertly as she gently probed the hound's wound. Abruptly, she raised her head and looked intensely at Keelin. "I indeed can find no serious internal injuries, though I find it odd, given this was a boar attack."

Keelin quickly averted her eyes. "I was certain Béar's wound was not fatal!"

Nuala gave the girl a withering glance. "Keelin, I want you to watch carefully as I close Béar's wounds. I will make interior sutures with this fiber. As the wound heals, the fiber will be absorbed into Béar's body." Nuala threaded a sharp needle with tough-looking thread. "After I complete my interior sutures, I will use a linen thread to make the exterior sutures. It is very important that the area remains clean and free from infection. You noted that I applied a powder to the wound, which should help prevent any pollution and festering. If no internal or external infection occurs, Béar should survive." Nuala completed the interior repair and adeptly closed the abdominal wound with neat, uniform stitches.

With her repair work complete and Béar placed on a blanket in front of the fireplace, Nuala looked pointedly at Keelin. "Béar's vital organs were not damaged. Though, as I said earlier, the wound was singularly peculiar. Infection is his only real threat. Now, let me look at you."

She examined the cut to Keelin's chest. "I am afraid this wound requires stitches and there will undoubtedly be a scar. You are lucky the boar was nimble and avoided doing more harm."

At Nuala's words, Séamus burst out, "You cannot believe how Keelin stopped the boar! It was charging her at full speed when she commanded it to halt, and it did! I still cannot believe it, though I saw it with my own eyes." Séamus regarded his cousin with admiration and pride.

"The boar undoubtedly stopped charging because of the threat from you and Brian, not Keelin's command," Nuala responded, dismissing Séamus's story without so much as a glance.

"Wild boars don't break off their charge, even when threatened," Brian proclaimed with authority.

"But they do break off their charge when a nine-year-old girl commands them to do so," Nuala said dismissively. "I have heard enough."

Looking defiant and angry, Brian shot Keelin a scathing

glance and, with a motion for Séamus to follow, strode out of the cottage. Nuala glanced up as they departed but said nothing.

THE WOUND FROM the boar's tusk did leave a crescent moon–shaped scar above Keelin's right breast. The scar was a constant reminder of how her life changed forever that day. She became Nuala's student and was propelled into the world of The Dagda. The priestess was quick to condemn Keelin's actions with the admonition to never display her gifts so openly in the future. "The gods did not bestow you with powers of the mind to save foolish hounds. We of The Dagda must use our powers wisely and always with discretion."

"But I am *not* of The Dagda," Keelin retorted when Nuala told her of The Dagda's law of secrecy.

"You will be one day," the priestess replied.

# CHAPTER FIVE

KEELIN TROTTED NELLIE INTO THE YARD OF A SMALL, neat farm. Two small boys were playing with one of the family collies near the pigpen and an older boy was harnessing their cart horse to a wagon. Sitting on a rail of the stable fence and watching her older brother was a small girl of nine. She had light blonde hair and round blue eyes that seemed too large for her delicate face. She was painfully thin, her spindly legs and arms partially hidden by a linen pinafore. When she and her brother saw Keelin, they both called a greeting, the little girl's face lighting up with a radiant smile. Despite her frail appearance, the girl's face was tinged with a healthy pink blush and her eyes were clear and sparkling.

"Keelin!" the little girl cried, jumping from the fence and running to greet her. "I've missed you so. Donal is going to let me go with him to the village because I am feeling so well."

Keelin's heart always swelled with love when she saw little Caitlin. She was one of Keelin's successes, seemingly cured, at least for now, of an evil disease that had threatened to kill her only six months earlier. Keelin jumped from Nellie's back and hugged Caitlin as the girl threw herself into Keelin's arms.

"I can see how well you are and how strong you are becoming. Here, take Nellie to the stable and give her some water. Then you can tell me all that has happened since I last saw you."

Keelin smiled as Caitlin led Nellie away. She walked over to Donal who also watched his sister as Caitlin and Nellie disappeared into the stable.

"So good to see you, Keelin," Donal said enthusiastically. "I promised Caitlin I would take her to the village today, and I am glad we were delayed or we would have missed you."

Just then Caitlin's mother, Maureen, emerged from the cottage and greeted Keelin. "Will you join me for a cup of cider, Keelin?"

"Thank you, but not today. Nuala is away and I have many visits I must make. I see that Caitlin needs nothing from me but I will visit with her outside for a while if I may."

"Yes, she does look well, thanks to the gods and to you, Keelin. She is still very tired by the end of the day, but I think that is only because she now wants to run and play with her brothers and perhaps she overdoes it. Nuala tells me not to fret and to let Caitlin enjoy herself, but I still worry so about her." Maureen's voice cracked and her eyes brimmed with tears. Embarrassed by her display of emotion, she averted her face and returned to the cottage.

"I gave Nellie a carrot and put her in a stall with a bucket of water," said Caitlin as she rejoined Keelin. The little girl took Keelin's hand and they walked across the sheep pasture to a large rock outcropping that rose above the neighboring farmlands. Nature had carved a smooth and encircling bench into the granite surface of the outcropping, giving it the appearance of a magnificent throne. Keelin knew it had always been Caitlin's favorite place to play before she had become sick. On sunny days the south-facing bench was warm and protected, and the view from its height spectacular.

When Caitlin was very ill, she had told Keelin of her "stone castle" on the hillside. "I dream I am a princess and all the land

I see from my stone throne is my kingdom," Caitlin had said, drawing slow, torturous breaths. The child had been deathly pale, her joints suffused with blood and her glands swollen. "I sometimes think I will never sit on my throne again, for I am no longer strong enough to visit my beautiful castle." Caitlin had gasped, coughing up flecks of blood.

"Nonsense," Keelin had said gently. "As soon as you feel a little better we will visit your castle. Donal will carry you and I will be your maid in waiting, ready to do your bidding, Princess Caitlin." The little girl giggled as Keelin curtsied with a flourish at Caitlin's bedside. Two months later on a sunny, breezy day, Caitlin, sitting on Donal's shoulders, showed Keelin her stone castle.

Today, Caitlin tugged at Keelin's hand, skipping along, excited to have Keelin all to herself. When they reached the castle, the two girls climbed up onto the throne and surveyed their surroundings. Caitlin sat down and leaned her back against the smooth granite wall, smiling happily. Keelin sat crossed legged facing Caitlin and began to gently massage the little girl's legs.

"Keelin," asked Caitlin shyly, "may I hold Rua while we talk?"

"Aye, my lady," answered Keelin, retrieving a small wooden box from her satchel. Inside the box, on a bed of soft wool, was an exquisitely carved wooden horse, its neck arched and its mane and tail flowing. The artist had captured the spirit of a mighty war horse in intricate detail with nostrils flared and muscles rippling, its powerful legs suspended in an animated trot. On Keelin's thirteenth birthday, Uncle Liam had presented the carving to her. "Here is your grand Rua," he said. "May his strength be yours forever. His mighty heart was gentled by your soft hands."

The carving of Rua became Keelin's talisman. It seemed to be imbued with magical powers to calm and heal. Keelin believed that as Uncle Liam carved the miniature, his sensitive fingers had been directed by the gods. Nuala had scoffed at the idea. "Whatever enchantment the carving possesses comes not from Uncle Liam but from your belief in it. Never forget your gift, Keelin."

Now, as Caitlin held Rua in her palm and chattered cheerfully, Keelin examined her with practiced hands and eyes. When Keelin had first visited Caitlin with Nuala those many months ago, she had been perplexed by the disease that plagued the little girl.

"An evil malignancy seems to be everywhere," Keelin had said, looking at Nuala with questioning eyes. "I can feel it flowing with her very life blood. How can that be?"

Nuala, with her enigmatic smile, responded, "Good, Keelin. The disease is rare but quite deadly and somehow inhibits the blood's ability to nourish the body. When it occurs in children, there is some hope that it will recede and allow them to reach maturity. However, the disease is only in abeyance and will reappear eventually. I have heard of cases where the disease never returns, but I have never seen such."

Caitlin had now been well for three months, yet Keelin could detect some evil that still lurked in the little girl's body, fearing she had only been granted a reprieve and not a cure, just as Nuala had warned. Keelin had fought Caitlin's disease with an intensity of emotion that Nuala thought unwise. She had lectured Keelin sternly but not without empathy. "Many of your patients will die and Caitlin is likely to be one of them. If you give so much to one patient, you will invariably neglect others. Moreover, you must remember that you are a healer and not a god. Who can say why some live and others die, no matter our efforts. Don't let your soul die piece by piece with each patient you cannot save."

"You know I never neglect any of my patients," Keelin had retorted. "And my soul would surely die if I didn't do everything in my power to save Caitlin." The priestess's pessimism was infuriating. Keelin had refused to accept the possibility of sweet Caitlin's death. It was too dark a reality to bear.

Today, as Keelin's fingers felt the soft glands of Caitlin's throat and massaged her legs, she found no sign of the disease. Keelin's heart quickened as she continued to examine her. No, she was not mistaken; the evil was gone, completely and forever. I cannot wait to tell Nuala, thought Keelin with joy and relief. Keelin laughed and hugged Caitlin impulsively, leaving the child nonplussed, since the story Caitlin had been relating was not particularly funny.

"Keelin, you were not listening to me," said Caitlin, somewhat offended.

"I am sorry, my lady, but I received the most wonderful news today and am somewhat distracted. We must hurry back now so you can travel with Donal to the village. We have left him waiting quite long enough." With that, Keelin stood up and jumped off the granite throne. Caitlin followed and the two ran down the hill laughing, both girls filled with a healthy exuberance.

KEELIN WAS JUST about to turn Nellie from a narrow path onto the village road when she saw a wagon approaching. Hidden by a large thicket, Keelin abruptly reined in Nellie and watched, the lessons of stealth taught by Nuala occasionally having some effect. A young man and woman sat side by side, and from the set of his shoulders and his wavy black hair, Keelin recognized Brian. He held the reins with one hand and the other was gesticulating with comical antics. The young woman's body pressed close to his as she broke into laughter. Brian then leaned down and kissed his companion soundly on the lips.

Keelin hastily clucked Nellie forward onto the road as the wagon pulled up alongside of her. Brian's companion was Brigid, arguably the most beautiful girl of the clan. She had exquisite features, big blue eyes, and golden blonde hair. And her figure, thought Keelin enviously, was that of a goddess.

"Keelin, how nice it is to see you," Brigid exclaimed disingenuously. "You won't believe my good fortune today. The axle of my wagon became fouled by a large rock. I was stranded just outside the village when who should happen along but Brian." Brigid smiled up at Brian and encircled her arm in the bend of his elbow.

"Yes, how convenient that your wagon should break down at such an opportune moment and this being the day and time Brian always travels home on the village road from his training with Pádraig," Keelin said, smiling sweetly.

Brian shot Keelin a wicked glance and pressed Brigid's arm against his side. "I cannot imagine a more pleasurable task than rescuing a damsel in distress. I had the miscreant rock dispatched in no time at all and now have the honor of accompanying the fair maiden home."

"Such is the life of a mighty warrior," Keelin sighed mockingly, annoyed that Brian was so eagerly playing along with Brigid's ruse. "It is fortunate that the rock offered no defense or the outcome might have been different."

"Indeed, I must improve my feint and weave techniques so as to better avoid all barbs that are thrown my way," countered Brian, smiling broadly. "But now we must be off if I am to deliver Brigid safely home before dusk. I will see you tonight, Keelin."

"Whatever for?" asked Keelin, irritated afresh. She was sure Brian had spoken his last words with reluctance.

"I promised your father that while he was away I would help your Uncle Liam with the farm. I am easily spared at home."

"Where is your father, Keelin?" asked Brigid, only slightly interested.

Ignoring Brigid's question, Keelin asked, "When did you see my father?" Brian's words had brought the Romhanach invasion as well as her foreboding dream crashing back into Keelin's consciousness. She had managed to quell the apprehension she felt when her father left for Tara at daybreak, and her happy visit with Caitlin had banished the worrisome thoughts completely.

"This morning at Pádraig's, just before he started his journey to Tara. Your father expects to be gone at least a fortnight, far too long for Liam to get by without help."

"How pleasant your company will be. I only hope my father is not delayed in his return," said Keelin sarcastically. With that she touched Nellie's side, sending the mare trotting off toward the village.

Curse it, thought Keelin as she rode toward the village. She felt oddly disheartened. For all her beauty, Brigid was calculating and devious. How could Brian be so deceived by her? Keelin was not sure she could tolerate his casual disregard should he dine with them each evening. On the other hand, at least her mother would be pleased. She mentioned just the other day how she missed seeing Brian. Keelin wished she could be more like her mother who faced life's troubles with equanimity and steadfast strength. But she was nothing like her mother. Keelin was different—arguably a little witch as Brian so often called her.

# CHAPTER SIX

EELIN SAT ON A BENCH IN FRONT OF NUALA'S cottage working on her Dagda cloak. She had always found sewing and mending tedious work offering little satisfaction. Creating her Dagda cloak was the one exception. As she painstakingly embroidered beautiful images with silver and gold thread on the fine wool cloak of deep purple, she let her imagination wander. She dreamt of performing heroic feats in strange lands, saving kingdoms from dreaded epidemics, and soaring through the heavens. She saw herself wearing her magnificent cloak, looking regal with her petite frame transformed by the cloak's enchanting powers. She also imagined *the* dream. She would finally stand before the man on the footpath and see his face.

It had rained throughout the night and into the morning. Keelin had spent the early hours of the day in Nuala's apothecary, which was connected to her cottage by a covered breezeway. The apothecary was a wondrous place to Keelin. Its stout door opened into a large room that was both Nuala's surgery and study. In the center of the room was an oak table, its smooth flat surface burnished and immaculate. Overhead hung oil lamps suspended from the rafters of the thatch roof. Bundles of herbs hung drying from hooks along the western wall and three windows dotted the south side of the building, shuttered today to keep out the rain but open during fine weather to let in fresh air and light. The opposite wall was lined with shelves that held pots and jars filled with tonics and medicinal herbs, each identified by name and purpose in Nuala's distinctive script. Other shelves held manuscripts detailing human anatomy and physiology, surgeries, medicinal formulas, and diseases. Many of the manuscripts were written in foreign languages with strange characters, while others were penned by Nuala. Most of the foreign manuscripts were Romhanach, and when Keelin asked Nuala how she had acquired them, the priestess replied, "When you are ready I will tell you." It was one of Nuala's many cryptic and illogical responses that infuriated Keelin.

Just before noon the rain stopped and the sky cleared. Keelin opened the apothecary windows and went to the cottage. After eating cheese and bread she had brought with her, Keelin retrieved her Dagda cloak from a large oak chest and went outside to finish her embroidery work. In the midst of a particularly fine fantasy, Keelin happened to look up and see Nuala striding toward her.

No one could help but be impressed with the priestess. Nuala was tall, standing nearly at eye level with the clan's most imposing warriors. Her frame, however, was not large, merely elongated, and she was thin almost to the point of emaciation. She had thick, dark brown hair that she partially swept up with a silver clasp; the rest tumbled down her back, glossy and reed straight. Her face was angular, like her body, with a straight, thin nose, prominent cheekbones, and a high forehead too austere for beauty. Nuala's skin was pale, almost translucent, and her piercing gray-blue eyes were those of a zealot. It would have been a chillingly ascetic face had it not been for her mouth with its full, beautifully formed lips. Perhaps, not surprisingly, few took notice of Nuala's individual features, such was the powerful, phantasmal aura that she presented.

Keelin was about to spring from the bench when Nuala called, "Stay as you are. I am pleased to see you are finishing your cloak, all the while dreaming of glorious deeds and grand victories, I might add." Nuala raised an eyebrow and smiled.

"I don't know what you are talking about," retorted Keelin, thinking how disconcerting Nuala could be. "I have been working in the apothecary all morning and thought I would put the finishing touches on my cloak this afternoon. It's beautiful, is it not?"

Nuala nodded in agreement. Nuala's own cloak was of the darkest pine, vivid and rich, with a beautiful scene of the stars, moon, and sun. The stars and moon were woven with precious strands of silver and the sun shone with threads of gold. Each cloak was reversible, the unadorned side always a muted brown. Normally, Nuala wore the unadorned side out. Today, the silver and gold threads on the deep green wool shimmered in the sunlight.

"But how is it that you have returned so soon from Tara?" Keelin asked. "Has my father returned also?"

"Your father has not returned. He will likely be gone longer than he first thought, perhaps as long as a full cycle of the moon."

"Is there trouble?" Keelin asked with alarm. "Have the chieftains rejected the call to unite?"

"Your father has yet to address the chieftains. However, he has a strong ally in Fionn, undoubtedly Eire's greatest warrior. Both men have like minds and together will argue for unification. They will face strong resistance but I believe they will prevail."

"And what of the Romhanach? Have we learned more of their intentions?"

"No. Some argue that we will not know whether an invasion is imminent until early spring. That, of course, is nonsense.

Agricola has grand ambitions. The only questions remaining are when and where his legions will invade. It is now up to The Dagda to seek the answers."

Keelin had been about to pepper Nuala with a flurry of her own questions but stopped short. "The Dagda?" she blurted.

"Yes, The Dagda. The high priest Fearghus has divined a means to aid Eire. Those of us with powers of the mind will gather details of the invasion so that Eire's warriors may prepare more effectively for the assault. Further, we have been given license to use our powers to coerce and confuse the Romhanach."

"How can we possibly aid our warriors on the battlefield using only powers of the mind?"

"Keelin, you are not listening, nor using your knowledge. We cannot aid our warriors on the battlefield. That is forbidden. We will, instead, become spies for Eire and manipulators of the mind. We may be able to influence Agricola. I, for one, am skeptical. But there are those of The Dagda who believe it possible. We shall see."

Keelin felt a rush of excitement course through her, intense and galvanizing. "Tell me all now!"

"You will learn all very soon. Now, however, I want to hear of our patients. Tell me what has happened here during my absence. I wish first to hear how the treatments of young Eoin are progressing."

Keelin regarded Nuala with frustration. "How can I calmly speak of our patients when you dangle such news before me? I cannot endure it!"

Nuala gave Keelin a sharp and reproving look but said nothing. She then turned and started toward the path that led away from her cottage.

Keelin could do nothing but follow her.

"A priestess will arrive this afternoon who will become your teacher for the foreseeable future," said Nuala casually. Keelin had finished telling the priestess of the events of the past week and the two had walked down to the creek that flowed near Nuala's cottage. They stood on large rocks that bordered the creek, watching the fast-moving water as it cascaded down from the mountain pass. Nuala had chosen the location to build her cottage well. It sat at the base of a sizable mountain range. The leeward face of the range and an oak grove afforded protection from strong winds and weather, and the creek provided fresh, clear water. There were no farms nearby and the lone cottage sat as a picturesque sentinel guarding the mountain pass.

"Another teacher? Your knowledge in the art of healing is without equal," responded Keelin with alarm. "I wish to study only with you." These last words escaped Keelin's lips unbidden.

"Do not fret, Keelin," said Nuala, sounding impatient. "You need not abandon your skills as a healer to develop your powers of the mind. Both will be needed in our defense of Eire. I have the power to read the thoughts of others. You have the ability to invade another's mind with your own thoughts. The priestess Deirdre has powers very similar to yours and can teach you far more than I can. You will begin studying with her at once." Nuala continued to gaze at the rushing water.

Her temper flaring, Keelin blurted out, "I am forever in the dark! You plot the course of my life as you please, never allowing me a voice. Now it seems I am to use my powers of the mind for the defense of Eire and yet I still know nothing. You did not even tell me of the Romhanach threat . . . I feel I have earned the right to your secrets."

Nuala was unmoved. "I will decide what secrets you will know and when you will know them. You must earn the privilege to stand as my equal."

"I have never betrayed your confidences nor revealed the powers the gods bestowed upon me."

Nuala regarded Keelin less sternly. "True. You have been most reticent about your gifts, which I believe is remarkable, given your nature. I must say that when you were very young I paid little attention to you. Your fits of temper and lack of intellectual curiosity did not endear you to me. That all changed after the day of the boar attack, and I must admit I have chided myself often for my early assumptions about you. I was too quick in my judgment." Nuala unfastened the brooch at the neck of her cloak. "Telling you of the Romhanach would have served no purpose until Déaglán's return. Only his news of the threat would hold credence with Eire's chieftains. Only then could we of The Dagda act."

"Why would the chieftains listen to my uncle and not The Dagda? You speak for the gods. What more powerful voice can there be?"

"We could share only vague auguries and visions. Our chieftains may honor the gods but do not necessarily pay them much heed unless it furthers their ambitions," responded Nuala with cynicism. "The chieftains hold your uncle in high regard and prefer his word to our omens."

"Yet you knew all and more of what my uncle reported before his return. How is that so and why share only *vague auguries*?" asked Keelin.

"We of The Dagda must protect our secrets and share nothing more than omens, lest our detailed knowledge of foreign lands cause undue interest in how we obtained it. Our powers are great but only if our possession of them is not known or fully understood. We are too few in number and are but flesh and blood, easily destroyed by those with ambition or evil intent."

"I am no threat and yet you said nothing to me. What powers have you kept hidden?" Keelin surreptitiously eyed the priestess absently touch the large ruby pendant that hung from an exquisitely woven gold chain around her neck. It was a gesture Keelin knew well, one that almost always meant the Priestess had decided to share something of import.

Nuala calmly dropped her right hand and the fingers that had traced the pendant lay perfectly still at her side. She turned and looked down at Keelin, her gray eyes intense. "I, as do some of my fellow priests and priestesses, possess the ability to pierce the veil of another world."

An unearthly chill swept through Keelin and she shivered. "Do you speak of the . . . Otherworld?"

The Otherworld was the sacred realm of the gods that afforded the souls of the dead passage to their next lives. Many imagined it as a dark and chaotic netherworld of unspeakable ordeals through which the souls of the dead must journey to reach their new lives. Keelin was sure they were wrong. She had always imagined it a place of verdant beauty and serenity, free from the hardships of life, where pain and suffering were assuaged and life was renewed. She had seen too much suffering in her young life. The gods could not be so cruel as to prolong that in death.

"Perhaps. We of The Dagda call it that. Although not the home of the gods, it is most certainly the world in which our souls travel from one life to another."

Nuala's expression softened and her eyes lost their zealotry. She smiled with something close to compassion and said, "It is neither frightful nor serene. It is merely a passage or, for our purposes, a window through which to view our world and the next. It is a realm where time and our bodily form have no meaning or consequence. You will travel there soon, once you are of The Dagda. You are only sixteen, too young to become a priestess, even too young to be ordained a novice in training. However, an exception has been made in your case because of the peril Eire faces. You will be seventeen next month, will you not?"

Before Keelin could answer, Nuala nodded and continued. "You will be formally ordained a novice at the festival of Samhain in two months' time. Because you are entering The Dagda before your eighteenth birthday, we must test your affinity for the Otherworld before your ordination. I have little doubt that you will be one with that world. In the meantime, Deirdre will help you develop your powers of the mind. We have little time to waste."

Keelin was hardly listening. She wondered if the Otherworld was as Nuala described it. The priestess was not above deception if it achieved the desired end. And Keelin knew full well that Nuala's plans for her led unwaveringly to The Dagda. More from her natural perversity than with any real conviction, she looked up at Nuala and said, "Whether or not I pledge my life to The Dagda is my decision, not yours."

Nuala eyed Keelin only briefly. "Circumstances and Eire's peril have made the decision for you. Whether you wish it or not, your fate is sealed. You will be ordained a novice."

Keelin felt as if she were suffocating. Indeed, duty and honor held her captive. She stood mute, watching the cascading water, knowing its journey would take it to the ocean and beyond the shores of this small island.

"Do not despair, Keelin. You have long wished to escape

Eire and its confining boundaries. The Otherworld will allow
you to do just that. You must trust the gods and their wisdom.
They chose you for a reason." Nuala turned from the creek and
motioned for Keelin to follow. "Now let us return to the cottage,
for I believe that Deirdre will arrive shortly."

❦

As KEELIN AND Nuala approached the cottage, a young
woman opened the door and stepped outside. When she saw the
two, she waved and walked briskly toward them.

"I wondered where you had gone. Nuala, I hope you do not
mind but I started a pot of stew and have some bread rising. I
have also brought with me the most wonderful fruit to sweeten
our palates after dinner." She smiled and turned to Keelin. "I
am so glad to finally meet you, Keelin. Nuala has told me so
much about you over the years but has jealously kept you all to
herself." At that Deirdre laughed and hugged Keelin with gen-
uine affection, the delicate scent of her perfume drifting through
the air.

"So you are already preparing a meal. Can you think of
nothing better to do with your time?" asked Nuala.

"Yes, occasionally." And then, with a conspiratorial look at
Keelin, Deirdre said, "Nuala believes me frivolous for relishing
the corporeal pleasures of life when spiritual rewards should
suffice. Perhaps her opinion has merit. I would find a mere existence of duty and self-sacrifice exceedingly dismal."

Keelin glanced quickly at Nuala, expecting her eyes to be
filled with censorial rebuke. Instead, the priestess smiled indulgently, with even a hint of mirth in her eyes. Keelin could not
believe it. Somehow this young priestess had managed to charm

even the dour Nuala. How could one such as Deirdre be of The Dagda?

"Keelin, I see something of the look of your Uncle Déaglán in you," said Deirdre. "Of course, you both have those marvelously beautiful eyes. Déaglán is such a fine-looking man. And I do believe he is one of the bravest men I have ever known."

Uncle Déaglán *fine-looking*, thought Keelin in astonishment. Her uncle was not in the least good looking and far too old for someone as young and vibrant as Deirdre.

"I would not forget, Deirdre, that Déaglán is still in love with his dead wife, Maeve," said Nuala.

"I have no illusions about Déaglán and his love for Maeve, but you underestimate the capacity of his heart if you believe there is no room left in it for me. Besides, he is a very sensual man and no doubt misses the comforts of a warm and loving woman," replied Deirdre with satisfaction.

"With you a priestess and him a seafarer, I see little hope or time for a romance," said Nuala.

"Quite the contrary! What better lover could either of us have? He is gone for months on his voyages and I am always occupied with my duties as a priestess. We can each look forward to those days and weeks when we can be together with neither one of us the sad and lonely lover who is left behind to pine."

"Has Uncle Déaglán made his feelings for you known?" asked Keelin.

"No, and I doubt he ever will," said Nuala. "Déaglán is content with his solitary life." The priestess's haughty conviction annoyed Keelin.

Deirdre laughed at Nuala's remark. "Well, the poor man has known little else for many years. He is wary of love and who can blame him. However, I have no doubt that before long I shall be preparing him sumptuous meals and he shall be sharing my—"

"That is quite enough, Deirdre," Nuala interrupted sternly. "We have serious work to do and Keelin should hear no more of your shocking words."

"My sense is that it takes much to shock Keelin," Deirdre offered, completely unintimidated by Nuala's rebuke. "But you are correct, Nuala, there is evil afoot and we must concentrate all our efforts to defeat the Romhanach. We can begin our work tonight. Keelin, will you be staying for dinner?"

"No, my mother is expecting me," replied Keelin with regret.

"Well, then, tomorrow is soon enough. It is a pity that you are not yet a novice but I suppose it cannot be helped. There is still much we can accomplish." Then, with a satisfied smile she added, "The three of us will wreak havoc on the minds of the Romhanach."

# CHAPTER SEVEN

*T*HE ENCAMPMENT SURROUNDING THE HILL OF Tara was teeming with men, horses, and dogs. Scores of makeshift hide tents and campfires dotted the landscape and a temporary forge had been erected and was billowing smoke, the smell of molten iron filling the air. Loose dogs were everywhere, their incessant barking and howling halted only momentarily by harsh commands from their masters. Raucous laughter, angry shouts, and the beating of drums added to the vigorous menace of the encampment. Horses were tethered in corrals fashioned with thick rope strung taut between huge oaks, the shrill cries of enraged stallions occasionally heard above the furious cacophony that enveloped this meeting of confident, deadly men.

Above it all was the hill of Tara and its ringed buildings of wood and stone, framed by concentric ditches that encircled the hilltop. From the outermost ditch rose a massive colonnade, its towering oak pillars joined by crossbars that reached to the heavens. From the north was the processional avenue, lined by another, less massive colonnade adorned with elaborate and beautifully carved pillars. The avenue led to Dumha na nGiall, the sacred passage tomb, guarded by the gods and venerated by

all since the time of the ancient *dark ones*. The priests and priestesses of The Dagda held all their conclaves at Tara, often extending invitations to Eire's finest poets, musicians, and historians.
All ordinations and ceremonial worship to the gods took place on
this hallowed site, and the beautiful, pure notes of the harp and
pipes accompanied the services. On the holy day of Samhain,
marking the end of one year and the beginning of the next, the
entrance to the sacred passage tomb was illuminated by the rising sun, drawing in the souls of all those who have died during
the year and granting them passage to their next life, reincarnated with a new body and existence.

It did not strike the chieftains or the priests and priestesses
of The Dagda as incongruous that very corporeal warriors were
assembled to discuss deadly combat at the base of Tara. The
assembly and its location mirrored the complex nature of the
people of Eire. Eloquent and savage, their love of art, music,
and lyrical poetry was ever at odds with their fierce passions,
fueled by defiant independence and a combative, martial spirit.

"The chieftains of the northeastern clans have arrived none
too soon," said Conall to Déaglán and Fionn as they watched
two young warriors joust with pugil sticks. Loud taunts and
fierce oaths were being shouted by a boisterous and drunkenly
riotous crowd of men as they cheered the fighters on. What had
started as friendly contests of skill and prowess had quickly de-
generated into boastful and brutal challenges of superiority.
Most of the chieftains had brought with them a retinue of clan
members that included their seconds, as well as two or three of
their finest warriors. With such a gathering of hard young men

born and reared for warfare, it was only the men's respect for the sanctity of Tara and the power of The Dagda that deterred mortal combat.

"Yes," agreed Fionn, "the men are growing restless. Curse Diarmuid and Niall for delaying the assembly. They are not to be trusted."

"Both chieftains had a great distance to travel," replied Conall, "though I suspect their late arrival was but haughty insolence."

"The swine!" exclaimed Fionn. "It was their purpose to keep us all waiting. They have even shown contempt for The Dagda by not immediately responding to the summons. Those two chieftains will be trouble. Mark my word."

"I have no doubt they will be. Diarmuid's high opinion of himself is exceeded only by his belligerence. Niall is far more dangerous. He has a keen mind and an indomitable will. He is contemptuous of all but the northern clans and rarely pays tribute at Tara. Niall will make a powerful ally if we can win him over. If not, he could spell our doom. Certainly, Diarmuid's stubborn resistance will be of little consequence if Niall joins our ranks."

"Let us rid ourselves of Diarmuid now," said Fionn with a dangerous gleam in his eyes. "He is nothing but a pig that should be slaughtered. I will challenge him to combat and smite him. It would give me great pleasure to cleave him in two and see him lying in the mud and offal where he belongs."

Conall nodded grimly in agreement. "Indeed, Diarmuid needs to die, but do not dull your sword on him today."

"No, today would not be wise, but Diarmuid's demise would ease my mind as well as warm my heart," replied Fionn.

Déaglán listened to the men's bloodthirsty words and said

nothing. He would watch Diarmuid and Niall for any signs of treachery. Agricola's spies may already be in Eire, perhaps even here at Tara. He was confident at least one of the chieftains or someone amongst the chieftains' retinues would betray Eire. It was his purpose to find the traitors. He smiled to himself. No one was better at finding and flushing out a scoundrel than he.

The three men were sitting on the trunk of a fallen oak that lay halfway up a hill overlooking the large arena where the young warriors were joisting. Déaglán's reverie was broken by a loud roar from the crowd as a massively built young warrior knocked another challenger to the ground. Even for a people known for their tall stature and intimidating presence, this young man was impressive. His giant frame was thickly muscled and his legs were built like tree trunks. He had red hair, a ruddy complexion, and a pugnacious face with thick features and a prominent jaw.

"Is not the big lad one of yours?" asked Conall, as the young man raised his fist in victory.

"Yes, that is Ruaidhrí, one of my most promising young warriors. As you can see, he is as big and strong as a bull. Unfortunately, he attacks much like a bull with little forethought," replied Fionn, shaking his head in regret.

Conall nodded. "Yes, he charges his opponents and foolishly exposes himself. He could also increase the force of his blows if he learned to move more effectively, better using those powerful legs."

"I agree. Unfortunately, he has bested all of the young warriors and many of the more seasoned men under my command and will not listen to my admonitions. His devastating strength has overwhelmed all of his opponents."

"Have you thought of challenging him yourself or have your second, Éamon, fight him?" questioned Conall.

"I have but would prefer to wait and see if there might be a younger man who can best him. That is why I had him accompany me here. He must realize that his lack of discipline will result in a loss when faced with a strong young warrior with exceptional skill. He is not one to take the measure of his opponent but rather is ruled by his fierce emotions. And, although not of vast intelligence, he is no dullard. Ruaidhrí could be a warrior of legendary might if he could but learn that battle is not only of the heart but also of the mind."

At that moment, cheers erupted from a crowd of men on the far side of the arena as a young warrior stepped out from amongst them and walked toward Ruaidhrí. Although perhaps a half head shorter than Ruaidhrí, he was nonetheless a tall man with a large, leanly muscled frame. He had wavy, chestnut-colored hair that fell to his shoulders and moved with leonine confidence and grace. He raised his right arm in challenge as he strode to the center of the arena, the spectators wildly shouting their approval.

"From the reaction of the men, it would seem Ruaidhrí may have met his match," commented Conall. "Is that young Seán? I have not seen him since he was a boy but he has the look of his father."

"Yes, that is Murchadh's younger son," replied Déaglán.

Murchadh was a strong chieftain of one of the western clans. He and Déaglán became friends when they were young, drawn together by their mutual love of the sea. Murchadh had recently been stricken with a wasting disease and many believed he would be dead before the year was out. He had chosen his eldest son, Ailín, to succeed him when the time came. Déaglán had been somewhat surprised by his friend's decision. Seán seemed the more likely choice to be chieftain with his superior mind and physical prowess.

"I have heard other chieftains praise Seán's strength and warrior skills. His look and presence seem only to confirm the accolades. This should be a grand fight," Fionn remarked with relish.

The two young men met in the center of the arena, standing several feet apart. Holding their pugil sticks in both hands, the men reached forward and knocked their sticks together, signaling the start of the contest. Then they stepped back, ready to begin the battle.

They circled, facing each other, Seán alert and tensely careful, Ruaidhrí fierce, his teeth clenched and his brows knitted against the sun's glare. It was Ruaidhrí who made the first move, rushing in to strike Seán with a blow to the head. Seán blocked the strike with equal force, easily fending off the attack. Ruaidhrí then attempted a body blow with a powerful swing of his stick. Seán deflected the blow and eluded his opponent's fury with quicksilver motion. Again and again, the clash of the pugil sticks reverberated through the air, though neither man was able to inflict serious damage. It was a match of brute strength and passion against superior skill and intellect, each man possessing heart and courage in abundance. The young men battled on with Seán feinting and slipping away from the most serious blows and Ruaidhrí, ever the aggressor, rushing and striking with deadly intent. Both men's bodies were dripping with sweat and there appeared to be no end in sight when Ruaidhrí, frustrated, made a fatal mistake.

Determined to end the contest, Ruaidhrí loosed all his fury and swung his stick like a pole ax at Seán's head, leaving himself open. Seán ducked away, avoiding the attack and then countered, landing a punishing blow to the side of Ruaidhrí's head. There was a resounding crack as wood hit bone and Ruaidhrí staggered and fell to the ground. There was a momentary silence and then bedlam ensued. Men shouted and cheered, some charging into the arena to congratulate Seán. Incredibly, Ruaidhrí quickly regained his senses and stood up, his expression murderous, blood flowing freely down the side of his head. Seán stood triumphant, his fists raised in victory. Before the jubilant spectators could reach Seán, Ruaidhrí warned them back with a threatening sweep of his arm. He then called for his axe and sword.

"The cursed, stupid fool," exclaimed Fionn, uttering a foul oath. "Has Ruaidhrí learned nothing from this beating?"

"It appears not. Instead he will die, for surely Seán will best him again," replied Conall.

Déaglán watched with resigned fatalism. He knew Fionn and Conall would not stop the fight and would allow two of Eire's finest warriors to battle to the death. We are cursed, thought Déaglán. Eire is never without conflict and it is of our own making.

The arena cleared, leaving Seán and Ruaidhrí to stand facing each other, waiting for their weapons. Suddenly, loud shouts were heard from beyond the trees to the west. The object of the alarm became clear when a runaway horse charged out of the trees and toward the men encircling the arena, knocking down one man who did not escape from the path of the crazed animal quickly enough. The horse's mad run would have sent it past the two young warriors had Ruaidhrí stayed where he was. Instead, with no consideration for the danger, Ruaidhrí stepped into the path of the stampeding horse and attempted to stop it. He had only time to raise his hands and shout, "Whoa fine fellow," before the horse, never slowing, hit him. The impact sent Ruaidhrí flying backwards through the air, landing with a sickening thud on the ground. The horse, stunned, staggered to its knees and collapsed. Two men ran to the horse and coaxed it to its feet where it stood trembling, its neck and flanks dark with sweat. One man took hold of its head collar while the other gently stroked the horse's neck, then they led the frightened animal from the arena.

Meanwhile, Seán had run to where Ruaidhrí was lying and bent over him. For some time Ruaidhrí lay motionless on the ground and Seán knelt down next to him, a hush falling over the crowd. Finally, Ruaidhrí stirred, lifting his hand toward Seán, who firmly grasped Ruaidhrí's offered hand in his own. The two young men appeared to be talking, with Seán bending close, then gesturing to where the frightened horse had been led. Ruaidhrí raised himself to a sitting position and Seán placed a steadying arm around his shoulders. The pair laughed at something one of them said. Ruaidhrí, instantly regretting his laughter, put his hand to his head. After several more minutes, Seán stood up and offered his hand to Ruaidhrí who took it. As Ruaidhrí slowly got to his feet, the men surrounding the arena roared with approval, some shouting, "Hail mighty Ruaidhrí!" All of the angry tension of the contest had dissolved and men were jesting and slapping both warriors' backs in congratulations. Ruaidhrí, still wobbly but enjoying the adulation, threw his arm around Seán and both men smiled broadly.

"Well, you can be sure there will be a song about this contest before the day is out," laughed Fionn.

"It deserves a grand poem, I am thinking," replied Conall. "However, I fear Ruaidhrí is badly concussed and will have a fierce headache tomorrow," he added, only somewhat bothered at the thought.

"Yes, but it is nothing, he has a thick skull," Fionn said, still laughing. Then he sobered and said, "Better concussed than dead, for I have no doubt that Seán would have won the contest."

Conall nodded. "I have a young warrior in my clan who has many of the same qualities that Seán possesses. Brian is young but in time his strength and skill will match Seán's. With warriors such as these, the Romhanach should be prepared to die. Because die they will, by the scores," he proclaimed with pride as the men watched the two young warriors walk from the arena, their arms around each other's shoulders.

IT WAS LATE the next morning and the mist and fog had almost disappeared. The day promised to be clear. Conall stood with Fionn and Fearghus, several feet above the crowd on the incline of a small hill with priests and priestesses of The Dagda flanking them. Niall stood below, slightly apart from the other chieftains, his warriors nearby. Seán and Ruaidhrí were standing side by side, a bond of mutual respect and friendship having arisen from the previous day's contest. Bellicose as always, Diarmuid was loudly deriding the assembly's purpose to those around him. Déaglán stood amongst a grove of trees at the crest of the hill, hidden but with an excellent view of all.

Surveying the crowd, Déaglán saw only a few openly hostile faces, but he knew that was of little consequence. The gathering was rife with enmity, chieftains of warring clans standing but paces from one another. Déaglán's watchful gaze kept returning to Diarmuid. He held a jug of ale, but as yet Déaglán had not seen him take a drink.

The high priest Fearghus stepped forward and called the

assembly to order. He then nodded to Conall and Fionn and addressed the chieftains. "All of you here are aware of the Romhanach threat. There is little doubt that Agricola, their commanding general, will order an invasion of our island. The manner in which we defend Eire against this invasion is in question. What you decide today is of vital importance and necessitates your most honest and thoughtful consideration. The fate of Eire is in your hands."

Fearghus stepped back, standing shoulder to shoulder with Fionn. Conall exchanged brief words with the two men, then he straightened his shoulders, stepped forward, and began.

"Yesterday, Fionn and I watched Eire's young warriors joist on this very spot. The contests we witnessed only confirm my belief that as warriors we have no equal. In single combat, no civilization can present a challenger who would triumph over the men who stand before us today. But the Romhanach care little for individual prowess or our ritual of single combat. They rely on vast armies and open-field combat. Their legions fight as one and with deadly effect. The Romhanach are contemptuous of our manner of warfare and trust that our internal strife will be to their advantage. They believe that we lack the discipline of command and can be drawn into battle on any pretext, thus making it easy for them to defeat us.

"The Romhanach's assessment may be accurate. We battle each other constantly and show no regard for battlefield tactics, let alone strategy, so confident are we in our superiority as warriors. But we have never faced a foe such as the Romhanach. If we are foolhardy enough to charge their lines with no forethought or coordination of forces, they will easily decimate our ranks before we can even engage them in hand-to-hand combat." Angry rumblings ran through the crowd and protests were sounded, the young men outraged and offended by Conall's affront to Eire's warriors. Fionn and Fearghus motioned for silence and many of the chieftains spoke harsh words of reproof to their men. When the angry murmuring died down, Conall continued.

"With this campaign, the Romhanach seek to gain a foothold on Eire by seizing the eastern harbors and conquering the midlands. They will then slowly but surely expand their territory and ultimately control Eire. They need not conquer our entire island with their initial invasion. They need only establish a strong fortress from which to launch future attacks. I have no doubt that the Romhanach will suffer defeats at the hands of our warriors during their campaign. But while we will leave the battlefield victorious and go home to rejoice and enjoy the comfort of our families, the Romhanach will retreat to the safety of their fortress, call for reinforcements, and devise a new battle plan. We must not allow them to establish that fortress. It is not sufficient for us to die trying to drive them from our shores. I know every man here would willingly give his life to protect his people and defend his home. That is not enough. We must triumph! We must deliver a defeat so devastating that the Romhanach abandon all notion of conquest. We must rip the heart out of their resolve. Let the blood payment we extract be more than they are willing to suffer for glory and power."

The same young men who had just protested now roared their approval, their bloodlust rising. The older men and the chieftains remained unmoved, stonily anticipating Conall's next words.

"There is only one way that we can achieve such a victory and that is to unite our warriors. Eire's warriors must fight as one with a chain of command and a carefully planned strategy.

We must understand and master the Romhanach open-field combat tactics. We must all follow the orders handed down to us. Discipline is of the outmost—"

Diarmuid shouted, "And you see yourself as commander of this mighty force? You would have us all do your bidding? See how Conall already vies for control of Eire!"

"All of Eire's chieftains will decide who is to command the warrior force," countered Conall. "That will come later, unless you speak for all of the chieftains and wish to vote for commander now."

"I speak only for my clan and declare that my warriors will never join a united force with dogs such as you!" Diarmuid bellowed.

"I should not say such words to a friend of mine," commanded Fionn, his steely gray eyes full of menace. "Hold your tongue or you shall regret it."

Diarmuid understood the deadly threat and had no wish to challenge Fionn, who he knew would gladly slay him. Diarmuid shifted on his feet, murmured an unintelligible apology, and backed down.

"Today, we are not here to decide who should command a united force but whether there will be one to command," continued Conall. "Today we must also agree to expand Fionn's band of warriors, drawing on the very best young men from each clan. The Fianna will supplement our united force, fighting in concert but with more speed and stealth."

"I agree we must strike the Romhanach with overwhelming power," stated Tuathal, a chieftain of a midlands clan. "However, I can raise a large force by relying solely on my clan and those men of friendly clans. Why would I choose to join forces with men I do not trust?"

"And who would your force of men be comprised of?" questioned Conall. "Would they all be trained and seasoned warriors, or would many be farmers and young boys with weapons no more deadly than the scythes they use in their fields? All of you have heard the tales of Queen Boudica of Sasanach, have you not?"

The crowd stirred, knowing of the horrors that befell the brave queen and her people. Enraged by Romhanach perfidy and brutality after her husband's death, Boudica had led her tribe and many other tribes in rebellion against the Romhanach. At first Boudica and her rebels scored victories, her overwhelming numbers and angry vengeance surprising the Romhanach. Yet the Romhanach recovered and, with a force far smaller than that of Boudica's, routed her undisciplined and untrained rebels. Tens of thousands were slaughtered, many of them farmers and tradesmen. The Romhanach also murdered the rebels' wives and children who were camped nearby. Unwilling to face the ignominy of capture and execution, Boudica took her own life.

Conall stood silent, forcing the men to imagine the carnage and destruction, willing them to understand the enormity of Romhanach retribution. When he spoke, he did so forcefully. "Do not let the fate of Queen Boudica and her people be ours. Do not let our internal strife and quarrels spell our doom. Only a united force of trained warriors under a central command has any hope of delivering a punishing defeat to the Romhanach. We must fight as one or perish!"

"What you say may be true," answered Tuathal. "Still, I cannot abide befriending my avowed enemies. How can I look on enemy clans with brotherhood and conciliation? That is impossible."

"I am not asking any of you to befriend your enemies," Conall assured them. "I would not expect you to forgive the wrongs committed by the men of rival clans. I do not ask you to embrace each other. What I do ask is that you stand shoulder to shoulder with them and battle together to defeat the Romhanach. Fight alongside all the warriors of Eire and defeat a foe who threatens what all of us hold so dear—our freedom."

Many of the chieftains nodded in agreement, others were less convinced, reluctant to concede, even now. An impasse appeared likely. Fionn was about to address the assembly when Niall stepped forward from his place on the periphery of the group and spoke.

"I made this journey to Tara with every intention of refusing any call to unite. All of you here today know I have no love for the southern clans. I would lose no sleep if a plague visited them and wiped out every man, woman, and child. I have only slightly less enmity for most of the northern clans. There is something I do love, however, to the core of my very being, and that is Eire. The thought of a Romhanach general setting even one foot on Eire's shores with visions of conquest is loathsome to me. I agree with Conall and Fionn. The Romhanach must not gain a foothold on Eire, no matter how small. The force with which we attack must stagger them and set them reeling. Those we do not butcher must flee to their ships, fearing our wrath and vowing never to return. If it is necessary to unite to achieve this end, so be it. If I must fight beside my avowed enemies, I will do so with a steadfast heart, for I know I will be fighting not for them but for my beloved land."

Murmurs and rumblings spread throughout the crowd, strong words and assured responses filling the air. There were none of the riotous shouts or war cries that customarily accompanied a call to battle. Instead, an almost somber resolve and uncharacteristic stoicism permeated the assembly. There was no longer any doubt as to the course of action.

The high priest Fearghus stepped forward and raised his arm, silencing the men. "Chieftains, you must now vote. Will you swear an oath to resist the invader as united warriors? Will you battle as one?"

# CHAPTER EIGHT

*D*ÉAGLÁN RELAXED, A MEASURE OF OPTIMISM easing the tension in his mind and body. He had just witnessed the impossible: Eire's chieftains had voted to unite forces in the face of the Romhanach threat. Perhaps a miracle was possible and Eire would remain free from foreign domination. He savored the notion of victory. The moment passed and his gaze returned to the spot where Diarmuid had been standing, only to discover the chieftain was gone. Déaglán cursed his momentary inattention, angry at himself. He had been home and safe too long.

Déaglán made his way toward Diarmuid's camp, skirting the assembly and using the oak grove as cover. He had no wish to draw the attention of others to his actions, even while in Eire. It was possible that the chieftain, disgusted with the vote to unite, had stormed back to his camp with no intention other than simply to drink himself senseless. But Déaglán's instincts told him the chieftain's motive was more sinister. He stopped once to search the crowd from a sheltered vantage point but still could not spot Diarmuid among the men now leaving the area.

Déaglán's pace quickened and he left the cover of the trees. His objective now was to reach Diarmuid's camp while the

chieftain was still there. Realizing he could not concern himself
with being seen when his prey was escaping, he walked purposefully, though unhurriedly. His years of stealth had taught him
well. He could hide in plain sight, and he made his way through
the crowd of men unheeded.

Diarmuid's camp was relatively quiet when Déaglán reached
it. A groom was currying one of the horses tied to a rope line.
The rest of the horses were grazing contentedly nearby, their
front legs hobbled so they would not stray too far. Several men
were seated next to a campfire. One was cleaning and sharpening his sword while others were finishing their morning meal,
the remnants of which appeared to be a boar. Another played a
cruit, the man's rough fingers remarkably light upon the strings,
the sound gently wafting through the air. Diarmuid, however,
did not appear to be there. Then, one of the grazing horses gave
the chieftain away. It lifted its head and stared toward the north,
its nostrils quivering as it attempted to catch the scent of its departed stablemate. The horse gave a mournful cry and waited.
Sure enough, a not too distant cry came in response.

Déaglán knew exactly where Diarmuid was headed. Off the
northern road was a dense forest known to be a refuge for
knaves and thieves. Few honest men dared venture into the forest, leaving the dark, moss-covered maze of trees and brambles
empty but for wild beasts and villains. Déaglán had explored the
forest many times and had grown comfortable with its eerie
dampness and shadows. He felt some affinity for the shrouded
solitude and loneliness of the place, though it could never match
the ocean's magnificent isolation. Nor could the forest even
closely approach the ocean's ruthless and unpredictable danger.
Déaglán sighed, thinking of the sea, the need to be once again
sailing upon it an ever-present and insatiable addiction.

The forest looked as forbidding as ever and Déaglán slowed his pace before entering. He had jogged from Diarmuid's camp, taking as many shortcuts as possible while trying to stay hidden. A flush of excitement surged through his body as he stepped into the shadows, the smell of decaying leaves and the damp chill immediately engulfing him. He was confident the chieftain's meeting would be in a small clearing that lay deep within the forest, where campfires and raucous meetings could neither be seen nor heard by the outside world. The dense growth gave the advantage to a man on foot, and he thought he could reach the clearing before Diarmuid. Déaglán moved cautiously as he made his way around the looming trees and gnarled undergrowth, his senses acutely in tune with every sound and breath of air. Several times he stopped to listen, certain he heard the stealthy movement of a large wolf. It was unlikely the beast was hungry, for it made no attempt to come closer. In truth, Déaglán's concern was with a far more deadly predator. He had no wish to have his throat cut by one of the murdering outlaws who called this wooded lair his home.

As he neared the clearing, Déaglán stopped short. Some distance ahead of him were two men standing at the clearing's edge and talking in hushed voices. He could not make out what they were saying but he knew who they were. Although dressed as natives of Eire, Déaglán was not fooled. One man looked vaguely familiar. His attire and presence bespoke a man of substance and, although not tall, he possessed a solid frame. The other man wore the plain dress of an attendant, but his muscled shoulders and disciplined bearing betrayed his military background. Though unusual, it was not unheard of for spies to travel in pairs. Déaglán believed the best and most successful spies traveled alone. He crept closer and listened.

Déaglán was just about to move to his left for a better view of the clearing when an almost imperceptible sound made him freeze. Instinctively he reached for the dagger secured by a thick leather belt around his waist. His fingers grasped the dagger's hilt and he slowly turned his head toward the sound's origin. Not thirty paces away, and watching the spies as he had been, were at least three, and perhaps as many as four, rough-looking men. Well concealed and standing some distance apart from each other, the men looked to be heavily armed. If he had moved even slightly to the left or closer to the clearing, he would have alerted them and exposed his position. Now all he could do was wait and see what drama would unfold.

It was not long before Déaglán heard an approaching horseman. The faint sound of breaking twigs and the rustle of leaves and bracken increased, and the telltale silence of the woodland birds told Déaglán that the chieftain was near. Déaglán kept a watchful eye on both the spies and the villains. Soon enough, the chieftain rode into the clearing, unhurried. He did not dismount and instead sat his horse and waited.

"I commend you for arriving so promptly. It is easy to get lost in this forest," said the well-dressed spy, as both he and his companion stepped into the clearing. They stopped several paces in front of the chieftain.

Diarmuid studied both men and then dismounted, his eyes never leaving them. He let go of his horse's reins and the animal's head dipped slightly, but he did not move from his master's side.

"I have hunted in the northern forests since I was a boy. Finding my way here was nothing," he said dismissively. "And who might your companion be?" Diarmuid spoke in a friendly tone but the question held a challenge nonetheless. He was taller than the men who stood before him and more muscled than even the purported attendant. The puffy bags under the chieftain's eyes and a certain thickening around his middle betrayed his love of ale and debauchery, but he was still a formidable warrior.

"Gauis is my attendant," said the spy, smoothly and with no hesitation. "A good man, though somewhat dim-witted. He does not speak your language and would understand little of the important matters we are to discuss even if he were fluent. Have no fear. You may speak freely." Gauis stood silently at his side.

"Is that so?" Diarmuid's eyes were hard and his expression inscrutable. Then he laughed abruptly, showing yellowed teeth and lines of cruelty framing his mouth. "We had best, then, begin our frank talk, should we not?"

"Yes, of course. I would offer you a seat if there were proper chairs. Alas, as there are only tree stumps, I fear we must stand."

When Diarmuid did not reply the spy continued. "I am not going to pretend I am unaware of the chieftains' vote to unite. I know it is so. The governor of Britannia will be informed of this consequence very soon. However, the vote means nothing unless actions follow intent. If the chieftains' resolve to unify Hibernia's clans does not hold firm, the governor wishes to know forthwith. Furthermore, it will be necessary to learn of the chieftains' battle plans and their strategies, regardless of whether or not they remain a united force."

"What is it you called my land?"

"Hibernia is Roma's name for your fair island. Truly a gem and soon to be a province of the empire. You have the foresight to see this eventuality. Your astute mind can envision a stronger and more prosperous—"

"I care little for empty flattery," interrupted Diarmuid. "What will I gain?"

"Your allegiance will be handsomely rewarded. After Agricola's victory, the enemies of Roma will be dead and their children enslaved. The wealth of their land will be divided among those loyal to the empire."

"And what might the empire demand in return?"

The spy hesitated for only an instant. "A reasonable tax on the land's bounty and nothing more of any consequence. It is a small tribute, really, when one considers what is to be gained in wealth, prosperity, and peace."

"I do not hold peace in high regard." Something in Diarmuid's voice warned Déaglán of impending mayhem. The spy sensed it also and stepped back, drawing his sword, as did the attendant. But it was already too late. The chieftain's arm swung up from his side and he hurled his axe at the bigger man. The blade hit the attendant full in the face and imbedded itself in his skull. His arms jerked spasmodically as he pitched backwards and fell to the ground, blood spurting from the wound. In an instant Diarmuid side-stepped toward his horse and grabbed the sword that hung from the animal's saddle.

The villains sprang into action, charging toward the clearing from their hiding places, their weapons at the ready. Déaglán ran after them and caught the man nearest him from behind. He thrust his dagger into the unsuspecting villain's back just below the ribcage and then upward into vital organs. The man let out a cry and then dropped to the ground. Déaglán picked up the dying man's sword and ran to aid Diarmuid.

The fight was over quickly, although it played out in slow motion to Déaglán. Images were magnified, and each parry and blow and every grunt and cry assaulted his senses. Afterwards he stood spent, trying to catch his breath. He glanced over at the chieftain who seemed not at all winded.

"You are Déaglán, are you not? Seafarer and spy?" Diarmuid's question was more a statement than a query.

"I am."

"One of those scoundrels escaped. No matter. Both spies are dead and two of the three thieves. A satisfactory result."

"Actually three of the four thieves. One never made it to the clearing."

Diarmuid barked a laugh. "You are skilled at killing with dagger and sword." He then looked more closely at Déaglán. "But I see you do not relish it."

"No, I do not."

"Well, I do," said Diarmuid grabbing up the cloak of the fallen attendant spy and wiping off the blood from his sword. He then pulled the axe from the man's face and wiped that clean as well.

"I thank you for aiding me but how is it you were in these woods?"

"I followed the spies here from Tara," lied Déaglán. Wishing to end Diarmuid's queries, he bent over the remains of the well-dressed spy and began to check for hidden pockets or pouches.

"You would check for a few pieces of gold? It is not worthy of you."

Déaglán paused in his search. "I am looking for any official letters or dispatches he might carry. It is unlikely but possible."

"Of course. I should have thought of that myself. I will check for the same on this faceless devil," said Diarmuid, as he turned and bent over the attendant spy.

Both searches proved fruitless. Diarmuid straightened up and surveyed the clearing. "Well, the wolves will have a fine feast this evening."

Déaglán nodded but said nothing.

"He was a presumptuous fool," said Diarmuid, nodding toward the spy Déaglán had searched. "He had the affront to threaten me with death should I not be loyal to his emperor! And then he offered very little. A promise of wealth and *prosperity*, as he called it, when all of Eire would be in bondage!"

"Men have turned traitor for far less," said Déaglán. He wondered if Diarmuid, for all his righteousness now, would have betrayed Eire if the prize had been greater. Perhaps not. Still, he did not like or trust the chieftain.

"We need no longer be concerned with spies or traitors. We have rid Eire of that threat." Diarmuid turned and walked toward his horse, who was now grazing at the edge of the clearing.

"No, we have not," said Déaglán. "I heard the spies speak of another while they were waiting for you. He will learn of what happened here today and be more careful."

"The scoundrel will be killed as these two have been." Diarmuid dismissed Déaglán's concern without so much as a backward glance. The chieftain reached his horse and patted the animal's shoulder. He then returned his sword to its scabbard and swung up onto the saddle.

"Will we head back to Tara together?"

"No, you go without me," Déaglán answered. "The spies' horses are tethered nearby. I want to search their saddlebags."

"As you wish." The chieftain reined his horse around and left the clearing.

Déaglán listened as the horse made its way carefully through the thick underbrush of the forest. When sounds faded away and the clearing was silent, Déaglán began his search for the horses. He had no idea if the spies came here on horseback, but he needed time to think and had no wish for Diarmuid's company. There was another spy; Déaglán had not lied about that. The danger had not passed. Déaglán's mind began to work, imagining what he would do if he were spying for Agricola. He soon located the horses and in one of the saddlebags found a dispatch confirming the existence of another spy.

# CHAPTER NINE

*K*EELIN STEPPED INTO NUALA'S COTTAGE AND WAS immediately greeted by the rich aroma of fresh bread and spices. Keelin's grumbling stomach reminded her that she had not yet eaten. The night before, Deirdre had insisted, "Now don't forget. Be here at dawn, my favorite time of day. You have much to learn." She had then kissed Keelin on the cheek and hugged her as though they had been friends all their lives.

Well, thought Keelin, as she trudged along the trail to Nuala's, the darkness enveloping her, dawn is not my favorite time of day. Bleary-eyed and sleepy, she had left home with the sky still black, not even the hint of a pink glow from the east. If the way to Nuala's had not been so familiar, Keelin would undoubtedly have become hopelessly lost. As it was, she stumbled on a tree root and nearly sprawled to the ground, snagging and ripping the sleeve of her dress on a clawing branch.

When Keelin finally reached Nuala's cottage, it had never appeared so welcoming, with the warm glow of lamplight seen through its open shutters and smoke curling from its chimney. Keelin stepped inside and was greeted with a smile from Deirdre who stood next to the fireplace stirring soup in a large iron pot. A fresh loaf of bread was cooling on a rack atop the hearth.

Keelin slumped down into a chair and watched Deirdre work, her hands moving with effortless grace. She wore a pale blue gown with lace sleeves that belled out around her slim wrists. The color of her gown matched Deirdre's eyes and a long spill of wavy, blonde hair fell to her waist. A large sapphire pendant held by a chain of delicate silver rested on her chest. Keelin wondered how the young priestess managed to remain so perfectly groomed and poised while cooking next to Nuala's sooty fireplace. She looked down at her rumpled, torn dress and decided to mull over less defeating thoughts.

Soon Deirdre poured the soup into large bowls and placed them, along with thick slices of warm bread and two full cups of milk, on the wooden table. "I find that the powers of the mind are always enhanced by a hearty meal," she said, smiling at Keelin as they sat down opposite each other. It was then that Deirdre noticed Keelin's rather disheveled appearance.

"Oh, you poor thing! What happened?"

"I stumbled in the dark while I was walking here this morning," Keelin admitted, feeling clumsy and unkempt.

"You walked here in the dark and damp?"

Keelin was momentarily nonplussed. "Well, I suppose I could have ridden Nellie or Bran, but that would have necessitated awakening even earlier so I could feed them before I left. As I am never at my best in the morning, that idea was unimaginably dreadful."

"How foolish of me," responded Deirdre. "Of course you had to walk and how inconsiderate of me not to have realized it."

"Furthermore, Nuala does not approve of me riding or driving the cart here. *One must have a healthy body as well as a sound mind, and that can only be achieved by rigorous exercise and conscious self-denial,*" Keelin said haughtily, quoting one of Nuala's favorite maxims.

Deirdre laughed. "I love Nuala, but her ways are not mine.

I have no wish to torture you with physical exhaustion or lack of sleep. I also have no desire to traipse around the countryside on foot, accompanying you on your patient visits as I teach you all I know. From now on, meet me here in the late morning and by all means bring a horse-drawn cart."

"Where is Nuala?" asked Keelin, looking around, only now wondering where the priestess had gone.

"At Tara. She mentioned something about treating a young man who had received a blow to the head."

"It takes days to travel to Tara from here—" Keelin stopped, realization hitting her. Now she understood Nuala's many mysterious absences. "Did Nuala journey to Tara through the Otherworld?" she asked eagerly.

"Yes, she did," replied Deirdre. "The Otherworld allows us to journey throughout Eire and beyond quite easily and with great speed. It will also allow us to spy on the Romhanach and plague their minds with our thoughts."

"Why would I be chosen to spy on The Romhanach? I am not of The Dagda and have never entered the Otherworld. *Divining the will of the gods and lurking in the shadows* hold no great charm for me." Keelin did not realize that Brian's words had stayed with her until she spoke them now.

"Nuala has told me of your reluctance." Deirdre frowned, then mused unexpectedly, "I wonder if it is The Dagda you loathe or Nuala's insistence that you must enter its realm."

Keelin was taken aback. It was true, Nuala was forever coercing her, but it was the secretive, duty-bound life of a priestess Keelin loathed. She would never reconcile her dreams of adventure with such a life, no matter the allure of the Otherworld. She would never become like Nuala.

When Keelin did not reply, Deirdre continued. "Nuala has

also told me your powers of the mind are formidable and, that
of late, she can rarely read your thoughts when you consciously
block them from her. Because of this, Nuala believes you will
have a natural affinity with the Otherworld, much like hers and
mine." Deirdre looked at Keelin earnestly for a moment. "If
truth be told, there are few of The Dagda who can enter the
Otherworld with ease, let alone travel great distances within it.
Among those, there are even fewer Fearghus trusts with the mission before us. While spying on the enemy is not expressly forbidden by The Dagda, it is seen by many to be linked indelibly
to war and therefore against the precepts of our law. Nuala has
assured Fearghus that you can be trusted without reservation."

Nuala rarely complimented Keelin and usually appeared
disappointed in her lack of scholarly talent. Now she learned
that the priestess had chosen her above all others to join in a
mission against the Romhanach. Keelin blushed with pleasure
but was immediately wary, both of Nuala and the Otherworld.
It beckoned to her and seemed to promise unimaginable freedom, but at what cost? She tried to suppress a vague disquiet,
not understanding why the Otherworld elicited in her such wildly
conflicting emotions. Almost involuntarily Keelin asked, "What
if I do not possess an affinity with the Otherworld as Nuala believes?"

"Then you will no longer be bound by your fate. You will be
free of The Dagda."

"When will I know?"

"When Nuala returns from Tara. We will travel to Danu's
cave where the Trial of the Otherworld is best performed. You
will know then."

❧

KEELIN AND DEIRDRE finished their meal and cleaned up, then went outside and sat down on the wooden bench in front of the cabin. A thick bank of fog hid the valley below and only scattered hilltops were visible, like lonely islands in a sea of gray mist. The two sat in silence for a time, enjoying the fresh morning air and the peaceful isolation of Nuala's remote aerie.

"Now we can begin," said Deirdre at last. "I am sorry I forced you to wake so early this morning. Mastering the art of the *starling* can be exhausting and requires intense concentration, for our art has nothing to do with magic but is instead an enhanced acuity of the mind."

"*Starling?*"

Deirdre sighed. "I see Nuala has told you very little. She did say, of course, that her sole purpose was to help you master the art of the healer. Still, she *should* have shared more with you."

"Nuala enjoys the power of her knowledge."

"Yes, she does. However, I think her reluctance to share knowledge comes from a deep reticence rather than from a quest for power over others. Would you not agree?"

Keelin nodded but thought Deirdre was being overly generous in her assessment.

"What Nuala failed to tell you is that, like me, you are a *starling*. We comprehend all manner of languages and can speak to both man and beast. We are messengers of the mind and often the harbingers of fate."

"I see little use for this gift against the Romhanach," said Keelin matter-of-factly. "Better a freshly sharpened sword through the heart."

"Perhaps, but we will aid Eire in a less bloodthirsty manner. There may be a better way to defeat the Romhanach than on the field of battle. You and I, along with Nuala, will attempt to forestall the invasion and hopefully prevent the blood-letting. For you see, Keelin, our power is immense. We have the ability to speak with our minds. We can convey our thoughts without speaking a word—"

"I cannot convey my thoughts without speaking," interrupted Keelin.

"You only think that speaking is necessary. It is not. Watch me carefully, Keelin, for *I can say everything I wish to you without speaking a word.* You can train your mind to do the same. Furthermore, I just spoke to you in my voice. You recognized it as mine, did you not?"

Amazed, Keelin agreed excitedly. "Yes, how do you do that?"

Deirdre smiled, looking very pleased with herself. Again, without speaking aloud or even moving her lips, she added, "*I can also communicate in a voice that is not mine or anyone else's, but instead gives one the impression of one's own thought.*"

Keelin shuddered. "One could wreak havoc on the minds of others with that power."

"Yes, we could. Perhaps that is why our power is so rare. You and I are the only *starlings* on Eire. At least the only ones The Dagda is aware of."

"So how can we use our *starling* power against the Romhanach?"

"Our primary purpose is to spy on them. We must learn their battle plans, their invasion site, and their strength in numbers. Granted, our powers of the mind will be less useful than Nuala's in this regard. We cannot read Agricola's thoughts, but we can, shall we say, *coerce* them."

When Keelin did not respond, Deirdre continued. "We will use our *starling* power to convey thoughts of doubt and defeat to Agricola and his officers. We now know Domitian denied Agricola reinforcements, although the emperor did not expressly forbid the invasion. Agricola must win a resounding victory in Eire if he is to maintain his position within the Romhanach military. If he fears defeat—and we will plant within him the seeds of doubt—he may abandon his plan for invasion. We could have even more success in influencing Domitian to order a halt to the invasion. The emperor's ill will toward Agricola can be easily exploited by us. Domitian has no wish for Agricola to add to his laurels with a victory in Eire. . . ."

Deirdre continued but Keelin stopped listening. She knew nothing of the politics of the Romhanach, and Deirdre's excited discourse left her mind numb. Her thoughts instead wandered, imagining an arid land with expansive valleys and distant mountain ranges.

"I see you have no interest in the political chess game I describe."

Keelin shrugged. "I hoped our mission would be . . . different. Also, how will *our* spying benefit Eire? Nuala has told me The Dagda can only share *vague auguries.*"

"In this regard we have an ally. Déaglán will convey all we learn to the chieftains. His knowledge of the Romhanach is not questioned, and even his supposed conjectures will be heeded."

"He knows of our powers?"

"I would say that what he long suspected about The Dagda was recently confirmed."

Keelin noted that though the young priestess's clear blue eyes appeared guileless, there was a devilish tilt to her lips.

"And, of course, Déaglán can be trusted," added Deirdre. "He can also tell us much about Domitian and Agricola. We must understand our enemies if we are to be effective spies for Eire." The young priestess placed her arm around Keelin's shoulder.

"But enough of that for now. Before we begin our lessons, I wish to know more about you. Tell me of your life."

"There is little to tell. I have no exciting tales or grand adventures to relate."

"Your adventures will soon begin, I can assure you."

Keelin's brows knit as she contemplated how best to describe her childhood before the boar attack, for everything changed after that. However, once Keelin began she found it refreshingly easy and comforting to share the details of her childhood with Deirdre. Long-forgotten events seemed to crowd her mind, and the words tumbled out as she excitedly told Deirdre of her family and friends, and of Rua, her magnificent stallion. Some of her fondest memories were of the times she spent at her Uncle Eirnín's and Aunt Meghan's farm. Keelin remembered the warm summer days she and her cousins spent fishing, swimming, or competing in a variety of games that her uncle would invent.

"After Uncle Eirnín was killed in the last clan battle, some of the joy of visiting my cousins left me," Keelin admitted. "However, by then I was already spending far less time at their farm because I had begun my studies with Nuala."

"And what of your gifts as a healer and *starling*? How did they influence you?"

"I suppose as a healer I have seen more of life and death than others of my age. However, I would not recommend my experiences to the faint-hearted or squeamish, for I have seen sights that can elicit the most fearful nightmares."

"And what of your *starling* gift?"

"It has always reminded me of how different I am from everyone else. It seems the gods were not content in singling me out with small stature. There were whispers that I was a fairy changeling, my parents' real daughter spirited away by evil demons. If my father were not the chieftain, I imagine the gossip and tales would have been worse."

"Were you teased when you were young?"

"Yes, but the boys who teased me paid a dear price."

Keelin rarely thought of the teasing and bullying anymore. The day it ended was a more vivid memory. She had been eight years old when Brian had come upon a group of village boys taunting her about her diminutive size. She remembered standing there as the boys mocked her and laughed. She was more angry than hurt and waited for an opportunity to strike. Her father had always told her that when facing overwhelming odds in battle, the element of surprise could shift the advantage. Suddenly, she lunged at the leader of the bullies, catching him off balance and knocking him to the ground, her hands punching and gouging. She did not hear the other boys roar in delight as the object of her wrath soon got the better of her. Nor did she immediately hear Brian when he stepped into the clearing and shouted, "Let her go, now!"

The boys looked over and, seeing Brian standing there, stepped back from Keelin. The boy on the ground slowly stood up, his eyes downcast, afraid to look at Brian. Keelin scrambled to her feet and gave the bully a swift kick in the shin, her chin jutting out in defiance as he grimaced in pain.

Brian strode toward the group, his face murderous. "Now, which one of you would like to repeat your taunts to me?"

The boys stood there, shifting from one foot to the other, silent with their heads down.

"No? Is it that you reserve your cruel words only for little girls half your size? Well, I give you fair warning. If you ever accost Keelin again, in any manner whatsoever, you will answer to me. I am sure Séamus and his brothers would also relish a good fight. Am I understood?"

The boys nodded, finally shamed into looking Brian in the eyes.

After the boys left, Brian offered Keelin his hand. "Come now, lass, I will walk you home."

Keelin refused his hand and brushed past him. After taking several strides away, she stopped and turned back, her head held high. "Thank you for your help but I can take care of myself. Dáire is a bully and the others just follow him. They are of no account." With her eyes now glistening with unshed tears, she blurted out, "And I am *not* a *little girl*! You are as bad as they are!" With that, she turned and ran off, not once looking back.

The memory of that day had always evoked humiliation, with her anger directed at Brian. Today she felt only regret.

# CHAPTER TEN

*K*EELIN, I WILL BE VISITING AUNT MEGHAN AND YOUR cousins today. Would you take these to the sacred hill?"

Keelin had been about to leave the cottage, excited to spend another day with Deirdre. Impatiently, she turned and looked at her mother. Saraid held out a small bouquet of flowers, their delicate petals vibrant with color. Keelin at once remembered: these last beauties from her mother's fading garden were to be placed on Uncle Eirnín's grave, commemorating the end of the last battle of the clans and her uncle's death.

"Of course I will take them," responded Keelin, taking the flowers then kissing her mother's cheek. Saraid put her arms around her daughter and held her close. Keelin still loved her mother's comforting embrace, never tiring of that special feeling of safety and calm.

"And if you see Brian at the sacred hill, be kind to him. He seemed distracted last night and left long before dawn this morning." Saraid's voice was gentle but Keelin could hear the underlying force of her mother's counsel. Keelin nodded, remembering Brian's brooding hostility and silence at dinner. She had not guessed the reason for his dark mood and now regretted her uncharitable thoughts of the evening.

"Well, be off then," said Saraid, lightly brushing a kiss on Keelin's forehead. In spite of the solemnity of the moment, Keelin couldn't help but reflect on how her mother still had to bend *down* to plant a kiss. Why did the gods choose to make me so small? she thought with resentment. Her happy mood of the morning was taking a decidedly bleak turn.

KEELIN HITCHED LIAM'S bay gelding, Bran, to the cart and was soon approaching the family's burial ground. It sat atop a small hill covered with closely cropped grass still burdened by heavy dew. Sheep grazed frequently on the hill but today there were none to be seen. Keelin saw only the stone cairns that marked each grave as she walked up the hill, having left Bran below to graze. She made her way to Eirnín's grave and placed her mother's flowers on top of the cairn. Then she sat down on the soft grass, heedless of its dampness, and recited a favorite prayer to the gods.

"Uncle Eirnín, we all miss you," Keelin said. She lowered her head so that her cheek was resting on one of the cold, smooth stones of the cairn. "I can't hear you anymore. You have passed to your new life and have left us behind. It should be thus but we still grieve." Then her mind slipped back in time to the day of Eirnín's death. It had been five years, but Keelin remembered every detail as though it were yesterday.

A truce had been called to allow both clans to treat their wounded and carry away their dead. The battle that morning had been brutal and the slaughter great, each side suffering fearful losses. To put an end to the bloodshed, her father had challenged the chieftain of the enemy clan to single combat, and that contest was to take place the next morning.

Keelin had been studying the healing arts with Nuala for almost two years and accompanied the priestess to the battlefield. The sights that awaited her would be seared into her memory forever. The ground was littered with the abandoned weapons of war and everywhere there was blood, its slippery wetness already congealing and its metallic stench filling Keelin's nostrils. The dead were scattered amongst the living, their bodies lying in grotesque positions, their white skin waxy, covered with rivulets of blood and flies. Moans and cries of pain punctuated an otherwise eerily quiet scene.

Keelin followed Nuala as they made their way from one downed warrior to the next, the Priestess assessing the damage and ministering to the living. Eventually, men began collecting the shields, spears, and swords of the fallen warriors and piled them at the edge of the battlefield to be claimed later by grieving families. Keelin quietly assisted Nuala, cleaning wounds, applying bandages, and carrying her satchel of medicines. Many of the wounded were carried from the field to be treated elsewhere. The more grievously wounded often required immediate attention, and Keelin's hands were surprisingly sure and her mind focused as she and Nuala worked desperately to save lives.

Keelin was standing next to Nuala as the priestess tended to yet another warrior when she glanced to her right and saw her uncle Eirnín. He lay flat on his back, his eyes mercifully closed. His shield lay upon his chest, covering much of his body and, undoubtedly, the wound that had killed him, for his face, arms, and legs looked unscathed. His sword had been driven into the ground next to him in quiet and stark tribute to his heroic death. Keelin suddenly felt an overwhelming sensation of nausea and weakness, the gruesome sights of the morning not affecting her nearly as much as the silent repose of her beloved uncle.

"Keelin! Do you hear me?" Nuala's voice entered her consciousness and she tore her eyes from her uncle.

"Keelin, please return to camp and tell one of the men to bring a wagon transport for this man. Then stay in camp and prepare beds and more bandages and supplies for surgery. I will return soon and no longer need your assistance here."

Nuala held Keelin's eyes and gently motioned her to leave, willing the girl not to look upon her uncle again. Stricken, Keelin stumbled back to camp where she hid behind a cluster of trees and retched until she felt empty and exhausted. She then smoothed her hair and quietly and mechanically began folding bandages and readying beds for more wounded.

"Dear Uncle Eirnín," said Keelin quietly as she straightened back up to a sitting position next to Eirnín's grave. She sat there quietly and then let her mind relive all of the wonderful times she had had with her uncle and his family. She was actually laughing silently when she felt someone's presence and turned to see Brian standing there. Their eyes met, hers soft with happy memories, his guarded and dark. Brian walked up beside her and knelt down on one knee, his hands clenched atop his left thigh, his eyes fixed on her mother's flowers.

"I thought I might see you here this morning," Keelin said. "I was just remembering how much Uncle Eirnín loved a good contest of speed and agility. He was forever designing the most difficult obstacle courses, and I would get so angry because I would never win."

"You were tough, though, even if you always finished last."

"I beat Séamus once," Keelin retorted.

"That was only because he cracked his head open when he fell and couldn't finish the contest. Don't you remember, he was swinging from one giant oak to the next when the rope broke and down he went."

"Well, perhaps," Keelin said, reluctantly conceding.

They sat there quietly for a moment and then Brian let out a ragged breath and whispered, "He was a grand man. I think of him every day and will miss him always, till I die."

Keelin heard the pain and hurt in Brian's voice, his customary veil of nonchalant bravado gone completely. She studied his profile—his head slightly bent, a strand of his black hair hiding his eyes. On impulse, Keelin stood up and kissed Brian's forehead, much as her mother had kissed hers earlier. She immediately regretted her action, certain Brian would direct some cutting remark at her spontaneous display of compassion. Instead, he remained silent and still, the only visible sign of a reaction seen in his hands, his tensely clenched fists relaxing and his fingers spreading out to rest quietly on his thigh.

Finally, he spoke, his eyes still downcast. "Thank you lass, now go. It is best I am alone."

Keelin turned from Brian and made her way down the hill then climbed up onto the cart. She picked up the reins and guided Bran to the road. There she stopped and glanced back at Brian. He still knelt at Eirnín's grave, silent and stark against a brilliant sky. Keelin sighed and lightly flicked the reins on Bran's rump, sending him trotting off down the road.

It was late afternoon by the time Keelin and Deirdre left what was no better than a bumpy cow path and steered Bran onto a wide country road. Deirdre heaved a sigh of relief when the cart rolled smoothly over the hard-packed rock and clay. They had just visited a remote farm where Keelin was treating a farmer's young wife who had suffered yet another miscarriage. The mournful pall that enveloped the household, combined with the rough jarring of the cart, had left both women's nerves frayed.

As was always the case, Deirdre recovered quickly. "I feel sure that young Saoirse's next child will be born healthy and strong. A boy, I believe."

Keelin, somewhat annoyed with Deirdre's optimism and not ready to abandon her dark mood, replied, "It that so? Are you a soothsayer as well as a *starling?*"

"In a manner of speaking, yes. I do not see the future but often I have feelings or visions, and sometimes dreams that foretell, or at least hint at, what might come. Admittedly, not all my visions come to pass. Still, I have learned never to regard them as mere flights of fancy."

Deirdre's words struck a chord with Keelin, unsettling and almost frightening her. Sometimes, when she successfully controlled her emotions, she could hear, feel, and sense things that were not real.

"Is it . . . possible," asked Keelin haltingly, "that I might *see* things as well?" They were now passing the crags of Loich's Gap and the sandstone cliff cast a dark shadow along the road.

"Undoubtedly. You are a *starling* and, as I have said, we are harbingers of fate, or at least of things that *might* be. I believe fate is not absolute. There is an ability within all of us to alter life's course. But tell me, have you already had such visions?"

Keelin was about to answer Deirdre when a falcon swooped low in front of them. Then the beautiful raptor banked, soaring up along the sheer face of the crag, finally alighting on the branch of an aspen high above.

Keelin halted Bran and exclaimed, "That is Bronach, my Uncle Eirnín's prized falcon!" Without hesitation, Keelin handed Deirdre the reins, jumped from the cart, and ran toward the crag's base.

"The bird is hopelessly out of reach, Keelin!" Deirdre called after her. "What is your purpose?"

Laughing, almost crying, Keelin shouted over her shoulder, "I am going to climb!" She did not have time to explain to Deirdre that Uncle Eirnín had taught her, along with his sons and Brian, how to climb these crags many years ago. It was great sport and Keelin loved it because her small size proved an advantage, and only Brian could consistently beat her to the top.

At the moment all she could think of was Bronach, her uncle's pride and joy who had flown off shortly after his death. Keelin and Brian had kept a tally of the times they had each spotted the falcon over the years. Often the sightings were near where Eirnín had taken Bronach to hunt, both man and bird reveling in the aerial chase. Keelin could not help but wonder if some divine instinct had brought Bronach here, five years to the day of Eirnín's death. She quickly reached the crag and tied her skirt up into makeshift trousers. Then she leapt up onto a low ledge and began climbing, her hands clawing the rocky holds and her feet digging into crevices as she pushed and pulled her way up the steep cliff.

It felt like hours before Keelin reached the top. She swung her legs over the ledge, scrambled to her feet, and looked up. There, still perched in the tree, was Bronach staring down at her.

"Oh Bronach, was it necessary for me to climb to such a

height to be near you? Yes, I suppose it was. Only at such a height are we kindred spirits. How I wish I could join you."

In answer, Bronach spread her wings and began flying in circles above the crag. Keelin stretched out her arms and reached for the sky, turning round and round as she followed the falcon's flight. Then Bronach dove down and glided by her, so close she could feel the swoosh of air from the raptor's wings. She watched Bronach fly off, past the crags and Loich's Gap. Without thinking, Keelin followed, running straight toward the cliff, stopping only when she was precariously close to the edge. Already her uncle's falcon was almost out of sight. Keelin sighed, feeling calm and at peace for the first time in days.

"Thank you, Bronach," whispered Keelin. "We have both honored Uncle Eirnín this day."

Keelin could now hear Deirdre calling up to her. She waved and stepped back from the cliff's edge, deciding to take a longer but easier and more gradual descent that lay some distance up the road. Focusing on all she had learned from Deirdre thus far, Keelin managed to communicate this without speaking a word. Deirdre raised her hands and clapped a resounding approval while communicating an unspoken, *Bravo*.

As Keelin walked along the cliff, she enjoyed the view this height afforded. She remembered her Uncle Eirnín proclaiming, "All of Eire can be seen from atop these crags!" Hyperbole aside and on a clear day such as this, the green expanse below certainly did seem endless.

In the distance she could see the north–south road, a main thoroughfare for merchants and travelers. Somewhat off its main track stood two horsemen. One man appeared to be of average height and sat a nondescript brown horse. The other man was tall and, even from this distance, looked imposing. The hood of the man's cloak covered his head and its skirt spread over his horse's rump. Odd, thought Keelin. There was no need for a cloak on this fine day. She squinted her eyes, hoping to sharpen her vision, but to no avail. As she did so, the men parted, the large man steering his horse north along the main road and the other choosing a narrow track that led toward an oak forest to the west. She watched as the men rode away, both unaware that she was spying on them. When the large man was nearly out of sight, she thought he pushed back the hood of his cloak but she could not be sure. An uneasy feeling swept over her and she hurried back to Deirdre, anxious to share what she had just seen.

"THERE ARE SPIES amongst us, to be sure," concluded Liam.

The family had just finished the evening meal, and the main topic of conversation had been the meeting Keelin had witnessed from atop the crags of Loich's Gap.

"More likely a spy and a traitor," responded Brian. "A messenger must be sent to Tara at once."

Keelin said nothing. She could not tell them that Deirdre left for Tara shortly after Keelin had described the clandestine meeting. In fact, Deirdre disappeared right before Keelin's eyes into the Otherworld, unnerving her. Whether she liked it or not, she was being drawn into The Dagda's shadowy world of secrets and sorcery.

"Are we not being premature? We have no proof of the men's evil intentions." Saraid had been quietly listening to the dinner conversation and saying very little.

"Do not fool yourself, Saraid," scoffed Liam. "We must increase our vigilance. At this moment, however, I will be saying goodnight to you. It has been a long day, with much to consider." He stood up and stretched, and turning to Keelin, said, "There is a new moon tonight and it is black as pitch outside. With not a cloud in the sky, the stars will be beautiful and bright. Walk back with Brian and me and stargaze for a while."

"That sounds grand," responded Keelin, pushing thoughts of The Dagda and war from her mind.

KEELIN SAT ON the split-rail fence with her uncle and Brian on either side of her. The sky was indeed brilliant with stars and looked like a mosaic of silver-white lace against the black heaven. Usually brimming with stories, tonight Liam was silent. Although Keelin could see nothing but his dark shape in the black night, she could nonetheless sense his nervous energy. His fingers fidgeted and moved as if he were tracing the lines of one of his wood carvings. Presently, he said, "I think I will be headed back to my workshop." He jumped down from the fence. "I am not sure the harp I completed this afternoon is quite to my liking. Good night to you both." With that he hurried off.

"Good, we are finally alone and you can tell me all about your sighting of Bronach," said Brian. "We have talked enough of spies and traitors for one night."

Keelin excitedly described every detail of the sighting, knowing Brian understood and felt as she did about Eirnín's falcon. After she finished, neither spoke.

Brian broke the silence. "Bronach is free and so too is Eirnín's soul. I wish . . . ." His voice trailed off. He shrugged and lifted his right hand from the railing, distractedly running his fingers through his hair. "I love Eire but cannot help but dream of more. How can one be confined to a small island when there is a world to explore? Look at the vastness of the heavens. And here we sit, shackled."

Before Keelin could reply, Brian gestured upward. "Look, Keelin. There is the North Star, the most important in the heavens for celestial navigation. We could travel the world with our knowledge of the stars."

"I would not rely on my knowledge," dismissed Keelin, not wanting to admit Brian's dreams mirrored her own. "I am woefully ignorant. I prefer Uncle Liam's stories of heavenly kingdoms and magical creatures and do not have the slightest interest in the 'science of the stars,' as Nuala calls it."

"If it is heavenly creatures you wish for, I will oblige. If you turn to your right and look up, you will see a group of stars."

Keelin turned, and as she did so her foot slipped off the lower rail, pitching her slightly forward. Brian easily reached out his arm and steadied her in the dark, his hand gently grasping her shoulder. He was now so close she could feel the warmth of his body next to hers. She raised her hand to push his away and then hesitated, confused by how his touch made her feel.

Without moving his right arm from around Keelin's shoulders, Brian pointed with his left. "See how that group of stars forms the body of a great horse with its long neck arched and its head set proudly?"

Forgetting her embarrassment, Keelin leaned more closely to Brian, trying to follow his line of vision.

"Do you see it?"

At first Keelin saw only clusters of stars with no distinct shapes. Then, with delight, she cried, "Yes, and I also see his legs. It appears he is at full gallop!"

"Beautiful, isn't he? We shall name our heavenly beast Rua, for never have I seen a stallion more grand than yours."

Keelin felt a warm flush of pride at Brian's words as she gazed at the magical vision. "Look at the stars hovering over his back. Might he have a rider?"

"Those are great wings of gold so he may soar through the heavens."

Keelin was sure Brian had opened up a window to her soul. Enchanted, she asked, "What else do you see?"

"Look to the left. Do you see the cluster of stars that hover together, each trying to outshine the other?"

"Yes, I think so," said Keelin, distracted by Brian's closeness and finding it difficult to concentrate.

"I imagine those are the young women of Eire, dressed up in their finery for the festival of Samhain, sparkling in their brilliance."

In spite of herself, Keelin was slightly irritated at the admiration in Brian's voice. The distasteful image of him kissing Brigid crowded her mind. "Yes, and I believe the most brilliant and beautiful one is Brigid, though it is a pity her mind doesn't shine nearly as brightly."

Brian gave her shoulder a playful squeeze. "Yes, I suppose that would be Brigid, for she is quite dazzling. However, I fear she is not bold enough to embark on a grand adventure with Séamus and me. Only you, my brave lass, may join us."

"And more's the pity, I am to be a priestess." Keelin felt rather than heard Brian exhale, then he casually dropped his hand from her shoulder.

"Indeed you are. Alas, Séamus and I must venture out on our own." Brian stepped down from the fence rail and offered his hand to her. "Here, let me help you. It is late and we have long days ahead of us. Our dreams will have to wait until after Eire's victory over the Romhanach."

Keelin returned to the cottage, a multitude of emotions swirling within her. She reached the cottage door and, before opening it, turned and looked to where she and Brian had been sitting. He still stood there, his dark form nearly blending into the black night. Then she gazed up at the stars, knowing he was doing the same.

# CHAPTER ELEVEN

EELIN LAY FULLY CLOTHED ON THE TOP OF HER
bed. After leaving Brian and returning to the cottage,
she had been restless and unable to sleep. Her thoughts kept
returning to the two horsemen and their clandestine meeting.
There was no doubt these men were enemies of Eire. A preter-
natural knowledge, more powerful and certain than instinct, told
her so. Deirdre had spoken earlier in the day about "visions"
and her ability to sometimes foresee the future or what might
come to pass. Keelin was beginning to realize she possessed similar, unsettling powers. She had two sights, one perceived by her
eyes and the other by her mind. She had always hastily dismissed these visions, thinking them fancies of her wild imagination. Moreover, Nuala's controlling nature and rigorous tutoring
in the art of healing left little time for any real introspection.
Deirdre was different; she did not teach as much as guide, encouraging Keelin to explore her mind and embrace her incredible
gifts. This measure of freedom had made Keelin more reflective,
though admittedly no less reckless.

Keelin knew the two men could not have traveled far before
darkness had set in. She had no idea where the traitor might be
but the spy would have few places to hide. Keelin smiled in the
darkness, knowing where the spy was likely to be. There was an

abandoned cottage hidden in a deep ravine bordering the oak forest near Loich's Gap. Trails leading to the cottage were choked with brambles and scrub oaks, discouraging even hunters who frequented the woods from sheltering there. Very few knew of its existence, and no one could remember who had been foolhardy enough to build it. When young, Keelin, Brian, and Seamus had discovered it while exploring the forest. Mysterious and isolated, the cottage had become a favorite destination where, within its humble walls, they planned grand adventures.

Getting up from her bed, Keelin crept across the floor, lifted her cloak from where it hung on a peg, and stepped outside. She carefully closed the heavy wooden door and winced when it creaked rather noisily. She listened anxiously for any sound from within the cottage but heard none. Her mother had not awakened. The air had grown cold and Keelin threw the cloak over her shoulders as she turned and hurried to the stable. She would ride Bran at least as far as the ravine and go the rest of the way by foot. Approaching the cottage by horseback would surely alert the spy.

She had almost reached the stable when a large shape loomed toward her in the darkness.

"Who goes there?" said Keelin with as much authority as she could summon. She peered into the darkness and could now see the shapes of a man and a horse.

"*Keelin?*" said Brian, his voice just above a whisper. He reached her and added with exasperation, "Whatever are you up to?"

"I might ask you the same thing," retorted Keelin.

"I am going hunting," said Brian. "I came to the stable to retrieve my saddle and bridle." He led Rónán by only a rope looped round the stallion's neck. The hood of Brian's cloak was down and his black wavy hair hung to his shoulders. His tunic was of soft, pliable leather and a dagger was sheathed on his belt.

"Hunting? And the prey?" Keelin knew his purpose. So often over the years, she and Brian had been of like minds and would plan remarkably similar adventures or deeds unbeknownst to the other.

Brian hesitated. "I believe the spy may be staying at the cottage near Loich's Gap. The other day I noticed that someone had been using the ravine's western trail. Moreover, he had attempted to hide his tracks. Very skillfully, I might add."

"You did not go down to the cottage?" said Keelin rather scornfully.

"No. There was not yet any talk of a spy within our midst." Brian handed Keelin the lead rope round Rónán's neck and made for the stable. "But I am wasting time. I intend to right my mistake and ride there posthaste."

"I will go with you," said Keelin, as excitement welled up within her. "I also believe the spy is hiding at the cottage."

Brian stopped and regarded Keelin in the darkness. "You will not!" he said with a vehemence that startled Keelin. "I have no desire to shield you from harm tonight."

"I am going and do not need your protection," Keelin spat back. "I am well able to take care of myself."

Brian stood without speaking, seemingly irresolute. Finally he said, "Curse you, Keelin. Tonight's affair is deadly dangerous. You must do just as I say and remain behind me at all times."

Dropping Rónán's lead rope and whispering something in the horse's ear, Keelin almost skipped past Brian. "I will go bridle Bran."

"You will ride on Rónán with me," said Brian, reaching out and grabbing her arm. He spun her round, though not roughly.

"I do not trust you. Go get Rónán's bridle only. We will have to ride bareback."

Keelin did not argue and hurried to the stable. She knew Brian was not beneath alerting her mother. Besides, the prospect of going to the cottage with Brian excited her. She relished the prospect of danger.

After bridling Rónán, Brian easily leapt onto the stallion's back, swinging his right leg up and over in one fluid movement. He bent down and offered Keelin his left hand and she sprung up almost as easily, settling herself behind him. Brian held Rónán to a walk until they reached the village road, and then softened his hold on the reins allowing the stallion a slow, steady trot. Neither spoke.

For her part, Keelin now wished she had insisted on riding Bran. She was no longer sure of her feelings for Brian. He had always been her friend and self-appointed protector. Their verbal duels and frequent annoyance with one another had never really threatened their bond of friendship. On any given day Keelin might despise Brian's insufferable behavior but her anger never lasted. How could she hate him? Brian mirrored her soul with his dreams. Now, however, their friendship had changed. Just as she began to see Brian as something more than a friend, he had distanced himself from her. He had become aloof and was seemingly indifferent to her. Yet tonight, while they stargazed, he had been more like the Brian of old—teasing, protective, and wonderfully imaginative—and now she fought a powerful urge to wrap her arms around his waist and rest her head upon his back. Startled by her wholly sensuous response to his closeness, Keelin recoiled, embarrassed by longings she knew Brian did not reciprocate. An instant later her temper flared, her invariable response to conflict or uncertainty of any kind.

"I can see nothing when sitting behind you. I should have ridden Bran," said Keelin testily, as she tried without success to wriggle away from Brian so she was not touching him.

"It is black as pitch. There is little to see," said Brian, unmoved. "And stop your squirming. Can you not just enjoy this night? It is as if we were moving in a dream, blind but for our instincts and acutely heeding all senses but sight."

"I smell only the dampness of your woolen cloak and Rónán," responded Keelin, unwilling to concede anything. When Brian began to hum a mournful dirge in jest, Keelin added, "And if you break into song I will surely murder you, for I also carry a dagger."

Brian laughed. "I do not doubt it, my bloodthirsty lass."

Keelin could not help but laugh as well. Reassured by the warmth in Brian's voice, she relaxed and they fell silent again.

They were nearing the oak forest when Brian said, "I visited the cottage this past spring, concerned the heavy rains of the season may have damaged it. I should have known it would be unscathed. Time and the elements seem to have little effect on our humble cottage." He sighed. "There were many nights when it sheltered me."

"Yes," said Keelin, softly. Brian had told no one, not even Séamus, of the nights he sought refuge there. He had suffered in silence at the hands of his stepfather, and when life became unbearable he escaped to the cottage.

"You knew?" asked Brian. "How?"

Keelin realized she had spoken aloud, lulled by the soothing cadence of Rónán's hooves on the hard-packed road. She had kept silent all these years. Slightly embarrassed, she admitted, "I followed you there." She had always doggedly trailed Brian and Seamus everywhere, afraid of missing a grand adventure. But that day had been different. She had felt Brian's pain and was concerned, her healer's instinct already a powerful force within her, even at seven years old.

"I should have known. You always found Séamus and me no matter how hard we tried to elude you. What a pest——" Brian stopped mid-sentence. "It was you who left food and supplies at the cottage for me," he said with certainty. "Those gifts brought me a small measure of happiness. I thought perhaps a woodland fairy watched over me. Indeed, it was so."

"I dreamed many a time of wringing Colman's scrawny neck," said Keelin, incensed. "Why did you never tell Uncle Eirnín?"

"I was too proud, perhaps. I did not want anyone fighting my battles for me. So I waited for the day when I would be big and strong enough to kill Colman with my bare hands. Alas, when that day came, I could not do it. Eirnín, over the years, had shown me what it was to be a man." Brian took a deep breath. "I sometimes wonder what would have become of me without him. He raised me as his own and taught me the importance of duty and honor. So, as much as I hate Colman, he is good to my mother and she needs him. Moreover, he never hit or ridiculed me in front of her. Thankfully, she knew nothing."

"No, I am sure she did not," said Keelin, wishing to allay the hint of doubt she heard in Brian's voice. He had always been very protective of his emotionally fragile mother. Áine was a lovely, sensitive woman who possessed little, if any, fortitude and faced life's trials with trepidation. When her husband died suddenly, leaving her with five-year-old Brian and vast landholdings, she collapsed into a grief-stricken malaise. Eirnín, who had been her husband's closest friend, quickly assumed stewardship of the estate and guardianship of Brian. When Áine eventually recovered, she seemed only vaguely aware of her small son.

Then, within months, she astounded everyone by marrying Colman, her late husband's estate manager.

They had reached the oak forest and Brian slowed Rónán to a walk. "It was a long time ago. Colman fears me now and is most cordial. Of more immediate concern is the question of how the spy learned of the cottage. Even within our clan, few are aware of its existence. It is likely we know the traitor."

"The spy could have stumbled upon it quite by accident," said Keelin. "Or someone may have unwittingly shared its whereabouts with him." She was not sure she believed either supposition but suggested them nonetheless. The idea of a traitor within their clan was too disturbing.

"We may know the answer before this evening is over," said Brian as they entered the forest.

Damp, fallen oak leaves blanketed the forest floor and, with each step, Rónán's hooves sank almost noiselessly into the spongy footing. Bats skittered through the night air, veering disconcertingly close to the horse and riders. But for these small, dark creatures the forest seemed empty and an eerie stillness enveloped them as they rode along. It was as though the tide of nocturnal life ebbed away as they approached and then flowed back behind them, just out of reach. The silence was broken only once when Rónán trod on a dried branch. The sharp snap startled the stallion and he leapt forward, his muscles tense in momentary alarm. Unprepared and pitched backwards, Keelin instinctively grabbed for Brian's waist to prevent herself from falling off.

"You must stay alert," warned Brian, his voice just above a whisper. "We have almost reached the ravine."

Keelin smarted at Brian's mild rebuke but could not fault him. She had not been vigilant.

Not long afterwards Rónán, without any signal from Brian, halted. They had reached the southern trail of the ravine.

"My good old man," said Brian, patting the horse affectionately. "It has been ages since we last used this trail and yet you remember." He swung his right leg up and over Rónán's neck and dismounted. Keelin hastily followed, but with less fluidity, and Brian steadied her as she hit the ground.

"If you can tolerate the cold, it would be wise to leave your cloak here," said Brian. He had already removed his and draped it over the outstretched branch of an oak. "Without them we can move quickly and with more stealth."

Without a second thought, Keelin lifted the woolen cloak from her shoulders and draped it alongside Brian's. She shivered slightly from both the chill and nervous anticipation. Brian looped Rónán's reins over the same branch and then walked toward the trailhead. Before them was a massive rock outcropping, a seemingly impenetrable wall. Along its base stood a cluster of scrub oaks. Many years ago Keelin, inexplicably drawn to the outcropping, had found a narrow passage in the rock, hidden completely by the bush-like oaks. The passage led to the seemingly unfrequented trail beyond. From the time of its discovery, the southern trail became the trio's preferred one, believing it was known only to themselves and the gods.

Keelin followed Brian to an oak whose branches pressed against the outcropping's rocky wall. There, Brian stopped and looked down at her.

"Now remember, keep behind me on the trail. I will approach the cottage alone when we reach it. Stay hidden but alert. Wait for my signal."

Years ago, as children, they had created a secret means of communication using animal calls, and they were still fresh in

Keelin's mind. She nodded in the dark and said simply, "Yes."

Brian turned and lifted one of the oak's branches. They both ducked under it and made their way among the trees and through the rocky passage. The trail was narrow but not over-grown as would be expected. Keelin, however, hardly noticed. Brian moved swiftly and it was all she could do to keep up with him. He stopped only once and listened as an owl screeched in the distance. Keelin could feel Brian's menace and thought she would not wish to be the prey he was hunting.

For most of its length the trail roughly followed the con-tours of the ravine, with only a gradual descent. Then, nearing its destination, the trail took an abrupt right turn and dropped precipitously down the ravine's steep slope. In daylight it was relatively easy to descend the rocky, stair-like steps. At night the going was treacherous. Even though Keelin's eyes had adjusted to the darkness, she could not accurately gauge the varying drops of the slippery stairs. Her diminutive size was an added disadvantage—the distance to each step farther than her legs could reach without jumping. She fell behind Brian more than once and each time he waited, continuing only when she had joined him. At the bottom of the ravine the trail all but disap-peared into a stand of alders. Beyond the trees was a fast-mov-ing creek and Keelin, her heart racing, stayed close to Brian as they made their way a short distance upstream, within sight of the cottage.

A dim light, most likely from the fireplace, escaped through the shuttered windows. Its only door, positioned between the two windows and facing south, was shut. The clearing in front of the cottage was empty and appeared untrodden, the sandy soil cov-ered only by sparse grasses. Keelin thought she heard the rustling of leaves nearby but could not be sure. The noise from the nearby creek's rushing water made it difficult to distinguish muted sounds and their origins. Brian, though, had heard something too.

"Unsheathe your dagger," he whispered. "If you see any movement, if you hear anything outside the cottage, alert me." Then, repeating his earlier admonition, he said emphatically, "Otherwise, stay hidden and wait for my signal." The next second he was gone, disappearing into the shadowy cover of the trees surrounding the clearing.

Fully intending to heed Brian's words, Keelin watched and listened. She heard nothing but rushing water, and though the faint light from the cottage windows illuminated the clearing somewhat, it only served to make everywhere else darker and less visible. Frustrated, she could not quell a growing need for action. Crouching down, she left her hiding place and crept along the periphery of the clearing toward the eastern side of the cottage, knowing Brian was approaching from the west. She had almost flanked the cottage when the dim light of the clearing behind her changed almost imperceptibly. She instinctively froze, her heart lurching into her throat. Someone had opened the cottage door. It must be Brian, she reasoned, every muscle in her body tense and ready to respond to his signal. Instead, she heard the clatter of rocks tumbling down an embankment from somewhere beyond the cottage. The image of the spy escaping on horseback flashed before her eyes.

"*Behind the cottage!*" warned Keelin, alerting Brian urgently and soundlessly, not using their childhood signals but her powers of the mind. She rounded the cottage running, now heedless of the danger that awaited. She heard rather than saw the startled skitter of a horse and the rider's sharp intake of breath and angry curse. Suddenly, the horse and rider's shape materialized, charging her with deadly malevolence. She dove sideways, trying to avoid being trampled, and then something hard hit the side of her head and everything went black.

KEELIN HOVERED ON the verge of consciousness, her mind muddled by images and sensations. She imagined someone gently brushing errant strands of hair from her forehead and then kissing it. The delicate scent of roses wafted about her and a fire burned and crackled in the hearth. She felt warm. Overshadowing all was a fearful pounding in her head, forcing her back from oblivion. She opened her eyes.

"You have decided to rejoin the living," said Brian, teasing, but Keelin could hear the relief in his voice. He sat next to her on one of only two rough-hewn wooden chairs in the cottage. She was lying on a crude leather and wood hammock with a rather dirty woolen blanket draped about her. Brian had lit a lantern and it sat squarely in the middle of a small wooden table. A fire glowed in the hearth. They both looked at her left hand which Brian held in both of his. Smiling sheepishly, he quickly released it.

Keelin tried to lift her head and immediately regretted her foolishness. The painful throbbing intensified and her body felt leaden and without strength.

"Lie still," said Brian. "You are concussed."

"Yes, I believe so," said Keelin, lifting her hand and tentatively touching the swelling on the side of her head. Nauseous and feeling quite ill, she dropped her hand to her side. Then she remembered and felt even worse.

"The spy?"

"Long gone," said Brian. "No doubt he also heard your

warning and, not knowing how many pursued him, wisely decided to escape while he could. By the time I reached you, all I heard was his horse scrambling up the western trail's embankment."

No, the spy had not heard her warning, thought Keelin. Then, almost to herself, she said, "I could not stop him. I am to blame for his escape."

"Perhaps," said Brian, in a voice surprisingly free of anger or accusation. "Though I am not certain the outcome would have been different even if you had not foolishly attempted to confront the spy by yourself."

"Do not humor me," said Keelin, disheartened. "I did not even see the spy leave the cottage. I moved too soon."

"You should not have moved at all," said Brian with finality. "But you would never have seen the spy leave the cottage because he was not there."

Keelin looked at Brian uncomprehendingly. She felt disoriented and dull, her mind not keeping pace. "What are you saying?"

"He had just returned when he attacked you. When I entered the cottage, the fire in the hearth had almost burned out and had not been tended nor the logs replenished for some time. Why? Because the spy was elsewhere. Indeed, I believe he had been escorting someone home, or at least as far as the village road."

"Why would he escort someone home in the middle of the night?" asked Keelin. "It makes little sense to me."

"It makes sense if his guest was a woman," said Brian. He leaned over and, gently lifting Keelin's head with one hand, pulled free the corner of a shawl acting as a cushion with the other. Then, with infinite care, he lowered her head back down, his fingers lingering for a moment in her hair. Keelin's head throbbed from even so small a movement, but she ignored the pain and eyed the shawl Brian held up for her to see. It was of dark green silk and beautiful, yet it was the shawl's fragrance that most enchanted Keelin. Perfume, though not unheard of in Eire, was rare and considered an extravagance by all but the very wealthy. And, until recently, she had not known there existed a perfume that smelled like the roses in her mother's garden.

"Deirdre wears such a fragrance," said Keelin. "It is made in Roma."

"And the shawl?" asked Brian.

"The traveling merchants often peddle shawls such as this. I have seen many of similar quality and color. And I suppose the scent may also have been peddled by merchants." Keelin could not remember seeing anyone wearing a shawl of precisely that shade of green. "It seems odd, though, that she would leave the shawl behind."

Brian shrugged his shoulders. "The lass forgot it."

Keelin sighed noncommittally. She could not think clearly. It seemed the answer was just out of reach.

"Perhaps your earlier supposition is correct and a lass from our clan unwittingly told the spy about this cottage," offered Brian. "The shawl and perfume may very well have been gifts from him." He rubbed the silk shawl between his thumb and fingertips and the fine cloth snagged slightly on the roughness of his skin. Then he frowned and shook his head. "No, I think not. Rather, it is more likely the lass is somehow complicit."

Keelin studied the shawl then met Brian's eyes. "I pray it is not so."

# CHAPTER TWELVE

*A* LINE OF HORSEMEN WAITED IN FORMATION at the near end of a large field, left fallow for the year and sprouting nothing but ankle-length grass. They faced a high, makeshift wooden barrier standing halfway across the field. When the order was given, two horsemen charged forward, galloping toward the barrier. One horse and rider, traveling at breakneck speed, reached the obstacle first. Instead of jumping, however, the horse ducked out at the last minute, swerving to the left. The rider was pitched off to the right and fell in a heap on the ground. Meanwhile, the other rider was even more unfortunate. His horse galloped gamely to the base of the obstacle and then planted his hind legs firmly in the turf and stopped dead. His rider was catapulted into the air and almost cleared the barrier without his steed. The man let out a howl as the sharp wooden ends of the barrier gouged his flesh. Again and again, pairs of horsemen charged the barrier, all with similar results.

"It is time to put an end to this folly before someone breaks his neck," said Fearghus, wincing at the sight of another horse and rider going down. "Even those horses brave enough to attempt the jump stumble and fall, either atop or on the other side."

Déaglán was unmoved. He knew it was not enough to triumph over Agricola's army on the field of battle. Eire's cavalry must breach the Romhanach's deadly repel formation and deny them an orderly retreat. Only then could Eire's warriors pursue the enemy to the sea and destroy them, handing Agricola an absolute and ignominious defeat.

"I have seen horses clear such obstacles in Roma. It can be done. With proper training, some of the horses that failed today will jump the Romhanach's more formidable repel barrier with ease when the time comes," asserted Déaglán.

"I do not share your opinion but will defer to it. Still, I would guess only one in fifty war horses has the skill to make such a jump."

As the high priest spoke, a long-legged, more finely boned gray sprang forward and settled into an effortless gallop. The rider had a steady, confident manner and both man and beast moved as one. The barrier was now only ten or twelve strides away. Seconds later, Déaglán and Fearghus watched the gray meet the obstacle and, without the slightest hesitation, clear it, though barely.

"There is our first one in fifty! More will follow, trust me."

Fearghus nodded. "Yes, I do trust you, as you trust me. When will you leave?"

"Tomorrow at daybreak." Last night Déaglán had agreed to share all he knew of Agricola and Domitian with Deirdre. In return, the priestess would supply Déaglán with critical updates on Agricola's invasion strategies. Somehow Déaglán was to relay these updates to Eire's chieftains without arousing suspicion as to their origin. When he had pressed Fearghus to tell him more, the high priest unequivocally refused.

Now, both men watched huge storm clouds approach the

field from the north. Already rain was falling in the distance, a thin gray veil obscuring the landscape.

"Do you know Deirdre helped me on Sasanach?"

"Yes, of course. It was I who ordered her to ensure your safe escape."

Déaglán was not surprised, though he was oddly disappointed. He wondered if Deirdre would have allowed him to die at the hands of the Romhanach without Fearghus's order. Shaking the thought off he said, "Well then, your pretext for secrecy is absurd."

"Perhaps. Still, I will tell you no more. The Dagda's secrets must remain thus." Fearghus looked up at the dark clouds, now almost overhead. "It appears our fine weather has come to an end. This storm will be quite fierce and last for days. Prepare for a drenching during your travels home. Give my best to your sister, Saraid. It has been two long years since I last saw her."

DÉAGLÁN LEFT TARA at daybreak the next morning. A light rain fell as he saddled his horse, dwindling to a mist by the time he set off. He began to wonder if the worst of the storm had passed overnight and Fearghus had been mistaken. By midday, however, the heavens opened up and Déaglán cursed his friend and the downpour. The roads became boggy and Déaglán's horse sloshed through deep pools of muddy water, stumbling occasionally in the treacherous and uneven mire. The trees that lined the roads blocked out what little light penetrated the thick storm clouds, their leaves heavy with raindrops, and their branches and trunks dark with wet. On the narrow paths, Déaglán had to steer his horse carefully through the gauntlet of the water-laden branches, any contact sending a heavy dousing of collected rainwater onto the already sodden horse and rider. His heavy woolen cloak provided some protection, its hood shielding his face and its wide cape spreading out to cover his shoulders and the horse's rump and flanks.

Déaglán's prolonged absence from the sea compounded his misery. Only spying atoned for his time on land, and he never tired of the deadly game of nerve and wit. But he was wary of the mission before him, knowing it promised neither the sea nor danger. The thought of seeing Deirdre caused him even more trepidation. The young priestess always saw more than he chose to reveal. She had been at Tara several days ago, bringing news of a spy near Loich's Gap. Déaglán did not see Deirdre, but even the thought of her so near unsettled him. Steeling his mind and returning to the task at hand, he pondered the report. If the spy was no longer at Tara, there was indeed a traitor within Eire's warrior forces. Tracking down both spy and traitor would be some recompense.

When his horse took an awkward step and fell to his knees in the mud, Déaglán cursed Fearghus yet again. He dismounted and ran his hands up and down his horse's forelegs, worried the poor animal may have pulled a tendon in the fall. Satisfied all was well, he led the horse back to an abandoned barn he had spotted earlier, just off the road.

As Déaglán sat in the barn waiting for the heavy rain to subside, he reflected on his many years of spying in Eoraip. It had all begun shortly after Maeve and their infant son had died in childbirth. Déaglán still could not clearly recall the bleak days following their deaths. Surely he had been mad with grief and drink. Fearghus had found him lying in his own vomit aboard his boat in the harbor at Fhianait. Déaglán had lifted his head and, slurring his words, said, "Go away . . . you meddlesome priest. I want none of your . . . sanctimonious counsel."

Without warning, the high priest had bent down and grabbed Déaglán, jerking him to his feet. "Is this how you honor your wife and son?" Fearghus exclaimed, his face red with anger. "So be it!" Then he picked Déaglán up and hurled him over the side of the boat and into the cold waters of the bay. "Save yourself or drown, it is of no account to me!"

Déaglán was never quite sure whether it was the shock of the cold water or Fearghus's angry admonition that had given him the will to climb back aboard and live again. Soaked and bedraggled, his lungs heaving, he made it up and over the side of the boat and collapsed in a heap. There, Fearghus sat waiting for him with a most intriguing proposal. He had asked Déaglán to become a spy for Eire, fearing that in the not too distant future, the mighty empire of Roma would threaten their small island.

"We *must* know our enemy," Fearghus had said with vehemence. "Only then will we have any hope of defending Eire. As a seafarer and wanderer, you have already traveled freely in Eoraip and speak all manner of languages. Furthermore, you are fearless and have a penchant for secrecy and deception."

Fearghus's observations that day nearly fifteen years ago had proved undeniably prescient. Almost at once, Déaglán realized he was peculiarly suited for and relished the life of a spy. He had made it his purpose to infiltrate the most elite imperial and military enclaves of Roma. Now, with the Romhanach poised to invade Eire, he had agreed to another of Fearghus's proposals and would share with Deirdre all he knew of the emperor, Domitian, and Agricola.

He had learned much about Domitian's character over the years. He knew Agricola less well. The general reminded Déaglán somewhat of Domitian's older brother, Titus. Both men were strong, confident military leaders who commanded respect and loyalty from their men. Déaglán chuckled to himself. In fact, Domitian's enmity toward Agricola was easily understood if one knew of the emperor's rabid hatred of Titus. Anyone even remotely reminding the emperor of his older brother was despised at best. Déaglán had witnessed the ugliness of their sibling rivalry while working as a groom in the imperial stables.

There could not have been two brothers more different than Titus and Domitian. Titus, the handsome heir to the imperial seat, was a bold leader and an eloquent orator. Domitian, distrustful and taciturn, was an able though unimaginative administrator. He was forever in the shadow of his charming and illustrious older brother. Déaglán saw more of Titus than Domitian at the stables. Titus was an excellent horseman and owned some of the finest stallions Déaglán had ever seen. In contrast, Domitian had a rough and heavy hand, and showed cruel disregard for his horses.

Déaglán quietly listened to the gossip of the stables and befriended some of the ladies' maids in the palace, who guilelessly provided him with the intrigue and scandals of the imperial household. He heard furtive whisperings and soon suspected that Domitian was conspiring to assassinate Titus. Domitian would often ride out at odd hours in the company of reputed mercenaries and scoundrels, men who sold their allegiance to the highest bidder and were loyal to nothing but their own greed. Domitian was a fool to think Titus was unaware of his nefarious plot, thought Déaglán. He could only wait and watch, knowing a deadly confrontation between the brothers was inevitable.

It happened early one morning as Déaglán finished feeding the horses and was preparing to clean and oil the bridles and saddles. Titus had been away visiting his estates in the country and was expected to return any day. Upon his return, Titus planned to remain at the palace for a week or more before setting out on a military expedition to quell unrest in conquered regions to the east. Déaglán had laid out the tack in preparation for cleaning when Domitian came striding into the stable yard excited, his eyes with a gleam that hinted at some recent triumph.

"You," Domitian ordered, "saddle Raven for me at once." Domitian did not look at Déaglán; instead, he fastidiously brushed some dust off his tunic, then his hands closed around the hilt of his sword, his lips curling in a malevolent smile.

"Raven, my lord?" questioned Déaglán. Raven was Titus's most magnificent stallion and his pride and joy. The stallion was coal black with not a fleck of white on his noble head or fine strong legs. Déaglán knew that Domitian had neither the skill nor the finesse to ride such a high-spirited horse.

"Yes, Raven, you fool. Are you deaf? Likely you are quaking with fright, cowering at the thought of what my brother will do to you when he learns that you have saddled that rogue stallion for me. If I were you, I would fear only my actions from this day forward!"

Déaglán nodded, keeping his head bowed, afraid that Domitian might see the anger and contempt that Déaglán was sure showed in his eyes. Déaglán noticed that Domitian wore viciously sharp spurs and knew that if Domitian dared use them on Raven, Titus, if he was still alive, would surely exact frightening revenge. Déaglán had no illusions about Titus. For all his charm and eloquence, Déaglán knew Titus was a ruthless and bloodthirsty general who showed little mercy and much cruelty to his enemies. Titus once remarked, when too full of ale, that he liked nothing better than the smell of his dead foes as they lay rotting on the battlefield. Yes, thought Déaglán, Titus inspired great loyalty but also immense fear.

Sensing danger, Raven was fractious as Déaglán saddled him, snorting and tossing his head as he pawed the ground and shifted his weight from one leg to another, starting at every noise, his massive body tense and quivering. Déaglán tried to calm the stallion with soothing words, but to no avail. Sighing in resignation, Déaglán led Raven out of the stable and toward the waiting Domitian.

"So, you black devil," exclaimed Domitian as he approached Raven, his face full of vitriolic revenge. "We shall see who triumphs today with Titus not here to protect and coddle you. It is the sting of the spurs that you need, and you would be wise to submit, for you have a new master now."

Alarmed at Domitian's words, Déaglán tried to hold Raven still as the stallion, his ears pinned flat against his head, reared up and shied away from Domitian, striking out with a vicious kick of his hind legs.

"Hold him still, you imbecile," snarled Domitian, barely avoiding Raven's lethal strike. Domitian then grabbed Raven's reins and with surprising agility swung himself into the saddle. Domitian was just about to dig his spurs into the stallion's sides when both men heard the sharp pounding of a horse's hooves behind them. Titus, his face taut and his eyes murderous, galloped full speed into the yard. Before Domitian could turn Raven and defend himself against his brother's charge, Titus reached

Domitian. With a swing of his fist, Titus knocked Domitian to the ground. Titus jumped from his horse and, pulling his sword from its scabbard, stood over his brother, the blade threatening.

"Stand up, you perfidious coward," Titus ordered with venom. "And if your spurs have harmed Raven, you are a dead man." Titus glanced over at Raven as Déaglán attempted to quiet the agitated stallion. Then Titus turned back to Domitian. "You did not wait long once you believed me murdered to take those possessions of mine you covet. Have you also tried to bed my mistress, or were you saving that for tonight?"

Domitian said nothing as he got to his feet, looking fixedly at the sword Titus held in his hand. Domitian then lifted his eyes and met those of his brother's. The two regarded each other with such naked hatred that even Déaglán was stunned.

"Did you actually believe you could conspire with villains to kill me and that your treachery would not be discovered? Do you think my guards are not ever watchful of your movements and associations, especially when you are in the company of murderers? Well, your knaves, though surprisingly bold, failed. My guards and I killed all but one. The villain we spared was more than willing to report my death to you in exchange for his life. I see that he played his part well, for you have wasted no time in claiming what is mine."

Titus waited for his brother to speak, and when Domitian said nothing, Titus swung his sword deftly, the tip of which sliced Domitian's left cheek, opening a deep cut. "Has your tongue failed you, brother? Have you nothing to say, or are you too terrified for speech?"

Though not naturally a brave man, Domitian was nonetheless emboldened by the powerful hatred he had nurtured over the years for his brother. Beyond fear and seeing no escape,

Domitian straightened his shoulders and stood facing Titus, blood running down his cheek and staining his tunic. "If you intend to kill me, do it now. I do not deny that I plotted your murder and wish you dead. I despise you and your charmed life. You are the anointed one, the heir to the imperial seat, the great soldier, the darling of the people. Meanwhile, I have been relegated to meaningless consulships with empty titles. You have maligned me since my earliest memory, convincing father that I am worthy of nothing more significant than administering to the building of roads or the laying of sewer lines. Yes, I conspired to murder you, but long ago you destroyed me in the eyes of our father. Now it seems you are the victor again. So slay me and finish the job you started so many years ago."

Titus laughed mockingly but there was a hint of admiration in his voice when he said, "So, little brother, there is some manhood in you after all. But you need not prepare yourself to die. I have no intention of killing you. Why, you may ask. I am not sure I know the answer, although I am loathe to break our mother's heart, for she adores you. Now, get out of my sight before I come to my senses." Titus started to return his sword to its scabbard then stopped. "Don't ever make me regret my decision to spare your life. I will not be so forgiving a second time." Titus's lips formed a smile that did not reach his eyes. "Cheer up, I am leaving for the eastern frontier next week. You can pray to the gods that I will die in battle."

It was not until Domitian was out of sight that Titus relaxed and realized that Déaglán, who he knew as "Tascus," was standing nearby, holding both horses by their bridles.

"Tascus, return Raven to his stall and then rub down Aquila. I rode him hard and do not want to hear later that he has colicked. Is that clear?"

"Yes, my lord," responded Déaglán. He then raised his eyes and the two men exchanged looks, Titus's gaze speculative and piercing, Déaglán's unwavering and inscrutable.

"Tascus, you have been a groom here for four months, correct? And you are from the north, are you not?"

"It has been five months, my lord, and yes, I am from the north."

"Umbria?" questioned Titus with nonchalance.

"No, my lord, I come from Gallia."

"Ah, yes, of course, I remember our discussion now. I remarked that your being from Gallia explained the light color of your eyes, blue being not uncommon in that region, although I have never seen anyone else with eyes quite the shade of yours." Titus looked once more at Déaglán, nodded, then turned and strode away.

Déaglán stood up and stretched, then walked outside the barn to survey the passing storm clouds. The rain had diminished to a light but steady drizzle. Déaglán decided not to push on even though there were still several hours of daylight remaining. His horse needed the rest, the exertions of the day having taken their toll.

A shadow of a smile appeared on Déaglán's weary face. His months as a groom at the imperial stables had been enlightening. He had quietly left the stables less than a week after the confrontation between Titus and Domitian, knowing that being a witness to the violent exchange would not endear him to either young man. Moreover, Déaglán had seen the speculative way that Titus had looked at him that day. Déaglán had guessed that Titus was suspicious and that the game was up. Rarely one to second-guess his own instincts, Déaglán slipped away one night and made for the coast.

Ironically, Titus did not die gloriously on the battlefield but in bed of an ague. He had been emperor barely two years when he was stricken, dying in the same country home where his father had died before him. Domitian wasted no time in proclaiming himself emperor, triumphantly establishing his authority before his brother's body was even cold. Domitian proved to be a repressive and despotic ruler who regularly executed his foes and real or imagined usurpers. Déaglán wondered whether Eire would have been safe from Romhanach invasion had Titus lived. Probably not. Titus, like Agricola, had been first and foremost a soldier always looking for new lands to conquer. Eire would have been merely another conquest to add to his tally.

# CHAPTER THIRTEEN

*A*s darkness fell, Déaglán started a fire and sat huddled next to it, the smoky flames from the wet wood irritating his eyes and providing little warmth. His horse had finished his grain and was standing in the corner of the barn, head hanging low as he slept. For the last hour, Déaglán had been thinking of Deirdre. Images of the young priestess had invaded his conscious thoughts unbidden and with increasing frequency since she had helped him escape. Tonight, as he sat near the fire damp, cold, and bone weary, Déaglán could almost feel her soft body next to his, remembering how she had pulled him close, sheltering him with her cloak and spiriting him to safety. It had always been his beloved Maeve he thought of when lonely and tired. When she died, his need for love died with her. There had been women over the years, of course, for he had no inclination toward celibacy. Still, it was only Maeve whom Déaglán thought of when he yearned for the comfort of a woman.

Now Deirdre constantly stole her way into Déaglán's mind, however much he tried to block thoughts of her. What was the matter with him, besotted with a beautiful young priestess who had so easily breached his carefully constructed wall of invulnerability? Déaglán had nothing to offer her, nor did he want such an entanglement. His passion for the sea and adventure would always win over the pull of a woman's charms. Looking back, he surely would have broken Maeve's heart eventually. Even when so young and in love, his wanderlust constantly intruded on his happiness, inexorably drawing him to the sea.

Tonight, however, Déaglán allowed himself to get lost in thoughts of Deirdre. Tomorrow, when he was rested and strong, he would suppress any affection he felt for the young priestess, controlling his emotions with cold calculation, an invaluable skill learned from his many years of solitude and spying. Déaglán assured himself that Deirdre would become only a chess piece for him to position in his deadly game with the Romhanach, nothing more.

Déaglán first met Deirdre two years earlier, when visiting Fearghus at the high priest's home in the north of Eire. Déaglán had recently returned from Eoraip, and the two men had just sat down for the morning meal when they heard a light tap on the front door. Fearghus was about to rise from his chair when the door opened a crack and a pleasantly musical voice called out, "Fearghus, may I come in?" Before Fearghus could respond, a young woman stepped across the threshold and into the room, only stopping when she saw Déaglán.

"Oh, there I go again, barging in without waiting for you to grant me admittance, and you entertaining a guest. How annoying I must be to you." The young woman, however, did not look at all repentant and gave both men a brilliant smile.

Fearghus, not looking in the least irritated, smiled broadly in response and stood up. With an outstretched hand he beckoned the girl forward.

"Deirdre, you are never annoying and always welcome."

Turning to Déaglán, the priest said, "Déaglán, I want you to meet the priestess, Deirdre, one of my former students and a very talented and remarkable young woman. Deirdre, this is my good friend Déaglán whom I speak of so often and whose voyages are legend."

Deirdre's face lit up at Fearghus's words, and she approached Déaglán. "I am so pleased to finally meet you, although I feel as though I already know you from all the stories of your adventures I have heard from Fearghus. What a wonderfully exciting life you lead."

Déaglán stood transfixed, momentarily speechless, his ready wit abandoning him completely. He was still taking in the image of this lovely young woman who had glided toward him with such grace and presence. Now, she was smiling patiently, obviously waiting for him to respond.

Déaglán came to his senses and, somewhat embarrassed, said, "The pleasure is all mine, Deirdre," and took the hand she offered him in both of his. With a wry expression and a gesture to Fearghus, Déaglán added, "But pay no attention to Fearghus. He embellishes my exploits with such abandon that I rarely recognize them as my own. Never has there been a better storyteller in all Eire than Fearghus, even though most of what he relates has occurred only in his dreams."

Fearghus laughed heartily. "Well, I only make the telling and the listening more enjoyable by spicing up those portions of a story that might send the audience into somnolence or weary apathy."

"Well, if even half of what Fearghus tells me of your adventures is true, I am still overawed by your daring." Again Deirdre smiled at Déaglán then glanced down at his hands, still firmly clasping her proffered one. Embarrassed afresh, Déaglán quickly dropped Deirdre's hand as if it were a hot coal.

Deirdre seemed not to notice Déaglán's discomfort and turned to Fearghus. "I baked the bread you are so fond of and am happy I brought two loaves, as there will now be enough for both you and Déaglán. Here, let me slice some pieces. I have also brought some wonderful fruit and a variety of delightful cheeses." She regarded the meal the two men were about to eat and shook her head dismissively. "Fearghus, let me prepare something more pleasing for you." Without waiting for Fearghus to answer, she removed the food from the table and began preparing a new meal, all the while chatting pleasantly with Fearghus, who was obviously delighted at the prospect of one of her feasts.

As Deirdre cooked, she shared her latest news with Fearghus, effortlessly including Déaglán in the conversation with an occasional question or comment directed to him. Déaglán welcomed the chance to study Deirdre while she worked, even as he silently chastised himself for behaving like such a dim-witted fool when introduced to the young priestess. Deirdre had caught him off guard. The vigilance and concentration he normally possessed when introduced to someone new had been regrettably absent. In his travels, he had developed an uncanny ability of quickly assessing everyone he met, determining whether they were friend or foe, harmless or dangerous. He knew the accuracy of this initial assessment was vital to his survival. However, when he was home in Eire, and especially among friends, Déaglán's vigilance relaxed.

Now he watched Deirdre, trying to understand this unusual young woman, instinctively wary of the effect she had on him. On close examination he realized that while Deirdre was pretty, she was not beautiful. Déaglán had seen far more handsome women in his travels, women with flawless features and exquisite bodies who graced the arms of the rich and powerful men of Eoraip. He admitted that Deirdre's figure was perfection, though its slender loveliness was nothing like the curvaceous women Déaglán was normally attracted to. Since Maeve's death, he had unconsciously shied away from any woman who resembled his fragile and willowy young bride, preferring instead robust, slightly plump women.

It was something else about Deirdre, not her face or her body, but a quality of absolute candor, of ready confidence, of natural poise, that intrigued Déaglán. Deirdre's face reflected an open sincerity and friendliness that was engaging, and with her smooth, rosy complexion she could easily be mistaken for a girl in her teens. Déaglán knew, however, that Deirdre must be at least in her twenty-first year, the earliest she could have been ordained a priestess. He guessed that she was probably several years older than that. For all her fresh-faced openness, Déaglán sensed Deirdre was no innocent and had powers of persuasion and influence that were formidable. He felt her pull, calming and soothing him, making him hopeful—and he wanted no part of it. Déaglán was content with the familiar rhythm of his life. He would not allow this alluring young woman to disrupt it. He smiled, casting a veil of impenetrable congeniality over the strong features of his face, his vigilance restored.

Déaglán came out of his reverie at the sound of his name. Deirdre had placed the meal on the table and was eyeing him expectantly.

"Please, Déaglán, sit here across from Fearghus and begin. I have already had my morning meal but will sit with the two of you so I may hear news of your latest voyage." Deirdre gave him a winning smile but her eyes were alert. Again Déaglán was disconcerted, left with the distinct impression that Deirdre had been watching him while he studied her.

After the men had eaten their fill and had pushed back their chairs from the table to stretch their legs, Fearghus said, "Déaglán, just before Deirdre arrived you started to tell me of your latest adventure—"

"Before you begin your tale, Déaglán," interrupted Deirdre, "I almost forgot the wonderful fruit I brought." She rose from her chair and retrieved a platter of assorted fruit that she placed on the table between the two men.

Déaglán eyed the fruit and looked at Deirdre quizzically. "These are exotic fruits grown in warm climates. They would perish in Eire's cold and damp. How did you come by them?"

"I am very resourceful," said Deirdre, regarding Déaglán with a clear, steady gaze.

"Indeed you are." Déaglán was fascinated, wondering how Deirdre had obtained fruit that was considered a rare delicacy even in the wealthiest homes in Eoraip. "I suspect you are also a sorceress to have conjured up such fruit."

"I told you that Deirdre is a priestess of extraordinary talent," interjected Fearghus. "However, let us not discuss the rarity of the fruit Deirdre brought but instead eat it. I am particularly fond of these sweet, succulent ones." Fearghus reached for a small, round fruit, pinkish-red in color. Using his knife, he sliced through the tough outer skin to reveal the juicy pulp within. He peeled back the skin from each half and popped the delicacy into his mouth, savoring its taste while greedily eyeing the remaining fruit on the platter.

If Fearghus had a weakness, it was food. He loved to eat and, while he appreciated fine food, he nonetheless would eat practically anything set before him. Fortunately, his big, raw-boned frame could accommodate some extra bulk, and it was only a slight paunch that betrayed his guilty excesses. Fearghus's face was round with a large nose, ruddy complexion, and brilliant blue eyes. His laugh was warm, hearty, and infectious, and never failed to bring a smile to even the most disgruntled of men. Naturally friendly and expansive, Fearghus was not only a fine storyteller but an excellent listener. Those who mistook his avuncular manner for weakness, however, lived to regret it. His warm blue eyes could in an instant turn hard, his friendly countenance deadly. Fearghus was a powerful force in The Dagda and its acknowledged leader. He was cherished by his friends and feared by his enemies, there being few individuals who were neither.

After consuming a second piece of fruit, Fearghus smiled in satisfaction. "Now, Déaglán, tell us of your travels."

"All in good time, Fearghus," said Déaglán. He then regarded Deirdre and held her eyes. "So, there is some sorcery at work here with the mysterious powers of The Dagda at play. I am disappointed. You appeared to be such a forthright and candid young woman. I now see that you enjoy The Dagda's mystery and ceremony of silence, even as it pertains to the acquisition of a mere piece of fruit." Déaglán wasn't sure why he was intentionally trying to provoke Deirdre; perhaps it was to gauge the point at which she lost her poised composure.

Deirdre's eyes widened slightly, but she returned his gaze without wavering then laughed good-naturedly.

"I am sorry to disappoint you. I do indeed love being a priestess of The Dagda and all that it entails. However, I enjoy mystery for its own sake. The truth is my secrets and hidden places please me as I suspect yours please you."

Déaglán blinked and then burst out laughing. When he had caught his breath, he inquired, "So, Deirdre, how are you at chess?"

Fearghus, who had been listening to this exchange with

amusement, chimed in. "Deirdre is an excellent opponent when I can cajole her to play, which is rarely. Now, Déaglán, will you please get on with your story."

Still chuckling, Déaglán reached for a cluster of grapes on the platter. He ate a few, spitting out their seeds and eyeing Deirdre with newfound respect. Here was a woman whose powers of perception and intuition rivaled his own. He would have to tread more carefully around this young priestess with the soft blue eyes and the razor-sharp mind.

Déaglán leaned back in his chair. "I think I will relate the events of the past summer. Fearghus, you will have no need to embellish what I am about to tell you today, although your creativity constantly amazes me." With that, Déaglán began his strange tale.

# CHAPTER FOURTEEN

*D*ÉAGLÁN HAD TRAVELED SOUTH FROM ROMA TO Campania in late spring and had settled in the coastal village of Salernum to fish in the Tyrrhenum Sea. There he had befriended a solitary old fisherman, Meles, who was considered slightly mad by the local villagers. Déaglán found Meles good company and something of a philosopher, more educated than he would have expected.

Meles considered the Tyrrhenum his sea and knew every island, port, and inlet along the Campania coast. He excitedly told Déaglán of waters where the fish "almost leapt into his boat," so abundant were they. Déaglán laughed at the time but had to admit that the old man was hardly exaggerating, such was the bounty of these waters. More importantly, Meles fished frequently near the islands of Capreae and Aenapria, both summer retreats of the Romhanach elite.

Déaglán was particularly interested in Capreae. The Romhanach emperor had not one but several villas there, the largest perched on a towering bluff on the northeastern tip of the island. Well accustomed to the beauty of the Tyrrhenum and the coast of Campania, Déaglán nevertheless marveled at the singular beauty and mystery of Capreae, its rocky cliffs and jagged coastline framed by a sea of cobalt blue, the color fading to swirling shades of azure when met by the shallows. The island was a natural fortress with no coves or harbors to safely dock a boat, and only one small shoreline and landing place, making it almost impregnable and adding to its mythical aura. Most remarkable, however, were the subterranean caves that honey-combed Capreae and were accessible only by boat.

Although imperial guards were stationed on Capreae even when the emperor was not in residence, Meles freely sailed its waters and was considered a harmless old fool, his comings and goings eliciting no remark or concern. Déaglán could not have befriended anyone with greater knowledge of or access to Capreae. He had been fishing with Meles for only a month when he learned the extent of his good fortune.

One evening, when the men sat in the old fisherman's hut drinking remarkably good wine, Meles said, "Tomorrow the waters will be calm and the tides will be low enough for me to take you into the hidden depths of Capreae to my secret retreat and cache of wonders. Are you interested in a little adventure, my friend?"

"Do you mean the Blue Grotto?" Déaglán was well aware of the large cave whose entrance had been discovered years before and was thought to be enchanted. Occasionally, lured by descriptions of the cave's beauty and tales of bewitching sirens, an intrepid fisherman would steer his boat through the small entrance. Few of these fishermen ever returned, but when they did, they told fantastic stories of a magnificent blue chamber inhabited by strange sea creatures, swearing they heard siren calls. While Déaglán did not doubt the grotto's beauty or mystery, he was not particularly interested in what lay beneath the island but what lay upon it. However, given Capreae's hostile coastline, Déaglán had abandoned any notion of successfully penetrating the island's defenses and spying on the Romhanach emperor and his retinue.

The old man's sun-browned face crinkled into deep lines as he smiled, his dark eyes full of wily mischief. "That cave is nothing. Beautiful and enchanted, yes, but useless. No, I alone know the whereabouts of my hidden refuge and it has allowed me to enjoy some comfort in my waning years, as you can see by the wine we drink tonight."

Déaglán was intrigued but cautious. What was Meles up to and why was the old fisherman sharing secrets with him, an acquaintance of only a month? Déaglán felt a quickening of his pulse.

"I am always ready for a little adventure, but how is it that only you know of this cave? And why would you trust me with the knowledge of its whereabouts?"

The old man cackled in delight. "Because I like you. It is as simple as that. I recognized your nature the first time I met you. We are kindred spirits, most happy when alone or braving the forces of nature, beholden and answerable to no one. I know you would not betray me unless I gave you good cause. Whatever your purpose for visiting Campania is or what aim you have, you mean me no harm. Besides, I am an old man and have lately had the need to talk and to reveal my secrets with someone who would truly appreciate them. The gods were very obliging when they sent you. So, tomorrow I will share with you my hidden retreat, you who are so like me in your love of solitude and danger."

THE NEXT MORNING while it was still dark, the two men sailed to Capreae, arriving at the southeastern reaches of the island not long after daylight. They followed the coastline, skirting towering rocks that rose from the sea. Meles made no attempt at stealth, steering his small boat as close to the island as was safe.

"Ever since I was a boy I have sailed these waters," said Meles. "I know this coastline better than any living soul, and yet I did not discover the opening of this cave until ten years ago. You will understand why very soon."

They were approaching the northeastern tip of the island, its high cliffs dropping steeply to the sea. As they rounded a rocky promontory, the emperor's villa came into sight. Déaglán never failed to be awed by the magnificent building whose expanse covered the entire top of a wide, high bluff. The villa appeared more like a city fortress, terraced along the natural slope of the land with winding stone paths that connected all but its steepest perimeters. The front of the villa faced north, its large portico supported by massive columns. There the emperor resided, high above the sea with an unobstructed view of the Bay of Neapolis.

"Rarely does the emperor visit the villa this early in the summer, escaping to Capreae only when the heat of the capital becomes unbearable," commented Meles as the two men gazed at the magnificent structure. "However, there are orders to always have the villa at the ready with plenty of food and wine. The emperor entertains lavishly while in residence and that is to our great advantage."

Before they reached the bluff where the villa stood, Meles steered his boat toward a steep-faced cliff. Though calm elsewhere, here the waters were rough and churning, with dangerous underwater rocks impeding the natural flow of the current. Déaglán watched Meles in disbelief as the old man continued to steer his boat directly toward the rocky wall and certain death, for there was no safe shore to swim to if the boat crashed and broke apart. The old fisherman was oblivious to all but the swirling waves, his hand steady as he carefully guided his boat through the treacherous waters. Just when Déaglán thought that all was lost, he noticed a narrow gap in the cliff that had not been visible just moments before. The small boat shot through the opening and Déaglán found himself in a tiny cove encircled by the towering cliff, its sheer rock face scarred by jagged vertical fissures, some small, others scaling nearly its entire height.

Meles laughed with joy and slapped Déaglán on the back. "I knew I had found a true adventurer in you, my brave friend. Never once did you attempt to stop me or pull my hand from the rudder as I steered for the rocks. Now we must wait for the lowest of tides to enter my cave." Meles noted the sun's position and smiled contentedly. "We have perhaps an hour to wait, maybe less."

"How did you ever discover the keyhole opening to this cove?" Déaglán asked, full of admiration. "No sailor in his right mind would dare risk his boat or life in these waters. I know I would have sailed clear of here had it been my boat."

"That is the beauty of this cove. Nature and the gods have conspired to hide it, surrounding its entrance with dangerous currents and a labyrinth of underwater rocks. All who sail in the calm waters well clear of the hazards see nothing but a solid granite cliff, the back face of the cove blending perfectly with the cliff's sea wall."

"It is as if the entrance opens up before your very eyes," marveled Déaglán. "One moment there is a sheer cliff wall and the next a magical gap appears. Again, how did you discover it?"

"The waters surrounding the cove had always puzzled me," Meles mused. "The currents seemed to move in odd patterns, and there was a small area of relative calm near the cliff where the whitewater did not spray high into the air as it met the rock wall. It was as if the waters were flowing into a hidden inlet and yet I saw no opening. Finally, my curiosity got the best of me and, determined to solve the mystery of these waters, I steeled my courage and steered for the calm. When I landed in this lovely and very secret cove, little did I know that what I had yet to discover would be even more remarkable. Fortunately, the tide was still going out that day while I sat enjoying the solitude. As the sea level dropped, I noticed a large gap appear at the base of one of the huge fissures in the cliff's face. Soon the gap was large enough for my boat to enter, the current carrying it safely through the opening and inside. The cave was high, narrow, and dark, nothing like the beautiful blue grotto. But my cave turned out to be a passageway to riches."

"Why haven't the emperor's guards discovered this cove? I understand the difficulty of discovering it from the sea. But the same problems would not be present on land."

Meles smiled serenely. "I believe this cove exists only for those brave enough to enter it from the sea. The gods have chosen to share it with no one else. The emperor's guards have not discovered it simply because they do not see it." Meles then lay down and closed his eyes, and for all Déaglán could tell, he drifted off into a well-deserved sleep.

True to Meles's words, within an hour the tide had receded enough to reveal a yawning hole in the cliff, large enough for a small boat to navigate through. Déaglán waited until the tide appeared to be at its lowest and then gently touched Meles on the shoulder to awaken him. Looking refreshed, Meles jumped up and motioned to the cave. "Would you like to take her in?"

Déaglán, his eyes bright, nodded and carefully steered the boat through the gap.

"We will dock some fifty yards in along the right hand side of the cave," said Meles, adeptly lighting a torch.

The torch's glow provided enough light for Déaglán to make out a high rock bench along the right side of the cave, widening in depth as the boat moved slowly forward. Just ahead bobbed a small canoe tied to an iron ring embedded in the cave's wall. As Déaglán steered the boat closer to the bench, he noticed that hanging from its walls were baskets, earthenware pots, and blankets. Metal sconces holding torches framed the area.

"I secure my things on the wall, fearing that the high tide could wash everything off the rock shelf—although I have never had that happen in all the years I have been staying here. Nonetheless, I take great care of this home away from home." As Meles spoke, he securely tied the boat behind the canoe, looping thick rope through rings. Holding his torch high, he pointed to steps carved deep in the rock leading up to the bench and signaled for Déaglán to climb them. "Please light one of the torches up top," he requested.

When Déaglán had complied, Meles extinguished the torch in his hand and with youthful exuberance joined Déaglán.

"Over the years I have accumulated all the comforts of home here." Meles took blankets and earthenware down from the wall and arranged them with precise care on the floor. "We can rest here and eat before continuing our journey." Meles settled on one of the blankets as Déaglán retrieved a basket of food from the boat. Meles opened a bottle of wine suspended from the ceiling in rope netting, then the two men ate a meal of bread, cheese, and smoked fish, sharing with each other their tales of the sea.

"If I were a man to put down roots, I believe I would settle here in Campania," said Déaglán, as he and the old fisherman finished their meal. "No land is more idyllic."

"Campania's bounty is both a blessing and a curse," said Meles, shaking his head regretfully while he poured the last of the wine into their wooden goblets. "Life here is too easy. The land is fertile, the sea is bountiful, and the region is safe from invading barbarians. Consequently, many of Campania's inhabitants have become self-satisfied and soft. They believe the gods have singled them out as deserving of special privilege, and so they live opulently in huge villas, thinking of themselves as highly enlightened. The men have become effete, no longer vigilant and strong protectors of their women and children. What they forget is how fickle our gods can be. The earth tremors are merely a warning, though few take heed. I fear the gods have grown tired of the decadent pleasures of Campania and will balance the scales somehow, reminding us all that we are mere mortals."

SOME TIME LATER, the men climbed down into the canoe. Déaglán picked up the paddle as Meles settled comfortably in front, holding a torch in his right hand.

"We have a considerable distance to travel as this cave meanders beneath Capreae for miles," Meles said. "The first time I ventured forth, I was sure I would become hopelessly lost or be consumed by a fearful sea creature. My fears proved unfounded. There is but one path in this cave and it leads to a large and quiet pool inhabited by nothing more frightful than small mullet fish." Meles said no more as Déaglán rowed the canoe slowly along the waterway, the only sound the splash and echo of water as the paddle glided through its surface.

After more than an hour, Déaglán thought he detected some natural light ahead, the dark walls of the cave illuminated by a faint golden glow. As he paddled toward the light, he also smelled the intoxicating scent of jasmine.

"We are almost there," proclaimed Meles. Soon there was enough light for Meles to extinguish his torch, and as they rounded a bend in the waterway a beautiful pool lay ahead of them, soft light filtering down from a large fissure high on the cave's wall.

"The smell of jasmine never fails to lighten my darkest mood," said Meles happily. "It always makes me think of this wondrous cave and the exciting times I have whenever I visit it." Meles tied the canoe securely and pointed to the steps leading up to the fissure. "I had a difficult time climbing up before I carved these into the rock. I don't believe I could scale the wall without them today." Meles started up and beckoned Déaglán to follow. Even with the steps, the ascent was daunting, yet Meles scaled the sheer wall with ease, exhibiting a monkey-like agility. Déaglán shook his head in amazement as he watched the old man move. Meles was a small man, his head not even reaching Déaglán's shoulders, and his dark, weathered skin was wrinkled and hung loosely on a slight frame. But he had lean, wiry muscles and was astonishingly strong. Déaglán waited for Meles to reach the top and then followed.

"We must wait here until dusk," said Meles when Déaglán joined him. Déaglán looked toward the source of the light and noted that the fissure angled upward, the passage narrowing and ending at a small opening some thirty yards away. The sun's light filtered through a blanket of jasmine, making the pathway appear ethereal and enchanted, leading to the heavens.

"We are very close to the emperor's villa," observed Déaglán.

Meles nodded. "I see you were able to keep your bearings in spite of the cave's twists and turns, though I suspect that long ago you guessed the source of my riches."

Déaglán smiled in acknowledgment.

Meles continued. "The cave opens on the southwest perimeter of the villa, very convenient for us because the servants' quarters, kitchens, and storerooms are located there. In the early years I braved this area of the villa during the day, enjoying the thrill. It was actually quite easy to blend in, with large numbers of servants busily coming and going, paying not the slightest attention to anyone. In more recent years, however, I decided that more discretion was advisable, especially since my object is to pilfer from the emperor's larder and wine cellar."

Déaglán feigned casual interest, yet his heart was beating rapidly with anticipation. "Have you ever ventured near the emperor's chambers and gardens?"

"Yes, for I can rarely resist the temptation of a little spying or the promise of riches. I used to visit the formal gardens regularly, though not as often in the last few summers. The way there is perilous and often the trek proves fruitless with no conversations to overhear or prizes to steal. However, it was in the gardens where I found my most prized possession—a wonderful volume of poetry and illustrations that I cherish above all else. I must show it to you."

"May we visit the gardens this evening?"

"Of course, though it is unlikely anyone will be there this early in the summer."

Just as it was becoming dark, Meles and Déaglán left the cave, both men with large linen sacks tied to their waists.

"These are for our bounty," Meles said, chuckling as the two men started along the passage.

Déaglán followed Meles through the blanket of jasmine, stepping onto a rock ledge perched on the side of a steep ravine. There was a narrow path leading from the ledge that zig-zagged up the hill, looking more suitable for sure-footed goats than men. Meles motioned for silence, holding his finger to his lips, and the two men trod cautiously, careful to avoid a fatal slip or telltale noise. When they reached the top of the ravine, Meles beckoned Déaglán to follow and both men quickly scaled a wall that bordered a wide stone path leading up to the villa. Before they reached it, they left the path and stole through a dense stand of trees, emerging opposite a large building.

"This building houses the larder and wine cellar and is where we will restock my pantry," Meles whispered, gleeful delight radiating from him, infecting Déaglán with the same euphoria. "However, we can save our thieving for later. Let us first visit the villa's gardens, for I sense that you are as anxious as I for some adventure."

Ever watchful, Meles and Déaglán weaved their way around buildings, over walls, and through copses, darting across lightened pathways and melting into the shadows. At length they came to a massive stone and mortar retaining wall that encircled the gardens, vines and honeysuckle trailing its height.

"Now we must go straight up," said Meles as he began to climb, grabbing the rungs of a sturdy trellis with Déaglán at his heels. At the top was a cluster of citrus trees, and the two men scrambled over the lip of the wall and crouched behind the trees, peering out onto the dimly lit garden.

"We are in luck." Meles pointed to the large banner that flew above the emperor's chambers, silhouetted against the sky. "The emperor is in residence, which is most peculiar. We must redouble our caution. The emperor's guards are everywhere."

The emperor's chambers blazed with light and voices could be heard through the night air, but the garden was quiet and unoccupied. When both men were ready to give up hope of seeing the emperor or any of his guests, they heard the sound of footsteps and could just make out the figure of a woman, her gown flowing around her, as she hurried in their direction. In the dim light Déaglán could not see her face, but by her slim figure and lithe walk he judged her to be young. Her hair was loose and fell on her shoulders and down her back. Déaglán was delighted—he knew there was to be a lovers' rendezvous here in this far, dark corner of the garden.

Soon, Déaglán heard the purposeful and heavy stride of a man approaching. As the man came closer, Déaglán repressed a sharp intake of breath, marveling at his good fortune, for he knew in an instant that it was the emperor Titus who was keeping this clandestine meeting.

"I knew you would come," the woman cried, her arms outstretched in greeting. Déaglán was incredulous, recognizing the voice of Longina, Domitian's wife.

When Titus reached her, Longina threw herself at him, pressing her body against the length of his. He grasped her upper arms and gently pushed her away, holding her momentarily at arm's length. "Longina, what is so secret that we must meet in this lonely place? And why your tragic voice? I thought you would be pleased to escape the city for a time, especially since my praetorian Plotius is also here on Capreae."

"Yes, I am overjoyed to escape, but from Domitian not the city. Life with him has become intolerable. He is so cruel to me, suspicious of my every move. He denies me all pleasures, yet he is free to enjoy his perversions with prostitutes and assignations with other men's wives. His touch makes my skin crawl. Let us not talk of Domitian but of us. Surely, you brought me here so that we could be together, away from the spying eyes of ene- mies." Longina's voice, at first shrill and petulant, took on a purring seductiveness with her last words, and she attempted to move closer to Titus.

Titus held up one hand, stopping her advance. "Longina, you are my brother's wife. Isn't it enough that I shield you from his wrath and help cover up your less than discrete love affairs?"

"You loathe him as much as I do," cried Longina. "You con- stantly belittle and torment him. Do not use brotherly loyalty as an excuse for not acting on the undeniable passion between us."

Titus sighed. "Whatever I think of my brother, there are certain lines I will not cross. Your affair with Plotius has given me enough cause for concern. You were ill-advised to choose a lover so closely associated with me. Why do you think I invited you to Capreae? Your trysts with Plotius would very soon have been exposed. At least here you are safe from Domitian's spies. You had best practice some discretion or Domitian will eventu- ally rid himself of you."

"I do not care if he sends me away. What prize is it to be the wife of Domitian, I, the daughter of a great general!" Long- ina was nearly screeching now, working herself into a frenzy. "It was always you I wished to wed, you I cared for, not your worth- less and despicable brother. I should be *your* wife!"

Titus laughed and shook his head. "I have always known you to be ruthless and fiendishly ambitious. It is not I you yearn for but the power of the imperial throne. I must admit that while I admire your lofty ambitions, your utter lack of scruples disturbs me. If we were wed, I should always fear of being mur- dered in my sleep, for you cannot control or manipulate me as you do my brother."

"You malign me and my intentions! You only deny me tonight because your *foreign* mistress is here," Longina hissed, her voice spiteful and venomous. "Berenice still has you mesmerized, doesn't she? You meet secretly with her on Capreae, deceiving the people, making them believe you no longer see that eastern temptress they despise. If I were to share my knowledge of your continuing love affair with that Jewess, your shining image would be sorely tarnished."

"Longina, do not forget to whom you speak." Titus's voice turned hard and deadly, his menace palpable, and Longina shrank from him.

"Please forgive me," she beseeched, tears streaming down her cheeks. "I would never betray you. It is only that I despair of my life with your hateful brother and the dismal years ahead." Longina grasped Titus's arm, clinging to him.

"Let go of me, Longina. You have tried my patience enough for one night. Go now to the arms of Plotius or sleep alone. It is of little consequence to me. I can almost pity my brother." With that Titus turned and strode back to the villa.

Longina called out to him, pleading for Titus to understand her sorrow. However, once he was gone and out of earshot, Longina's crying stopped abruptly. She cursed his name and muttered, "I will make you pay for my humiliation of this night, Titus. You are no better than your brother. We will see who ultimately triumphs."

DÉAGLÁN AND MELES made several more trips to Capreae over the long summer. When the sun faded below the horizon, the men raided and stalked with the skill of nocturnal predators, never once arousing any alarm. Déaglán heard little more of interest when visiting the gardens, instead finding the idle talk of the emperor's guards more enlightening with battle victories, military expeditions, and imperial gossip figuring prominently in their conversations.

Late in the summer, Déaglán reluctantly said farewell to his good friend Meles and traveled to Misenum, a Romhanach naval port on the northwestern tip of the Bay of Neapolis, staying there briefly before returning to Eire. Déaglán would learn some months later about the cataclysmic eruption of Mount Vesuvius. Shortly after his departure from Misenum, the mountain had rained death and destruction over Campania. He would not learn for years whether or not Meles had survived the conflagration. It seemed the grizzled old fisherman's prophecy had played out in horrifying detail.

# CHAPTER FIFTEEN

EELIN RODE UP TO NUALA'S COTTAGE WITH THE
sun still high. After a fortnight of dark, stormy weather,
blue sky joined scattered clouds. Keelin had recovered quickly
from the blow to her head, but she and Brian had all but abandoned any hope of discovering the whereabouts of the spy. He
had simply vanished. Brian had continued to scout the forest
and surrounding countryside until the storms and heavy rain made
tracking impossible. Nor had they identified the young woman
who had visited the spy that night. If he had indeed given her
the perfume, she had thus far not betrayed herself by wearing it.
In truth, Keelin had little time to ponder any of this. Nuala still
had not returned from Tara, and the care of the sick and injured fell solely on her shoulders. Deirdre, ever perceptive, had
recently declared that she had little left to teach Keelin and suggested they meet only in the afternoons at Nuala's cottage.

Jumping down from Bran's back, Keelin removed his bridle
and patted him on the rump. "Now go and enjoy the grass I saw
you eyeing so longingly in the upper pasture." Bran turned, and
with decided alacrity, trotted back down the hill. Keelin watched
him for only a moment, then walked toward the cottage.

"Deirdre," called Keelin as she opened the door and stepped
inside. Usually the young priestess greeted her before she even

had time to open the door. Strange, thought Keelin, when both the cottage and the apothecary proved empty. She walked to the small barn where Nuala kept chickens and an old milk cow and peered inside.

From behind her a stern voice sounded, "Deirdre is not here."

Keelin jumped noticeably and turned to see Nuala standing there.

"Nuala, you gave me a fright, sneaking up on me so."

Nuala made no apology and instead looked at Keelin appraisingly. "Deirdre tells me you have learned the art of the *starling* quickly. I am pleased though not surprised." Turning back toward the cottage, she added, "Come, we have much to accomplish today. Have you completed your cloak?"

"Yes, I made the finishing touches on it last week."

"Good, though we will not use it today. I must get a few items from my apothecary, and then we will leave for Danu's cave. Deirdre also tells me you are impatient to test your affinity for the Otherworld. Today you will learn whether or not your powers of the mind are strong enough to transcend our natural world." Reaching the cottage door, Nuala stopped and turned abruptly. Keelin, scurrying to keep up with the priestess's long stride, almost slammed into her.

"Wait here," Nuala ordered.

Keelin stood fidgeting, excitement and dread dueling within her. The past weeks with Deirdre had clarified nothing. She was no closer to reconciling her dreams of adventure with a secretive, duty-bound life within The Dagda. Still, the magic and allure of the Otherworld was undeniable and Keelin hoped she had the power to break through its barriers. But therein lay her dilemma. If she possessed an affinity with the Otherworld, her fate was sealed. She paid little heed to Deirdre's assurances that novices were not compelled to take their final vows. Keelin could feel—almost viscerally—the powerful pull of The Dagda. Overshadowing everything was the threat to Eire.

"You will accomplish much with your powers. Never regret possessing them." Nuala looked down at Keelin reprovingly, hearing her thoughts, and then brushed past her, striding toward the winding path that led through the mountain pass behind her cottage. Keelin followed, heartily disliking the priestess and yet knowing she spoke the truth. Now was not the time to bemoan her fate. Keelin took a deep breath and glanced up at a small cloud as it passed in front of the sun, darkening the landscape. After the cloud moved on, she set out at a run and soon caught up with the priestess, settling into a jog behind her.

Shortly before Keelin and Nuala reached the entrance to the cave, they met Deirdre sitting in the shade on a large boulder alongside the path. She had been inspecting the contents of a small leather pouch when she looked up and saw them.

"There you are. I was beginning to wonder what happened to the two of you," Deirdre said, pulling the ties of the pouch tightly closed and knotting them securely. She picked up two other pouches that lay on the boulder next to her and walked toward Nuala and Keelin.

"I see you have brought the ceremonial essences," said Nuala. "Did you have any difficulty obtaining them?"

"No, I visited Fearghus. He always has any potion or essence necessary for every ceremony. I have also readied the cave with fuel for the fire and have lit the lanterns along the passage."

Keelin listened to their exchange and felt her stomach knot

with nervous anticipation. She noticed that Deirdre, who usually wore exquisitely tailored dresses of the finest cloth, wore a drab brown linen dress with no adornment whatsoever. Trying to shake off her nerves, Keelin feigned surprise and said, "Deirdre, I would never have believed you owned such a dress, much less that you would wear it."

Deirdre looked down at her simple frock with dismay.

"It is dreadful, isn't it? I keep it for occasions such as this when I must perform ceremonies in dark and dirty caves, caring little if I stain or damage it irreparably."

She looked at Keelin's lovely blouse and skirt with regret. "If I had known sooner about today's ceremony, I would have warned you to wear one of your old dresses. I would also have given you some time to prepare your soul." Deirdre shot Nuala an annoyed glance. Something passed between the two priestesses that Keelin could not read, and she was surprised to see Nuala glance away first.

"Samhain is but a month away, and one's sensibilities cannot always be considered," said Nuala. She hesitated only an instant. "Furthermore, Keelin has a courageous soul. She needs no coddling."

"Please do not speak of me as if I were not present," said Keelin. "I am quite able to speak for myself." She expected Nuala to bristle at her words. Instead, the high priestess looked pleased and cast Deirdre a triumphant look. "Indeed, you are."

"Yes, Keelin, you are our equal and will be treated as such," said Deirdre.

Nuala shook her head and approached the mouth of the cave. "No, you are not our equal yet, Keelin. By the end of the day, however, we will know if you are."

Nuala, Deirdre, and Keelin sat cross-legged in a circle on the cold earth, their hands intertwined. Nuala was reciting a poem in the ancient tongue of The Dagda that spoke of lost heroes and gods, of liberty and peace. The poem was endless and Nuala's chanting was discordant and eerie. Keelin did not enjoy listening to the ancient language of The Dagda, finding its harsh tone jarring to the ear. The spoken language of Eire, in contrast, had a lyrical, lilting beauty. She let her mind wander far from the cave and Nuala's tedious recitation. She saw Brian walking along a cliff's edge. He was singing but she could not discern his words. Instead, she felt an overwhelming sense of isolation and despair. Frightened, Keelin yanked her consciousness back to the cave and realized the chanting had ended. Nuala and Deirdre were looking at her expectantly.

"Did you not hear me?" questioned Nuala.

"No . . . I did not."

"Then I will ask you again. Do you wish to enter the realm of The Dagda? Will you abide by and uphold the edicts of The Dagda? Will you protect the secrets of The Dagda?"

Keelin fought back the urge to scream, "No, I do not want such a life!" And then she thought of Caitlin and her uncle Eirnín. She thought of the young men who would fight and die battling the Romhanach. She thought of how her seeing, her *power*, would help them. "I do. I wish to enter the realm of The Dagda, abiding by and upholding its edicts and protecting its secrets."

"Very well, then, we shall continue." Nuala and Deirdre rose and walked over to where a large pile of kindling and peat lay in the middle of the vast cave, beckoning Keelin to follow.

The priestesses lowered their heads and whispered a prayer of gratitude before lighting the ceremonial fire. Keelin wiped her sweaty palms against the fine linen of her skirt and watched the flames, the smell of the smoke blending with the musky dampness in this hidden sepulchre of earth.

Into the vibrant flames Nuala sprinkled basil for protection, celandine for freedom, and bluebell for truth. She tilted her head up toward the ceiling of the cave and closed her eyes. "May Keelin be protected by the gods, may she seek wisdom and find truth in the world, all in the name of The Dagda." Then Nuala and Deirdre began circling the fire, swaying in a rhythmic dance, their faces feline and glowing in the amber light.

Keelin instinctively moved her body, following the graceful flow of the priestesses, engaging in a primitive dance as ancient as the gods. As Keelin circled the fire faster and faster, she could feel herself lifting off the ground, no longer using her body to move. Even the walls of the cave began to ripple and wave, as if the earth were following her movements. She was sweating now, lightheaded and tingling. She closed her eyes, trying to block the bizarre images, not wanting to faint. When she opened them again, Keelin realized she was no longer in the cave but soaring through a black night, devoid of clouds. She glanced down and saw only the dark shadows of hills and the iridescent sparkle of lakes, all becoming mere specks as she flew farther away from her island home.

Keelin breathed in the night air, feeling its chill; she explored every one of her senses: the reflection of the moon on her pale skin, the raised hair on her arms, the weightlessness of her body. She could have traveled for hours or days or centuries, she did not know. Keelin eventually noticed the first rays of sunlight begin to break through the blanket of night, promising a new day. The outline of a coast emerged, and she immediately recognized the scenery from her recurring dream. She began her descent to the sharp cliffs of the coastline, expecting to find the cottages and the familiar path and the man whose face was always blurred by distance. This time, Keelin thought, I shall see his face, regardless of whether the gods will it or not. However, as soon as she neared the vista, Keelin was propelled past the cliffs with an intensity so great she was forced to shut her eyes. When she opened them, she was blinded by a white light much brighter than anything she was accustomed to.

Keelin looked around and found herself hovering above a room with smooth white walls, lit with enormous, blinding lamps suspended from the ceiling. Everywhere were strange boxes of varying sizes displaying moving images, symbols, and lines that were constantly changing. Everything—the lights, the boxes, the images—was focused on the center of the room where a surgery was taking place, yet no surgery Keelin could ever have imagined. The four healers administering to the patient were clothed in plain blue long-sleeved tunics that reached below their knees. Each wore a cap that hid their hair and a small white mask over their nose and mouth, secured with two ties. The patient's chest cavity was open, and a delicate procedure was being performed on his heart. How was it possible for the heart to be still, not beating, yet the patient lived? Transfixed and disembodied, Keelin suddenly felt the blue tunic against her skin, could smell the astringent odors through the white mask. In a language heretofore unknown, she asked one of the healers for a scalpel and held the finely wrought instrument in her gloved hand. She was no longer observing the surgery. She was performing it! In the next instant, everything went black.

❦

KEELIN WOKE TO find herself in the cave with Nuala and Deirdre staring at her.

"What happened . . . how long was I . . . away?"

"Only for a short while," Nuala answered, "but time is continuous."

Keelin's mind was reeling and her stomach unsettled. She looked down at her blouse and skirt, both stained and ruined by the damp clay of the cave. She pushed her hair away from her face and noticed the soot on her hands. Nothing seemed real. She wondered now if she had fainted and only dreamt the magic.

"What did you see, Keelin?"

Keelin could hear the urgency and impatience in Nuala's voice but could not yet respond. Why did Nuala not read her mind? Never in the past had the high priestess shown any reluctance to do so. Keelin wished to be spared the need to speak until she regained her equilibrium, fearing she might vomit. "I . . . read my thoughts, Nuala. I feel quite ill."

"Your mind is in a muddle. I can hear nothing," said Nuala. The high priestess abruptly stood, and in the fading glow of the ceremonial fire, she looked like a demon. Keelin shuddered and turned her head away from the apparition.

Deirdre stood also and lightly placed a restraining hand on Nuala's arm. Then she turned from Nuala and bent down, offering her hand to Keelin. "Here, I will help you up. Let us move outside. You will feel better when you can breathe clean, fresh air."

Keelin stumbled out of the cave, holding fast to Deirdre's hand. They made their way to a grove of oak trees nearby. The oaks formed a natural and hidden amphitheater, with a small meadow nestled in the center of the grove. Once they were within the shelter of the oaks, completely hidden from view, Deirdre led Keelin over to the trunk of a fallen tree and invited her to rest upon it. Nuala, without unhesitating, sat upon the damp grass of the meadow facing Keelin. Deirdre frowned in consternation at the ground but nonetheless sat down next to Nuala.

Keelin immediately began to feel better. She breathed in the damp, sweet-smelling air and the fogginess of her mind cleared. Preferring to sit on the ground as well, she slid off the tree trunk and leaned her back against it. Soon her stomach stopped its frightful lurching.

"Well," she began slowly, "it was all very strange." She paused, not sure how to describe what had happened and whether the priestesses would even believe her. "I closed my eyes while dancing in the cave, fearing I would faint. When I opened them again, I found myself flying swiftly through the night air, away from Eire. As dawn approached, the same scenery in a dream of mine appeared—the beautiful coastline and the high granite cliffs." Keelin then described the strange room and surgery in as much detail as she could remember, marveling afresh at what she had experienced.

Nuala and Deirdre listened intently. When Keelin was finished, the priestesses exchanged a glance. Then the high priestess looked at Keelin, her gray eyes gleaming. "You are one of us, easily able to pass into the realm of the Otherworld. You are of The Dagda."

"So I truly experienced these wonders . . . I was not sure. I feared you would not believe me."

"Of course we believe you," said Deirdre.

"When did I enter the Otherworld? I felt . . . odd as I danced round the fire."

With uncharacteristic solicitude, Nuala explained, "You became faint because you had entered the Otherworld. You must
have closed your eyes at the precise moment you left the con-
fines of the cave."

"Did you enter the Otherworld with me?"

"Yes, Keelin," said Deirdre. "We accompanied you."

"This is madness," muttered Keelin to herself. She couldn't
recall any changes to her surroundings as she danced. She
frowned, trying to remember. That was not exactly true. She had
felt a strange chill hit her, even though she had been sweating
from the heat of the fire and her dancing.

"I felt suddenly cold and then lightheaded. I am not sure if
the chill hit me before or after the walls of the cave began to
move."

Nuala nodded. "You felt the chill as you entered the Otherworld, and you undoubtedly felt ill because of the scarcity of
life-nurturing air within it. One's body feels robbed of substance
and oddly buoyant within its boundaries. The mind is, at first,
sluggish and faint. It will take you some time to adjust to the
strangeness of the Otherworld. Soon, though, you will be able
to enter and leave at will, with no ill effects."

"I did not see either of you once I left the cave. Why?"

Keelin, even in her somewhat befuddled state, sensed a certain hesitancy in both priestesses to answer her question. Finally,
Deirdre said, "We would have stayed with you had we been able.
We were not. When you left the cave and disappeared through
time, you were alone. You traveled to one of your future lives,
not ours."

"Neither of you ever mentioned the possibility of time travel
within the Otherworld. Why?"

"I told you time was of little consequence within the Otherworld. I saw no need to explain more . . . then." Nuala's tone was dismissive as she shifted her gaze uneasily from Keelin.

"Well, I need to know and understand now. What are both of you not telling me?"

Nuala's fingers lightly touched her ruby pendant. "Deirdre, tell Keelin. She will learn the truth soon enough."

Deirdre hesitated, then spoke. "Keelin . . . we are aware of no one who has traveled to a future life during a ceremony to test affinity for the Otherworld. There are only a few of us within The Dagda who have ever traveled through time. In truth, we have done so only during Samhain and with the magic of our Dagda cloak to aid us. It is then that the boundaries between life and death are broken, as are the barriers of time, allowing the souls of the departed to pass through the sacred passage tomb and be reincarnated. For reasons only the gods know, it is also during Samhain when a select few of The Dagda can travel to the future. We have no control over the life we visit, being always pulled to the same place and time. I can only believe it represents a future existence in which we achieve the ultimate realization of our souls. Of course," said Deirdre, glancing at Nuala, "this is only my belief."

"You have each traveled to your ultimate life?" Keelin addressed both priestesses but she looked directly at Nuala.

Nuala raised an eyebrow. "I traveled to my future life several times when I was young and foolish. Almost everything captivated me. Man will create the most remarkable and magical conveniences, some of which, I must admit, left me awestruck. However, I was never given more than a glimpse, a few seconds to take in the vision before I was hurled back to the present."

Deirdre nodded. "My experience was very similar to yours, Nuala. The glimpses into my future were always brief and, seemingly, without purpose. Enticing, miraculous, but ultimately use-less in living my present life."

"But I not only viewed my future life, I was *living* in it," marveled Keelin. "I spoke in a strange language, handled the surgical instruments, and performed the surgery. What does it mean? Are there no others of The Dagda like me?"

"There was one priest who, it is said, could pass easily be-tween his present and future lives," offered Deirdre. "However, he is long dead and few speak of him now. Perhaps, you, Nuala . . ."

Keelin eyed Nuala expectantly. "Did you know him? Can you tell me anything about his life?"

"I can tell you nothing about him," said Nuala. "You must find your own answers. Come, we should head back to the cot-tage. It will soon be dark." Nuala stood and offered Keelin her hand. Surprised, Keelin took it and rose, facing both priestesses.

"So it seems I am doomed to be different, even from those of The Dagda."

"You are not different from us, Keelin," said Deirdre, "only more gifted."

# CHAPTER SIXTEEN

*I* THINK I WILL JOIN YOU AND YOUR FAMILY FOR the evening meal tomorrow night if I may," said Deirdre as she and Keelin walked back to Nuala's cottage from their favorite place near the mouth of the gorge. The shadows of dusk darkened the narrow path and the air had grown chilly and damp. It had been several days since the ceremony in the cave and the rhythm of Keelin's days went on as before. Nuala had departed for Tara shortly after the ceremony, leaving Keelin to visit and treat patients every morning and pass her afternoons with Deirdre. Yet, Keelin knew she would never be quite the same. Her experience in the Otherworld had freed her. She no longer resented being, admittedly, *different*. Somehow, learning she was different even from those of The Dagda had given her confidence. After the Romhanach were defeated, she was determined to choose her own path and destiny.

"Of course you may," said Keelin, surprised. In the early days, Keelin had frequently invited Deirdre to dinner but she rarely accepted. "Dear Keelin," she would say, "I would like nothing better than to dine with you and your family, but unfortunately my evenings are rarely my own." Nuala's ardent and tireless devotion to her obligations as a priestess was easy for Keelin to understand; Deirdre's cheerful dedication was more difficult. Nonetheless, the young priestess was steadfast in her commitment to The Dagda and the people of Eire and Keelin respected her for it.

"You have had news of Déaglán's impending arrival? Or have you been following his progress from Tara via the Otherworld?" Keelin teased, knowing full well she, herself, would shamelessly use her power in such a way.

Deirdre laughed. "I admit I am not above such amusement but there is never enough time. Instead, I have felt Déaglán's presence for days. Truthfully, I have sensed the nearness of his soul."

"You hear the souls of the dead as well and converse with them, do you not?" asked Keelin, though it was more of a statement than a question. She had guessed her friend's other "gift" some time ago but had said nothing, reluctant to talk of death and dying.

"Yes, I do, since I was a child," answered Deirdre simply.

"I am sure I would not like that."

Deirdre shrugged slightly and smiled, taking no offense. "I am accustomed to hearing the voices of the dead, while you, as a healer, are accustomed to seeing the suffering of the living. We are not so very different in our desire to alleviate pain, whether it is of the body or the soul." Deirdre knitted her brow. "I am not sure how to explain my gift, but I can feel my thoughts and words soothing others, the healing power of my mind giving them some respite from sorrow and anxiety."

"I feel the same thing with my hands," said Keelin. "I can lessen my patients' pain by simply touching them. My hands are more powerful than my eyes when determining an injury or disease." Keelin looked at her small, delicate hands outstretched in front of her, marveling at their power.

"We are peculiarly special," said Deirdre airily, pirouetting gracefully on the grassy pathway.

Taking Keelin's hands, Deirdre kissed them. "It is well you and I rejoice in our gifts. They burden us with enormous responsibility. Even I, on occasion, chafe at the bonds my powers place on me. Fortunately, most souls are eager to enter their next life, starting anew. They feel buoyant and free, no longer suffering the indignities of advanced age or the pain of a lengthy and debilitating disease. These souls have little need of me."

"It is true about the very ill and dying," said Keelin, her mood becoming dark. "Even those who are the most determined and strong at the outset of a disease become weary of the pain and the constant struggle for life. I wish to fight for them but they no longer want my help." Keelin thought of little Caitlin, who had been so close to death, so ready to die. At least in Caitlin's case, thought Keelin, death had been cheated.

"At some point," said Deirdre, "death is a release for the beleaguered soul. However, when sudden and unexpected death strikes the young or those in their prime, there is often extreme anxiety and regret. Many souls are tormented with fear for their families, by injuries or injustices they caused or endured, words left unsaid. They call out to me for help and I do what I can to aid and soothe them."

"Our gifts will be sorely tested when the Romhanach invade."

"They will, indeed," said Deirdre. She put her arm around Keelin's shoulder and squeezed gently. Then she abruptly stopped walking and turned to Keelin, her eyes bright with excitement. "Enough of this distressing talk. We deserve some relaxation and I know just where to take you."

"We are going somewhere tonight?" Keelin asked, bemused, her mind still lingering on the dead and dying. She could not so easily dismiss her dark thoughts. Deirdre's irrepressible optimism often confounded and sometimes annoyed her.

"Yes, tonight. Far to the west, across the ocean there is a vast expanse of land, nearly uninhabited. On its southwestern edge is the coastline where warm, dry winds blow in the late summer and fall, though sometimes I have felt them in the first months of winter. The skies are almost always clear and the ocean is pleasantly warm by late summer, and even into the fall. There we can swim and lie in the sun, and revive our spirits."

"And how do you propose we travel there?" asked Keelin.

"Through the Otherworld, of course," said Deirdre.

"I am not yet of The Dagda. The law prohibits such travel. Only in matters of life and death could I accompany you." Keelin saw Deirdre's eyes widen and could not help but laugh. "Do not look so surprised. I can recite quite accurately every Dagda restriction regarding travel within the Otherworld. Before she left for Tara, Nuala insisted I commit the tedious law to memory."

"Well, Nuala has a rather strict interpretation of Dagda law. I, on the other hand," said Deirdre mischievously, "choose to follow the spirit rather than the letter of the law. You have already traveled greater distances within the Otherworld than most of The Dagda's priests and priestesses could ever dream of. The Otherworld welcomes you. Therefore, I am not truly breaking Dagda law. Rather, I am simply ignoring convention."

"Nuala would likely say otherwise," said Keelin with conspiratorial delight.

"Well, Nuala is not here," said Deirdre. "There will still be hours of daylight where I am taking you. We will travel so quickly and so far that we will turn back time and experience the day all over again, with the sun high in the sky.

❧

Keelin and Deirdre stood just out of reach of the tide, gazing at the ocean. The small waves lined up one behind the other two and three deep. As one wave crested and broke, another humped up, ready to follow, the rhythm and flow of the waves amazingly consistent. There was an offshore breeze, but it was too weak to catch the waves and send saltwater spraying upwards and back. Instead, dry air from the inland deserts lingered along the coastline, strong enough, at least for the day, to hold back the fog, ensuring warm temperatures and clear skies. The beach was wide, the sand ending only at the base of a low plain that spread gently to distant hills. Large trees, their yellow leaves signaling autumn, followed the meandering line of a dry creek through the surrounding plain of sparse grasses baked golden by the sun.

Keelin dug her toes into the wet sand and closed her eyes, lifting her face to the sun. She savored the gritty feel of the sand between her toes, the salty smell of the ocean, the warmth of the sun. It was the clean, dry air, however, that filled her with happiness and a wonderful sense of freedom. Both new and familiar, this was where she belonged. It was surely the coastline in her dream.

"Did I not tell you the weather would be fine," exclaimed Deirdre, putting her arm around Keelin's shoulder and pulling her close.

Keelin sighed. "It is perfect, the most beautiful day. In fact," she said, a good-natured challenge in her tone, "it is a perfect day for a swim."

Deirdre laughed. "Yes, a perfectly wonderful day for a swim." She turned and walked back to where they had left their cloaks, safely beyond the reaches of high tide. There she undid the ties of her dress and lifted it over her head, folding it neatly and placing it on top of her cloak. Standing there in only her fine linen shift, Deirdre braided her hair in one long plait, securing the end with a jute string. "Well, what are you waiting for?" she teased.

Quickly, and much less methodically, Keelin stripped to her shift, not bothering to braid her hair.

"Shall we?" invited Deirdre, running toward the water with surprising abandon. Keelin sprinted after her, stopping only when the chilly surf reached her knees.

"You told me the water here was not cold," cried Keelin, just as a wave broke in front of her, sending whitewater splashing up against her body. Keelin laughed even as she shivered, far too happy to feign annoyance.

"No, I told you that in summer the water was mild and that even in winter it was not frigid. Who is the prissy lass now?" Deirdre turned back to the waves and steadily made her way out into the surf, diving through a wave as it crested in front of her.

Keelin watched Deirdre with admiration. Not wishing to endure the agony of slowly and steadily wading through the surf as Deirdre had, Keelin charged forward and flung herself head first into a wave just as it broke, getting tossed and tumbled in the whitewater. When she finally surfaced, she found Deirdre near, laughing at her.

"I see that I must teach you how to dive *under* the wave after it has broken, not through it. I will also teach you how to ride them to the beach. It is grand!" Deirdre looked beautiful; Keelin thought she resembled a sea goddess, looking more comfortable and at home in the sea than on land. It was the first time Keelin had ever seen her friend so uninhibited, Deirdre's poise and refinement replaced by something more instinctively free.

The young women stayed in the ocean until their legs and

arms became leaden with cold, their fingers white and numb. Deirdre was the first to make her way to the shore. Keelin soon followed, riding a small wave until she was only knee deep in whitewater. Standing up on wobbly legs, she waded through the surf as it retreated, holding her shift high above her knees, then joined Deirdre on the beach. She dropped down onto the warm, dry sand and lay flat on her stomach. Her hair, a tangled mess with a piece of seaweed adorning it, collected a coating of sand in the process. Keelin rested her head in the sand, feeling its warmth on her cheek. Looking up at Deirdre, she asked, "How does one leave here, once visited?"

"With difficulty," Deirdre said simply.

They lay there in silence for some time, listening to the low rumble of the waves and the screech of the seagulls. Then, grabbing her dress, Keelin balled it up and rested her head upon it. Almost to herself, she said, "Uncle Eirnín's soul spoke to me, soon after he was killed."

"Yes, I know," whispered Deirdre.

"His soul is the only one I have ever heard. Talking with him helped lessen the pain I felt at his passing. Also, he entrusted me with an important task. Uncle Eirnín was frightfully worried about . . . someone. I am thankful I was able to carry out his wishes and allay his fears, bringing him solace."

KEELIN REMEMBERED HER uncle Eirnín's burial as if it were yesterday. He lay on a funeral bier, dressed in warrior garb and covered with leafy branches of birch. His family stood solemnly round him. Aunt Meghan's face was deathly pale and her children wept as a chorus sang a mournful dirge. Above the other singers rose Brian's beautiful voice; not a tear escaped his tormented eyes. Keelin's heart ached as she listened, knowing he was suffering the loss even more than she.

To Keelin's knowledge, Brian never shed a tear. Instead, in the weeks following Eirnín's death, Brian fought—constantly. He was relentless, forever challenging the young men of the clan to fisticuffs. It mattered little whether there had been any provocation for the fight. Brian needed none. It seemed only physical pain helped ease the anguish of his soul. He always sought out superior opponents, attempting to banish all his demons with each blow given and received, enduring horrendous punishment.

Within days of his death, Uncle Eirnín spoke to Keelin. His foremost concern was for Brian. Eirnín asked Keelin to relay a message to the boy, praying it would help lessen his pain and give him renewed purpose and strength. Keelin tried several times to approach Brian during those first weeks, but he had warned her off with savage anger. Undeterred, she waited and watched for the right moment to reach him, forcing herself to be patient.

It was Aunt Meghan who gave Keelin an excuse to seek out Brian. Somehow her aunt had learned about a particularly brutal fight Brian had provoked. He had taken the worst of it and Meghan was both worried and incensed. With her hands on her sizable hips, she declared, "I understand Brian is full of sorrow. We all are. However, Brian shames my Eirnín's memory with his fighting and blood-letting. It must stop." Keelin heard her aunt's voice quaver slightly and saw tears fall unchecked down her freckled cheeks.

"I will find him, Aunt Meghan."

"You are a healer. Please treat his injuries. Perhaps you, alone, can also treat his damaged soul. He has always loved you so."

Keelin dismissed her aunt's words. She knew Brian found

her annoying and somewhat of a nuisance. Still, the words had inexplicably pleased her.

Keelin found Brian squatting by the side of a stream, spitting out blood from his ravaged mouth. Even from a distance Keelin could see his battered and bloody face. When he looked up and saw her, he smiled slightly and then his mouth hardened. He turned back to the stream and splashed water on his face and head. In an offhand manner, he said, "So you have escaped Nuala's servitude for the day, I see. Can you find nothing better to do with your freedom than to pester me?"

"And can you find nothing better to do with your time than to get yourself beaten to a pulp? You look ghastly." Keelin shook her head and pursed her lips in reproof, though she felt only tenderness. She slid from Nellie's back and walked over to Brian to kneel by his side.

Stretching out her hand, she attempted to touch Brian's bruised and split cheek but he brushed away her hand. "Curse you, Keelin! Just leave me alone. I don't need your help."

"You most certainly do need my help," said Keelin. "Aunt Meghan sent me to find and fetch you. She heard about your fight—do not ask me how. You know very well it is impossible to keep anything from her. If she were to see you as you look right now, you may wish that thug had finished you off because nothing is worse than one of Aunt Meghan's tongue lashings."

Brian laughed, causing him to grimace with pain. "You make an excellent point. But if I learn you were the scheming tattletale . . ."

Keelin refused to grace Brian's words with a response. She would never betray a friend. Instead, she returned to where Nellie was grazing and retrieved her satchel. "Take off your shirt," she said matter-of-factly, "if it is not too painful to lift your arms."

"I will do no such thing. Next, I suppose, you will be demanding that I remove my trousers as well."

Keelin gave a derisive harrumph. "Your shirt is soaked in blood, and I am going to wash and lay it out to dry while I patch you up. Trust me, I have no wish for you to remove your trousers, although I cannot imagine that you have anything I have not seen before. You forget that I am a healer."

Somewhat embarrassed but appeased, Brian removed his shirt gingerly and handed it to Keelin, quietly watching her as she washed it in the stream, wringing out as much moisture as she could before hanging it on the branches of a nearby bush to dry.

"Now, let me see what I can do to make you more presentable to Aunt Meghan," Keelin said, looking at Brian appraisingly. She knelt down next to him and stretched out her hand, running her fingers along his ribcage. "Just as I thought, three of your ribs are cracked." Keelin gently pressed her hands against the damaged ribs, making Brian flinch. Soon, though, he relaxed and Keelin knew her touch was easing his pain.

"I am going to wrap this area," she said, indicating Brian's ribcage, "and please do not remove the wrap until I see you in a couple of days." After she finished attending to Brian's cracked ribs, Keelin turned her attention to his bruised and bloodied face, at which point Brian waved her off again. "Enough. I hate being fussed over."

"You will just have to endure my fussing, as I must close these wounds so there will be no scarring. Also, I am sure you are aware of the fact that your nose is broken and must be put back in its proper place. That, I can assure you, will hurt."

Keelin spoke with the authority of a practiced healer, sounding not at all like a twelve-year-old girl. With herbal remedies, salves, and her busy, skillful fingers, she cleaned and closed Brian's cuts, soothed his swelling, and with a quick snap, popped his nose back into place. All the while Keelin chatted, sometimes explaining what remedies she was using or what she was about to do, and other times speaking of inconsequential things, managing to keep Brian amused and interested during her ministrations. Caring and gentle, Keelin tended to his battered face, her hands working their strange magic, her sweet voice acting as a welcome balm to his battered psyche. At length, Keelin stood and stepped back, viewing Brian's face much like an artist would a completed painting. "Well, I cannot perform miracles, but you do look better than before. How do you feel?"

"Far better, thank you. I do believe you can work miracles, you little witch," said Brian, smiling.

Keelin did not bristle; instead, she kept her head down, busily collecting and sorting jars of ointments and powders, several strange metal implements, and needles of varying sizes, returning them carefully to her satchel. She did not know how she would tell him of Eirnín.

"I have never seen so many different potions and odd instruments. Do you carry an entire surgery in that huge satchel?" Brian's words were meant to tease but Keelin could hear the admiration in his tone.

"*One must always be prepared for any contingency*," Keelin responded, delivering one of Nuala's many maxims.

Brian laughed, grimacing only slightly. He stood and gingerly made his way to a large oak, where he sat down again, leaning against the trunk and lazily watching Keelin.

When Keelin finished packing up her satchel, she plopped down next to Brian, sitting cross-legged and watching the stream, all the while twirling and twisting a lock of her hair round and round with her forefinger. They sat there in companionable silence for some time before Keelin spoke.

"I . . . had the most wonderful, curious dream last night in which Uncle Eirnín visited me, talking to me for what seemed like hours and hours—"

"I have no wish to hear about your dreams," interrupted Brian.

"You must and you will," retorted Keelin. "Eirnín spoke mostly of you—"

"Hold your tongue, Keelin! I do not want to hear of your fanciful conversations with Eirnín. Did Aunt Meghan put you up to this?" Brian's brown eyes flashed threateningly. "Let me grieve privately."

Her anger rising, Keelin took a deep breath and struggled to compose herself. "I was not completely honest with you a moment ago and I apologize for that. Eirnín did not speak to me in a dream. He spoke to me when I was very much awake. I *heard* him, just as if he was standing next to me. He asked that I might convey a message to you. Laugh and think me mad, hate me, but you *will* listen to what Uncle Eirnín told me. He deserves nothing less."

BRIAN LISTENED TO Eirnín's words and they saved him. Thereafter, Brian fought only as a warrior of Eire in defense of his people and clan.

Keelin cherished the memory of that day. She had always thought it was because she fulfilled her promise to Uncle Eirnín. Now she realized it was also because of Brian and how he had listened to her.

# CHAPTER SEVENTEEN

*D*ÉAGLÁN'S HORSE WALKED ALONG THE VILLAGE road, deeply rutted by the wheels of heavy carts. It had not rained in several days but the damage done to the road during the rainy, foul weather would take months of hard labor to repair in the spring. There was a chill in the air that heralded the onset of winter. Déaglán shivered in spite of himself, not wishing to spend the next months in Eire with its bleak dampness and cold. He thought of the blue waters of the Tyrrhenum and longed to be sailing upon it. But the prospect of seeing Saraid and Keelin cheered him and he pushed thoughts of the sea from his mind.

He had not gone much farther when he heard shouts and approaching horses from behind. He turned in the saddle and saw Seán and Ruaidhrí riding toward him, leading two fine-looking horses. The men urged their mounts into a trot and all four horses somehow navigated the rutted road without tripping. Déaglán reined Banner around and faced the men. He noted Seán and Ruaidhrí looked considerably less road weary than he felt.

Ruaidhrí greeted Déaglán first. "Good afternoon to you, Déaglán. We did not expect to meet you on our travels." Seán nodded a hello, halting his horse alongside Ruaidhrí's.

"I could say the same about the two of you. You left Tara shortly after the chieftains' vote. Have you not yet told Brian he is to join the Fianna? Your mission was to return with him posthaste to begin training with Fionn."

"Do not fret, Déaglán. We have the long winter and much of the spring for training. Moreover, did you not also task us with an important, though apparently secretive mission?" Seán looked pointedly at Déaglán and then at the horses he and Ruaidhrí were leading.

"Indeed, I did." Déaglán eyed the two geldings appraisingly. They were sleek and long-legged. Although slightly different in type, each horse's confirmation was impeccable. He was pleased. After rigorous training, these bay geldings might very well be capable of jumping the Romhanach's repel barrier.

"We found more than a dozen likely beasts on our travels. Most have already been taken to Tara by their owners, and we will fetch the rest on our return trip. These two we bought for a tidy sum from a farmer who seemed reluctant to part with them. We paid the man his price and quickly departed." Ruaidhrí regarded with pleasure the geldings standing quietly on loose leads.

"They are, indeed, fine-looking animals," agreed Déaglán. He *had* asked Seán and Ruaidhrí to look for horses but did not think they would spend so much time doing so. Hoping to learn of the whereabouts of the spy, he had made several detours during his travels and left Tara a fortnight ago. Seán and Ruaidhrí had been wandering the countryside for nearly a full cycle of the moon. Déaglán's inquiries had been, with one exception, fruitless. He had spoken to a traveling merchant who had, perhaps, seen something of significance. The man claimed to have seen a stranger riding away from an abandoned cottage just before dark. The merchant described the rider as a "tall, broad-shouldered man, almost certainly a warrior, and riding a big bay horse with a white off-hind leg." The stranger's cloak covered his head and shoulders, making it impossible for the merchant to comment on the stranger's attire or the color of his hair. When the merchant reached the cottage, he was certain he heard another rider trotting away to the south but could see nothing in the waning light.

"We are headed for Conall's training fields," said Seán, shortening his horse's reins in preparation to depart. "We would be honored to have you ride with us."

"I am headed to my sister's farm but will ride with you until then," said Déaglán, his eyes sweeping over the horses Seán and Ruaidhrí were riding. Seán was astride a dark brown mare with no white markings whatsoever. Ruaidhrí's bay had a wide white blaze on its face and an off-hind white leg. Of course, thought Déaglán, many bays have off-hind white legs. He reined his horse alongside Ruaidhrí's and the three men headed down the road.

Déaglán rode into the farm's yard and almost immediately saw his sister. Saraid was in her garden, bending over the remnants of what had once been thriving herbs and vegetables. Even as a girl, Saraid had tended her flower and vegetable gardens with something akin to maternal devotion. Déaglán used to tease his younger sister, saying she enjoyed working in her garden more than anything else. She always smiled dismissively and shook her head, though the look in her eyes gave him pause. Today she was inspecting a particularly forlorn cabbage when Déaglán called out a greeting to her.

"Déaglán," she cried, her face lighting up with joy and relief. She straightened up and approached him. Déaglán jumped
from his horse and grasped Saraid's shoulders in his hands, gently kissing her pale cheek.

Saraid, in turn, kissed Déaglán's bearded cheek, searching
her brother's face.

"Is all well at Tara? You must tell me everything that has
happened. I long to hear of Conall."

"Conall is well and as irascible as ever." Déaglán noted with
concern the lines of anxiety etched on his sister's brow, the blue-
gray shadows under her eyes, and the colorless hue of her beautifully formed lips.

"Are you ill, Saraid?" Déaglán questioned with alarm, unaccustomed to seeing his sister tremulous and vulnerable.

"Don't be silly. I am very well, though perhaps a little tired.
I am only impatient for more news from Tara. You must tell all
you know at dinner tonight. Brian can hardly contain himself,
knowing he is to be a Fian and waiting for the arrival of Fionn's
warriors. They have most certainly been delayed by the heavy
rains."

"Brian knows, then, that he will join the Fianna?"

Saraid nodded. "He is impatient for battle and the chance
to prove his worth." Almost to herself, she whispered, "Young
and foolish."

"Yes, perhaps, though Eire needs warriors such as Brian.
Without them we will all surely perish." Déaglán was not surprised Brian had heard he would fight with the Fianna. Nuala
would have found a way to relay the news from Tara to Conall's
family and clan. He glanced again at Saraid, sensing her distress, but the beautiful face revealed nothing more of her concern.

"Yes," she said, acknowledging the truth of his words. "Now take your horse to the barn and wash up. We will eat soon." Saraid gave Déaglán another kiss on the cheek and then turned and walked toward the cottage.

DINNER WAS A lively affair, with Déaglán relating much of what had occurred at Tara before he left. The mighty Fionn had been elected supreme commander of Eire's warriors, with Niall enlisted to command the northern clans and Conall the midlands and southern. Each chieftain was challenged with assessing the strength of his clan's warriors and what, if any, special skills they possessed. This assessment proved contentious with many chieftains making false claims, reluctant to share such intelligence with enemy chieftains. It was only through the influence of the high priest Fearghus and after threats by Fionn that reasonably accurate assessments were made.

"Most likely," said Déaglán, "Agricola will field only one legion and employ a very straightforward formation, believing our forces inferior and our tactics and strategy nonexistent. Still, he is careful and will undoubtedly position formidable reserves behind his assault forces to counter any flanking threat our warriors may pose."

"We will flank and slaughter them nonetheless," responded Liam with a deadly gleam in his eyes.

"Perhaps, but only if we can devise a strategy that surprises Agricola. We must draw him in, bolster his confidence. He must commit his legion before he learns of our strength."

"This damnable rain and the approaching winter will hinder our training and readiness," said Brian. "And what of the spies? How can we surprise Agricola and draw him in, with his spies still wandering around somewhere in Eire, learning our secrets?"

"Do not begrudge the winter. It is all that stands between us and Agricola's invasion. He must wait to cross the channel until late spring or early summer when the seas are less hostile. The winter buys us time to plan and, yes, train." Déaglán did not mention it was possible a dispatch had already been sent to Agricola, informing him of the chieftains' vote to unite. Nor did he speak of the spy Diarmuid had killed. He noted his sister's pallor and steered the conversation away from war. He would speak to Brian and Keelin tomorrow about the spy who had eluded them near Loich's Gap.

Turning to Saraid, Déaglán said, "I expect Conall to arrive any day. He plans to remain here until just after Samhain, when all the chieftains will again assemble at Tara."

As Déaglán expected, his mention of Samhain turned the conversation to the festival, and the mood in the room lightened considerably. The communal feasts, the lighting of the bonfires, the games of sport, including the most prestigious horse race of the year, were discussed. Although he added an opinion or answered a query occasionally, Déaglán was free to study those in the room. He consciously avoided looking too often at Deirdre, for she invariably roused strong and unwanted emotions. Instead he focused much of his attention on Brian, whom Conall had spoken of so highly at Tara.

It had been many years since Déaglán had last seen Brian while visiting Saraid. The tall, sturdy boy Déaglán remembered had grown into an imposing young man, bearing a striking resemblance to Cormac, his father. Cormac had been an imposing man, with wavy black hair, broad shoulders, and a deep, resonant voice. He had always seemed larger than life: handsome, wealthy, charming, and not one to be visited by tragedy, surely not a victim of a premature death. Nonetheless, Cormac had collapsed and died suddenly when Brian was near five years old, leaving his young wife bereft and the boy fatherless.

Déaglán had heard of Brian's struggles over the years, first battling a brutish stepfather who was jealous of him and then enduring the grief of Eirnín's death. Not surprisingly, Brian grew up angry and had a penchant for violence. Of course, thought Déaglán, anger in a warrior was a powerful weapon, provided it could be harnessed and directed at the enemy. He sensed Brian would be lethal on the battlefield, an instinctive leader, inherently bold and courageous. Déaglán was no less impressed with Brian's keen mind and understood why Conall had recommended him for the Fianna. Tonight, Déaglán also noted Brian's restlessness and agitation, his pent-up aggression. The young man is ready to explode, thought Déaglán, wondering at the cause. Perhaps it was only Brian's impatience for battle. Déaglán ventured a stealthy glance at Deirdre, who was knitting what appeared to be a shawl made of fine silken yarn, lavender in color, gossamer in weight and texture. Perhaps Deirdre knows what plagues Brian, reflected Déaglán.

Invariably, the conversation soon focused solely on the famous Samhain horse race, and Déaglán was drawn into a debate on which horse was likely to win it this year. There were some fine young stallions who were entered but none seemed likely to outrun Rua, Conall's magnificent red stallion.

Turning to Keelin, Déaglán asked, "Will you ride him this year?"

"No, not this year. I wish . . ." Keelin's voice trailed off and she shook her head, looking quite miserable.

Deirdre came to Keelin's rescue. "I plan to place a tidy sum on Rua to win the big race, even without Keelin riding him." Standing up, she announced, "Now we must have some music and dancing. I hear Liam has completed the harp he plans to present to The Dagda at Samhain and I can no longer wait to play it. If truth be told, I have thought of little else all evening." She glanced around the group. "Saraid, you look tired. Don't get up. Brian, go fetch the harp while Déaglán and Liam move the table so there is room for dancing. Keelin, you and I can move the chairs and get the other instruments."

The men sprang enthusiastically to their feet. Brian hurried off to Liam's workshop to get the harp and Déaglán and Liam moved the heavy oak table from the center of the room. Deirdre had a way of making people want to do her bidding, thought Déaglán, wondering if she had cast a spell on him years ago.

# CHAPTER EIGHTEEN

*D*EIRDRE'S FINGERS MOVED LIGHTLY OVER THE
strings of the exquisite harp, testing its sound, playing
wisps of melodies, varying her touch, and delighting in the pure
notes and resonance. Déaglán held a drum at the ready, Liam a
fine set of pipes. Once Deirdre had acquainted herself with the
harp, she played a lilting melody, with Déaglán punctuating the
chord changes, keeping time with muted beats of the drum.
When the song ended, Deirdre smiled radiantly, running her
fingers over the beautiful wood carvings on the neck of the
harp.

"Liam, never have I played such a harp. You are a genius! I
shall love you always for creating this treasure."

Liam turned red, more from embarrassment than pleasure
at Deirdre's words. As affable and ebullient as Liam was around
his friends and family, he had always been painfully shy and
awkward with women, at least those he found attractive. Liam
was a confirmed bachelor, very happily burying himself in his
art and never missing the mysterious aspects of women and
their strange ways.

"I . . . had some trouble with the harp's design but was able
to correct its flaws. I am . . . pleased with its sound," Liam

stammered. "Perhaps you would accompany Brian so he may sing a song."

"Of course," responded Deirdre and turned to Brian. "What would you like to sing?"

Brian chose an ancient ballad chronicling a great boar hunt, the music rousing and strong, the lyrics lauding the skill and bravery of the hunters and the power and ferocity of the boar.

Those in the room listened to Brian sing, captivated by the poetic beauty of the words, even as they told the tale of a brutal hunt. Brian's voice had great range and his high, clear tenor notes were beautiful. When the song ended, Déaglán, with sincere appreciation said, "Brian, if your prowess on the battlefield even approaches the beauty and power with which you sing, the Fianna will be lucky to have you."

Brian nodded. "Thank you, Déaglán."

"Deirdre, Keelin, it is time for some dancing," said Saraid. She picked up her flute and began playing. Déaglán enthusiastically accompanied her on the drum, beckoning Deirdre and Keelin onto the dance floor with a sweep of his arm. When Deirdre laughingly protested, the men shouted words of encouragement, cajoling her to join Keelin, who never needed any encouragement to dance. She pulled Deirdre out of her chair and into the middle of the room.

The two young women could not have painted more strikingly different pictures as they danced to the lively tune—its tempo ebbing and flowing, quickening and slowing. Deirdre danced with exquisite skill, her movements poised, her steps light, following the rhythm and beat of the music with effortless grace. Keelin, far less skilled, yet every bit as captivating, moved with complete abandon, surrendering all conscious thought to the atavistic response the music awakened in her. She swayed with wildly exaggerated movements, her body and arms undulating in intoxicating waves as she spun around the room. Whereas Deirdre's leaps and pirouettes were airy perfection, Keelin sprang into the air with feral energy, her tiny feet outstretched, her toes pointed, her thick auburn hair flying about her. With each leap it was as if Keelin were about to shed the bonds of her small human form and be transformed, shapeshifting into some enchanted, bewitching creature.

When the tune ended, Déaglán immediately resumed the beating of the drum, signaling a new jig. Liam followed the drum's lead with the pipes, his foot tapping the floor, his fingers moving expertly over the stops. Deirdre laughed and, feigning exhaustion, pulled Brian to his feet and toward Keelin who had already begun to dance to the new tune.

Brian was at first reluctant, but Deirdre was undeterred. "I am exhausted and Keelin still wishes to dance. We will see if she can dance you into the ground as well."

Brian glanced skeptically at Keelin who welcomed him, her lips curved into something very close to a smile. Her cheeks were flushed and her violet eyes sparkled. Brian needed no further prompting and took the hand Keelin offered. The two danced, Keelin spinning around Brian as his feet tapped a martial cadence, forceful and strong. Stepping high on her toes, Keelin twirled and weaved to within inches of Brian, only to retreat as he took her hand, pirouetting within the arc of his outstretched arm. Then, facing each other, they stepped in unison as they circled the room, Keelin springing high into the air, Brian tapping, clicking his feet with amazing speed and dexterity, matching Keelin's animation and exuberance.

When the music finally stopped, Brian's back was to those in the room, hiding Keelin from view. Keelin laughed and impulsively hugged Brian. She then stepped back, her eyes brilliant, tiny beads of perspiration glistening along the line of her temples and upper lip, her hair hanging in silken tangles down her back. Brian searched her face and then settled fixedly on her mouth. Tentatively, he lightly touched the bow of her lips with the tip of his forefinger.

Liam suddenly shouted his approval at the pair's inspired dancing and Déaglán punctuated Liam's whoop with a drumroll finale. Brian snatched his hand away as if he had been shocked, and Keelin, also jolted back to reality, lowered her eyes in embarrassment.

Though he had not seen Brian's gesture, Déaglán noticed Keelin's uncharacteristic reticence when she returned to her chair, as quiet now as she had been wild just moments before. Puzzled, he glanced at Brian but Deirdre distracted him. "Your touch on the drum is commendable if not brilliant. You must have few occasions to play so your mastery is even more impressive."

"I have played the drum since I was very young and, once learned, it is a skill that has stayed with me. But you are correct. I rarely play, especially when I am here," said Déaglán with a wry laugh. Saraid and Liam joined in the laughter.

"What amusing secret am I not a party to?" questioned Deirdre.

"When Conall is home," explained Liam, "he always insists on playing the drum, much to the distress of the other musicians present. For a man with such subtlety of mind and eloquence of speech, he is an oafish bull on the drum, pounding indiscriminately and drowning out all other instruments, let alone the voice of any singer. He possesses no musical talent whatsoever, yet still plays with enthusiastic abandon, completely enjoying himself and making true musicians miserable."

Saraid smiled but protested. "Conall's playing is not that dreadful, though I must admit his approach is unorthodox. Liam exaggerates for effect."

Liam scoffed, warming to the subject. "If you wish only to hear the drum pounded on with maniacal fervor, likely conjuring up all the evil fairies and witches of Eire, then Conall's manner of playing will appeal to you. Surely it is terrifying to witness Conall beating the drum and Keelin dancing, both behaving as if possessed by demons. Many a time I have thought that Keelin, in the midst of one of her wild leaps, would screech like a banshee while Conall ushered in some dreadful augur with his frightful pounding."

"I love Keelin's dancing. It is beautiful," said Saraid, coming to her daughter's defense when Keelin remained silent. "She feels the music completely, never allowing artistic convention to interfere with her emotional response."

"Well, I for one am glad Conall was not here tonight accompanying Deirdre. The harp's sound and Deirdre's playing were perfection," remarked Déaglán, smiling at Deirdre.

Deirdre's eyes twinkled as she thanked Déaglán with a politeness equaling his own, then turned to Liam. "Has Conall always insisted on playing despite your protests?"

"When Eirnín was alive, he always played the drum. Eirnín was a grand musician, playing both the pipes and drum brilliantly. He also had a handsome singing voice, though not as fine as young Brian's here."

Brian sat rigidly upright, staring at the glowing embers in the fireplace.

"Was not it magic when the two of you sang?" Liam asked. "Eirnín with his deep baritone, and you with your tenor?"

"Yes," agreed Brian rather stiffly, "those are some of my

fondest memories, singing with Eirnín." Then, seemingly stirred by his reminiscences, Brian added, "Eirnín was a grand teacher, showing me how to use and train my voice, treating it as a fine instrument. I know I would never have developed my range or power without his careful guidance."

"I am sure Eirnín was very proud of you," responded Deirdre warmly. With that, Deirdre stood abruptly. "And now I must start back to Nuala's cottage. I thank you, Saraid, for a most enchanting evening."

"Do not be silly," responded Saraid. "You will stay here tonight. It is far too late, and too dangerous, for you to travel to Nuala's alone."

Roused from her reverie, Keelin agreed with her mother. "Yes, please stay, Deirdre. You can accompany me on my patient rounds tomorrow morning."

"I would love to stay, but I have much to do tomorrow morning. I really must travel back tonight." Deirdre gave Keelin a slight smile.

"Déaglán," said Saraid, "please ease my mind and escort Deirdre home. You can take the cart and Liam's gelding. Bran knows the way to Nuala's well and will get you there and back easily."

"Yes, Bran should take you safely to Nuala's," said Keelin. "However, I had Bran out all day today making my patient rounds, and it would be unfair to ask him to make the return journey tonight. Why not stay in Nuala's apothecary tonight, Déaglán? She often has guests sleep there when they visit. There is a shed behind the cottage where you can bed down Bran for the night."

Liam, looking affronted, was about to speak when Saraid concurred. "That is an excellent plan, Keelin. Deirdre, don't protest, I know that Déaglán would be only too happy to escort you home and stay the night."

Déaglán glanced resignedly at his sister and, with only the slightest hesitation, turned to Deirdre. "I would be honored to see you safely home, Deirdre."

Deirdre smiled at Déaglán and then shot Keelin a mischievous glance, exchanging what could only be conspiratorial delight. Déaglán was about to protest, sensing he had been reined in and hobbled by these two young witches, when Keelin jumped to her feet and, carefully avoiding Brian's eyes, made for the door. "I will go hitch Bran to the cart and tell him that he is to take you both to Nuala's."

After Déaglán and Deirdre had left the cottage, Liam was no longer able to contain his irritation. "Keelin unjustly maligned my fine Bran. She knows very well that he is indefatigable and could pull that cart from sunrise to sunset with ease." After voicing his umbrage, Liam grew even more incensed. "I will set Keelin straight on Bran this instant!"

Saraid put her hand soothingly on Liam's shoulder, restraining him. "Keelin is well aware of Bran's stamina and meant him no offense. Her real concern lies with Déaglán, knowing that he has grieved for Maeve long enough. Now help Brian move the table and chairs back into place."

Liam swore to himself that he would never understand the illogical thoughts of women. Shaking his head, he dutifully helped Brian move the furniture.

## CHAPTER NINETEEN

*D*ÉAGLÁN AND DEIRDRE SAT NEXT TO EACH OTHER in the cart, neither speaking as Bran trotted briskly out of the farm yard and down the track that led to the village road. The night was clear and the moon nearly full, making the two lanterns, each affixed to the leading corners of the cart, almost unnecessary. Unfamiliar with the narrow track to Nuala's, Déaglán had lit them before leaving, even though Keelin assured him that Bran could find his way.

"You need not waste the precious oil. Bran will take you safely to Nuala's," she had said, gently stroking Bran's sleek neck.

The silence between Déaglán and Deirdre lengthened, with only Bran's hooves adding a muted, two-beat cadence to the night sounds. Déaglán, his senses heightened and his guard up, felt tense. In contrast, Deirdre seemed content to sit quietly, as composed and poised as ever. Déaglán knew he must break the silence first, if only to distract himself from the inevitable thoughts and feelings that her closeness evoked. Although Deirdre sat demurely on her side of the seat away from him, she was still tantalizingly near. Déaglán was acutely aware of her slightest movement, once venturing a glance at her lovely profile, her skin like porcelain in the moonlight. Occasionally, the night breeze caught and gently lifted wispy tendrils of her hair, the faint scent of roses drifting through the air.

"So, I have orders from Fearghus to tell you all I know of Domitian and Agricola," said Déaglán. "You, in turn, will keep me apprised of Agricola's preparations throughout the winter and spring. Somehow, I must relay the particulars of your spying to the chieftains without arousing suspicions as to my omniscience. I must say, I am beginning to wonder why I have risked life and limb all these years when you can so easily acquire what was so hard won for me."

"You are indeed brave," said Deirdre, "though I suspect your spying is not prompted solely from an altruistic desire to help Eire."

Déaglán sensed rather than saw Deirdre's smile, and it irked him somewhat that she should know him so well. He spied because he loved the challenge and relished the deadly game of nerve and wit, never sure when the axe might fall. "Perhaps," he said. "I nevertheless wonder why The Dagda will only now help protect Eire and spy on Agricola. The powers to do so have always been there."

"Only now is the threat dire enough to warrant the risk," Deirdre replied.

Déaglán raised his brow. "Do not be deceived into believing that none suspect the powers of The Dagda."

"I am not, but suspicions are just that. So we will continue to protect our secrets, even from prying, though loyal, spies such as yourself."

As Deirdre spoke, Bran slowed and turned off the village road, heading north on a track that appeared to be little more than a cow path. Déaglán took a firm grip on the reins and checked Bran. "So much for Bran knowing his way to Nuala's. Instead, I believe he intends to graze in this pasture."

"But this *is* the way to Nuala's," Deirdre countered, "though a rather bumpy shortcut. Keelin always uses this route and I have become accustomed to it, even though it rattles my teeth somewhat." Deirdre took hold of the seat's railing with her right hand, anticipating the inevitable jostling of the next mile or so.

"I should have believed my strange little niece," said Déaglán as he softened his hold on Bran, letting the gelding resume his purposeful trot. "Keelin is a wild lass, probably more in commune with animals than people."

Déaglán had always had an appreciative affection for Keelin, seeing something of himself in her. Whenever he visited over the years, she was invariably covered with scrapes and bruises, the result of falling off her horse or out of a tree, always trying to keep up with her bigger, older cousins.

"Keelin has great empathy for all living creatures, man and animal alike. You forget that she is a gifted healer," said Deirdre.

"Nevertheless, she possesses an untamed spirit. I have no doubt she finds her small island home of Eire a gilded cage."

"Are you speaking of Keelin or of yourself?"

Déaglán laughed. "Both of us, though I suspect Keelin is far more impulsive than I have ever been. I cannot imagine her as a priestess of The Dagda, shackled by its laws and formalities."

"Keelin does take frightful risks, courting danger with alarming frequency," said Deirdre, ignoring his reference to The Dagda. She then related their sighting of Bronach, Eirnín's falcon, and Keelin's perilous climb to the top of the sandstone cliffs of Loich's Gap.

"Grand!" said Déaglán.

"I found nothing *grand* about Keelin's boldness at the time. I was sure that at any moment she would slip and fall to her death. And then, when it appeared she would follow Bronach as the falcon flew off . . ." Deirdre shuddered and did not continue.

"You would not have let Keelin fall that day. Your feigned alarm is just that. You forget to whom you speak."

"No, never."

They both were silent for several moments, unspoken thoughts enveloping them. Déaglán broke the spell forcibly. "I will speak with Keelin tomorrow about the clandestine meeting of spy and traitor that day. Was she able to describe the horses the men were riding?"

"As I recall, they were both bays, or perhaps one was bay and the other dark brown."

"Any white markings?"

"I believe so, but you will have to speak with her. Do you . . . know who the traitor might be?" Deirdre's voice faltered slightly.

"No, though I believe there have been others who have spotted him." Déaglán heard Deirdre sigh and asked, "What is troubling you?"

"I don't know. Keelin's fate seems to be irrevocably tied to the battle, whatever the outcome. I have a vague sense of unease, and your mention of the traitor only heightens my troublesome fears."

Déaglán nodded. "The fate of each of us on Eire is tied irrevocably to the battle."

"Yes, of course, how foolish of me. Pay no attention to my fanciful notions."

"I would not fret too much on Keelin's accord. She can take care of herself. Besides, I believe Keelin's immediate fate may lie with young Brian. They are most definitely enamored with each other."

"Yes," Deirdre agreed, her optimism returning, "though I am not sure either of them is quite ready to admit their love for one another,."

"I would not be surprised if Keelin has bewitched poor Brian as you have bewitched me."

"And how would I have managed that?"

"That is for you to tell me. More sorcery to be sure."

"You do Keelin and me a disservice if you believe we must resort to enchantments in matters of love."

Déaglán wanted no more verbal sparring. "Tell me, then, of the night you aided my escape from the Romhanach fortress, conjuring up a violent storm and spiriting me to safety. Did Fearghus order you to do so?"

"I did not conjure up the storm. It came of its own accord, though Fearghus does have an uncanny ability to foresee such things. You must ask him how he divines nature's vicissitudes. As to his order—"

Before Deirdre could continue, Déaglán extended his arm and with no gentleness, grabbed Deirdre around the waist, pulling her tightly against him. "Do not trifle with me, Deirdre. Did you save my life on Fearghus's order alone? Had our bodies never touched, perhaps I could be indifferent to your answer. Now I find it impossible."

Instead of recoiling at Déaglán's rough manner and harsh voice, Deirdre relaxed, leaning against him, melding her body with his. "It was I who went to Fearghus and told him of your peril. I asked for his permission to aid you and he gave it. I would risk all to see you safe, even my vows to The Dagda. You see, I have loved you since the day we met."

Déaglán's grip on Deirdre softened and he kissed the top of her head. He had never felt such peace and overwhelming love, yet Déaglán's elation quickly turned to regret when he foresaw the inevitable heartache for both of them. Even then, he hesitated before saying, "You and I—it is impossible, doomed."

"Why?"

"I am accustomed to being alone, of coming and going as I choose. No woman wishes her rival to be the sea. I tell you now that she will win every time, my lovely Deirdre. I cannot change who I am."

"I would never wish you to be anyone other than who you are. Visit me when you can. That will be enough. And I might occasionally visit you, for as you know, my powers of sorcery are great."

DÉAGLÁN AWOKE THE next morning just before dawn to find himself alone, Deirdre no longer lying next to him. He was disappointed, already missing her. There was something infinitely sweet and reassuringly constant to awake with a beloved woman nestled close. He had forgotten the contentment and intimacy of early morning when the mind is still calm, the body warm and languid with sleep. He wished he could draw Deirdre close and they could speak of nothing and everything, content to simply be in each other's arms.

Just then, Déaglán heard muted sounds coming from the next room and smelled freshly baked bread. His stomach gave a protesting growl and he realized he was hungry, though moments before, food had been the furthest thing from his mind. Reluctantly, Déaglán rose and pulled on his trousers, then walked to the bedroom door, which was slightly ajar, and carefully opened it.

Deirdre stood next to the fireplace, intently stirring something in a large pot hanging over the fire. The shutters on the south side of the room were open, letting in the cool morning air. A glowing lantern sat in the middle of the dining table, the only other light save that from the fireplace. Deirdre had already bathed, her wavy blonde hair still damp, hanging loosely down her back to her waist. Her cheeks were slightly flushed and the skin of her freshly washed face clear, with a healthy and youthful vibrancy. She wore only a loose white shift of a material and weave so fine as to be almost transparent. Standing silhouetted against the light from the fireplace, her small waist, the curve of her hips, and the swell of her breasts were exquisitely outlined. Déaglán felt the muscles of his stomach contract and his pulse quicken as he studied Deirdre, at once demure and erotic, far more alluring than if she had been standing there naked.

"Good morning, my love," greeted Deirdre brightly as she looked up and saw Déaglán. "Breakfast is almost ready and there is just time for you to bathe. You will find the bath water still pleasantly warm."

Déaglán smiled. "I am not hungry for food just now," he said, walking toward her.

Deirdre held up one hand, halting his advance, and gave him a warm smile. "Bathe first. You will feel refreshed and I can finish preparing breakfast."

When Déaglán returned from bathing, indeed feeling refreshed and no less amorous, Deirdre was setting the table.

"Now we will eat. How I love having a man to cook for."

Déaglán walked over to Deirdre and stood just behind her

as she placed a fresh loaf of bread on the table. Brushing aside her hair, he gently kissed her neck, then ran the back of his right hand lightly over the tip of one breast. Encircling her waist, he pulled her against him.

"The meal . . ." Deirdre sighed in feigned protest.

Turning her to face him, Déaglán, his voice husky, murmured, "You know very well the meal can wait."

# CHAPTER TWENTY

*I*T WAS MID-MORNING BY THE TIME DÉAGLÁN reached the village road and reined Bran south toward the warriors' training field. He had been reluctant to leave Deirdre but it was she who urged him to go, telling him Conall had returned and might already be waiting for him. Déaglán did not bother to ask Deirdre how she could possibly know this. She was a sorceress and her secrets were now his. He had not gone far when he saw Brian astride his beautiful bay, Rónán, waiting by the side of the road.

"I'm surprised you are not yet at the field," said Déaglán as he reached Brian.

"I'm waiting for Séamus."

"And where might Séamus be?" Déaglán followed Brian's gaze as he scanned the landscape but saw no one approaching.

Brian turned back to Déaglán. "He is undoubtedly with a lass, though he is rarely late for training. He knows better than to rouse Pádraig's anger."

At that moment, both men were alerted to an approaching rider when Rónán suddenly neighed a loud greeting. The stallion tossed his head and pranced handsomely when a shrill cry came in response. Even at a rather advanced age, Rónán was still in good flesh and his coat shone.

Brian shook his head and patted the horse's sleek neck. "Pay no heed to Rosie, old man. You know she is a big tease with a nasty disposition." Brian took a tighter hold of the reins and he and Déaglán waited as Séamus rode up on a gray mare, long-legged and elegant.

Séamus first greeted Déaglán and then turned to Brian as he reined Rosie alongside Rónán. "I was hoping you would wait for me this morning. I have no wish to face Pádraig's wrath alone." The stallion snorted and tried to greet the mare, who squealed and lunged at him, baring her teeth and just missing the mark as Rónán shied away.

"Curse you, Séamus!" You know better than to bring that bitch of a mare too close to Rónán. Why you tolerate her is beyond me."

"Well, you are in a fine humor this morning," responded Séamus, unfazed. "I love my dear Rosie, even if no one else does. Besides, she runs like the wind and there is none braver over fences. Even you must admit that." As Séamus said this, Rosie pinned her ears flat against her head, swishing her tail and glaring malevolently at Rónán.

"Well, keep her clear," said Brian, somewhat appeased, the edge off his voice. Then, almost as an afterthought, he said, "I suppose there is no need to ask why you are late. What lass are you pursuing this week? Is it still the pretty Sinéad with the big green eyes?"

"No, not Sinéad. All she talked of was marriage and children. It quickly cooled my ardor for her. No, I fancy Maureen, you know, the buxom lass with the rosy cheeks and wild nature."

Déaglán listened to the exchange without comment. The two young men were soon laughing and joking as they rode toward the field. Of course, thought Déaglán, it was difficult for anyone to remain angry with Séamus for long. He was good-natured, optimistic, and thoroughly likable. When he occasionally exhibited a lack of discipline and dedication, Brian was always there to cover for him. In turn, Séamus bore the brunt of Brian's angry outbursts with amazing equanimity. They had been close friends since childhood and their bond of brotherhood was steadfast and enduring.

WHEN THE MEN reached Pádraig's, Brian and Séamus dismounted and hastily led their horses to a barn at the edge of the training field. Déaglán had no sooner halted Bran than a young groom approached him. "Sir, let me care for your horse. The chieftain is waiting for you."

Déaglán nodded and jumped down from the cart. He handed the reins to the groom and approached the field. There, training was in full swing, the shouts of men and the clashing of swords filling the air. The vast field was divided into different sections, each designated for specific disciplines. In the near sections, wrestling and boxing arenas were laid out; the middle sections were focused on fighting with pugil sticks and the weapons of war; and the far sections were reserved for the teaching of horsemanship and the training of war horses. Boys from as young as ten to mature, seasoned warriors trained and fought, sweat and struggled, perfecting their deadly skills. It was an impressive and invigorating sight to behold and never failed to stir Déaglán's more atavistic impulses. He quickly found Conall and Pádraig watching a wrestling match. Standing with them were Seán and Ruaidhrí.

Before Déaglán had reached Conall, the chieftain strode toward him and warmly grasped his hand. "We have much to discuss. Already our newfound unity is showing the cracks of enmity. But first, let us watch this wrestling match. It is grand sport."

Brian and Séamus soon joined the men. Pádraig, seeing who it was, frowned. "You are late," he exclaimed, condemnation in his voice.

Brian immediately stepped forth. "I apologize. The fault is mine."

Séamus gave Brian a sideways glance and then stepped forward. "It was I who caused us to be late, not Brian, though I am sure that does not surprise you."

"No, sadly it does not."

Conall, equally angry but remembering his guests, addressed the two young men by his side. "Seán, Ruaidhrí, I would like you to meet Brian and Séamus, two of our finest young warriors." Then, addressing Brian, he added, "Seán and Ruaidhrí arrived from Tara yesterday and will be accompanying you back to Fionn's training camp. I expect you to make our clan proud."

The young men shook hands, Seán saying, "Ruaidhrí and I have heard grand things about you Brian, and we welcome you into the Fianna."

"Thank you. I am honored."

"Well, then, now that you two have finally graced us with your presence," said Pádraig pointedly, "you had best get started. Séamus, you will box with Ciarán. I have noticed lately that your defensive skills need sharpening. Your superior quickness and foot speed will not save you if you leave yourself unprotected, dropping your hands as you do. Ciarán is sure to cure you of that folly. You will find him working with the young stallions in the far field. Go fetch him and begin at once."

"Yes sir," Séamus said, apprehension briefly showing in his

eyes. Ciarán was one of the finest warriors of the clan and far outweighed Séamus. Ciarán also had the reputation of being a merciless boxer, granting no quarter. It would take all of Séamus's considerable skill to survive this match, but only if he boxed defensively. Déaglán knew Séamus could not win. Déaglán also knew Pádraig meant for Séamus to pay not only for his sloppy defense but also for being late. Pádraig had always been a hard taskmaster, demanding absolute commitment and effort, often pushing his men to the brink of their endurance. Now, with the threat of a Romhanach invasion, it seemed he had redoubled the intensity of the training. War and battles were not for the weak or ill-prepared. Déaglán thought of the carnage that lay ahead for these men and it sickened him.

As Séamus departed in stoic resignation, Pádraig turned to Brian, who, thought Déaglán, was wondering what punishment was to befall him.

"I have heard that Seán is one of the finest wrestlers of the Fianna, having won many matches while attending the chieftains' gathering at Tara. What better opportunity to test your skills, Brian, than to challenge Seán to a bout. If you are agreeable, Seán, we will commence at once. I see the match we were watching has finished."

Both Brian and Seán stripped to the waist, revealing their strong, leanly muscled frames. Although Brian was the taller, Seán had a decided weight advantage. However, Brian had been wrestling all of his life and did not appear intimidated by the older, more seasoned competitor. Déaglán had no doubt the match would be a good one.

The young men shook hands and then stepped back as they waited for Pádraig to signal the start of the match. Their eyes were fixed on one another, their knees bent, elbows almost touching their thighs in a crouching stance, ready to attack. When Pádraig raised his hand, both men shot forward, Seán trying unsuccessfully to snap and control Brian with a front headlock. Within seconds Seán attacked again, locking his arms around Brian's upper body. Brian counterattacked with lightning speed, wrapping one hand around Seán's head and grabbing Seán's leg with the other, simultaneously pulling and twisting. In a flash, Seán was off-balance and down, Brian pinning him.

Ruaidhrí shouted his approval, barely able to restrain himself, eager to join the fray. Pádraig acknowledged the takedown and the bout resumed, this time with Seán more mindful of Brian's quickness and strength. The rest of the long bout was fought to a draw, neither man able to score a clean takedown, though Seán would probably have been judged the victor had Brian not scored the early takedown. When Pádraig finally signaled time and separated the two men, Ruaidhrí rushed over to Brian and grabbed his arm, raising it high in victory and slapping Brian on the back, nearly knocking him over. Seán, his lungs heaving, offered Brian his hand and the younger man grasped it appreciatively. Ruaidhrí was now vigorously slapping both their backs.

Seán staggered and coughed, then said, "Ruaidhrí, I have just endured much abuse, I do not care for more. I have no doubt Brian feels the same."

"'Tis a grand day for sure," shouted Ruaidhrí, oblivious to his strength and beside himself with glee. "Though I am fond of you, Seán, I must say it pleases me exceedingly for young Brian here to have bested you. I have hoped that someone would avenge my sorry loss to you at Tara."

"I had a horse to help me that time," responded Seán, laughing along with Ruaidhrí. When Brian gave a quizzical look, Seán said, "It is a long story and best told after we get cleaned up. Right now congratulations are in order. I misjudged your strength and speed and paid the price. You have great skill. I commend you."

IT WAS LATE afternoon when the war games and training ceased and the field was at last empty of its society of men, the rough and hardened warriors of Eire. Conall and Déaglán had departed much earlier and Pádraig was discussing the day's training with his ranking officers. Brian, Seán and Ruaidhrí had saddled their horses and were about to set off for the village pub. From the far end of the field they heard Séamus shout out to them. They waited and he galloped up on Rosie, a big smile on his face. Séamus's left eye was swollen nearly shut, with a nasty cut above his eyebrow, clear evidence of Ciarán's handiwork.

Seemingly unfazed by his appearance, Séamus proclaimed, "Finally, this taxing day has ended! You must all join my family for dinner tonight. In truth, my mother would never forgive me if I should appear without you, grand Fianna!"

"You only hope we will protect you from your mother's tongue lashing when she sees you in such a sorry state," said Brian.

"You should see Ciarán . . . not a mark on him. Very discouraging. At least he did not kill me. Think how the warmhearted Maureen would have mourned. Seeing me thus, she will undoubtedly want to shower me with tender loving care, something I am very amenable to."

"Is Maureen your betrothed?" questioned Ruaidhrí as the young men rode away from the training field.

Séamus looked aghast. "No, nothing so immutable as that!"

Brian laughed at his friend's dismay. "Maureen is just one

of Séamus's many conquests. He pursues all the lasses for miles around. Pretty ones, plain ones, it seems to matter little to Séamus. It is the variety that pleases him."

"True, true," said Séamus.

"One at a time is more than enough for me," said Ruaidhrí.

"Speaking of lasses," commented Seán, his gaze fixed on an approaching wagon, "If my eyes do not deceive me, an unbelievably beautiful one is headed our way."

Brian looked down the road and nodded. "Yes, that would be Brigid."

"Yes," seconded Séamus, "the exquisite Brigid."

Brigid drew her wagon to a halt when she reached the young men, favoring them with her most dazzling smile. "Well, I always know that if I want to see the handsomest men for miles around, I have only to visit Pádraig's. Though, perhaps, I should not even speak to you, Brian. You failed to show up for dinner last night."

"Did you not get my message? I sent a word of regret with your brother," said Brian.

"Yes, I received the message, but I should have preferred that you deliver it personally," Brigid said with pique. "But let us not be impolite. Please introduce your companions to me." Brigid's gaze quickly passed over Ruaidhrí and settled on Seán.

"Of course. Brigid, please meet Seán and Ruaidhrí, warriors of the Fianna. They have traveled from Tara, arriving yesterday." Then, with a flourish, his arm sweeping toward Brigid, Brian bowed in the saddle. "And this is Brigid, one of the loveliest women in all Eire."

Both young men greeted Brigid, Seán following Brian's lead, chivalrously bowing. "I am delighted to make your acquaintance, fair Brigid." Ruaidhrí merely nodded in greeting and remained oddly silent.

"Thank you, sir," responded Brigid, her eyes lowered in feigned modesty. "Had I known, Brian, that you had such important visitors, I would have insisted you all join my family for dinner. However, Pádraig will be our guest tonight. You know how Mother adores him, and, to my dismay, insists on playing the matchmaker." Brigid frowned ever so slightly, but she had purred Pádraig's name. She then turned to Ruaidhrí and Seán and asked, "Is it true all warriors of the Fianna are from illustrious families, destined to someday become chieftains? Or is this just hearsay?"

Ruaidhrí scoffed. "I would hardly call the son of a blacksmith illustrious, though I am a proud warrior of the Fianna, giving my allegiance to the mightiest chieftain who ever lived, the great Fionn. Seán, here, comes from finer stock."

Seán smiled somewhat ruefully. "I am but the younger son of the chieftain Murchadh, my older brother being the heir apparent. However, I can imagine no better life than that of a Fian."

"'Tis a grand life to be sure," agreed Ruaidhrí. "We fight and feast, never staying in one place for very long, our musicians and poets traveling with us."

"So as to chronicle your heroic deeds, I suppose," said Brigid dismissively. She turned to Brian. "I see no reason why you, Brian, should join the ranks of the Fianna. Your home and lands are here. Your duty is here—with your people. Furthermore, I have heard many say the Romhanach will not invade. It would seem wise for you to wait until the Romhanach land, if indeed they do. All this training and talk of war is excessive."

"I should fear for that slender white neck of yours, lass, if we wait until the Romhanach land on our shores," declared Ruaidhrí, his eyes hard.

Brigid bristled. "I have no fear for my life or my honor with the warriors of *my* clan to protect and defend me."

"It may very well be that the Romhanach do not invade. Still, we must prepare now," said Seán. "But know this, lovely Brigid: you need have no fear for we, the Fianna, will also protect your life and honor—to the death."

Brigid graced Seán with her most beautiful smile, her deep blue eyes sparkling. "I have no doubt you will, brave sir. Perhaps I will see you at the marketplace tomorrow?"

"Nothing would give me greater pleasure," said Seán.

Brigid smiled and idly brushed a lock of her golden hair away from her face and neck. Without another word, she flicked the reins on her horse's rump and continued on her way.

THE YOUNG MEN had ridden some distance when Seán remarked, "What a beauty is Brigid! She has the presence of a queen even as she sits in a farmer's wagon. I am surprised you have not claimed her for your own, Brian."

Brian shook his head. "I am afraid Brigid is more enamored with my lands than with me. It is not love or lust that prompts her affections but ambition. I grant you that Brigid is enticingly, maddeningly alluring, but she is also miserly with her favors. Still, she will find no willing dupe in me. I have no plans to marry her."

Ruaidhrí barked a loud laugh, then he gave Brian a hearty pat on the back. "I am liking you more and more, young Brian. That Brigid is a crafty and covetous wench, for all her beauty. She reminds me of a beautiful mare my father owned when I was young. Wicked, Síle was, terrorizing all the other mares of the herd—"

"I will not listen to you compare Brigid to a horse, however lovely the mare may have been," interrupted Seán. "And there is nothing wrong with ambition. I admire Brigid for that. She will seize what she wants in life."

"I have no doubt she will, trampling over those in her way. I should stay clear of that one if I were you," said Ruaidhrí to his friend.

Seán laughed. "You will learn that Ruaidhrí is forever comparing the lasses he has known or bedded to animals, usually a favored horse or dog, though in one case he compared a poor girl we met on our journey to a pig!"

Ruaidhrí's blue eyes twinkled. "Well, you must admit she was rather stout—with a singularly peculiar nose. But I meant no real disrespect. I prefer big women. Look at me, what would I be doing with a dainty, delicate lass? If only I could find a big, strong girl with a sweet and loving disposition, I would marry her tomorrow." Ruaidhrí smiled wistfully, an almost benign look on his face. Within an instant, however, his face turned hard. "Though perhaps not. First we have some killing to do and a battle to win."

"Describing how he plans to slay the Romhanach, in particularly gruesome detail, is another of Ruaidhrí's favorite subjects, I might add," remarked Seán.

"A man after my own heart," said Brian.

# CHAPTER TWENTY-ONE

EELIN LOVED THE MONTHLY GATHERING OF farmers, shopkeepers, and merchants held at the northern end of their village. The marketplace was bustling, noisy, and always crowded, drawing people from the far reaches of the clan's land and beyond to barter and sell their goods. Farmers brought in their produce and livestock, merchants peddled household wares, clothing, and healing ointments and tonics. Women brought their laces and embroidery to sell and display, often stitching their intricate work at the marketplace itself. The itinerant tinkers were never without horses for sale, some being fine animals, others merely sad, broken-down nags.

Tables and booths lined both sides of the main street and the livestock were corralled in a grassy field bordering the village. Food was everywhere, the smells of fresh breads and savory stews mixing with the powerful odors from the pigs, sheep, and cattle. Farmers discussed the weather and their crop yields, and tinkers and horsemen had heated disputes over the quality and age of the horseflesh. Women carefully inspected the goods and produce for sale, strolling from one booth to the next with their youngest children in tow. The older children gathered in front of the street jugglers and musicians or played games of tag in and around the village. Old men sat drinking ale and talking of

bygone days, their stories and feats of bravery increasingly em-
bellished with their imbibing of spirits. Others sat playing chess,
balancing boards between them on their knees. Their wives sat
nearby, gossiping and knitting, some selling their beautiful
woolens. One old woman, still with an ear for a lively tune, was
dancing to a jig played by the musicians, her bony fingers holding up the hem of her dress, her step still amazingly nimble.

Keelin knew that her village market did not compare to the
annual fair of Tailltenn that drew people from all of Eire, not
only to buy and sell goods but to participate in contests of physical prowess and endurance. The Tailltenn games included sports
of every description, from boxing, wrestling, and running to
swimming, archery, and horse racing. Keelin had visited Tailltenn once with her parents years ago and was entranced, caught
up in the excitement and energy of the fair. However, she still
loved the far less grand but happily familiar liveliness of her
clan's marketplace. Since she was young, she had frequented the
monthly gathering with her mother. When Keelin began studying the art of healing, Nuala accompanied her, teaching Keelin
to identify all of the exotic herbs and dried plants the traveling
merchants were peddling and to differentiate those with medicinal qualities. Now, Keelin often visited the market alone, enjoying
a pleasant reprieve from the drudgery of studying and Nuala's
teachings of restraint and duty. Keelin always found things to
delight in: sometimes a rare healing herb or flower, other times
parchments or fresh fruit and vegetables. Occasionally, she pur-
chased more than was necessary for Nuala's apothecary, pleased
at the prospect of annoying the priestess.

Today, Keelin made what for her was an unusual purchase.
When visiting the booth of one of the traveling peddlers, Keelin
noticed a silk shawl woven with threads of royal blue and teal.

The pattern of the weave made Keelin think of the waves in her dreams and the silk was of the finest quality, soft to the touch and exquisitely woven. Even as Keelin inspected the dried herbs and flowers also on display, her gaze kept returning to the beautiful shawl.

The old peddler noticed Keelin eyeing the shawl and picked it up, gently placing it around her shoulders. "The colors suit you to perfection with those glorious eyes of yours. Feel the fine silk. There is none to compare with it."

The peddler then looked round nervously and stepped back, a small muscle below his left eye twitching spasmodically.

"Have no fear, the high priestess is not with me today," said Keelin, knowing the peddler found Nuala unsettling. No doubt because she always knew when he made false claims about his merchandise.

The peddler relaxed and smiled, showing his yellow, crooked teeth. "And will you buy the shawl, lass? None other than you would do it justice."

Keelin ran her hand lightly over the fabric. "Yes, I will. It is indeed lovely."

With the beautiful shawl resting lightly around her shoulders and a basket in hand, Keelin strolled through the marketplace feeling decidedly happy. She was enjoying her freedom, knowing it would not last much longer. Samhain was drawing near and the festival would mark her entry to The Dagda, however transitory. She was resigned to taking her novitiate vows and doing her part to defeat the Romhanach. In truth, she was excited at the prospect of using her powers of the mind against Eire's enemy. Moreover, she could not deny the pull of the Otherworld. It promised an escape from the confining boundaries of Eire. In her more fanciful moments, Keelin imagined Otherworld adventures with Brian and Séamus. However, the mere thought of Brian now sobered her. She had not seen him since the night they had danced together, and her father said Brian was leaving tomorrow to train with the Fianna at Tara.

Keelin was inspecting some dried herbs when she looked up and spotted Brian across the marketplace. He was standing with two unfamiliar young men, one of them partially blocked from her view. Her pulse quickened and she tightened her grip around the basket handle. Brian looked handsome and relaxed, obviously enjoying himself. She dragged her eyes from him and turned her attention to the young men. One was large and bulky—though not in the least fat, an intimidating presence. He laughed rowdily, gesturing to Brian and the other man, who was leaning against a post with his feet crossed in front of him, only his profile visible. She was so busy scrutinizing the big red-headed man that she failed to notice when the other stranger turned and stared straight at her. His gaze staggered her, for he was quite possibly the most handsome, perfect-looking man she had ever seen. Embarrassed, she dropped her eyes. However, she quickly recovered and shot a defiant glance toward him before turning her attention pointedly to the herbs she had been examining.

When Keelin looked up again, the young men were walking toward her. She watched as they made their way through the throng of people, imagining a cowardly escape. She had admittedly avoided Brian since the night they had danced, as he had seemingly avoided her. She feared the depth of her feelings for Brian. Even more, she feared he did not share those feelings. Why else would he avoid her? Curse him, she thought, angrily, her temper rising. *I can make my way very well without him.* She stood resolutely, waiting for Brian and the young men to reach her.

"Keelin, my friends wish most earnestly to make your acquaintance," said Brian. "Seán, Ruaidhrí, this is Keelin, a healer of renown and the daughter of our chieftain, Conall."

"I spied you across the marketplace and was captivated, fair Keelin," said Seán, bowing.

"Pleased to meet you, lass," said Ruaidhrí. "I am indebted to your teacher, the priestess Nuala, who came to my aid at Tara."

Nodding a greeting to both men and enjoying Seán's gallantry, however disingenuous, Keelin looked more closely at the two Fianna. Seán was even more handsome than he appeared at a distance, and his eyes were not blue as she expected but green, with flecks of amber. Ruaidhrí was indeed a giant of a man and she wondered how Nuala had come to his aid. Then she remembered. Addressing him she asked, "Are you the warrior who sustained a blow to the head?"

"The very same warrior, I must admit," said Ruaidhrí rather ruefully. "Seán, here, bested me in a contest of pugil sticks."

"It was a grand battle," said Seán.

"The outcome would be different should we fight again," said Ruaidhrí.

Seán shrugged. "Perhaps."

Keelin could not disagree with Ruaidhrí. There was something menacing about the bigger man that gave Keelin pause. "Well, I wish to witness the next contest if ever it comes to pass," said Keelin.

"You are interested in such things?" questioned Seán.

Keelin heard both surprise and skepticism in Seán's tone and she bristled slightly.

Brian nodded. "Keelin is a bloodthirsty lass, for all that she is a practiced healer. When we were young, Eirnín had his sons and me box and wrestle, long before we started training with Pádraig. It was all Eirnín could do to keep Keelin from jumping into the fray. As it was, she would stand on the sidelines and shadow box, yelling both words of encouragement and taunts to the contestants. I might add that the taunts were usually directed at me."

Keelin frowned slightly and then laughed, conceding the truth of Brian's words.

"I do enjoy such matches. I have never been a very good spectator. Instead, I wish to be part of a good fight. Uncle Eirnín always let me join in on all other competitions of agility and strength, although Aunt Meghan frowned on it all, saying that it was 'frightful, shocking, to allow such a young lass and poor Saraid's only child, to join the lads in such rough and tumble sports! Truly shocking!'" Keelin had placed her hands on her hips, mimicking Aunt Meghan perfectly.

Both Brian and Seán laughed heartily, but Ruaidhrí had not been listening and was instead staring across the marketplace where a group of men stood.

"Who do you see?" asked Brian as they all followed Ruaidhrí's gaze.

"A man I thought I saw at Tara several times," said Ruaidhrí. "I believe he belongs to one of the midland clans."

"Why would he be here?" asked Seán. "Let us go question him."

"No, I was wrong. He is not the same man, though very similar in stature and carriage to the other at Tara. Besides, he has already departed and I see no reason to search for him," said Ruaidhrí, dismissing his friend's suggestion. "Instead, I wish to find Moira." Looking down at Keelin, he said, "Do you know where your cousin might be selling her cheeses? I promised her I would come visit."

Keelin had been about to question Ruaidhrí about the stranger, a prickly sensation running along her spine. At his mention of Moira, however, the stranger vanished from her thoughts. Moira was Uncle Eirnín and Aunt Meagan's oldest daughter and looked like her mother. But the similarity ended there, the girl being sweet, shy, and obliging. Keelin had shamelessly bossed Moira around when they were little, even though her cousin was two years her senior. Of late, Keelin had come to respect the unassuming Moira. Now it seemed the intimidating Ruaidhrí had taken a fancy to her.

"Moira's booth is at the other end of the marketplace," said Keelin. "I would be happy to show you, but first there are several booths I must visit—"

"Do not be bothering yourself, Keelin," responded Ruaidhrí. "No doubt I will find her with little trouble." With a nod to Keelin, he turned and left them, striding purposefully away.

"Last night it was clear Ruaidhrí was enchanted by both Moira and the wonderful meal she prepared," said Seán. "I only hope his intentions are honorable, for I have no doubt her fierce mother would gladly cut out his heart while he sleeps if they are not." Seán smiled, his eyes twinkling, but Keelin could hear the concern in his voice. She turned to Brian, her eyes questioning.

"Ruaidhrí seems genuinely taken with Moira. But do not worry too much about your cousin. I believe she possesses the iron will of her mother without the fearful temper. Moira is well able to take care of herself."

"Yes, I believe she is," said Keelin, smiling up at Brian. He smiled back and seemed about to say something before thinking better of it.

"Well, I for one much prefer your company, Keelin, to that of the besotted Ruaidhrí," said Seán, bowing with a flourish and offering Keelin his arm. "Let Brian and me escort you through the marketplace."

Keelin nodded and, shifting the basket to her left hand, took Seán's offered arm. Brian stepped around to her other side and the three set off.

KEELIN ENJOYED STROLLING from booth to booth flanked by Seán and Brian. The two young men were quick-witted and their conversation was amusing. Keelin joined in occasionally but for the most part simply savored these carefree moments. She was surprised how easy it was to show only friendly affection for Brian. She caught him studying her once but he had quickly looked away, his veiled eyes telling her nothing of his thoughts.

The three had not yet reached Moira's booth when Brigid approached them. Keelin noticed that both Brian and Seán watched her expectantly, and in spite of her best intentions, she felt her combative instincts surface. She quite unconsciously dropped her hand from Seán's arm. The joy of the afternoon vanished in an instant and she dreaded the thought of politely tolerating Brigid's presence.

Seán was the first to speak as Brigid reached them. "What a pleasure it is to see you again so soon, Brigid. We are on our way to Moira's booth. Would you care to join us?"

"I can think of nothing that would please me more." Brigid

smiled at both young men and, stepping between Keelin and Brian, possessively took his arm.

Brigid turned to Seán and said, "You undoubtedly met Moira last night and sampled her superb cooking. The cheeses she sells at the market are delicious, though I am afraid she consumes far too much of her own merchandise. She is looking more like her mother with each passing day and it worries me so." Brigid sighed, her lovely brow etched with concern. "Moira is such a dear, sweet girl, but far too shy and timid, finding comfort only in food. It breaks my heart to think of her alone, but I am afraid that might very well happen."

"I would not worry any further about Moira," Seán assured Brigid, "for my friend Ruaidhrí is determined to keep her company."

"Is that so? How *perfectly* wonderful." Dismissing the topic of Moira and Ruaidhrí with the toss of her long blonde hair, Brigid gazed up at Brian and squeezed his arm. With conspiratorial delight, she proclaimed, "You will never guess my exciting news! Mother's people have invited us to Tara for Samhain. Pádraig was kind enough to offer mother and me escort when he heard of our proposed journey. In fact, Pádraig was especially eager to do so now that my brother Cillian will be riding his young stallion in the horse race there." She then acknowledged Keelin's presence for the first time. "What a pity, you will miss the celebration at Tara. Pádraig has told me that all of the Fianna warriors will be there this year, including our handsome companions." Brigid squeezed Brian's arm again while casting an alluring eye at Seán.

"But I will be traveling to Tara," Keelin said, enjoying the effect her words had on Brigid.

"Whoever will you be journeying with? I understood your

father is to remain here, readying our warriors for the *supposed* invasion." Brigid did not try to hide her annoyance at such a thought.

"I am to accompany the priestesses Nuala and Deirdre," said Keelin. "We will leave in a week."

"For what purpose?" questioned Brian sharply, his abruptness startling both Keelin and Brigid.

"I am to participate in Samhain's ordination ceremony and will be recognized as a novice of The Dagda."

"You are too young to be a novice. One must be eighteen and you just turned seventeen." Brian looked down at Keelin, disbelieving.

"The threat of invasion has prompted even The Dagda to ease their strict rules. I am needed, my . . . gifts being useful." Keelin glanced at Brian, but he was now staring straight ahead and made no response. She wished she had kept silent.

"Well, it seems I am in exalted company today—*dear little* Keelin nearly a priestess and two brave Fianna warriors." Brigid sighed and then her expression brightened. "Here we are at Moira's booth. It appears she still has some of her cheeses left."

Keelin took their arrival at the booth as an opportunity to take her leave. After greeting Moira, she said, "I must go now. I have patients to visit at outlying farms."

With uncharacteristic boldness, Moira urged, "Please stay, Keelin. And you must come for dinner tonight. Mother has been asking after you and wondering why you have not visited in so long."

"Please send your mother my regrets and tell her I will see her soon. Now I really must be off." Keelin turned and hurried toward the animal pens where her horse and cart waited. She paid no attention to several greetings along the way, intent only on escaping the marketplace. She had been very close to losing her temper and wreaking havoc on Brigid's mind with her *starling* powers. She imagined the most fearful and delightful mind torments to inflict and could not help smiling to herself rather malevolently. Reaching Bran, she patted him on the neck, gave him a carrot, and quickly hitched him to the cart. She was heading out of town, her anger simmering, when she heard a horse approaching from behind. Turning, she saw Brian cantering Rónán toward her. She halted Bran and loosened her grip on the reins.

When Brian reached her, she said, "Did you not wish to stay with the lovely Brigid? Such a *kind* heart she has."

Brian cursed and shook his head. Keelin could feel her hackles rise and sat up in the cart a little straighter.

"Did you think I would not challenge your asinine decision more vehemently? You are a fool, Keelin. You are no more suited a priestess than I a farmer. It will be torture for you."

"Do not presume to know what I am or am not suited for," retorted Keelin, picking up the reins in preparation to depart. "And, though it is none of your concern, I have no intention of becoming a priestess like Nuala."

"But what of your gift as a healer? Is that not your passion to the exclusion of all else?" Brian's voice was rough with emotion. "Long ago, Eirnín told me to protect you because the gods had singled you out for a higher purpose. I have tried. When we were young it was easy. Now . . . it is not."

"And what of Brigid and all the other lasses you court?" Keelin asked, unwilling to concede his selflessness. "I am a healer but I am also a woman, and seeing you kiss the detestable Brigid is not easy for me."

Brian looked at her hard, his scrutiny intense, but she glared right back. After several seconds, he abruptly smiled, his eyes at once friendly. "Well then, I will see you at Tara?"

"I will be busy and have no time for the likes of you," said Keelin, still angry.

Brian chuckled and reined his horse back around. "Nonetheless, I will see you there, lass."

IT WAS DUSK and dark shadows hid the rider from view, his horse standing amongst a stand of trees just off the main road. The man heard something behind him and turned quickly toward the sound but could see nothing. Impatient and tense, he rolled his shoulders and neck, trying to ease the tightness of his muscles. Then, almost as a ghost, another rider was beside him.

"You would do well not to surprise me like that again." He spoke cordially enough but the threat was evident.

"Your advice is taken," said the second man.

"You sneak around in the dark but foolishly showed yourself in the marketplace today. Are you mad or just simple?"

"You know I am neither. The marketplace held no danger. Strangers from parts near and far were present. I was but one more. Now tell me what more you have learned about Fionn's plans for the defense of Eire. I have no doubt Agricola is impatiently awaiting my dispatch."

# CHAPTER TWENTY-TWO

EELIN WAS HOVERING AT THE EDGE OF SLEEP and consciousness. The drone of discordant chanting at first stole into her dream and then jarred her awake. She opened her eyes to darkness and cursed under her breath as she listened to the familiar prayer recitations of Saoirse, a particularly devout novitiate who seemed to pray endlessly.

"Cease your incessant praying and let me sleep!" hissed Keelin. Her eyes swept the darkness and she could detect no movement. All the other novitiates are sound asleep, she thought with disgust. Saoirse's praying actually soothed them, such was their unwavering devotion. Keelin shuddered, thinking of what life would be like with these dreary souls.

When Saoirse paid her no heed, Keelin spoke soundlessly. "*The gods are not pleased.*"

Saoirse stopped abruptly, startled by a voice she did not recognize. She then started up again with increased fervor. Keelin could only imagine the girl believed the gods were scolding her lack of enthusiasm.

Now fully awake, Keelin got up, threw a woolen shawl round her shoulders, and crept outside. Patches of ground fog scattered the campsite and thick clouds hovered overhead. She could see the dark shapes of priests and priestesses already moving about and several campfires were being set. No one seemed to notice her as she left the camp and headed toward the hill of Tara.

Keelin had been at Tara for more than a week and could feel herself being drawn inexorably into the web of The Dagda. Since the moment she arrived, the tomb of passage had beckoned her, alluringly mystical and promising. This morning in the dark, she walked with sure steps toward the sacred site atop the hill, never faltering or losing her way. The tomb granted the souls of the dead passage to their new lives and Keelin sensed it held the key to her fate. She also felt tantalizingly close to the Otherworld when near the tomb. Deirdre had told her that to enter the Otherworld, the soul must transcend the body. It was necessary to clear the mind of everything but its spiritual essence. Only then could the body's substance fade, allowing the soul to move freely from one world to the next. Keelin, not being particularly spiritual, thought such a feat would be impossible for her. Yet standing at the tomb's entrance, she could almost feel her soul reach out for the Otherworld. In those moments she felt disembodied, more a specter than a flesh and bones woman.

On this morning, Keelin was determined to enter the Otherworld, regardless of any Dagda law forbidding it. Several times during the past week, she had come very close and felt cold, lifeless air hit her face for but an instant. Then the veil between the worlds closed, shutting her out. Now, as Keelin approached the tomb, she closed her eyes and kept walking. She stopped just short of its entrance and stood absolutely still. Instead of forcibly ridding her mind of all thought she relaxed, and slowly her dreams, worries, and desires melted away. She felt the Otherworld's cold air touch her and still she kept her eyes shut. Finally, she opened them and found herself floating not far above the tomb. Cloaking the entire hill of Tara were clouds, limiting the view to only her immediate surroundings. Keelin did not care. An intense feeling of triumph swept over her. The next moment she found herself sitting on the damp grass out-side the tomb.

"The Otherworld is not to be conquered but respected."

Keelin looked up and saw Nuala standing there, looking like a malevolent wraith. Surprisingly, though, the priestess's tone of voice had not been entirely censorious, and she held out a hand to help Keelin to her feet.

"All week the tomb has called to me . . ." Keelin's voice trailed off. When Nuala did not respond, Keelin said, "I entered the Otherworld and do not regret it." Then, with vehemence, she added, "I broke no law."

The priestess sighed and shook her head. "No, you broke no law. The gods have granted you great power, though I am at a loss to understand why. You have yet to demonstrate the wisdom that such power demands."

"I did not wish for any of this."

"Indeed you did not. Yet the Otherworld welcomes you. You have managed to enter its realm without benefit of The Dagda's blessings or cloak, without even taking your novitiate vows. There has been only one other with such powers."

"The priest who could travel freely back and forth in time? The priest you spoke of outside Danu's cave?"

"Yes."

"Please tell me about him."

Nuala did not respond. Instead, the priestess turned and said, "Deirdre, you have finally arrived. I thought perhaps you had forgotten."

Deirdre wore her Dagda cloak and looked resplendent, even in the dim light of dawn. She regarded Nuala and Keelin, then smiled. "So you invited Keelin after all. I am glad you agreed she should take part in our planning."

"I did not invite Keelin," responded Nuala. "Instead, I found her here, just as the Otherworld expelled her."

"You are truly gifted!" proclaimed Deirdre. She hugged Keelin and whispered in her ear, "Pay no heed to Nuala's displeasure."

"I see no purpose for your whispering," Nuala commented. "I can hear everything in your mind."

"Yes, I know," said Deirdre, looking unwaveringly at Nuala.

"Well, we will talk later, after Keelin has taken her vows. Perhaps it is wise to include her in our plans for the Romhanach." Nuala looked once more at Keelin and then turned away. Her tall figure was soon lost in the mist.

"Now I may ask you, Keelin," said Deirdre, "what were you doing here before dawn? I know quite well you are not an early riser."

"I would still be happily asleep were it not for Saoirse and her praying. I cannot abide the novitiates and have absolutely nothing in common with them."

"They are a decidedly gloomy lot, to be sure."

"Sometimes I wonder what the gods were thinking when they gave me such powers," said Keelin, "why they made me so very different. This is not how I imagined my life. Yet now I believe my powers may allow me to live a better one."

"And how did you imagine your life?"

Keelin smiled, remembering. "When we were young, Brian, Séamus, and I used to dream up the most wonderful, exciting adventures in faraway lands. Well, perhaps just Brian and I. Séamus has always been happy with his life on Eire. Still, he was determined to accompany Brian on all of our adventures."

"So your dreams always included Brian?"

"Not always," replied Keelin. "Yet, we understand each other. He is a restless soul . . . as am I." Keelin paused, pondering her future. "Perhaps the gods bestowed upon me these powers so that I might determine my own destiny, whether as a priestess of The Dagda or not."

"Well, everything should become clearer at the ordination ceremony tomorrow. The Stone of Fáil may enlighten you. What has Nuala told you about the ordination?"

"She detailed the order of events, how and when I will take my oath. She also told me that Fearghus will bless my cloak, giving it powers to aid my travel to and from the Otherworld. I know nothing of the Stone, except that I must place my right hand on it while I say my vows. What has Nuala not told me?"

Deirdre eyed Keelin intently. "When you place your hand on the Stone, you will not only pledge your loyalty to The Dagda but you will also be given a glimpse into your future, for the Stone has the gift of foresight. Usually, this portent is visual, though it can be manifested in other ways, such as a spoken message or even as a powerful premonition. For some, the portent is maddeningly vague or seemingly insignificant, and years may pass before its importance is revealed or understood. For most, however, the portent already has profound significance."

Keelin was not sure she liked the idea of seeing into her future. She felt a vague disquiet and laughed nervously. "As long as my future does not include the solemn Saoirse reciting verse, I will be immensely happy."

THE PROCESSIONAL AVENUE leading to the sacred tomb of passage on the hill of Tara was lined three deep with the priests and priestesses of The Dagda. Those standing along the outermost and elevated perimeter of the avenue held flickering candles, the only illumination against the darkening skies of dusk. Even in the fading light, the beautiful Dagda cloaks worn by all created a phantasmal mosaic of rich, vibrant colors. The strong voices of the priests resounded in the open air, singing recitations of honor to the gods. As the priests sang the final notes of their stanzas, the priestesses would answer, celebrating the power of the land and its endless cycle of life, death, and rebirth. With the end of each recitation and response, the singers would join in a refrain, their voices accompanied by the haunting chords of a hundred harps.

Keelin stood at the far end of the processional with the other young men and women who would be ordained this evening. She was already feeling uncomfortable and apprehensive, shifting from leg to leg, wondering when this interminable ceremony would end. Granted, the voices of the priests and priestesses were beautiful, but they sang in the ancient tongue of The Dagda and the music had none of the lilting, melodic beauty that Keelin loved. Had she been taller, she could have studied the many faces of the priests and priestesses. As it was, she saw only the faces of those closest to her, and those solemn individuals were singularly uninteresting.

After what seemed like three lifetimes, the novitiates were summoned to the processional avenue and formed a single-file line leading toward the high priest Fearghus and the Stone of Fáil. Keelin walked slowly up the avenue, seeing nothing but the cloak of Saoirse, who stood in front of her. She was nonetheless stirred by the sound of Fearghus's deep voice as he blessed the novices and their cloaks. It was not until she stood at the front of the line, watching Saoirse recite her vows, that Keelin actually got a good look at the high priest. She was awed.

Fearghus looked magnificent in his Dagda cloak of rich burgundy. Down the middle of the cloak ran a dazzling lightning bolt of fine gems, with a golden sun glowing from the left and a silver moon and stars shining from the right. On the third finger of his left hand was a magnificent ruby ring, its thick gold band etched with intertwining scrolls. Fearghus himself was imposing, exuding power and knowledge, and embodying both the mysticism and wisdom of The Dagda.

Keelin was nervous and wanted to bolt like a frightened rabbit. Instead, she stood waiting. Shortly thereafter, all was quiet and she looked up into the clear blue eyes of the high priest. All her fears vanished in an instant as she felt the warmth of his soul. Keelin stepped forward and firmly placed her hand on the Stone of Fáil and began reciting her vows. When the vision came, portending her future, Keelin's eyes widened in surprise. It was as unexpected as it was familiar.

# CHAPTER TWENTY-THREE

EIRDRE'S DEFT FINGERS DRESSED KEELIN'S THICK hair, pulling it away from the girl's forehead and temples. The priestess then braided the upswept locks, weaving in sprigs of evergreen and silver ribbon. Finally, she wound the plait into a bun at the back of Keelin's head. Masses of glossy, auburn hair still tumbled down Keelin's back and spread like a veil to her waist.

Keelin sat impatiently as Deirdre fussed over her, knowing all of her friend's efforts would make little difference. Keelin knew she would never be beautiful, even pretty for that matter. Her eyes were too big, her jaw too square, and her irregular features defied all measures of traditional beauty. She now heartily regretted allowing Deirdre to dress her for tonight's festivities at Tara. The priestess had been twittering for days about the beautiful gown she had sewn for Keelin, saying repeatedly, "It will enhance your beautiful eyes and your otherworldly allure!"

Keelin had been drawn into Deirdre's excitement, wondering whether she could indeed be transformed. But with her backside slowly going numb, reality was now intruding and she wished she were anywhere but sitting there as Deirdre tried to work miracles. Just as Keelin's patience was at its limit, Nuala entered the cottage. She looked splendid in her Dagda cloak and carried a satchel filled with essences for the night's ceremony.

"I see neither of you is ready to walk with me to the hill of Tlachtga. While I have been preparing for Samhain and the lighting of the first fire of the New Year, the two of you have been engaging in foolishness." Nuala looked with displeasure at both young women, and at Deirdre in particular. But the young priestess only smiled, a mischievous twinkle in her eyes.

"Walking to Tlachtga will take hours. Why would you consider such toil when the Otherworld is readily available?"

"A holy task is at hand. Walking is not toil but a respite from the disquiet of life. It cleanses the soul. I can meditate and prepare for the coming year. The two of you would be wise to do the same. When will you join me?" Nuala started to open the cottage door.

"As soon as I have finished readying Keelin for this evening," said Deirdre. "As for Keelin, she will not attend the ceremony at Tlachtga."

At Deirdre's last words Nuala stopped, her hand still on the latch of the door. She looked sharply at Deirdre, ignoring Keelin.

Keelin stood and faced Nuala. "As only a novice I cannot take part in the lighting of the fire at Tlachtga, and I wish to join in the festivities here at Tara."

Keelin was expecting Nuala's censure. Instead, after an appraising look, the high priestess said, "Well, I suppose it is not necessary for you to attend. You conducted yourself quite admirably at the ordination ceremony yesterday. Enjoy the evening. You will have little rest in the months to come." Without a backward glance, Nuala stepped outside and closed the door behind her.

Keelin watched Nuala leave then distractedly sat back down

in the chair, remembering her ordination and the Stone of Fáil vision. Addressing Deirdre, she said, "Can you tell me about the priest who had the power to readily travel back and forth in time? The priest Nuala mentioned that day outside Danu's cave. She will tell me nothing."

Deirdre hesitated, then pulled up a chair and sat facing Keelin. "Aidan was a powerful priest and admired by everyone. He was also Nuala's great uncle. I am told the two were very close when she was a young girl. He did not think her odd and unsettling, as did most of the villagers—and even her own parents. Nuala adored him and, in turn, he protected her and helped her develop her extraordinary gifts, even though she was but a child. Of course, I know nothing of this firsthand. Fearghus has told me most of what I know about Aidan. When Nuala was only eight years old, he disappeared for nearly a year. For some months before his disappearance, he had been traveling within the Otherworld, briefly visiting a future life. Almost no one knew then of the ease with which he traveled back and forth in time. Little Nuala was likely one of his only confidants. When he returned from his year-long absence he was different, more secretive, even with Nuala. Whispering and speculation soon began within The Dagda, especially after he disappeared several more times over the next few years, often gone for weeks at a time. The last time he disappeared he never returned. The pull of his future life was apparently too great."

"Nuala must have suffered when he did not come back home," said Keelin. She knew how isolated and different she had often felt while growing up. Yet she had always had her family and Brian. Life would have been intolerable without them.

"Yes, I imagine she did. That is perhaps why she chooses not to speak of him."

"I feel the pull of the Otherworld," said Keelin. "Especially when I venture near the passage tomb. Yet, perhaps it is not the Otherworld that beckons me but my future life. The one I visited that day."

"I would not dwell too much on what the future may hold but cherish these moments in the present," replied Deirdre, concern in her voice. Then, hastily changing the subject, she said, "And now your dress." She walked across the room to a large, beautifully carved cedar chest.

"Stand up and close your eyes. Do not open them until I tell you." After Keelin had complied, she heard Deirdre open the chest, then felt her carefully slip the dress over her slender neck and shoulders, tightening the laces that ran down the gown's back.

There was a pause, then Deirdre said with satisfaction, "Now you may look."

Keelin opened her eyes and turned anxiously toward the mirror of highly burnished metal. The sight she beheld was startling and she drew her hand to her mouth in surprise, barely recognizing herself. The beautiful gown fit Keelin to perfection, gracing her curves. Its feminine neckline revealed her delicate collarbones and the dark indigo color accentuated her white skin. Dipping elegantly low in the back, the gown's skirt fell to the floor like liquid silk. Keelin's fingers traced her figure in the mirror and, reaching her face, she studied her reflection. Her violet eyes sparkled and the sharp angles of her high cheekbones were softened by the blush of her cheeks. Her lips were tinted with a subtle rose-colored stain. Delicate earrings of sapphire and silver hung from her ears.

"You are a vision," Deirdre said proudly. "No one at festival tonight will look as splendid as you, my fairy princess!"

Keelin at first could not tear her eyes away from her reflection. At length, she turned and smiled shyly at Deirdre. "Thank you, Deirdre. I look . . ."

"Beautiful," added Deirdre simply.

Keelin decided at that moment she would go to the great hall where the Fianna would assemble to feast before the ceremony. "Do you think anyone will recognize me?"

"Brian most assuredly will, but you may not recognize him or his Fianna friends unless you visit the great hall where they feast. After supper they will don masks and light the bonfires of Tara. I would hate for you to choose wrongly and dance with a man not of your choosing tonight."

"I think that highly unlikely. Besides, you will be there to help me."

"Not I," said Deirdre. "I never stay at Tara during Samhain. As soon as the fire is lit at Tlachtga, I will leave for my home in the north."

"Why not stay and enjoy the night?" urged Keelin. "You love to dance."

"Samhain is a frightening time for *starlings* such as I, especially at Tara. You forget that I hear the souls of the dead. During Samhain the boundary between our world and the Otherworld is penetrable. Souls of the dead are awakened this night and move freely back and forth, waiting to begin their next life. Souls of those who have died during the year and souls of those long dead are everywhere. They converge on Tara, pulled inexorably toward the sacred tomb of passage. The souls of those long dead can be the most alarming. They are only tenuously bound by their mortal, earthly memories and cry for deliverance to a new life, wreaking havoc and tormenting the living with their wailing. That is why I never stay at Tara after the bonfires are ablaze, wishing to spare myself much grief. I will see you and Nuala at her cottage tomorrow."

"Where did you say you will go tonight?"

"I have a small cottage nestled amongst the rocks on a cliff in northern Eire. It is there I go when I need peace and rest. Tonight Déaglán will be waiting for me. I can think of no better way to celebrate Samhain."

"I am to travel back to Nuala's alone . . . through the Otherworld?"

"Your cloak will aid you. You are already skilled beyond understanding and know what to do. Remember, traveling from here to Nuala's cottage is no distance at all, akin to walking across this room," said Deirdre, dismissing Keelin's concern with a wave of her hand.

AIDED BY HER Dagda cloak, Keelin traveled to Tara's great stone fortress through the Otherworld, entering the assembly hall like a ghost and hovering above the many long tables. Most of the revelers had finished eating and were now drinking ale. Some have already imbibed too much of the drink from the looks of them, thought Keelin with a wry smile. When she spied Brian, he was sitting next to Ruaidhrí with Seán and Pádraig on the bench opposite them. Keelin's heartbeat quickened and she whispered his name soundlessly. She had fooled only herself for a long time. She watched Brian stand and scan the hall, seemingly distracted, before sitting back down. Keelin then left the hall, found a dark alcove in an anteroom to conceal her cloak, and stepped from the Otherworld onto the stone floor of the fortress.

Soon back in the hall, Keelin walked lightly and agilely,

making her way between the tables and sensing many eyes upon her. Before she reached him, Brian was on his feet and striding toward her. Keelin stopped.

"I was hoping to find you this evening," she said, smiling up at him.

Brian bowed and took her offered hand in his, searching her face. Then he brought her hand to his lips and a thrill ran through Keelin. The kiss was lingering and his lips felt warm against the back of her hand. Quite involuntarily, Keelin moved closer to him.

Brian straightened back up and reluctantly released her hand with a slight frown. "I thought perhaps you were an apparition . . . it has been a strange night. I felt your presence, heard you earlier." He laughed and shook his head, studying Keelin once more, his eyes sweeping over her. "You are beautiful." He lightly traced the line of her jaw with his fingertips. "Curse all these prying eyes," he said.

"Will you dance with me tonight?" asked Keelin, her eyes bright.

Before Brian could answer, Ruaidhrí reached them and, throwing his burly arm around Brian's shoulders, exclaimed, "I know, Brian, that Keelin here is the loveliest lass in the hall, but we have work to do and wooing her will have to wait until later. Already the Fianna are assembling on the hill of Tara, their masks and torches at the ready."

Sure enough, Keelin noted that the hall was slowly emptying, young men from every table excusing themselves, some happily boisterous, others intoxicated and combative, and all formidable, deadly.

Keelin said farewell to Ruaidhrí before turning to Brian. "Remember, I wish to dance only with you."

"That will be a trick, dear Keelin," said Ruaidhrí. "We will all be wearing masks, and you will not know Brian from the rest of us. And," he remarked over his shoulder as he walked away, beckoning Brian to follow, "I can assure you, there will be many wishing to dance with you this evening, looking as bewitching as you do."

"Pay Ruaidhrí no heed," said Brian.

"I will know you, whatever your disguise," Keelin said hurriedly to Brian, noticing Pádraig and Seán approaching. "And if you dance with anyone else this evening, I shall never forgive you."

"Why would I ever dance with anyone but you, my beautiful witch?" Grinning, Brian lightly brushed Keelin's cheek with the back of his hand, then turned and followed Ruaidhrí out of the hall.

KEELIN BREATHED A sigh of relief as she made her way surreptitiously back to the anteroom and the dark alcove, thinking that tonight was the first time she had ever been happy she was small. Wishing to speak to no one after Brian left, Keelin quickly slipped behind three imposing Fianna warriors as they made their way out of the hall, avoiding the necessity of having to make idle conversation with anyone. Reaching the alcove, she hastily retrieved her Dagda cloak from the shadows and vanished as easily and silently as she had appeared. In a matter of seconds, she was safely on the firm ground of Tara, looking toward the hill of Tlachtga.

Keelin purposely chose to stand some distance from the crowds assembled on Tara, watching Tlachtga expectantly as the shadows of dusk lengthened. As soon as the sun had dipped below the horizon, all fires throughout Eire were extinguished, symbolizing the end of the year. Tara was cloaked in darkness and the crisp air of nightfall brushed against Keelin's cheeks. She shivered slightly, as much from excitement as from the cold. She then stood mesmerized as she watched torch after torch lit at Tlachtga.

The priests and priestesses of The Dagda, standing close to each other and holding the burning torches high, formed a circle around the unlit pyre. Breaking the circle's link and walking slowly, they spiraled out from the pyre forming three concentric rings and creating fluid, undulating waves of brilliant orange and yellow light. Keelin felt irresistibly drawn to the flames and to Tlachtga, as if some powerful, atavistic instinct were taking hold of her. One by one the torches were extinguished until only a single torch burned against the black sky. Fearghus, the high priest of The Dagda, circled Tlachtga's pyre, igniting the dried kindling at its base every few strides. Once the bonfire was blazing high into the heavens, a roar of celebration erupted on the hill of Tara. The Fianna warriors, each disguised in a mask resembling one of the mighty beasts of Eire, lit a line of three pyres, all of which quickly rivaled the bonfire at Tlachtga. As far as Keelin could see, other fires were lit, from distant hill to distant hill, until all of Eire was alight with the flames of rebirth.

No sooner had the bonfires on Tara been lit than the music began. Pipes and drums, fifes and horns filled the air with a martial beat as the warriors danced round the pyres and one by one threw their torches into the flames. Dressed in black, the men looked demonic—seemingly half man, half beast—silhouetted against the conflagration. Keelin's feet were already tapping, keeping time to the beat, and she moved closer to the bonfires,

joining the revelers who were also caught up in the rhythmic cadence of the drums.

Suddenly, the music stopped and the warriors' voices rang
out, chanting a tribute to the dead and calling upon them to join
in the celebration. Keelin was sure she could hear Brian's voice
and she stood on her tiptoes, trying to spot him. When the music
resumed, the harps, pipes, and drums played a lively reel, and
Keelin began to dance, abandoning all caution and reserve, an
elfin beauty who sprang into the air as if she had wings.

As it turned out, Keelin did not have to look for Brian. It
seemed she had been dancing only moments when he was beside her, his arm about her waist, pulling her close. Keelin knew
instantly it was Brian, both from the boldness with which he held
her and the intensity of emotion that sparked between them.
When Keelin saw that Brian wore the mask of a wild boar, she
laughed, happy he had chosen the visage of that beast above all
others. Then they were dancing together and everything else
faded away into a blur of light and sound and motion, all sense
of time vanishing as they were swept up in the magic of the
night and each other.

It was only when the music stopped abruptly once more that
the spell was broken. Momentarily bemused, Brian instinctively
put his arm around Keelin. Quickly, though, Brian realized what
was about to take place.

"The Fianna will now light the remaining three bonfires.
Come," said Brian, leading Keelin by the hand toward the unlit
pyres. Stopping at a place where Keelin would have an unobstructed view of the spectacle, Brian lightly grasped her shoulders in his hands and ordered, "Now stay here while I help light
the fires. I should not want to search for you again in these
crowds."

Keelin raised her chin defiantly, her natural impishness resurfacing. "I *might* wait, but only if you hurry back."

"Did I ever tell you that you are a mighty pain in the arse?" Brian said as he turned to join his fellow Fiann.

"I do not believe that you have," called out Keelin, "though I have thought as much and worse of you many times."

Keelin watched as Brian headed swiftly toward his comrades, all of whom held unlit torches at the ready. When Brian joined them, the warriors divided into three groups, each approaching one of the blazing bonfires. As the warriors thrust their torches into the flames, the horns sounded and the drums rolled. Holding the glowing torches high above their heads, the Fianna shouted a salute to the gods and marched toward the unlit pyres that formed a line opposite the blazing ones. As each new bonfire was lit, a roar erupted from the crowd, anticipating the ritual that would follow. Quickly the new bonfires raged, forming a narrow passage between the walls of fire. One by one, the warriors danced through the fiery gauntlet and the crowd went mad, chanting, singing, and urging men amongst them to join the Fianna in the age-old ritual.

A man toward the front of the crowd took the hand of a lovely young woman standing next to him, kissing her soundly on the lips and pulling her toward the flames. The crowd erupted again as the two started their run through the passage, the man holding his frightened yet elated sweetheart close to him.

Keelin could barely contain herself as she watched, shouting praises to the bold as they dashed through the passage, jeering and taunting those less willing to brave the flames. When she saw Brian approaching her, Keelin did not hesitate. She ran to him and, grabbing one of his hands in both of hers, pulled him back to the fire. Brian needed no encouragement and they danced between the fiery walls, Keelin bouncing and twirling, heedless of the burning embers cast out by the flames and Brian dancing right behind her, shielding his willful, exuberant lass as best he could. When they emerged safely with nary a singe, Brian put his arm around Keelin's shoulders and led her through the crowd, beyond the bright light of the bonfires to a shelter of oaks that stood midway down the hill. Pulling off his mask and dropping it to the ground, he abruptly scooped her up, his arms locked just below her hips, and carried her toward a large oak tree. Keelin laughed delightedly, grabbing for the sleeves of his shirt to steady herself. Brian set her down on a horizontal bough of the oak, where she sat nearly at eye level with him.

"Now this is as it should be," Keelin said, smiling contentedly. She unfastened the clasp of her cloak and let it fall away from her shoulders.

"I knew you would be pleased." Brian took her face in his hands and gently kissed her lips. Dropping his hands from her face, Brian ran his fingertips along her pale skin, tracing the neckline of her dress, his hand trembling slightly. When his fingers reached the visible tip of her scar he stopped and, lowering his head, kissed the scar with infinite care. Keelin could feel his warm breath on her skin. The tender intimacy of that simple kiss bespoke of a shared memory, both cherished and enduring.

Keelin sighed happily, remembering, and ran her fingers through Brian's wavy black hair. "I was very angry with you that day. You were being particularly insufferable."

Brian laughed in mock affront. "You were angry with me? I wanted to wring your neck. Had you not been along, Séamus and I would have hunted the wild boar with Eirnín and Conall. Instead, we were forced to keep watch over you, an almost impossible task." Brian hesitated, then added, "You gave me a horrible fright."

"Poor Béar, he never proved to be much of a hunting hound," admitted Keelin.

"Singularly worthless is a more apt description," said Brian, and they both laughed. He leaned toward her and they kissed again, their lips barely touching. It was at that moment they heard the laughter of another couple approaching the oak grove. Brian cursed, taking a deep breath. Keelin giggled and playfully kissed his cheek, whispering, "If you are agreeable to a walk of perhaps a mile or two, I know where we can be alone."

"I welcome the walk, for I want you all to myself," murmured Brian into Keelin's ear as he gently lowered her to the ground, taking her hand in his. The two, hand in hand, left the shelter of the oaks and walked down the hill.

# CHAPTER TWENTY-FOUR

*T*HE SPRING GRASSES IN THE HIGHLAND PASTURE were knee high and lush. The footing was firm, though occasionally rocky under the cattle's hooves, with the bogs of the lowlands left far below. The predawn sky was a mosaic of stars and promised a cloudless day. It was cold on the mountain but a warm breeze occasionally wafted through the air, as if heralding the miracle of rebirth. The winter had been long and hard, darkness and frigid air hanging over Eire and its barren fields like a death shroud. Yet even then, nascent life abounded. Safely hidden in soil beneath the frozen ground lay the seeds of spring, waiting for warmth and light.

Déaglán listened intently and strained his eyes, hoping to detect any unusual sound or movement in the shadows. He sat on a rough cowhide and leaned against the trunk of a large fir tree. Beside him lay a young herdsman fast asleep, his deep breathing rhythmic and peaceful. Most of the cattle were also asleep, some lying down, others standing quietly with their heads hanging low. A few were already grazing contentedly, including the lead cow, a bell hanging from a rope around its neck. They had been brought up to the pasture the day before without benefit of wolfhounds or even cattle dogs. Déaglán had come upon the small herd in the early afternoon and had cursed the fool who sent the herdsman up to the pasture alone. He was little more than a boy and would have been defenseless against an attack by wolves or men. With the spring had come cattle raids and the isolated highland herds were the most vulnerable.

Déaglán feared it was only a matter of time before one of these raids became deadly and a battle ensued between belligerent clans. Eire's unity was tenuous at best, and with each passing day of this unnatural peace, its chances for survival diminished. Agricola would not invade before summer; Deirdre had brought Déaglán the news when last they met. The winter that had ravaged Eire was similarly harsh in Britannia, and Agricola's army would need the spring to prepare for the invasion. Fionn and his chieftains also needed the spring to prepare for the defense of Eire, but all would be for naught if war broke out among the clans before Agricola's army even reached the island's shore.

Déaglán's disquiet was heightened by his failure to apprehend and silence the spy. The elusive devil had stayed just out of reach, winning the game of cunning and wits thus far. Two of the spy's dispatches had reached Agricola before the winter storms rolled in. Deirdre confirmed the general knew both of the chieftains' vote to unite and that Fionn was in command of Eire's warriors. Agricola had not yet learned of Fionn's defensive strategies or his battle plan, and, even in Eire, only Conall and Niall were privy to their details, having helped Fionn develop them.

Now, with the invasion looming, all of the chieftains and their seconds would have to be briefed. That meant it was likely the traitor, whoever he may be, would learn enough to share damaging intelligence with Agricola's spy. The element of surprise would be lost and so too would any hope of victory for Eire's warriors. Time was of the essence. With calmer seas, a dispatch could easily reach Agricola before his army left Britannia. The traitor must be unmasked and the spy silenced—now. Déaglán knew he should, at this moment, be pursuing them both. Instead he was sitting in a highland pasture watching over a young herdsman and his cows. Protecting one foolish boy would not save Eire, thought Déaglán grimly, disgusted with himself and his sentimentality.

Perhaps Deirdre's latest news might shed some light on the traitor's identity. Déaglán was to meet Deirdre at Tara in two days' time. He shook his head and smiled in the dark, thinking of Deirdre and her conspirators, Nuala and Keelin. They were splendid sorceresses who had become critical to the defense of Eire. Deirdre did not detail the nature of her powers to him and Déaglán did not ask, though he had surmised most. Again he smiled, remembering the day he first saw her. Just thinking of Deirdre made him feel better; even when apart, she mesmerized him and gave him hope. He relaxed and watched as a faint glow appeared in the east and he heard the boy stir next to him.

Déaglán's horse trod along the muddy road, carefully stepping on firmer ground where river rocks had been laid like cobblestones. Déaglán would not reach Tara until early afternoon; he was impatient to arrive but dared not go faster. The road had been empty save for an occasional farmer's wagon. Still, he could not enjoy the peaceful isolation of the day. He looked up when he heard the loud honking of geese flying in formation overhead, marveling at how graceful they looked—a marked difference to their waddling gait on land. When his gaze returned to the road ahead, he was startled to see Deirdre standing alongside it, not ten paces away. She wore her Dagda cloak of rich royal blue, its hood down. Her fair hair shone in the sunlight, with most of it swept back in a bejeweled clasp. Her pale skin was clear and her lips were curved into a bewitching smile. Déaglán was captivated, wondering how Deirdre always looked so elegant in the most rural and rough of places.

"Your sudden comings and goings are most disconcerting," said Déaglán, jumping down from his horse and kissing Deirdre soundly on the lips, encircling her in his arms. "We were to meet this afternoon, though I welcome the sight and feel of you now."

"I could wait for you no longer, as I have important tasks elsewhere. Here is as good as anywhere to give you news, my love." Deirdre's eyes were soft with tenderness. She glanced around and frowned in dismay. "Well, perhaps not, for there is no comfortable place to sit. It seems we must stand."

"No matter. What news do you have?"

"First, rest assured. Agricola still knows nothing of Fionn's battle plans and has not received a dispatch since the fall. In truth, he fears his spy may have come to grief."

"I hope his fears will soon be realized. Has there been any mention of Eire's traitor, by name or clan?" Déaglán had asked Deirdre this same question each time they met, only to be disappointed. Still, he could not help but ask again.

"Unfortunately, no. I do have good news, however. Agricola received a dispatch from the emperor, Domitian, denying reinforcements. That will leave the Romhanach in Britannia vulnerable if Agricola invades Eire with his existing forces. Keelin's and my efforts were quite successful with Domitian, though we had hoped he would veto the invasion outright. It is possible, even without the veto, Agricola may still abandon his plans to invade."

"Agricola will not abandon his plans. Only Domitian's veto or

Agricola's death will halt the invasion." Déaglán, frustrated and angry by Deirdre's apparent naiveté, added, "Agricola is a general. He leads armies, he conquers, and he subjugates. All of your efforts will not change who he is and what drives his soul."

"You sound like Keelin," said Deirdre with the slightest reproach in her voice. "Indeed, Agricola's soul is that of a conquerer. I acknowledge as much. Nonetheless, one must first do all one can to prevent bloodshed. Our efforts have proved wanting and yes, Agricola will invade Eire." Deirdre looked at Déaglán, her eyes now full of sorrow. "Many will die when Agricola's army lands on Eire's shore. Young, strong, brave souls. How can I rejoice, even if our warriors are victorious? I would not be true to my vows as a priestess of The Dagda if I did not do all within my power to prevent such a tragedy."

Déaglán's anger evaporated and he pulled Deirdre to him. He would not speak of something she already knew. A worse fate than bloodshed and death threatened Eire's people. More devastating was the loss of freedom and the evils of slavery. Instead, he held her close. Neither spoke for some time. Finally, Deirdre gently dislodged herself from his embrace.

"Not all of Keelin's and my efforts with regard to Agricola were unsuccessful," said Deirdre, brushing back a tendril of hair that had escaped the clasp. "He will land his army in the harbor whose surrounding countryside is most beneficial to Fionn's battle plan. The wide plain also has its benefits for Agricola, though it was not his first choice. For some time he seemed reluctant to abandon his preferred harbor but Keelin was most persuasive, visiting him in his sleep and sharing thoughts of great victory should he land, instead, in the southeastern harbor."

Déaglán had long known of Deirdre's powers of the mind. He had experienced them the night of his escape from the

Romhanach fortress. However, imagining his little niece wielding such otherworldly powers over the likes of Agricola and Domitian still left him awestruck.

"Agricola is confident of victory, again in part due to Keelin's efforts, and will invade with only one legion," continued Deirdre. "Of course, it seems he never seriously considered fielding more than one against our warriors—"

Deirdre stopped abruptly, her whole being alert. She turned her head toward Tara and seemed to be listening to something, though Déaglán could hear nothing.

"Hurry, we must go," said Deirdre, turning back to Déaglán and clasping his hand in hers. "Keelin is in urgent need of us."

"Keelin?" asked Déaglán, dumfounded. "What is she doing at Tara?"

"Keelin is everywhere of late."

With Deirdre still holding his hand, Déaglán made a move toward his horse.

"There is no time," said Deirdre, her voice barely above a whisper. She dropped his hand and pulled her Dagda cloak round him as best she could. In an instant the quiet roadside disappeared, and in the next they were standing in a thickly wooded forest, little of the sun's rays filtering through to the damp ground of fallen leaves. Just ahead of them was Keelin, kneeling over the body of a man, her head almost touching his, her hands staunching the flow of blood from his neck.

Déaglán took a step toward his niece but Deirdre's hand touched his arm and she shook her head. "No, wait," she whispered.

At last, Keelin stood and walked slowly toward them. Her hands, which hung limply at her sides, were covered in blood.

"I could not save him," she said haltingly. "The damage was

too great." It was then she noticed the blood dripping from her fingertips. She stopped and, bending down, used the leaves at her feet to wipe off most of the blood. She then returned to the body and retrieved her satchel. From one of its pouches she pulled out a clean linen cloth and wiped off the remaining blood as best she could. When she started back toward them she had regained her composure.

"Keelin, dearest, what happened?" asked Deirdre.

"I was in the forest searching for a particular fungus that grows here. Its medicinal qualities are quite remarkable," said Keelin, acting more like the spirited, fairy-like lass Déaglán had always known. "I had just spotted some of the fungus when I heard the desperate cry of a man. I ran toward the sound and found him here." Keelin gestured for Déaglán and Deirdre to follow her back to the body. "Perhaps one of you may know him?"

Deirdre shook her head. "No, and his soul does not speak to me."

Déaglán looked at what had been a powerfully built man, though not exceedingly tall. His neck had been slashed, and only slightly more force would have severed it altogether. There were lesser wounds to his chest and arms but none as gruesome as the wound that killed him. It appeared he had put up a valiant fight.

"No, but he is surely a warrior and will be known at Tara," said Déaglán. "What more can you tell us?"

Keelin bent down and, with great care, closed the man's eyes. Then, straightening up, she said, "As I reached this place, I saw one man walking swiftly away and heard another, walking in the opposite direction. I did not follow either man. I could not. I was . . . compelled to aid him," she said, nodding toward but not looking down at the fallen warrior. "As fate would have it, I should have pursued his murderers. If I had, the spy would now be captured and the traitor unmasked."

Déaglán's heart rate quickened. "The spy and the traitor? How do you know this?"

"When I reached him he was still alive, though barely. I was able to stop—or at least slow considerably—the bleeding. He was conscious and desperate to tell me what had happened. He had seen a man acting suspiciously and suspected him of being a spy. He followed the man here and confronted him. It was then Eire's traitor appeared. The spy smiled and said, 'Yes, I am a spy for Agricola and you will not live to reveal my identity.' Our warrior battled the traitor but was no match in strength or skill. He could not name his murderer, though he knew him to be a Fian. Then, he repeated the word 'lion' over and over until he breathed no more."

"He could not possibly have spoken to you with such a wound," said Déaglán disbelieving, looking again the bloody ruin on the ground before him.

"He nonetheless conveyed to me all that I have just shared with you," responded Keelin, her violet eyes steely. Déaglán was taken aback. For the first time, Keelin reminded him of her father, Conall.

"I should not have doubted you. Forgive me."

Keelin nodded and her eyes softened, though only slightly.

"What did he wish to convey with the word 'lion'?" asked Deirdre.

"I do not know," said Déaglán. There was *something*, he thought, but it was buried deep in his memory and he could not grasp it.

"He meant to identify his murderer as best he could," said

Keelin, studying the ground around them. "I think, though, his battle to the death might tell us more. The traitor must have sustained some injury, however slight. There should be a blood trail leaving here."

Sure enough, Déaglán quickly discovered small drops of blood and followed them for some distance to a more sparsely wooded area. Then the drops abruptly stopped. The cursed traitor must have bound his wound, thought Déaglán. He tried but failed to pick up the trail again. He was not surprised. The man, however loathsome, was a Fian, able to hide his tracks better than the most elusive beast. Not wanting to waste time on a fruitless search, Déaglán headed back the way he had come. He did so, however, with the knowledge his quarry would be running scared. The spy had gotten careless and had been exposed. The traitor was wounded. Déaglán could smell blood and felt certain no additional dispatches would reach Agricola.

# CHAPTER TWENTY-FIVE

*K*EELIN SAT IN NUALA'S COTTAGE, IMPATIENTLY waiting for the priestess to arrive. After Déaglán had assured her that he would return the warrior's body to Tara, Keelin had gone back to gather the fungus. Its medicinal qualities were indeed remarkable and very much needed. Agricola's impending invasion did not suspend the ebb and flow of everyday life and she still had her responsibilities as a healer, treating the sick and injured. In fact, she now had patients throughout Eire. The Otherworld enabled her to visit even the most distant regions of the island in a matter of seconds. Still, there was never enough time. Nor were her powers strong enough to heal most of the sick or to stop Agricola. Sometimes she wished she had remained in Eire, blissfully ignorant of what was about to befall her people. She wanted to believe Eire's warriors were invincible, that the invaders would be easily repulsed. Instead, the likelihood of a Romhanach victory stole into her thoughts all too often and an icy, dreadful fear would sweep over her.

Initially, Roma had stirred in Keelin a strange reverence. The empire's network of roads and bridges, aqueducts and grist mills, were beyond anything in Eire, and Domitian's palace with its lush gardens, sunken courtyards, and pools of sparkling water faced in marble and gold was truly awe inspiring. She could have gazed for hours upon the beautiful paintings and life-like marble statues adorning the palace and imperial buildings. Yet it was the Romhanach medical practices and innovations that most captivated her. Keelin visited the surgeries as often as she could, watching and listening with growing wonderment.

Nuala had accompanied Keelin everywhere at first, both in Roma and on the island of Sasanach. After the two had observed a particularly innovative surgery, the priestess had said rather sternly, "Never forget at what cost in human suffering these medical advancements were achieved." Nuala hesitated, as if contemplating whether or not to say more, then continued. "If it were not for the empire's campaigns of conquest, we would not have witnessed such a surgery today. Military physicians gained valuable experience and knowledge treating the gaping battlefield wounds of living men, the soldiers' agony no less though they were Romhanach."

"I can only think of the lives I will save in the future," said Keelin. During those early days in Roma, she had refused to heed Nuala's cautionary tales.

Keelin's reverence for Roma soon vanished. While visiting one of the many marketplaces in the imperial city, she and Nuala had witnessed a public slave auction in which men, women, and children were treated as cattle, affording them no dignity. Keelin had seethed with impotent rage as Nuala held her arm in a vice grip, preventing her from leaving the safety of the Otherworld and attempting to halt such an abomination.

"Most of those slaves are vanquished foes, the spoils of Romhanach victories," said Nuala, loosening—though only slightly—her hold on Keelin's arm.

"Our warriors will triumph over Agricola's army. Such a fate will not befall Eire's people," asserted Keelin.

Nuala did not reply and, for the first time since arriving in Roma, Keelin felt a vague disquiet.

When Nuala showed Keelin the Romhanach's military garrisons, her disquiet turned to alarm. The armies were terrifying for their sheer numbers alone, and their weaponry was generally superior to that of Eire's. Then she traveled with Nuala to Sasanach and watched Agricola's army quell minor uprisings. The soldiers under his command were disciplined and highly trained. They were also unwaveringly loyal to their general, and, in turn, Agricola led with authority and great skill. From that moment on, Keelin had made it her purpose to stop Agricola by whatever means possible. She had failed unequivocally. Using her powers of the mind, she had only succeeded in shifting some of the advantage away from his invading army. But it was not enough.

Now, as Agricola was poised to invade Eire, Keelin had never felt so tired. There had been too many nights of little sleep, yet she could not afford to rest. Today she had allowed the spy and traitor to escape. Her instincts had told her to follow the man she had seen walking away. Instead, she had attempted to save the dying warrior. "Lion," she whispered, convinced the warrior's last word would ultimately expose the traitor. She whispered it again and looked up to see Nuala standing in front of her.

"I have just spoken to Déaglán. Do not find fault in your actions. You are a healer," said Nuala, dismissing any notion of Keelin's guilt with the wave of her long arm.

Keelin shrugged and stood, making no effort to hide her thoughts from Nuala.

"Come, we must go visit Agricola," said Nuala, picking up Keelin's satchel from the bench and handing it to her, solicitously. "We need only spy on the general now, a rather simple task. We

have done all we can with our powers of the mind. Your nocturnal sojourns, your influence, have banished all doubt from
Agricola's mind and he envisions an easy conquest to add to his
tally. He underestimates our warriors and such miscalculation
may save Eire—"

"Curse *influence!*" spat Keelin. "I want to stop him! Slay him!
Agricola and his legion must not set foot on Eire's shores."

Nuala stood perfectly still and studied Keelin. The priestess's eyes then inexplicably softened and she lightly touched her
ruby pendant. "You would murder Agricola now, before he has
even set sail for Eire? Before he has ordered any sword to be
raised against Eire's people?"

"Call it murder if you wish. But let us not quibble over tim-
ing or Agricola's intentions. I have imagined many ways I might
kill him. You know it is true, for I am sure you have listened to
my murderous thoughts."

"Yes, I have listened. Your mind can be unsettling to visit at
times. I also know you have the soul of a healer, even if your
heart is that of a warrior. I have grown accustomed to your
bloodthirsty thoughts. I used to despair but I do no longer. Your
soul will always prevail." Nuala clasped Keelin's hands in hers.
"Now, let us go. And do not look at me with those fierce eyes of
yours. You know I speak the truth."

"Eyes," murmured Keelin, her memory jarred. Distracted,
she pulled her hands from Nuala's grasp and held them to her
temples. Something Ruaidhrí had said. . . . Then she remembered. Keelin, numb, could only whisper, "A lion's eyes." She
looked at Nuala. "I do not want to believe he could be . . ."

"Eire's traitor," said the priestess.

"We must be certain."

"Yes, then we will act."

⚘

THE FIAN ENTERED the great hall quietly. For such a large man, he moved with easy grace. His entire presence bespoke power and an unhurried confidence. Without removing his cloak, he heaped wood in the hall's massive fireplace and then lit several sconces along the opposite wall. Lighting a torch from one of the sconces, he returned to the fireplace and lowered the torch's flame to the wood. Soon, warmth began to permeate the damp expanse of the room. He stood for some time in front of the roaring fire with outstretched hands, warming them. The flickering light from the flames caught the droplets of dew on his hair and cloak and his dark frame glistened iridescently. Finally, he turned from the fire and removed his cloak, hanging it atop the back of a large chair.

Hearing his name called, he turned toward the door from which he had entered but saw no one. Then he heard the loud creaking of an interior door. Nuala, accompanied by Keelin, stepped into the room, then closed the door behind them.

"Nuala, Keelin," he said. "I thought I heard my name called, though not from your direction. What brings you here so early? Dawn has just broken."

"I might ask you the same question," said Nuala.

"The Fianna are to meet here this morning. I arrived early in an attempt to warm up this cavernous hall."

"I was aware of no such a meeting," said Nuala. She walked over to his damp cloak and laid her hand upon it. She shifted her gaze from the cloak to his wet hair, and then she stared unwaveringly into his eyes. "How is it you are nearly wet through, walking only from your quarters to the hall?"

"There is much to consider as the invasion nears. I was restless and went outside to walk and clear my mind. I realized my folly after a time and retraced my steps, coming here where at least one may get dry if not warm." He smiled without a hint of alarm, his charm very much in evidence.

Keelin witnessed the exchange with grim fascination. Seán's leonine eyes did not shift, even slightly, from Nuala's gaze. He had murdered the warrior nearly a fortnight past. Two days ago Fionn had shared his battle plan with the Fianna and Eire's chieftains. Just hours ago, Keelin and Nuala had listened as Seán betrayed his people, detailing the plan to Agricola's spy.

"Yes, you have indeed been walking, though for a traitorous purpose."

Seán took several steps toward Nuala, his hand instinctively grasping the handle of his dagger. Then he stopped and the hand holding the weapon relaxed and dropped to his side. But his eyes remained fixed on the priestess. He had shed all semblance of the chivalrous gallant and looked predatory, poised to attack. Keelin, alarmed, hastened to Nuala and stood alongside her. Seán regarded them sardonically. "The two of you come here alone and question my honor. Most unwise."

"There is no longer any question as to your honor," said Nuala, the hood of her Dagda cloak casting eerie shadows on her face. Undaunted by Seán's menacing presence, she stared back at him. Keelin could feel the force of Nuala'a mind boring into his soul. The hall fell silent except for the crackling and hissing of the fire. Finally, Nuala shifted her gaze and calmly continued. "Before dawn this day you met with Agricola's spy and shared with him Fionn's battle plan. I will repeat, if you wish, each traitorous word you spoke. And, no, the spy did not escape. He was no match for Brian."

Seán said nothing, but his eyes swept over the hall and he

cocked his head slightly toward the door from which he had entered. Then he smiled, some of his old charm resurfacing, and said with certainty, "All of the doors of this hall are guarded, are they not?"

"Indeed they are."

"You are a crafty old witch." Seán laughed and shook his head.

"Why, Seán? Why would you betray your people?" asked Keelin, appalled at his utter lack of remorse.

Seán looked at Keelin as at a simpleton. "Nuala already knows the answer, seems to hear my thoughts. But for you, fair lass, I will oblige." His lips curled with bitterness. "My father, who stubbornly refuses to die of his strange malady, has chosen my brother to succeed him. My brother, who has neither my intellect nor prowess." He sighed and chuckled to himself. "Though, perhaps my father chose wisely. I would never have been content as a mere clan chieftain. I have always had loftier ambitions. I would have been ruler of all Eire after a Romhanach victory. I believe such power would have been worthy of me. Now, it seems, I shall never know." He turned to Nuala and, without trepidation, asked, "So tell me, what is to be my fate?"

"Better than perhaps you deserve. Single combat."

"I hope you have chosen my opponent wisely. I can best nearly all of Eire's warriors, including their chieftains."

At that moment, the heavy interior door swung wide open and slammed against the adjoining wall. Fionn strode into the hall and faced Seán. "You will battle me, to the death."

# CHAPTER TWENTY-SIX

*T*HE EMPEROR DOMITIAN WAS SEATED ON A cushioned chair in his private chambers attempting to read the latest reports regarding the construction of fortresses and military roads along the empire's frontier, which roughly followed the Rhenus and Danubia rivers. Instead, his eyes kept returning to Agricola's report from Britannia, lying on the table beside him. The pages of the report were curled and the ink smudged, having been handled and read repeatedly. Domitian finally set aside what he was holding and compulsively reached for Agricola's report, but his hand stopped in midair, as if frozen. Then he grabbed the papers and flung them across the room. "Curse you, Agricola! I will not rest until I bury you!"

Domitian could not know that Deirdre and Keelin were watching him or that his innate antipathy for Agricola had been carefully tended and cultivated by the two young women. Keelin had been particularly effective with the thoughts she conveyed, emphasizing Agricola's similarity to Domitian's dead brother, Titus. The emperor had gone as far as denying reinforcements for Agricola but had yet to veto the invasion of Eire. Both Nuala and Deirdre had told Keelin on numerous occasions that, at this late date, Domitian was unlikely to take that decisive step. Keelin reluctantly agreed but would not openly admit defeat. She still regularly visited his dreams and she and Deirdre occasionally spied on him, relaying any valuable intelligence to Déaglán.

Breathing heavily, his face contorted with anger, Domitian stood up from his chair and paced restlessly around the room, eyeing the strewn pages of the report as though they were vipers. Finally, he stopped and surveyed the room more calmly. He picked up each page and placed it on top of the table. He then sat down in the chair and leaned back against its soft cushions. He sighed and, with reluctance, reached for the reports on the frontier and resumed reading them. Believing they would learn nothing today, Deirdre and Keelin were about to leave when there was a knock at the door and Longina—before her husband granted entrance—stepped into the room.

The emperor's wife was undeniably attractive, having a sensuous, feline quality that many men found irresistible. She was not beautiful, not even pretty in a conventional sense, and yet few noticed. Longina's magnetism and her ability to charm overshadowed the imperfections of her face. She could bewitch both men and women, captivating them with her laugh, her witty stories, and her undeniable zest for life. Even those seemingly impervious to her charms were often impressed with the sheer force of her appeal, sometimes being drawn in despite knowing of her insatiable ambition, her amoral selfishness.

Longina stood briefly at the threshold gazing at Domitian, one eyebrow raised in mild irritation, and then approached him, the silky fabric of her pale green gown draping her curves provocatively and fluttering with each step. Reaching her husband, Longina stopped and glanced distastefully at the report in his hands. "I had hoped I would find you resting after the evening meal. Instead you are reading one of those infernally incessant reports from the frontier. You have capable officers who are well rewarded to oversee such matters as logistics and tactics, leaving you to confer with your generals on broader, grander strategies. Why must you always muddle your mind with details rightly entrusted to officers in the field?"

"Spoken like the daughter of a great general," Domitian responded. "I have often thought it a pity that your esteemed father relied on others to manage the details of his own estate, leaving you and your mother veritable paupers at his death. Yes, quite a pity. But no matter. I saved you from penury." Domitian took one of Longina's hands, kissing the back of it. He smiled rather unpleasantly and continued. "As it happens, I have been distracted from these scintillating reports by just such a strategic consideration as you would prefer I limit my thoughts to."

As Domitian spoke, Longina's mouth hardened almost imperceptibly. In an instant, however, her lips curved into a perfect smile, even as she pulled her hand from her husband's grasp and sat on the footstool in front of him. "Pray, tell me what weighty concern is foremost on your mind."

Domitian laughed, eyeing his wife not unkindly. "I fear that our legion's strength on the frontier, both to the north and east, is inadequate, and my generals concur. The Dacian tribes in particular are troublesome. They have found new life and organization under Decebalus and threaten our garrisons in the east. We must mount a strike on them soon, before they have time to consolidate and strengthen their fledgling army. The question, of course, is where can we draw additional legions from? It is necessary to have seasoned men, those who have shown their ability on the battlefield. The obvious answer would be Agricola's legions in Britannia." In spite of Domitian's condescending manner with Longina, both Deirdre and Keelin knew that he often shared his concerns with her, particularly on military matters.

"Agricola's legions must still subdue the rebels in the highlands of Britannia," said Longina with a hint of scorn. "And what of Hibernia? I have heard he plans to invade the island in early summer. Surely he cannot spare any of his legions, most particularly since you failed to send him the reinforcements he requested."

"Britannia's highland rebels are only annoyances, much like fleas on a dog. They do not threaten the empire's hold of the island. In fact, most Britons seem quite amenable to our rule, having prospered by it. As for Hibernia, I find such an invasion a waste of good men. Agricola is launching the campaign without my express approval and with a legion that should rightfully be sent to the frontier. Even if his forces triumph, he has given me reason enough to recall him. I will then appoint another general to complete the conquest of Hibernia." Domitian raised his hand to silence Longina, who threatened to interrupt. "If he should suffer a defeat . . ." He paused and smiled malevolently. "I will not only recall him but strip him of his command."

"You need no reason, no excuse, to recall Agricola," said Longina forcefully, not attempting to hide her disdain and anger. "Need I remind you who you are? You are emperor! Everyone must bow to your will!"

"For a woman of such keen intelligence and breeding, your lack of subtlety has always surprised me," chided Domitian. "Absent in you is a certain refinement that I find very appealing in a woman. Can you not appreciate a more deft touch when wielding power? Will you never learn that it is rarely necessary to resort to such unseemly and abrupt demonstrations of authority? You often assail my sensibilities with such outbursts."

Longina regarded her husband for several moments, her nostrils flaring slightly, her eyes predatory. Apparently coming to a decision, she replied, "Sometimes bold action is not only appropriate but necessary. However, I would agree that often a more subtle approach, one requiring cunning and patience, is far more effective to achieve one's ends. A case in point would be the rather premature demise of your dear brother Titus." At this, Domitian raised an eyebrow and Longina smiled with satisfaction. "Of course, I have heard the rumors of your unsuccessful attempt to rid yourself of him years ago, but it would have been indelicate of me to make mention of such a humiliation. Would you not agree? Instead, I decided to take the matter of your loathsome brother into my own hands. I fortunately had an ally within the ranks of Titus's praetorian guards, someone I could trust without question. I waited patiently for my opportunity—"

"Titus died of an ague, having caught a chill on his way to our family villa in Sabini," interrupted Domitian with a dismissive sweep of his arm. "We have only the gods to thank for his demise." However, the look on his wife's face gave him pause and he sank back in his chair, his impatience giving way to wary silence.

Pleased to have Domitian's complete attention, Longina continued. "Yes, the attending physician concluded that Titus had died of an ague and there was no evidence to the contrary. I know many whispered that somehow you had hastened Titus's death but such was not the case. Nor were the gods responsible. It is I you may thank."

"How is this possible? Titus did suffer an ague . . . my spies confirmed as much."

"I have just told you that I was very patient. There was to be no hint of foul play. My trusted ally, who, I might add, was once a loyal officer of my father, had instructions to only deliver the fatal potion should Titus become ill with a natural affliction. I must admit that because of your brother's strong constitution, the wait for such an eventuality was particularly long and tiresome. However, when Titus finally did fall ill, his affliction could not have been better suited to mimic the effects of the deadly poison, easily mixed with the physician's healing elixir." Longina had become so absorbed in her chilling tale that she failed to notice the dark look on her husband's face. Expecting his admiration and appreciation, she was taken aback by Domitian's cold, accusatory stare.

Domitian grasped one of Longina's wrists, squeezing it painfully when she tried to pull away. "I would be pleased with your admission and attribute your murder of my brother only to your ravenous ambition and your dreams of being empress if it were not for that look of satisfied vengeance on your face. What have you not told me? Were your murderous plans prompted by something other than thoughts of power and grandeur?"

Longina instantly became contrite. "I am sorry for trying to deceive you. I forget how well you know me. I was prompted not so much by ambition but by a need to avenge your honor. I, better than anyone, know how Titus dishonored and disgraced you, threatened by your ability and promise. I hated him for his vile treatment of you and, yes, I wanted vengeance for every tortured look I saw on your face, knowing he was the cause." As she spoke, Longina kissed Domitian's hand and moved from the footstool onto his lap, pressing herself against him, meeting his eyes imploringly.

Domitian searched his wife's face for any sign of duplicity. Suddenly, he smiled agreeably and encircled his hands around her slender neck. "I have always been captivated by you and cannot imagine my life without you. Even after all these years, you still have the ability to rouse me like no other woman can. I should hate to lose you, to send you away. However, know that I will do so if you give me cause." Domitian smiled again and, removing his hands from Longina's throat, stroked her breasts, the silky material of her dress revealing the hardening of her nipples.

From their hidden space, Keelin turned to Deirdre and said silently, *"Let us leave for your cottage before I become quite ill."* Deirdre nodded in agreement and they were gone.

DEIRDRE'S COTTAGE IN northern Eire was perched on a narrow ledge halfway down a rugged cliff that dropped precipitously into the sea. Below was a small cove, just large enough for a boat to dock in relative safety. Steps had been carved into the cliff's granite face, leading to the cottage. At low tide a small spit of sand was revealed if the sea was calm. The cottage's exterior was hewn of rock and hard wood, blending almost invisibly into its surroundings. Only upon entering the one-room cottage was Deirdre's influence apparent. The room was lovely and comforting, and everything in it was beautifully crafted, from the bed, with its intricately carved frame and delicate lace and linen bedspread to the round table of highly burnished oak and the two chairs of fine yew wood. The place settings were of silver, etched with the weaving tendrils of the sacred thorn bush, upon which sat tiny birds or, more precisely, starlings.

The first night Keelin had stayed with Deirdre, a frigid wind and driving rain battered the cottage, and yet the room was pleasantly warm even before Deirdre had lit a fire in the hearth.

Keelin had looked around, enchanted, as she removed her heavy Dagda cloak. The charming room seemed impervious to the brutal storm raging outside.

"How do you keep the damp sea air from seeping into every crevice? The room is wonderfully dry, without even a hint of dankness," remarked Keelin. She had never liked the cold dreariness of Eire and imagined a land of warm, dry winds and clear skies. The land she often visited in her dreams.

"Knowing a little sorcery is one of the advantages of being a priestess, although I cannot wholly take credit for this cottage. It was my great-grandmother's, and it was she who created this lovely refuge. It fell into disrepair after her death and not a soul visited it for years. My father brought me here when I was only ten years old, knowing that, like his grandmother, I had been touched by the gods, singled out as their messenger. The cottage was in ruins, yet there still emanated a dry warmth from its walls, even with the rain and the sea air invading its tattered roof and broken shutters. I fell instantly in love and visited the cottage often, engaging in the necessary repairs to make it habitable. When I became a priestess, I brought it back to its original splendor. I was told my great-grandmother kept even the exterior of the cottage pristine, though I prefer that it look uninviting, thus discouraging anyone who might be tempted to brave the treacherous steps to its door."

Tonight, after leaving Domitian, Keelin hardly noticed the cottage's inviting warmth. "Ugh!" Keelin grimaced as she tossed her cloak on the bed, then slumped onto one of the chairs. "I wish we had not stayed to hear all of that. I feel as if I need to bathe to wash off the stench of their souls."

"They are a decidedly malignant pair, though I find Longina the more evil of the two," responded Deirdre with an almost philosophical objectivity. "However, I am pleased we remained. Domitian's words confirmed to us how successful we have been in influencing him. Although he will not veto the invasion, neither will he send reinforcements. Moreover, he will abandon the campaign and recall Agricola if the initial assault fails. Our warriors have only to defeat Agricola's invading forces and Eire will be safe." Deirdre had also removed her cloak and was busily putting some cheese and bread on the table, along with a fine wine from Campania.

Keelin eyed her friend irritably and frowned. "How will our warriors possibly defeat Agricola's legion? So many will die and we cannot stop the bloodshed."

"Never doubt the might of Eire's warriors, Keelin," said Deirdre with surprising vehemence. "They will fight as one with much more than justice on their side and will triumph. We— you, Nuala, and I—have done our part. Our influence as well as our spying have given Fionn the advantage of foresight, whereas Agricola will learn nothing from his spy or the trai—" She corrected herself. "Or from Seán."

"Well, perhaps a victory is possible," said Keelin, grudgingly. "Still, I find your cheerful optimism most annoying. You are far too . . . *serene*, given the circumstances."

Deirdre smiled and poured the wine into two beautiful pewter cups. "Well, it would not do to have both of us ill-tempered. Now stop your scowling and let us eat."

"I am not hungry. I think I will return home," said Keelin, picking up her cloak.

"You may not be hungry but I am." Deirdre sat and took a sip of the wine, then absently brushed a lock of her blonde hair away from her face before slicing a piece of bread and placing it on her plate.

Keelin reluctantly dropped her cloak back onto the bed and glanced at Deirdre, who looked as tired as she felt. Keelin had been so absorbed in her own thoughts and worries the last few months that she had not looked particularly closely at Deirdre. Always slender, Deirdre now looked almost gaunt, her dress no longer fitting to perfection. Her face was pale, almost translucent, with not a hint of color in her cheeks. Her eyes were as blue as always but without their appealing liveliness. Keelin had always believed that Deirdre was somehow immune to worry and anxiety and had, again and again, selfishly relied on her friend's perpetual good humor and strength. How foolish she had been to imagine that Deirdre did not fear for Eire as much as she did.

Silently scolding herself, Keelin returned to the table. "In truth, I am hungry as well."

At that moment, there was a knock on the cottage door. Keelin opened it to find Nuala. Keelin stepped aside and the priestess entered the cottage, nodding a greeting to both young women but saying nothing.

"What a pleasant surprise," said Deirdre. "Keelin and I were just sitting down to supper. Please join us."

"No, I haven't the time," said Nuala, even as she removed her cloak and allowed Deirdre to hang it on a peg near the door.

Keelin looked uneasily at the priestess. "You have news?"

"Yes." Nuala gazed at Keelin solemnly. "Fionn has ordered your father to gather his forces and march toward the invasion site. As you know, Niall has already assembled Eire's northern forces and should arrive there within a fortnight."

"What of Agricola?" Keelin felt a rush of dread run through her. She had been focusing all of her efforts on Domitian and had not visited Sasanach or seen Agricola for many weeks.

"Preparations for the invasion are nearly complete. Agricola is very thorough and it will be several weeks before he gives the final order to depart. By then, Eire's forces will have taken up position and be at the ready."

"The battle is upon us," said Keelin, almost to herself.

"Yes, and therefore we have no time to brood or wish for what is naught," said Nuala abruptly. "The field camps and infirmaries are now of utmost importance. Keelin, have you managed to gather all the medicines and instruments we will need?"

"Yes," said Keelin, "and all the bandages and dressings as well." She had purloined much of Eire's needs from Roma hospitals and infirmaries, the Romhanach none the wiser.

"Your skills are limitless," said Nuala with satisfaction. "As a thief you are both fearless and cunning. I applaud you."

Keelin was taken aback. Nuala so rarely praised her. But the priestess had turned to Deirdre.

"What of the field camps? Will we have adequate food and supplies to support our warriors?"

"Yes," said Deirdre. "It seems we will have foodstuffs and livestock from even the most remote regions of Eire. Carts and wagons full of supplies have been arriving daily. Women of all ages, as well as old men and boys, have already taken it upon themselves to establish the camps. I and my fellow priests and priestesses have been little more than observers. Our warriors will want for nothing."

"It is settled, then," said Nuala. "We will not be deterred by thoughts of defeat. We will remain vigilant and steadfast." She turned to Keelin and said earnestly, "To the brave belong all things."

"And to the bold," said Keelin, nodding. "It is the waiting that bedevils me."

"Yes, waiting burdens us sorely, for we know what lies ahead." Nuala eyed both young women for some time and then frowned, the fingers of her right hand touching her ruby pendant. "You are both exhausted and in need of rest. You must regain your strength." Addressing Deirdre, she said, "Déaglán is at Tara. Go to him and bring him back here if you must. He is no stranger to the Otherworld."

"I will," said Deirdre, some of the liveliness returning to her eyes.

Nuala turned to Keelin. "Your father will arrive home tomorrow but will not stay for more than a day, as he must assemble the midland and southern forces. I know you will wish to see him."

"Of course," said Keelin, her heart pounding. "But what of the Fianna?"

"Brian and Ruaidhrí have been given leave to accompany your father home and stay, perhaps several days, before returning to their posts. I had little trouble convincing Fionn to give the two leave, especially given Brian's role in dispatching the spy." Nuala smiled, her beautiful lips softening. The priestess smiled only rarely but when she did it transformed her face, making it lovely and tender, revealing the depth of her empathy and compassion.

Tears sprang instantly to Keelin's eyes. She ran to the priestess and hugged her. "Thank you," she said simply, resting her head against Nuala's chest.

Nuala, somewhat awkwardly, returned Keelin's embrace. "You will freely choose your own destiny. I should never have doubted you. Surely the gods do not."

KEELIN AND BRIAN sat on a cowhide blanket, finishing a picnic lunch. Rua and Rónán were grazing companionably nearby on the grasses of Keelin's meadow. The day was chilly, even though patches of blue sky were visible as the storm clouds that had opened up the night before were quickly passing. Every so often, the sun's rays brightened the landscape but did little to warm the air or the newlyweds. They had both shed their cloaks when they reached the meadow, though Keelin wore a woolen sweater over her dress and Brian had on a thick linen shirt and leather breeches. Keelin's hair fell in a loose braid down her back. Errant auburn tendrils had escaped, framing her face.

They had been married the day before, Nuala performing the ceremony at dawn on the very spot where they now sat with only Rua and Rónán as witnesses. A heavy mist blanketed the ground, and the damp air hid and sheltered them from the outside world. They had barely been visible, even to each other, as they rode side by side up to the meadow. When they cleared the rise, Nuala was waiting for them, standing perfectly still, an eerie sentinel. Overcome with emotion during the ceremony, Keelin had been only faintly aware of Nuala's words, as they were caught in the mist and held for only the three to hear.

Now, as Brian and Keelin finished their lunch, she smiled, remembering. "I could not have imagined a more perfect wedding ceremony, private and sacred, here in my meadow. And to have Nuala agree to marry us . . . I could never have dreamed of such a day."

"I never liked Nuala, nor she me," said Brian. "I suppose I will have to reassess my opinion of her. Years ago she warned me off, saying you were destined for a life in The Dagda. I feared such a life might crush your spirit. Still, she and Eirnín had entrusted me with your safety and nothing else. I would have defied

Nuala but not Eirnín. When I saw your passion for healing, I believed you wanted to become a priestess for that reason alone."

"I never wished to become a priestess, though now I suspect my reluctance stemmed more from defiance," said Keelin. "I resisted and fought Nuala, constantly. I could never be a priestess like her, or even Deirdre. But perhaps I can serve the gods in a different way."

Brian patted his stomach contentedly and lay back, using Keelin's folded cloak as a pillow. "For the present, I wish you to serve only me." He laughed and grabbed Keelin around the waist, pulling her on top of him.

Feigning annoyance, Keelin freed herself and sat back up primly, a wicked smile playing on her lips. "You are insufferable." She gazed down at him and ran her fingertips along his chest, feeling the rough texture of his shirt and sensing the strong beating of his heart. "I am not of a nature to make a good, dutiful wife. You were very foolish to fall in love with me."

Brian peered up at her. "Whatever would make you say something so daft?"

"Well, I am admittedly contrary by nature and not one to follow your lead. And, I am *different*," said Keelin as she continued tracing the lines of his chest with her fingertips. "I have secrets I may never be able to share with you."

"Perhaps," said Brian, unperturbed. "But ever since you kicked that bully Daire in the shins, I knew you were the only lass for me. Besides, I have always known you were a little witch. And, if you do not stop running your fingertips thus, I will be forced to ravage you, for I have only so much self-control."

"*Finally*," murmured Keelin as her fingers trailed down his stomach. "I was wondering how long it would take for you and me to be of like minds."

❧

Some time later, Keelin awoke. She was curled up in Brian's arms, her head resting on his chest. Brian had pulled his cloak up over them, and she felt warm and safe. "I must have fallen asleep," she said, realizing that Brian was awake.

"Yes, I did as well and woke only a short time ago." Brian chuckled and patted Keelin's hip, then squeezed her closer.

"That was a very self-satisfied laugh," said Keelin indulgently. "Need I ask the reason?"

"Very satisfied with you. I have always known you to be bloodthirsty. It is my good fortune you are pleasingly wanton as well."

"I shall take that as a compliment. I am too happy and comfortable to allow you to vex me."

"As well you should." Brian said nothing for several moments. When he did speak, his tone was more serious and his words heartfelt. "I never dared even to dream that we would be together one day or that I could be this happy. I love you, Keelin."

"And I love you, Brian. Always."

They lay there contentedly, neither wishing to move, neither prepared to let the afternoon end.

Finally, Brian sighed deeply and said, "I must journey back tomorrow. Ruaidhrí and I plan to leave at dawn."

Keelin's happy, comfortable world vanished in an instant. She had forcibly banished all thoughts of the battle to the deepest recesses of her mind the past two days, and now all the fear and anxiety came flooding back tenfold. "Stay," she pleaded.

"You know I cannot. Ruaidhrí and I were granted leave only because we were to accompany your father. Already we have stayed too long. We must be prepared for the Romhanach and our duty is with our fellow Fianna." Brian stroked Keelin's hair, still holding her close. "Do not fear. I promise we will be together again. Our warriors will triumph, of that I am sure. Trust me."

"I trust you but I fear for you also. The Romhanach are powerful, more powerful than can be imagined. I know. I have seen their might." Keelin's tears flowed freely and she kissed Brian frantically.

"I suspect you have, my little witch. We will fight nonetheless, and you would not have it otherwise. Do not doubt our strength. It is far greater than the enemy believes."

The truth of Brian's words rallied Keelin and she felt a small measure of optimism. "Yes, we are ready for Agricola," she said. "Nothing more can be done." She held him tightly and when they made love again, it was with a mingling of heartache and bliss.

# CHAPTER TWENTY-SEVEN

*I*T WAS EARLY SUMMER WHEN THE ROMHANACH fleet was spotted off the coast, moving inexorably closer, toward a large bay in southeastern Eire. The sight of so many ships, their large square sails billowing in a friendly wind, was both terrifying and magnificent. The weather had been mild for several days. There were only a few high clouds and not a hint of the normally omnipresent drizzle. The clear skies allowed those on hilltops to see the approaching ships, extending far out to the horizon, more than one hundred and fifty strong. It seemed that even the gods of the sea were favoring the Romhanach. Crossing the channel had presented no difficulties and all the ships had made it safely to Eire. The protected waters of the bay and the flat, accommodating beaches promised a smooth anchorage and landing. Lush farmland fanned out from the shoreline, surrounded by gently rolling hills. Stands of oak trees dotted the rises. It seemed the perfect amphitheatre for a display of Romhanach military might.

Agricola stood on the tower of one of the foremost ships, his prefect, Aquila, standing alongside him.

"Sir, we should have our men on shore before dark," said Aquila, surveying the bay. "There could not be a more likely site to launch a campaign."

Agricola nodded. "Initially, I did not prefer this landing site. Additional review is sometimes necessary. It was most assuredly so in this instance."

"The gods favor you, sir," said Aquila with admiration.

Agricola chuckled. "Perhaps. I welcome their favor, though I would not wish to rely on it. The gods, on a whim, may abandon me. No, I will rely on my own judgment and on the strength of my men, molded by training and discipline, and tempered by battle."

Their ship was now well within the waters of the bay. Near its northern reaches was a small village, and the surrounding countryside was largely uninhabited with only a scattering of sheep and cattle.

"The village looks deserted, as do the farms," observed Aquila. "It is as though they have long known of our arrival."

"On a fine morning such as this, our fleet would have been sighted long ago. No doubt the inhabitants have all fled to safety."

"Of course, sir. We have already struck fear in their hearts. Our landing and encampment will be all the smoother for it."

"It is likely only the women and children fear us," said Agricola in measured tone. "These Hibernians are a warlike people and they will be defending their homeland. We will face strong resistance initially, from warriors who battle with unparalleled ferocity. However, they cannot sustain such resistance for long. Their chieftains' attempt to unite the island's warring clans seems to have failed. The last report I received indicated as much. Unfortunately, I have heard nothing from my spies since early spring and therefore must rely, again, on my own judgment."

"I believe the spies are dead, sir."

Agricola nodded. "I know they are dead. If not, we would

have heard from them. It is regrettable. They were good men and will be sorely missed. However, their reports were not essential. Even united, Hibernia's warriors are no match for my legion. They are barbarians with little notion of strategy and no forethought. They will charge our line mindlessly and we will defeat them with relative ease. I envision a great victory." Agricola's expression hardened. Under his breath he muttered, "And Domitian be damned."

FOUR MEN SAT on horseback among a stand of oaks, watching the Romhanach fleet's approach. From their vantage point it was possible to see the entire bay, which was now occupied by many of the fleet's ships. Small landing boats had already been lowered from the anchored ships and were being rowed to shore, filled with supplies and men.

"The arrogant bastards!" spat Niall, affronted. "They have arrived in full daylight!"

"Yes, and uninvited," commented Fionn grimly. "But no matter. We will be accommodating hosts and most willingly offer our presumptuous guests a taste of sword and axe."

"Indeed, Agricola will not be expecting the reception we have planned for him," added Conall as he scanned the bay. "Judging from the size of the fleet, it appears he will field a legion against us, with perhaps as many as five hundred cavalry troops."

Fionn nodded in agreement and addressed Déaglán. "You have again proved your worth as a spy. I believe you are something of an oracle as well. In each particular you foretold Agricola's intentions."

Déaglán did not offer an explanation and he knew Fionn did not expect one. Perhaps later, if Eire triumphed, his uncanny knowledge of Agricola's invasion plans might prompt questions. If that time came, he would gladly deflect any suspicion away from The Dagda and its three sorceresses. In truth, he would die before revealing their secrets.

Fionn shifted restlessly in the saddle. "We know our enemy and have chosen our battlefield. He believes we are no match for his legion. We will soon disabuse him of such a notion."

"Niall and I will alert our men to remain vigilant but cautious, keeping well out of sight," responded Conall. "The chieftains and their warriors know their positions and all are at the ready."

"Good, it will be necessary for us to exploit every advantage," said Fionn. "First, however, before a drop of blood is shed, we will greet our visitors and advise them of the foolhardiness and injustice of their campaign against Eire. One must always appeal for peace. If our offer is met by deaf ears, we will gladly make war."

"Will we send a delegation to the esteemed Agricola this evening?" questioned Niall, an edge to his voice.

"No, let Agricola and his officers anchor all of their ships and establish their beach camp. Tomorrow evening will be soon enough for me to lead our welcoming party."

"You cannot lead the delegation. It is far too dangerous for you to enter the enemy's encampment," protested Niall, appalled. "You are Eire's finest warrior, our leader."

"All the more reason for me to represent Eire. I will not be absent from any part of this conflict. Furthermore, I relish the opportunity to match wits with such a man as Agricola."

"It is foolhardy to trust Agricola to act honorably," said

Conall. "You could very well be held hostage or worse, jeopardizing our carefully laid plans."

Fionn shifted in the saddle again and rubbed his thigh, grimacing slightly. Glancing between Niall and Conall, he said, "So both of you believe it would be prudent of me to send an emissary of lower rank to Agricola's encampment rather than to go myself. You believe our defense of Eire would suffer without me. Yet, either of you would readily lead the delegation should I request you to do so, even though your absence on the battlefield would be felt no less than mine. Why? Because we are not men to step aside."

Yes, thought Déaglán, these men were bold nearly to recklessness, very different from the brave, methodical man who led the army they would soon face. Fionn still suffered pain from the wounds he sustained during his battle with Seán. Had it not been for Nuala and Keelin's immediate treatment of Fionn's wounds, he may very well have been left a cripple. As it was, he could barely sit his horse and only recently could he walk without a limp. Despite this, he was Eire's finest warrior and leader of the Fianna, and his reputation had spread far beyond the reaches of their small island. Agricola and his officers would know of Fionn's exploits.

Breaking the uneasy silence, Déaglán said, "I agree with Fionn. He should lead the delegation."

"Are you mad also?" questioned Niall. Both he and Conall looked murderous.

"No, Déaglán, you are not mad, though your purpose is different than my own," said Fionn, eyeing him speculatively.

"It is," responded Déaglán. "If I am to enter the Romhanach encampment unnoticed and obtain the intelligence we seek, a diversion would help, the grander the better. Fionn, I suggest

Fearghus accompany you, along with a dozen or more of your most powerful and intimidating Fianna. The benefits of such a grandiose display will be twofold. It will provide the cover I need and it is sure to give Agricola's men pause, knowing they must soon battle such formidable warriors."

FIONN AND THE high priest Fearghus walked side by side, followed by twenty Fianna, as they were escorted to Agricola's tent by two Romhanach centurions and a contingent of soldiers. Fionn was dressed in warrior's attire but without shield or mail, and armed only with a short, double-edged sword secured in a sheath that hung from his wide, intricately carved leather belt. He was a tall, broad-shouldered man with a square build that bespoke both power and agility. Fionn wore his blonde hair long, pulled back from his forehead and secured at the nape of his neck with a leather tie. Around his neck was a torc, fashioned from a single band of twisted gold, each end of the spiral decorated with an ornately molded golden ball. His pale blue eyes missed nothing as he followed the centurions to Agricola's tent, even as he appeared to look only straight ahead.

Equaling Fionn in height and far exceeding him in girth, Fearghus wore the simple garments of a priest with the resplendent side of his Dagda cloak hidden and the plain brown woolen side in view. It was only from the hood of the cloak resting against his back that one caught a glimpse of the rich burgundy color beneath. Fearghus's expression revealed none of his natural good humor and warmth. Instead, there was about him an air of ominous solemnity, an augury of doom.

Were Eire's two most powerful men not intimidating

enough, the Fianna who accompanied them, including Ruaidhrí, would have caused even the boldest man to hesitate. The
Fianna, like Fionn, were dressed in their warrior garb except
they carried shields and were armed with their weapons of war.
Towering, powerfully built, and menacing, the Fianna marched
boldly through the encampment as though they had already
achieved a great victory. The hustle and bustle of the camp
stilled noticeably as Eire's delegation passed by, muted curses
and low murmurings replacing the shouts and laughter of
Romhanach soldiers, an unnatural, eerie hush following in the
wake of Fionn and his warriors.

When the delegation reached Agricola's tent, one of the
centurions waited outside with the men while the other entered
the tent to announce Fionn's arrival. Within moments, Agricola
emerged and faced Fionn. Though a much smaller man, Agricola
exuded the authority and confidence of one long accustomed to
giving orders and leading men into battle. "I see there was no
need to send couriers to find you and request a dialogue. You
have found us," said Agricola politely. He then glanced briefly at
Fearghus before his eyes swept over the Fianna. "You are undoubtedly Fionn Mac Mathúna, are you not?"

Fearghus effortlessly translated Agricola's words into Gaelic,
and Agricola looked sharply at the priest, surprised.

Fionn nodded and replied in Latin, "Indeed I am. And you
are Gnaeus Julius Agricola. My esteemed companion, the high
priest Fearghus Ó Néill, has accompanied me to aid us in our
dialogue. Though I speak your language, my understanding is
rudimentary at best. Fearghus will ensure that any subtlety of
meaning or thought will not be lost on either of us."

Agricola was momentarily taken aback. Then his eyes swept
over Fionn's warriors and he smiled slightly. "You need not have

brought armed warriors with you, their number being too many for mere ceremony and too few to defend you should I not be an honorable man. I assure you I am, and would not, at least this evening, cause any harm to befall you. So please, join me inside so we may begin our conversation." Agricola gestured courteously toward the large tent, the hide flaps of its door held open at each side by Romhanach guards.

Fionn nodded in assent and he and Fearghus entered, the general following a step behind, the hide flaps released when the men passed the threshold. Inside, the tent was sparsely furnished with table and chairs at its center and a simple cot in the far corner. None of the opulence one would have expected from a general of Agricola's stature was present. Two of Agricola's senior officers stood at attention, and once the formality of introductions was complete and refreshments had been offered and refused, the men sat down. Agricola and Fionn faced each other across the heavy table. Agricola's officers sat on either side of him and Fearghus sat to Fionn's right.

Agricola took the lead. "Although your island is remote, far removed from the influence of our civilization, I have no doubt that you are well aware of the purpose of this landing." Agricola paused and, when Fionn did not readily respond, he continued. "It is to secure Hibernia as a territory of the Roman Empire. Tonight, you are in the position to negotiate the terms with which your country joins our empire. Tonight, you are in a position to choose peace and prosperity rather than war."

"I am well aware of your motives, Agricola," responded Fionn. "Your ships have sailed into Eire's waters and your soldiers have landed on her shores to make war. Of that I am certain. The peace and prosperity of Eire's people be damned. It is unworthy of you to feign a sympathy you do not feel. Let us speak frankly or not at all. It is Eire's rich soil and gold you covet."

Agricola nodded. "Very well. I will speak with more openness, though my message remains unchanged. Tonight you can save your country from destruction. Many nations far stronger than yours have succumbed to the might of my legions. Negotiate a surrender, the terms of which need not be harsh. Our rule will bring order and civilization to your country and an end to the dangers of your clan warfare."

"I will never negotiate the terms of my people's enslavement," said Fionn with deadly calm. "Only if you abandon your campaign and set sail will there be no war. You were ill-advised if you were led to believe I would ever forsake freedom and honor for a peace that comes with chains."

Agricola smiled wryly, though his eyes were hard. "You are in no position to speak of freedom and honor. That is a conversation reserved solely for equals. Instead, you must accept the inevitable and take what concessions I am willing to give you. Surrender and avoid a war that will lay waste to your land, spell death to your men, and slavery for your women and children."

"Now at last you speak openly," exclaimed Fionn, an insolent glint in his pale eyes. "To utter such threats you must be supremely confident of victory. I would remind you that the battle has not been fought. Your soldiers have yet to prove themselves as mighty as your words. They have never fought Eire's warriors, men whose deadly skills are without equal."

Agricola stared at Fionn with disdain. "I admire your pride even as I scorn your folly. The Fianna warriors who accompanied you tonight look formidable, but how many such men will take the field of battle tomorrow? How many of your warring clans will come to your aid? Very few I suspect. You will be vastly outnumbered, both in men and materiel, and for all of your warriors' size and strength, they are still made of but flesh and bone and will die just as readily from sword and spear as men half their size. Now it is time for you to speak openly with me."

"It matters little whether you believe our numbers are adequate to take the field, we shall do battle nonetheless," countered Fionn. "My Fianna are prepared to die, as are the warriors of the clans who chose to follow me. For it is not the prospect of death we fear but the loss of our honor and freedom."

"I warn you a final time, said Agricola, his dark eyes merciless, "if it is not surrender tonight, it is death tomorrow."

"Then we agree." Fionn spoke with maniacal pleasure, looking quite mad. "Tomorrow the bloodletting will begin."

MEANWHILE, HAVING ASSUMED the disguise of an officer's attendant and taking advantage of the distraction caused by Eire's delegation, Déaglán slipped easily into the encampment, identifying the key centurions of each cohort and the colors of their standards. Well acquainted with the duties of an attendant, Déaglán, keeping his head lowered and his eyes and ears sharp, blended seamlessly into the bustling activity of the camp. Long after Fionn and his men had departed, Déaglán listened to the soldiers and overhead a few chance remarks from their officers, noting with satisfaction that Fionn's visit had been successful on all counts. Before any Romhanach was the wiser, Déaglán, armed with the intelligence he had sought, melted into the shadows and disappeared.

# CHAPTER TWENTY-EIGHT

*J*UST BEFORE DAWN, KEELIN WALKED THROUGH the makeshift infirmary, noting all was ready to receive Eire's wounded once the battle began. It mattered little that there were three other healers of The Dagda and a half dozen physician's attendants present, Keelin personally and meticulously inspected everything for readiness. The infirmary had been set up in a temporary field camp several miles northwest of the bay where the Romhanach had landed. The camp, one of three such camps providing food, shelter, and medical aid to Eire's warriors, was situated in a wooded glen, hidden from the field of battle by low hills. Even in the dim light of predawn, the women of the camp were busy, folding bandages, preparing food, tending to the livestock, and milking the cows. Old men and young boys were working at the forge, sharpening weapons. There was little talk, everyone intent on their duties with thoughts of what was to come foremost on their minds.

After one more inspection of the infirmary reassured her that everything was as it should be, Keelin went in search of Deirdre, who could usually be found supervising the cooks or preparing some delectable stew that seemed to feed far more men than the size of the pots would indicate. Initially, the women of the camp had looked with suspicion at the young priestess with her beautiful dresses and exquisite jewels. Now they all loved her, not only because of Deirdre's warmth and charm, but also because she enthusiastically shared all of her delectable recipes with them. As always, Deirdre had a calming influence on those around her, and she helped still the frayed nerves of the wives, mothers, and daughters of Eire.

Keelin was greeted with smiles and nods as she walked through the camp, several women stopping what they were doing to exchange a few words. Only a fortnight ago these women had been strangers; now they were comrades, united in a common purpose. As Keelin approached the cooking area she caught the mingling aromas of freshly baked bread and savory stew. Perhaps she would try to eat something, even though she was not in the least hungry. Keelin's stomach was in knots and she feared losing whatever she attempted to eat. She decided to take some bread and cheese back to the infirmary and eat it later, once the battle had begun. It was the waiting that was most disturbing to Keelin, the helpless anticipation. She was disgusted with herself, for even her hands trembled. Conjuring up the most frightful scenarios, she would not be freed of their torment until she could be active, fighting to save lives. She knew that only then would her hands become steady and her mind calm.

Where was Brian at this very moment? Where were her father and Séamus? Keelin had seen her father and Séamus occasionally in the camp but had been unable to exchange more than a brief word and hug with either of them. Brian was with the Fianna and had not been in her camp at all. Only once, late at night, Keelin had searched for him, traveling through the Otherworld. She found him asleep and had an overwhelming desire to brush errant locks of his dark hair from his forehead and kiss it. Instead, she remained hidden, murmuring words of love and then departing, an ache in her heart. Keelin knew she would see none of her loved ones until after the battle, and she dared not think what the end might bring.

FIONN SURVEYED EIRE'S warriors, who had assembled a final time before taking up their battlefield positions. Conall and Niall, both mounted, were at the front of their battalions, their officers flanking them. Those Fianna not attached to either Conall or Niall's warriors formed a small contingent of both cavalry and infantry, and stood to Fionn's right. It was shortly past dawn and the fighting would soon commence. Eire's warriors are ready and the battle is coming none too soon, thought Fionn grimly. The men had become restless and irritable over the past weeks, unaccustomed to the discipline and order necessary to field a force of such unprecedented magnitude. Fights were becoming ever more frequent as clan rivalries and deep-seeded antipathies surfaced. Still, even as tempers flared, the majority of the men stifled their individual sentiments for Eire's cause.

Fionn raised his right arm. A drumroll sounded then abruptly halted.

"Men of Eire!" shouted Fionn, his voice booming in the early-morning air. "The enemy is on our soil. They have come to conquer and destroy, to murder and enslave. Instead, at our hands they will falter and die!" A deafening roar erupted from the men, and Fionn waited a moment before continuing.

"Their soldiers fight not for country and honor but for gold.

We battle as free men, in defense of Eire and our people! The enemy believes our warriors no match for their legion of mercenaries and presumes we lack the resolve to mount a united resistance. We, the men of Eire, know better!" Again, a roar erupted and many raised their spears in salute. Fionn saluted in kind.

"The fateful day is upon us and the battle is now. I will not deceive you. The peril is great. The sovereignty of Eire and the lives of our women and children are mightily threatened. Today, men will die and blood will flow. But we will triumph! The blood of Eire's warriors will dampen the earth, but it will be the lifeblood of the enemy that flows in rivers to the sea. It will be the enemy who turn from battle and flee for their lives!"

Over the shouts and war cries of Eire's warriors, the martial beat of drums and the call of pipes and horns resounded, the fearful tumult carrying through the air for miles. In the Romhanach encampment, Agricola's soldiers hesitated at their duties, listening to the ominous din, which seemed to come from nowhere and everywhere, an unearthly portent. Centurions quickly barked orders at their men and work resumed, yet the dreadful sounds continued and the soldiers' edginess increased. However, neither fear nor foreboding slowed the formation of the Romhanach battle lines. Column after column of infantrymen marched out of camp grouped in their respective cohorts. The cavalry led the columns, positioned on the wings to protect the legion's flanks. The strict discipline of the centurions and the unquestioning duty of the soldiers was the strength of the Romhanach legion, and nowhere was it more apparent than on that cold and damp morning in Eire.

THE WARRIORS OF Eire and Agricola's soldiers faced one another, a span of lush farmland separating the vanguard of each force. A Romhanach horseman braved the lonely expanse, furiously galloping halfway across and halting, waiting for his enemy counterpart to reach him. Once the message was delivered, the intrepid messenger waited alone for a response. Eire's courier delivered Agricola's curt demand to Fionn: *Surrender now. Lay down your weapons or face certain death and defeat.* Fionn's reply was no less terse: *Surrender is foreign to the warriors of Eire.*

Upon receiving Fionn's response, Agricola cursed silently, thinking once again that Fionn was not only a fool but mad, a man willing to sacrifice his warriors and condemn his women and children to slavery, all in the name of freedom and honor. Fionn must realize, thought Agricola, that I will grant no quarter or clemency, that I will not hesitate in my ruthless retribution. Agricola's own code of honor extended only to the conduct of war and the empire's order of law. He was first and foremost a soldier and believed that compassion and mercy equaled weakness, dangerous luxuries in the brutal game of war and conquest. Swift and terrible vengeance and the fear it elicited was a necessary aspect of conquering a recalcitrant people.

Agricola was not troubled by such simple notions as the sovereignty of nations or freedom. The strong conquered and the weak submitted. Agricola knew that only when all those of a rebellious and independent nature were dead or enslaved would a vanquished territory be truly safe for exploitation and rule. Even as Agricola was merciless, however, he took no fiendish delight in the destruction and death meted out at his orders. Rather, he had acquired a cold and fatalistic acceptance of its necessity, a detached executioner and arbiter of fate. Sighing, Agricola gave the command to engage the enemy.

Once the order was given, the legion's light infantry advanced. The cavalry was on the wings, hiding the main body of heavy infantry that marched a short distance behind. The light infantry's advance was methodical, the men maintaining a strict checkered formation, their shields protecting their bodies and their spears at the ready. Eire's warriors advanced in kind—with less precision but with infinitely more outward menace. Their vanguard was terrifying, the warriors being imposing and powerfully built, every aspect of their countenance fierce. Mounted on a bay stallion Niall rode at their lead, a small contingent of cavalry at the wings. The gap between the combatants quickly closed and, upon a shouted command, the Romhanach front line halted. Lead centurions judged that the enemy was now within range of their *pila*, deadly throwing spears intended to thin the ranks of Eire's vanguard.

Before the Romhanach soldiers cast their *pila*, Niall gave the order to attack. With deafening shouts and war cries, Eire's warriors charged forward, brandishing their swords and running easily, in spite of their size and the weaponry they carried. When the hail of *pila* reached them, some warriors staggered and fell, mortally wounded. Others, ignoring their wounds, continued their wild charge. Still others lost the use of their shields, the iron point of the *pilum* piercing the shield's thin layer of bronze and firmly embedding in the thick hide of its core. Unable to quickly loosen these murderous spears, the warriors disdainfully cast their shields aside. Defying prebattle orders to fall back between the ranks if their shields were rendered useless by the *pila*, most warriors charged forward, heedless of their vulnerability, their rage and bloodlust banishing all caution.

The collision of the two armies was horrific. The clash of metal, the roar of the men and screams of the horses reverber-

ated through the air. The much smaller force of Eire's warriors
fought with far greater skill and ferocity, pushing the Romhanach
line back. The warriors who fought without their shields parried
blow after blow, feinting, dodging sword thrusts, smiting their
opponents again and again. Finally, however, as fatigue slowed
their movements, the warriors were cut down, their thin, finely
woven coat of mail being no match for the Romhanach double
edged sword. Eire's front line wavered and the forward push
slowed as the murderous fighting continued. The ground became slippery with blood; those men who lost their balance and
fell were quickly run through with sword or spear. It was then,
as Eire's warriors faltered, that the second line of the Romhanach
legion hurled their *pila* over the heads of their front-line soldiers
and onto fresh columns of enemy warriors advancing to relieve
their exhausted comrades.

In the early stages of the battle, Agricola had been in the
thick of the fighting, much to his senior officers' dismay. Mounted
on his gray stallion, he led the right wing of the cavalry charge
and then dropped back, returning to the second line of infantry
who waited for their orders to engage the enemy. From there he
directed the battle, always on the move, receiving front-line updates, shouting orders to centurions, and assessing when best to
launch the legion's second line, the powerful heavy infantry. The
order to advance the second line must be given before the legion's front line was completely spent and threatened to break,
but ideally not until the enemy weakened or hesitated. Agricola
knew from years of experience that a legion's heavy infantry
could easily overwhelm a tiring enemy, even an enemy as for-

midable as the Hibernians. Not until he gave the order for the second line to advance did Agricola finally leave the field of battle and gallop his horse to safety.

Still mounted, Agricola positioned himself and his aids on a hilltop just southeast of the battlefield from which he had a clear view of the fighting. He noted with satisfaction that the legion's heavy infantry had pushed the barbarians back, reversing the enemy's initial gains. Agricola admitted to himself that he had not been completely prepared for the extraordinary skill and strength of Hibernia's warriors. This was in spite of a report from his spies the previous summer that included warnings of both the might and bloodthirsty nature of these barbarians. Of course, the report also detailed their complete lack of order and discipline and their penchant for killing each other, clan battles being a way of life. Still, with a much smaller force, the Hibernians had pushed back his legion's front line and had threatened to break it for a time. The enemy had also demonstrated a rudimentary understanding of tactics, holding back several columns of their warriors, advancing them only when their front line tired and wavered. However, such simple tactics would be of no avail to Fionn's warriors or his cause of freedom. It will all be over very soon, thought Agricola grimly. The enemy's line was weakening and would soon crumble. In spite of Fionn's confident posturing, he had been unable to unite Hibernia's warriors and field a force large enough to challenge a Roman legion. Granted, the force was larger than Agricola had expected but still wholly inadequate.

There were only two aspects of the battle that troubled Agricola at this point and gave him pause. First, where were Fionn and his Fianna? Fionn had not led Hibernia's charge nor had he been seen on the battlefield. After the fighting had begun, Agricola sent scouts to reconnoiter both the hills to the east and west, certain Fionn and his Fianna were secreted somewhere close by, waiting to attack one or the other of the legion's flanks. Agricola was not overly concerned, yet he wanted to know from which direction Fionn would attack so his centurions on the targeted flank could redouble their forces.

Scanning the terrain, Agricola guessed that Fionn would attack from the east, using the rising sun to his benefit. However, the scouts reconnoitering the eastern hills had found nothing. Looking down from a particularly high summit, the scouts noted scattered oak groves on the reverse slopes of the hills but saw and heard nothing. Not satisfied, they ventured down to the closest grove, bravely entering its shadowy depths to find only a frightened doe and her fawn. The scouts reconnoitering the western hills were met by a dense forest not far beyond the base of the hills. Even though his scouts had reported no obvious threat, Agricola's instincts told him Fionn would attack soon. Agricola felt a vague sense of unease even as he reasoned that any such attack by Fionn and his Fianna would be both fruitless and suicidal.

More disturbing to Agricola, however, was not Fionn's absence or the threat from the Fianna, but reports that many of the legion's highest ranking centurions had been mortally wounded. In every battle, centurions were lost. Sometimes their ranks suffered heavy casualties. But the deaths of so many of his finest centurions could not be simply fate or coincidence. Agricola had the utmost respect and admiration for these courageous men, Roma's most indispensable soldiers. Battle-hardened and experienced, centurions inspired both loyalty and fear in their men and always led from the front. Now they were dying at an alarming rate and, if the reports were accurate, their deaths were at the hand of towering Hibernian warriors whose skills and strength even the mightiest centurions could not match.

Well, thought Agricola angrily, that explains where at least some of the Fianna are, and the devils are targeting my centurions! It was well that his legionnaires were now advancing and that the battle was almost over. With a vengeful passion Agricola rarely felt, he sent the order to press the enemy harder and to expect an attack on the right flank. He also gave the order to spare no one, neither women nor children, once the enemy was in retreat and the battle won.

As AGRICOLA'S ORDERS were delivered, Ruaidhrí, with several other Fianna, had found his target, the highest ranking centurion in the legion, the *primus pilus*. While his comrades kept all other Romhanach soldiers at bay, fending off even the bravest defenders of their centurion, Ruaidhrí, with a nod of his head, challenged his foe to mortal combat. The powerfully built centurion, a man of no ordinary courage, was ready and nodded in kind. At first the men parried sword thrusts and blows with equal skill and power, Ruaidhrí demonstrating uncharacteristic patience. He fought with measured and deliberate precision, judging his opponent's lethal range and movements, waiting for the opening to strike. Ruaidhrí knew he must not fail and could not afford to be careless. The course of the battle was desperate and he had been given the supreme mission of slaying the mightiest of the centurions.

When his opening came, Ruaidhrí struck with lightning speed, his sword hitting the base of the centurion's neck where it met the shoulder. For a split second the centurion remained standing, then his knees buckled and he pitched forward, blood spurting from his neck. The fatal blow was struck with such force that it would have cleaved the centurion in two had it not been for his chest armor. Ruaidhrí quickly pulled his sword from the dead man's body and turned to join the other Fianna battling around him.

At that moment, horns sounded and cries of alarm were heard over the deadly commotion of battle. Looking to the east, Ruaidhrí shouted in triumph as he watched Fionn and a small band of Fianna galloping their horses down from the hills and toward the battlefield. Turning to the west in anticipation, Ruaidhrí spotted Conall and his battalion of warriors just as they crested the western summit. The warriors hesitated only a moment before spurring their horses forward, charging recklessly down the steep slopes to join the fray. When Conall's warriors reached the battlefield, the infantrymen amongst them leapt from their horses with their swords at the ready. Conall, remaining on Rua with his horsemen, protected his infantry from being cut down by the Romhanach cavalry.

The right flank of the legion had been prepared for an attack, but the Romhanach soldiers protecting the left flank were taken by complete surprise. In the confusion, lower ranking centurions tried to restore control and order. The simultaneous attacks badly rattled the Romhanach ranks, and during their hesitation and disarray, the warriors of Eire pressed forward. Though still outnumbered, Eire's warriors nonetheless had the advantage. They were more mobile and independent and were not limited to fighting within strict formations. With many of their leaders dead and their battle line already firmly entrenched, the Romhanach heavy infantry could not quickly change tactics and shift positions. Instead, the order was sounded for the legion's third line and most experienced infantrymen, their *triarii*, to engage the enemy and help defend the legion's left flank in a desperate attempt to avert disaster.

R UA   REARED   UP and sprang forward, airborne, as Conall delivered a lethal blow to his opponent's head, knocking the soldier off his horse. Conall then reined Rua back and settled the stallion before turning to join Brian and Séamus who battled nearby. The Romhanach line was weakening but had not yet broken and the battle continued, relentlessly taking its toll in blood. Conall had seen Pádraig fall, had seen so many others wounded and dying. With a rage he had not felt since his brother Eirnín's death, Conall had fought savagely, his conscience banished, his mind focused only on killing the cursed invaders. Now the end was close at hand. The Romhanach could not hold their line much longer.

Conall allowed himself a brief respite before joining his men as they pushed forward. He stroked Rua's neck, noting with pride that the great stallion was hardly damp and that he trembled impatiently, wishing to be off. It was then that the arrow hit Conall, high on the right side of his chest, driving through his coat of mail and piercing his lung. Conall fell from the saddle and Rua screamed and reared, his hooves pawing the air as a Romhanach horseman advanced upon the stallion's fallen master. Out of nowhere Brian and Séamus appeared, charging the Romhanach. Brian knocked him to the ground, then leapt from the saddle and ran the fallen Romhanach through with his sword before turning to Conall. Séamus was already at his side and had managed to help Conall into a sitting position.

"Knocked out of my saddle by a cursed archer," said Conall haltingly. He tried to smile but coughed instead and tasted blood in his mouth. "You killed the bastard, I hope."

"I did, sir." Brian glanced quickly around, worried about another attack. "Conall, we have to move you, get you from harm's way. Do you think you can ride if we help you onto Rua?"

"I can try," responded Conall.

"Should we not try to pull the arrow out first?" asked Séamus, his arm around Conall's back, supporting him.

"No, the arrow has pierced his lung," said Brian frowning, noting the blood on Conall's lips. If you can stand the pain, Conall, I would leave it be for now. Pulling it out could cause you to lose more blood."

"The pain is tolerable," responded Conall. Séamus helped Conall to his feet and Brian led Rua to Conall's side. Conall hesitated, looking at Rónán who stood nearby, his head hanging low, his neck and flanks drenched with sweat.

"Help me on Rónán instead," ordered Conall. "The old horse looks as spent as I feel. Brian, you take Rua. He is fresh and ready for more."

Brian nodded, whistling to his brave old stallion. Despite his fatigue, Rónán trotted over and stood quietly while Brian and Séamus helped Conall onto his back. The three men rode slowly from the battlefield, stopping only when they had reached the summit of a small western hill.

"Go, now!" ordered Conall with as much vehemence as he could muster. He watched as Brian and Séamus galloped away, back to the bloody melee. There is something gloriously terrible about war, thought Conall. Yes, war was ghastly and brutal, yet at this moment he would not have wished to be anywhere else. He was no longer afraid to die. He would stay on this hilltop and watch Eire's warriors triumph. The cold fingers of fear that had clinched at his gut just before battle had been quickly banished by predatory rage and aggression. Now, even the rage was gone. He coughed involuntarily and grimaced with pain, bloody foam at his lips. Well, pain was a good thing, he supposed, smiling wryly. It meant he was still alive and would live to see his men victorious.

By the time Brian and Séamus reached the battlefield, the Romhanach line was crumbling. Shocked by the surprise attacks on both fronts and demoralized by the deaths of their centurions, many of the Romhanach soldiers lost heart. The legion's strength, its discipline and cohesiveness, had been irreparably broken and with it the soldiers' will to fight. It mattered little that the legion's numbers were still far superior. The tide of the battle had turned. Now the remaining centurions' only goal was to effect an orderly retreat.

From his hilltop vantage point, Agricola watched the disaster—at first with incredulity and then self-recrimination. He had been too confident. His legion was facing an ignominious defeat. Fionn and his warriors would triumph this day. Retreat and entrenchment were all that was left, and Agricola's only hope was to protect what remained of his legion. Already Agricola's aids were urging him to abandon the hilltop and gallop to safety. He gazed upon the battlefield a final time—his heart full of bitter regret—and then reined his horse toward the sea.

Commands to withdraw were shouted and horns sounded, and yet the vicious fighting continued. As infantrymen fell back, Eire's warriors mercilessly pushed forward, and some of the legion's soldiers panicked, dropping their weapons in their mad flight, only to be cut down by their vengeful pursuers. Still, most Romhanach managed an orderly retreat, many escaping slaughter. Eire's horsemen gave chase, their infantrymen no longer needing protection. It was then, over the din of battle, that everyone, warrior and soldier alike, heard the horns sound once again, followed by the Romhanach command for *repellere equites*, the formation to resist the enemies' cavalry. Responding to the command, the *triarii* began to close ranks and form the deadly wall of spears and shields that would prevent Eire's horsemen from pursuing the legion's retreating soldiers.

Hearing the *repellere* command, Brian spurred Rua on, knowing that the Romhanach must not be allowed to escape, must be pursued to the sea.

As loud as he could, Brian commanded, "Charge, Repel!"

Nearby, Séamus shouted the same and the command spread like fire from one horseman to another. They knew they must reach the wall before the *triarii* managed to form the second line, before the wall became too wide and too high for the horses to jump it, before the spears were poised to impale. But had not the warriors and their mounts practiced jumping over such obstacles for months? Had they not prepared for a moment such as this?

Brian felt Rua lengthen his stride and urged him still faster. The great stallion dug in, the sounds of his breathing and the pounding of his hooves being all that Brian heard. Séamus had charged forward with Rosie now at Rua's flank, her ears flat back, her long stride effortless. Both young men knew they were racing against the building of the wall, racing against the *triarii* who had as yet only formed the line of kneeling infantrymen, their spears angled upward. From all directions Eire's horsemen galloped, riding recklessly, leaping over the dead, racing past the living, following Brian and Séamus's lead, heedless of everything except this final challenge and their fate.

Brian was no more than ten strides out when the *triarii* attempted to position their second line of standing infantrymen—their spears pointing directly at the charging horses. Brian let out a blood-curdling yell and Rua surged forward, covering the distance to the wall of spears in an instant. The stallion bunched his muscles and, without breaking stride, soared through the air as if with wings, far above the deadly spears. Séamus was next, and then horseman after horseman jumped the cursed wall as the stunned and disbelieving *triarii* looked on, their resolve broken and the formation collapsing. The breach made, Eire's infantrymen charged through. The *triarii* quickly abandoned their wall and attempted to rally the retreating soldiers and make a final stand. But when the wall gave way, the Romhanach soldiers lost any remaining sense of order and discipline and fled, panic-stricken. Eire's warriors gave chase and mercilessly pursued the retreating enemy to the sea.

KEELIN FELT THE sweat trickle down her temples and off the tip of her nose, and she hurriedly wiped her face with a dry rag. In spite of the damp chilliness of the day, Keelin was perspiring both from her exertions and the sense of urgency that pervaded the infirmary. Not long after the battle had begun, the infirmary received its first casualty, a warrior whose wound from a *pila* proved fatal. Since then, a steady stream of battlefield casualties had arrived, and Keelin and the other healers had worked unceasingly to save lives. Everyone in camp was enlisted to help. The women boiled bloodied and soiled rags to be used again and readied new cots. Others held the hands of dying men, listening to halting reminiscences or pitiful moans. The old men and boys worked in relays, driving carts to designated rest stations to recover the wounded and take them back to the infirmary. And still the wounded and maimed, the dead and the dying, kept arriving, the blood and gore unspeakable. There were so few who could be saved, their wounds being horrific. The loss of blood and the subsequent shock killed many before they even arrived at the field camp.

When news of Eire's victory reached the camp, there was no wild jubilation or celebration. Instead, there was immense relief and a pride that would prove enduring. Everyone had seen what price Eire's warriors paid for victory, had seen firsthand the suffering and death. Many of the women in camp waited anxiously, not knowing whether their men had survived, becoming ever more frantic as time passed without word. When Keelin saw her father ride up alongside a wagon filled with the wounded, an arrow protruding from his chest, a host of emotions swept over her. She felt relief, but that was followed quickly by alarm and fear. She saw in an instant that her father's condition was critical, that the arrow had pierced his lung. Despite this, he had ridden all the way to camp, refusing a place in the wagon.

"The cursed wagon would have rattled me to death," growled Conall as he was helped down from the saddle. He coughed and staggered once on the ground, and he would have fallen had a wiry old man not been holding him tight about the shoulders.

Noticing Rónán for the first time, Keelin panicked, a new fear grabbing at her gut. "Brian . . ." she said, unable to continue.

"Brian is riding Rua. Rónán and I were spent." With these words, Conall finally gave way and lost consciousness and was quickly carried into the infirmary. Keelin was not allowed to operate on her father but nonetheless assisted a priest, who with sure hands and a calm, steady manner, removed the arrow and cleaned and cauterized the wound. With luck, and if no infection set in, her father would live. Recovery would be slow and painful as with all sucking chest wounds. But still, there was hope. It was not until after the surgery and her father had been bandaged and taken to the recovery area of the infirmary that Keelin felt a vague disquiet. Images of a long-forgotten dream resurfaced, images of Brian riding Rua away to battle. Keelin also remembered the fearful foreboding of the dream, how she had been powerless to prevent Brian and Rua from leaving her.

Distracted and lost in her disturbing recollections, Keelin was startled when a young woman rushed up and grabbed her hand, pulling her toward the surgery.

"My husband, Diarmuid, has just been brought in. He is grievously wounded and needs you. Please, Keelin, *hurry*," she beseeched, tears streaming down her freckled cheeks.

Keelin did not hesitate and ran back to the surgery, thoughts of the dream banished from her mind. After that, Keelin lost all track of time. Diarmuid would live but so many others would not. With the battle over, warriors arrived at the camp in droves. Once, when using a procedure she had learned from watching a Romhanach surgery, Keelin was struck by the irony of it all, that she would save this man's life because and in spite of the enemy. She had just finished stitching up and bandaging the arm of a young warrior who had suffered severe lacerations when Nuala suddenly appeared at her side. The priestess was responsible for the infirmary in the eastern field camp and Keelin was surprised to see her.

Frowning, Nuala said, "Your camp has been receiving more of the wounded and I have come to help. You are exhausted and must be hungry. I can care for the men in your stead for a time. Go and find Deirdre and get something to eat."

"I am not tired or in the least hungry," protested Keelin. Then, seeing Nuala's raised eyebrow and stern expression, Keelin conceded, smiling wanly.

Instead of searching for Deirdre, however, Keelin left camp and started down the road to the rest station, hoping to get word of Brian. She had just left the woods when she spied a group of warriors in the distance, making their way toward her. She strained her eyes and started to run toward them. She was now sure that the man in front was Ruaidhrí, since he was at least a half-head taller than the other men. Also, his red hair and beard stood out like a beacon. As she drew nearer, Keelin recognized Séamus walking slightly behind Ruaidhrí, leading a horse. Where was Brian? Keelin knew Brian's walk, the way he held his head, yet could not see him amongst the men. Why did he not run to meet her? Fear seized her and she ran faster until she was almost upon them. Keelin stopped abruptly when she saw the men's expressions, saw that Séamus's horse pulled a litter.

"Keelin, lass," said Ruaidhrí taking a step toward her, his hand outstretched. "Do not be—"

"*NO!*" wailed Keelin. She dodged Ruaidhrí as he tried to grab her hand and ran past Séamus to the litter.

Keelin froze as she looked down on the ravaged, broken body that had been Brian. She dropped to her knees and with a trembling hand reached for a lock of hair that lay against the pale, bloodless brow. Lovingly, she brushed it aside and kissed Brian's forehead, then rested her cheek against his. Lost in her grief, Keelin had only a vague notion of strong hands gently grasping her shoulders, pulling her away from Brian and lifting her up, comforting her.

The men resumed walking and no one spoke. There was nothing to be said, nothing left to do but bury their friends. They walked slowly, these grim, exhausted men, and at their lead were Ruaidhrí cradling Keelin in his arms and Séamus, intent only on bringing his friend home.

# CHAPTER TWENTY-NINE

*D*EIRDRE HELD THE INFANT IN HER ARMS, humming soothingly as she studied the pink face with its pursed lips and prominent chin. A shock of red hair crowned the rather high brow, and it appeared the deep blue of the child's eyes would not change. After a very fussy and colicky interlude, the little boy was now almost asleep, content in Deirdre's arms. The young priestess had only just arrived when Saraid handed her the crying baby. "Here, Deirdre, take little Fionn. Keelin tells me you can soothe the most troubled soul. Perhaps you can also soothe a colicky baby."

"You have a way with Fionn," commented Moira as she nursed his twin brother. "He is the more demanding of the two, although not by much. Brian was born first and I think Fionn will be forever trying to catch up with his older brother. What a pair these two will be, if they are anything like Ruaidhrí." Moira said this not with concern but with pride, and she touched Brian's cheek lovingly with her fingertips.

Saraid laughed. "Brian and Fionn are going to be terrors, no doubt."

The three women sat outside Saraid's cottage, enjoying the warmth of the summer sun still high in the sky. The scattered, wispy clouds floated around the sun at a respectful distance, never dimming its brilliant light.

"Where are the men this fine day?" asked Deirdre.

Ruaidhrí is helping Conall and Liam pull tree stumps in the lower meadow," said Moira. "They should be back in the late afternoon with hearty appetites."

Deirdre's face brightened. "Do you need help preparing the evening meal?"

Shaking her head, Saraid said, "I know you did not come here to help us cook but to visit Keelin, though I appreciate your offer. Will you stay for dinner?"

"Yes, I would love to. I believe Déaglán will be arriving soon. Is there enough food for him as well?"

"There is always more than enough food when Saraid and I cook," said Moira.

"How is Keelin?" asked Deirdre. "My duties have kept me away too long. I pray she is doing better."

"Yes, I believe so," answered Saraid. "The twins have helped, have given her joy." Saraid's eyes glistened with tears. "Keelin will now smile and laugh, sometimes with real mirth, yet she will not speak of Brian, cannot bear to hear others do so. I still occasionally find her sitting in Rua's empty stall, Brian's cloak wrapped around her. It breaks my heart. She disappears for days at a time and offers no explanation as to where she has been. Oddly, she seems happier upon her return and I no longer worry as much about these absences." Saraid smiled warmly at Deirdre. "I know she will be delighted to see you."

"And I, her," said Deirdre, standing. "Do either of you know where she might be?"

"Shortly before you arrived, she returned from her patient visits and jumped on Rónán, bareback I might add," offered

Moira. "She and Brian's old stallion seemed quite happy as they trotted away. She did not say where they were headed."

"I think I may know," said Deirdre, carefully handing little Fionn to Saraid.

"When do you expect Déaglán to arrive?" asked Saraid.

"Any time now," said Deirdre, smiling as she looked toward the road, beyond the cottage yard.

Saraid's eyes followed Deirdre's gaze and within seconds they saw Déaglán appear, cresting the rise, riding toward them. "Deirdre, you have the most uncanny ability to know when my restless and wandering brother will grace us with a visit."

"Yes," said Deirdre without explanation, and the three women watched as Déaglán approached.

KEELIN TROTTED RÓNÁN along the village road, her spirit buoyed by the bright sunshine. Warm days in Eire were infrequent and to be savored. Keelin lifted her face to the sun and closed her eyes. She sighed and thought longingly of her coastline far to the west where the hot winds and the clear skies made her feel free, banishing her dark thoughts. Brian would have loved her coastline and the huge expanse of land it bordered. They would have had grand adventures and started life afresh. Keelin sighed again and smiled, opening her eyes. Yes, Brian would have loved her coastline.

There were more and more days such as this, days when she could think lovingly of Brian without blackness descending upon her. Yet nights were still frightful and she often slept only fitfully and rarely woke refreshed. For months Keelin had railed against a fate so cruel as to take Brian and Rua after the victory had been won and the enemy in retreat. Keelin could not remember when the anger disappeared. In its place a deep sorrow had burrowed into her soul, more devastating than the anger. But then, Keelin began to have *the* dream again and it rescued her. She now understood the dream and how it had long ago foretold her fate.

"So my fine Rónán, shall we fly?" asked Keelin as she reined him off the road and onto an open field. The old stallion pricked his ears and bounded forward, the desire to run bred into his blood. Keelin had to admit that on flat, open land no horse could touch Rónán for speed, not even her beloved Rua or the remarkable Rosie. She felt the wind against her face, listened to the stallions's rhythmic breathing punctuating his powerful stride, and she was happy, invigorated by his strength and heart. Before Rónán tired, Keelin slowed him, cooling him out at the walk, and the two followed the path up to the meadow.

Keelin did not at first see Deirdre sitting on the trunk of a fallen oak. It was only when Deirdre stood and approached her that Keelin noticed her friend. Jumping down from Rónán and slipping off his bridle, she ran to Deirdre and the two embraced fondly.

"How did you know to find me here?" asked Keelin.

"When Moira told me you had ridden off on Rónán, it was not difficult to imagine where the two of you would end up." Deirdre hesitated, then added, "Little Brian and Fionn are quite a pair. And I can attest to Fionn's strong lungs."

"You saw the twins, then?" asked Keelin. "Are they not beautiful? Brian . . . would be honored that Ruaidhrí and Moira chose to name their firstborn after him." Keelin's voice wavered a bit but she felt almost serene. It was good to speak of Brian without a wave of emptiness pummeling her.

"Indeed Brian would," responded Deirdre. "I held little Fionn and quieted him, though it was not easy. He has a fierce temper, that one."

"You would not wish to be present when both boys are unhappy. Their discordant shrieks are not for the faint-hearted. During those moments, I quickly remember a patient I must see and escape," said Keelin with some of her old impishness.

"It is good to see you smile again," said Deirdre.

"I am hopeful. I know what I must do." Keelin inclined her head toward the fallen oak. "Let us sit. There is much I have to tell you."

Once seated, Keelin wondered how to begin. She felt at peace sitting next to Deirdre, watching Rónán as he grazed in the meadow. She was not yet ready to speak of her decision and knew Deirdre would not press her, would sit quietly for as long as need be. Keelin's mind wandered, freely moving from one moment in her life to another, some important, others inconsequential, all shaping who she had become. She was not sure how long they sat there without words, Deirdre displaying infinite patience and Keelin enjoying memories no longer clouded by Brian's death. Finally, she turned to Deirdre. "You will not be happy with what I am about to tell you."

Deirdre frowned, looking puzzled.

"For many years I could not understand why the gods gave me the powers I possess. I wanted no part of The Dadga and a life of devotion and self-sacrifice. Admittedly, I thought only of myself and my dreams. When Eire was threatened, everything changed. I entered the Otherworld and learned my affinity for its realm is extraordinary. There are only a handful of others in The Dagda who are so welcomed. Even more rare are those who can travel through it without benefit of their Dagda cloaks as I do. I know only of you, Nuala, and, of course, the high priest Fearghus." Keelin sensed a change in Deirdre and expected a challenge.

"I believe there are two others with such ability," said Deirdre, almost reluctantly. Her soft blue eyes betrayed both anxiety and a hint of indecision. "However, if I am to be honest, I would have to say none of us possess your affinity. It is . . . most uncanny."

Keelin laughed. "You should rightfully have said 'disturbing,' for I am sure that is what you are thinking."

"Please do not tell me you have acquired Nuala's powers of the mind as well," said Deirdre, laughing along with Keelin, the tension of the moment broken.

"Most assuredly not," said Keelin. "My existing powers burden me enough. Before the battle I believed the gods had granted me such powers for a purpose. They did not wish me to be bound by The Dagda or its law. I had the freedom to determine my own fate. I foolishly believed the life I imagined would still be open to me after the battle." Keelin smoothed the folds of her linen skirt, her fingers trembling slightly. "It was not," she said, her voice barely audible. "Yet the gods did not deceive me. The Otherworld had already given me not only a glimpse of my future life but, for a few brief moments, allowed me to experience what my life could be. The gods have always known what my struggle would be. Now, so do I. I had to choose between the life into which I was born and the life I was destined to live."

Deirdre eyed Keelin sharply. "What is it you are saying?"

"I have chosen my future life," said Keelin, calmly.

"Your *future* life?"

"Yes, the life I visited . . . experienced, when I traveled to my future during the ceremony in Danu's cave. You know very well of what I speak."

"Keelin, what you suggest is madness, even if it were possible," cried Deirdre. "Your home, your family and friends, your *life* is here, in *this* time and place."

"No, I have never truly belonged in this life, in this time. I have always been different, have chafed under the restraints of this life and have yearned for something more. Brian felt as I do. We were never meant to stay in one place, to live on Eire, however beloved."

"Of course, you feel different from others. Those of us who have been singled out by the gods *are* different. You have suffered a great loss. Yet abandoning all you know will not heal your wounds. You will be alone in a strange world, without solace. You cannot do this," implored Deirdre, clasping both of Keelin's hands in hers.

"I am not unafraid. Sometimes my decision terrifies me. Yet I cannot stay here. There is another reason I must leave." Taking a deep breath Keelin said, "Only in my future will I be with Brian. He is there, I know, waiting." Keelin searched Deirdre's face for understanding and saw only concern. With a lopsided smile, she said, "You think me mad and perhaps I am, though only slightly."

"I am not amused," said Deirdre. "You do not know if Brian will even exist in that time or place, or what he will look like. Your reasoning is flawed at best."

"I know I will find Brian. He is the man walking on the cliff's path above the ocean, the man whose face I could never quite see in my dreams. Everything is very clear to me now. I have not told you but when I touched the Stone of Fáil at my ordination, it was the coastline of my dream I saw. In particular, it was the vision of the man walking down the cliff's path. Now, when I have the dream, I feel Brian's soul near me. Sometimes I even feel his touch."

Deirdre looked intently at Keelin. "I imagine Nuala already knows of your decision?"

"Yes," said Keelin, smiling. Nuala had become her staunchest ally. "She is helping me."

"Undoubtedly Nuala believes your journey is possible."

"I have already traveled to my future several times. Granted, I was given only quick glimpses from the safety of the Otherworld. It was like viewing beautiful Romhanach murals," said Keelin, her eyes shining. "However, I could not enter, was not present there. Nuala believes I must wait until Samhain, when the veil between this life and others is truly open. She told me her uncle Aidan first traveled to his future during Samhain. Later, when he was more skilled, he could travel with only his Dagda cloak aiding him."

"Nuala spoke to you of Aidan?" Deirdre's eyes widened. Then, embarrassed by her curiosity, she said, "I am sure Nuala spoke to you in confidence. She trusts your discretion and always has."

"Nuala is most reticent," said Keelin, nodding. She thought of Aidan's small journal, safely stored in an inner pocket of her satchel. Nuala had given her the journal not so very long ago. When Keelin had tried to refuse the precious gift, Nuala had placed it in her hands, saying, "My uncle's journal chronicles his travels and will help you immeasurably. He gave it to me when he said goodbye for the final time. I have memorized each line he wrote and can recite them as I do Eire's histories. I want you to have it, and so too would Aidan." Nuala had then smiled and added, "You are like him in so many ways."

Both young women were silent for several moments, deep in their own thoughts. Finally, Deirdre sighed resignedly and took Keelin into her arms, squeezing her tightly. "You are braver than I, a true adventurer." Deirdre stood and reached for Keelin's hand. "Come, let us visit our favorite coastline and watch the sun rise. There, you can tell me all."

In an instant the two disappeared, leaving Rónán to enjoy the grasses of the meadow until they returned.

# POSTSCRIPT

In 85 A.D., Domitian (Titus Flavius Caesar Domitianus Augustus, 51–96 A.D.) recalled Agricola from Britannia and, despite the general's illustrious career, he never again held a military position. Gauis Cornelius Tacitus, a Roman historian and Agricola's son-in-law, claimed that Domitian recalled his father-in-law because his successes in Britannia had outshone the emperor's in Europe. The invasion of Eire was officially recorded as a reconnaissance mission.

Eire would remain secure and undisturbed for another 800 years, until the arrival of Norse raiders.

On 18 September 96 A.D., Domitian was murdered as he sat reading a report in his chambers. The conspiracy to assassinate the emperor was alleged to have been orchestrated by Domitia Longina, the emperor's wife.

There is no written record of Keelin or her family.

## ACKNOWLEDGMENTS

I would like to thank two people in particular who contributed to the writing of this novel. First, my daughter, Katie McGrath Shuler, who was my early writing partner. She helped me with much of the initial research on ancient Ireland, and with the vision for both the storyline and the development of its characters. Scenes in several of the early chapters were either written or outlined by her. Although Katie became too busy with her young family and photography career to continue our writing partnership, her ideas and creativity were invaluable to me. Second, I would like to thank Jennifer Sawyer Fisher, my extraordinary editor. Her knowledge, guidance, and wonderful suggestions helped me beyond measure. From Jennifer I learned it was not enough to write well. One must also tell a compelling story. With each editing round I learned something new and, almost without exception, grudgingly agreed with her edits.

Special acknowledgement goes to those kind souls who read my first draft and gave me helpful feedback and encouragement. Roger McGrath, Duncan Shuler, Allison Bennett, Holland Hunter, Faith Heinemann, and Yuna Erickson waded through what I would soon realize was a *very* rough draft needing much work. Thank you!

I would also like to thank Sara Parriott and Lucinda Dyer for encouraging me to "go for it" and publish the novel. Their support has meant a great deal to me. Finally, my heartfelt thanks to Stacey Aaronson, my copyeditor par excellence. Stacey helped me publish my grandfather's WWI diary and has now done a similarly beautiful job with this novel. Stacey, you are truly a gem!

## ABOUT THE AUTHOR

A native Californian, S.C. McGrath grew up in western Malibu, riding her horse on the beach and in the hills, weaving stories and daydreaming. Now, many years later, not much has changed. McGrath still rides in the Santa Monica Mountains—either on a horse or a motorcycle—enjoying flights of fancy along the way.

Made in the USA
Las Vegas, NV
15 October 2023

79168998R00198